The Green Man's Gift

The Green Man's Gift
Juliet E. McKenna

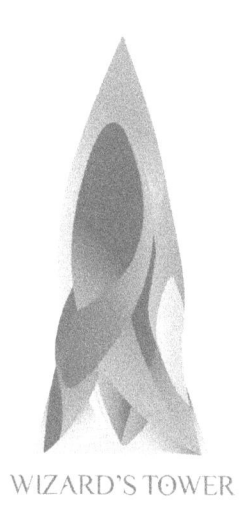

WIZARD'S TOWER

Wizard's Tower Press
Trowbridge, England

The Green Man's Gift

First edition, published in the UK October 2022
by Wizard's Tower Press

© 2022 by Juliet E. McKenna
All rights reserved

Hardcover ISBN: 978-1-913892-41-8

Cover illustration and design by Ben Baldwin
Editing by Toby Selwyn
Design by Cheryl Morgan

http://wizardstowerpress.com/
http://www.julietemckenna.com/

Contents

Praise for the Green Man Series	8
Chapter One	13
Chapter Two	19
Chapter Three	25
Chapter Four	30
Chapter Five	36
Chapter Six	46
Chapter Seven	55
Chapter Eight	62
Chapter Nine	72
Chapter Ten	81
Chapter Eleven	91
Chapter Twelve	101
Chapter Thirteen	107
Chapter Fourteen	112
Chapter Fifteen	118
Chapter Sixteen	124
Chapter Seventeen	132
Chapter Eighteen	140
Chapter Nineteen	151
Chapter Twenty	160
Chapter Twenty-One	171
Chapter Twenty-Two	181
Chapter Twenty-Three	192
Chapter Twenty-Four	201
Chapter Twenty-Five	210
Chapter Twenty-Six	220
Acknowledgements	227
About the Author	228

JULIET E. MCKENNA

For Toby

Praise for the Green Man Series

Praise for The Green Man's Heir

Finalist for The Robert Holdstock Award for Best Fantasy Novel, the British Fantasy Awards 2019

"... any way you look at it, the book is a delight from start to finish. [...] It's one of my favorite books so far this year." — Charles de Lint in *Fantasy and Science Fiction*

"I read this last night and thoroughly enjoyed it, more please!" — Garth Nix on Twitter

"I really enjoyed this novel!" — Kate Elliott on Twitter

"Juliet McKenna captures the nuances of life as a stranger in a small town in much the same way as Paul Cornell does in his splendid Lychford series, with the local gossips, the hard-pressed police, the rampaging boggarts and rural legends come to disturbing life. Thoroughly enjoyable; a UK fantasy author branching out (oh god, sorry for the inadvertent and terrible pun!) and clearly having a great time doing it. Highly recommended." — Joanne Hall

"So far up my street it could be my house." — K.J. Charles on Goodreads

"*The Green Man's Heir* is a thoroughly engaging, at times almost impossible to put down, tale which, despite besides its titular character, is peopled with an impressive array of interesting and intriguing women." — *The Monday Review*

"After a stumbling start, I found myself unable to put down *The Green Man's Heir*. If you're looking for a book to read on your summer holiday, then this is it." — Charlotte Bond via The British Fantasy Society

The Green Man's Heir is a straightforward fantasy story, with a lively pace and characters who wonderfully come alive. It starts as *Midsomer Murders* set in the Peak District but with added supernatural element and turns out to be the book you won't put down because you enjoy it too much." — *The Middle Shelf*

"I hope this turns into a series. I'd love to read more about Daniel's adventures." — N.W. Moors in *The Antrim Cycle*

"And she has absolutely nailed it. This is a complete and utter joy." — S.J. Higbee in *Brainfluff*

"I'm certainly on board for reading more such novels." — Paul Weimer in *Skiffy and Fanty*

"Brilliant concept, compellingly told" — Virginia Bergin on Twitter

Praise for The Green Man's Foe
Finalist for Best Novel, the British Science Fiction Awards 2020

"I loved *The Green Man's Heir*, and while I expected to thoroughly enjoy *The Green Man's Foe*, I did not expect it to be even more satisfying than its forerunner. Which was foolish of me, I admit – I should know by now that McKenna is more capable of outdoing her previous tales in a series." – *The Monday Review*

"If you've read the first book then I'm pretty confident you're going to love this one, and if you haven't read the first one then you need to remedy that straight away." – Naomi Scott

"This is one of my outstanding reads of the year." – S.J. Higbee in *Brainfluff*

"*The Green Man's Foe* is a great addition to what is becoming a great series. I was entirely caught up in it for a couple of days. It is a must read if you have enjoyed the first one, and a great reason to start on this series if you have missed it." – *The Middle Shelf*

"*The Green Man's Foe* is a tasty serve of mystery and myth that has done quite enough to cement this series as one I'll be reading and cheerleading for from now on." – Imyril at *There's Always Room for One More*.

"What I loved reading this tale is how genuinely real McKenna makes the story feel." — Matt at *Runalong the Shelves*

Praise for The Green Man's Silence

"These Green Man books provide a wonderful blend of British folklore and ordinary people trying their best to make the world — or at least their corner of it — a better place. The characters are likeable, while the mythical creatures are earthy, dangerous, and full of that Sense of Wonder that makes fantasy such a pleasure to read. Recommended." — Charles de Lint, *Fantasy & Science Fiction*

"Highly recommended for fantasy fans who are looking for well-written fae adventures with a difference." — S J Higbee in *Brainfluff*

"This is undoubtedly one of the best books I've read this year and I thoroughly enjoyed it. I can hardly wait for the next book!" — *The Monday Review*

Praise for The Green Man's Challenge

Finalist for Best Novel,
the British Science Fiction Awards 2022

"I don't usually review every book in a series, but I'm so taken by this one by McKenna that I want to keep touting its virtues so that people will, I hope, buy each one of them." — Charles de Lint in *Fantasy & Science Fiction*

"Wowee! That was one hell of a ride. A fantastic ride, both the main tale and the bonus short story at the end." — Pers at *Goodreads*

"It is also a delight to read a novel written by someone who knows her genre so well and works at finding different ways to exploit its tropes. The threat in *The Green Man's Challenge* is a giant: the hero doesn't have the strength to match the foe, so other ways must be found, ancient knowledge must be discovered again. By doing so, McKenna consciously subverts the expectations of a certain kind of fantasy: no lone hero, no unbelievable physical prowesses, no amazing powers (political or supernatural)." — *The Middle Shelf*

"Ms McKenna has a glorious sense of place" — Jacey Bedford

JULIET E. MCKENNA

McKenna has brilliantly utilised the likes of the giant figures cut into chalk hillsides and some of the numerous folk stories around hares to add to her intriguing Brit rural fantasy tale. — S.J. Higbee in *Brainfluff*

THE GREEN MAN'S GIFT

JULIET E. MCKENNA

Chapter One

I'm useless at telling lies. I get that from my mum. It cuts both ways though. I can usually tell straight away when someone's trying to bullshit me. This particular morning, I definitely reckoned Eleanor Beauchene wasn't telling the whole truth, even if I didn't think she was lying as such.

That was odd. Really odd. For a start, Eleanor's not much better at telling lies than me, even if her dryad blood comes from the seven-greats-or-so grandmother in her family tree, instead of direct from a parent who's spent centuries tending the oak trees in the Warwickshire nature reserve where my dad's the resident warden.

For another thing, Eleanor and I don't keep secrets from each other. We share them. At least, we do when it comes to dryads and naiads and the other scary things we can both see thanks to our greenwood blood. For a long time, neither of us had anyone to talk to about this stuff, not without risking a referral to whatever the latest cuts had left of local mental health services.

Then there was quite a while when it was just the two of us keeping an eye open for threats no one else would notice until disaster struck. Dealing with those was how our paths had crossed in the first place. We've fought things no one else would believe, and we've always had each other's backs. You trust someone after that, and you don't keep secrets. Ignorance isn't bliss for people like us. It can be sodding dangerous, even lethal.

On the other hand, we each have our own lives, and that's how we like it. If I'm away for a couple of days, she'll ask me how things went when I get back, and I'll say 'fine', and that's that. When Eleanor comes down to Blithehurst House for her monthly visit from Durham, I'll ask how things are going up there. She'll say 'fine', and that's all I need to know.

At least, that's how it had been until the world went weird. After a year and a half of uncertainty and upheaval, things had settled into a routine this summer, but anyone talking about life getting back to normal was kidding themselves as far as I'm concerned. You never know what's around the corner, and I don't only mean viruses or whatever. So I really didn't like the feeling that Eleanor wasn't being straight with me.

She had told me this Tuesday morning that she wanted me to take a look at the dog kennel in the old castle courtyard. I'd said okay, and I fetched my tools from my workshop in the old dairy yard. She's my boss, after all, managing the business on her family's behalf since her father retired. I'm the handyman, estate carpenter and woodsman working out how to turn a profit from the different trees that grow on Beauchene land – pronounced 'Beechen' these days. I also carve wooden trinkets and ornaments from fallen wood I find around the estate. They sell well and Blithehurst takes a cut, so everyone comes out ahead.

I took the path that crosses the gravel sweep at the front of the Tudor manor house. That goes past the grand entrance porch before heading down the gentle slope of the valley side. The path passes the hollow where building stone for the manor house was quarried. The Edwardian Beauchenes turned that scar on the land into a decorative rock garden. It was a pleasantly warm, sunny day. I could hear bird song, the wind in the trees and the distant mooing of the rare-breed cattle grazing in the wooded pasture on the other side of the river. Apart from a couple of the garden staff picking up litter and tidying the colourful flowerbeds, the manor house grounds were empty.

The quiet was a relief. I know, I shouldn't complain. After a year and more of lockdowns and shutdowns, the business needed all the visitors it could get. Blithehurst House had been the Beauchene family home for centuries, but these days the Tudor manor house is a privately run visitor attraction. Thankfully so far this season, the numbers coming through the gates were way up on previous years. I'd get used to it. I was getting used to it. I mean, it's not as if there was any alternative.

Anyone with any sense wasn't risking a foreign holiday when there was no guarantee sudden new restrictions wouldn't leave them unexpectedly stranded. Then there were the endless new reports about traffic mayhem and sky-high prices in Devon and Cornwall and pretty much anywhere around the coast. So tourists were heading to places like Staffordshire and Derbyshire in droves. On the border between those two counties, Blithehurst now found itself ideally placed for visits from people desperate to see something besides their own four walls.

There's plenty to see. Up by the road and the car park, the old stables have been converted into a restaurant, gift shop and garden centre. The rest of the estate doesn't only offer the Tudor manor with its portraits, ornaments and polished furniture to entertain families looking for a historical day out. I crossed the lawns where various Victorian Beauchenes had planted exotic trees they had brought home from their travels. I was heading for the old castle's ruins. Well, that's what everyone calls it, but it's a bit of an exaggeration.

Strictly speaking, to begin with, Eleanor's ancestors had built themselves a moated fortified house. William the Conqueror had handed the estate to Sir Graelent de Beauchene as a reward for cracking Saxon skulls. It was the Tudor Beauchenes who finally got sick of the damp in the valley bottom and built themselves a smart new house further up the hillside. That's what Eleanor says, and she should know. She's the family archivist as well as a graduate student doing a history PhD up in Durham. That was another reason why she'd offered me a job, so she could go back to university and do her doctorate.

But whatever historians might call Sir Graelent's house, the modern footbridge crosses a moat fed and refreshed by water from the little river that carved out the valley. The bridge leads to a battlemented gatehouse flanked by two solid towers. Go through the stone arch and you're standing in a cobbled courtyard looking at the ruins of a great hall. As far as most people are concerned, it's a castle.

Some romantic poet of a Regency Beauchene demolished a lot of the old buildings to make a more picturesque ruin, but someone with more sense at the time had insisted the gatehouse was left intact. These days, it's a cafe serving drinks and sandwiches to people who can't face the walk back up to the restaurant. The kitchen's on the ground floor of one of the gatehouse towers, and the room on the other side of the arch has tables and chairs for the punters on the days when it's raining.

All the doors and windows were open and I could hear voices inside. Blithehurst used to be closed on Mondays and Tuesdays, but as soon as the business reopened, Eleanor cut that back to only shutting on Mondays. With the added footfall this summer, that means there's a lot to get done each week before we unlock the car park gates again. Not that any of the staff are complaining. After months of furlough and short hours, they're relieved to have their jobs back, and Eleanor works out a rota to make sure everyone gets enough time off.

Eleanor works as hard as anyone else, even if she is the boss. Maybe because she's the boss. She does the books. She hadn't said anything specific, but when she came down from Durham and told us she'd be staying on through July and August, I got the distinct impression the business was on a knife edge financially.

I caught a bracing waft of bleach as I went into the courtyard. The door to the Ladies loos was open. Sarah, who's in charge of the cafe down here, came out with a mop and bucket. She grinned at me, cheerful as always. 'Everything all right, Daniel?'

She talks to me like I'm one of her kids, which is fair enough. She must be about the right age to be my mother, if my mum wasn't an ageless tree spirit.

I hefted the toolbox in my hand. 'Eleanor's asked me to make sure the old kennel is still okay for kids to play in.'

Sarah looked surprised. 'I haven't had anyone complaining about splinters or skinned knees.'

I shrugged. 'Better safe than sorry. Health and safety and all that.'

'I suppose so.' She smiled again and headed for the cafe kitchen.

I headed for the kennel. It's just inside the courtyard, on a stone plinth and close by the gatehouse wall. This particular doghouse could be two hundred years old or even older. Wood lasts, especially oak. It gets harder as it weathers, and especially when some piece of joinery has been well made and kept in a sheltered spot. This kennel ticked all those boxes. Up in the main house, I'd seen black-and-white photos that went back to the early days of cameras. When the estate gardener and his family had lived in the gatehouse, their dogs had slept out here.

There's easily room for a couple of German Shepherds or the like. So there's plenty of space for pre-school kids who can't resist taking a look inside, and climbing in once they see it's empty. Parents, grandparents or whoever takes photos of their little darlings sitting in the doorway, grinning from ear to ear. Why not? It's a handsome piece of work, with an ornate carved ridge where the shingles meet on the roof and decorative scrolling around the entrance.

As I examined all four sides, I wasn't surprised to find every joint was still perfectly watertight. Whoever had made it had known his trade. I can tell. I did my own apprenticeship with a master joiner after a year of university convinced me that an earth sciences degree wasn't for me. I've made my living working with wood for over ten years now.

I supposed there was some chance the inside had been damaged. Some idiot kid with a penknife whose parents hadn't wanted to own up could do a lot of mischief. Did parents give their kids penknives these days? My dad had given me my first one when I was pretty young. He told me I could keep it as long as I didn't cut myself. If that happened, he said, he'd put it away somewhere safe until I was a little bit older. My dad's old school though. Most of his friends were already grandfathers by the time I was born. Still, his style of parenting never did me any harm. Since I knew the rules, Dad didn't have to take that first little knife off me. I've still got it somewhere in the bottom of my toolbox.

I crouched down to look through the kennel's doorway. I definitely wasn't going to get inside. I wasn't even going to get my shoulders through the entrance. Dryads' sons are as human as the next man, mostly anyway, but we do tend to be tall and strong. I'm six feet four, and I have to buy most of my clothes online these days because so many shops don't even bother carrying XXL stock.

That does mean I've got long arms. I could reach a good way inside the kennel and have a cautious feel of the floor, the walls and the roof. My fingertips found smooth, dry wood, polished to silkiness on the floor by untold generations of contentedly curled-up dogs. I got a torch out of my toolbox and shone it inside to look at the bits I couldn't reach. There was no sign of anything wrong. So why the hell had Eleanor insisted I come down here and check it over?

About to stand up, I braced myself with a hand on the stone plinth. When some ancestral Beauchene had decided his dogs deserved a decent shelter, someone had had the bright idea of raising that first kennel up off the ground by around a foot. Another reason this latest kennel had lasted so long was the plinth kept the wood out of whatever rain puddled on the cobbles.

I took a closer look. Something had changed. Something was different, though I didn't know exactly what. I studied the woodwork again. No change there. Then I took a closer look at the kennel's base. I traced my finger along the dark line where the silvery wood met the tightly fitted masonry.

That line should have been green. There should be a faint growth of moss along there. I remembered seeing it last year. I'd mentioned it to Eleanor. I was going to come back with a stiff brush and clean it away. Moss wouldn't damage the wood on its own, but the moisture it held could eventually cause a problem. But it hadn't been urgent, and other things had driven it out of my mind.

Come to that, the gold and grey spots of lichen I recalled had been scoured off the flat surface of the stone as well. I supposed someone might have decided to take care of the moss and not thought it was worth mentioning, but there was no good reason to get rid of the lichen. I walked around the kennel and checked all four sides. There was no moss and no lichen anywhere on the top of the plinth, though both were still growing undisturbed on the sides.

The kennel had been moved, I realised. Who had done that, and why? Well, I guessed Eleanor must have done it. I'd find out why when I moved it myself. I braced my feet on the cobbles and took hold of the back of the kennel, close to the gatehouse wall. I wasn't working at the best angle, but I moved it easily enough. It slid across the plinth until the front half teetered on the edge of the stone. I shifted my hold, taking the weight and easing the front gently down onto the cobbles. Now the kennel was propped at an angle, I could see the top of the plinth.

It was immediately obvious the stonework wasn't a solid block built in regular courses. There were two larger slabs on the top, and one had a fractionally wider gap along one edge. I knelt down and looked in my toolbox for the old, battered screwdriver I use when I want a bit of leverage on something. I eased the end into the gap, and a bit of a shove got it under the slab. I lifted the stone up and got hold of the end with my other hand. Dropping the screwdriver back in the toolbox, I used both hands to lift the slab away. It was heavy, and I put it carefully down on the cobbles.

This must be what Eleanor hadn't been telling me. I'd uncovered a hollow that held a wooden box. I got to my feet and took a step back so I could see the cafe door.

'Sarah?' I waited a moment and then shouted louder. 'Sarah!'

She appeared in the archway, mildly concerned. 'Dan?'

'Come and take a look at this.' I realised what Eleanor had wanted when she sent me to find this. Witnesses. To what? I had no idea, but I trusted her.

Sarah came to stare at the box tucked into the hollow in the stone. 'What's that then?'

'I have no idea.' That was the honest truth.

Chapter Two

I studied the box. A skilled joiner had used mahogany, maybe, or some other hardwood. The top was dull with dust and one corner had a faint dark stain, but it had once been highly polished. Even without looking closely, I could see it was beautifully made. Someone had spared no expense.

Sarah fished her phone out of her jeans back pocket. 'Shall we open it up? Or maybe we should call Eleanor. Oh blast, there's no signal today.'

The mobile phone reception in the bottom of the valley comes and goes. Everyone else complains that the local cell towers are too far away to be reliable. They say something should be done about it. Eleanor and I are more inclined to think mobile phones shut down when the local dryads are in a bad mood. They can travel unseen through the air and sense the earth's magnetic fields in the same way as birds. That means they can screw with modern technologies very effectively when they decide to, even if they are centuries old.

'You could take some photos,' I suggested.

'Right.' Sarah poked and swiped at her screen, and held out her phone at arm's length.

I heard the fake camera shutter sound that reassures people they've taken their pictures.

'What's going on?' Lynne came out of the kitchen, wiping her hands on a tea towel. She's a bit younger than Sarah. I think they're some sort of cousins.

'Dan's found something.' Sarah walked backwards a bit and took another couple of photos to include the whole plinth and the tipped-up kennel.

Lynne looked at me, bemused. 'What on earth were you doing?'

'Making sure the kennel was still sound.' That wasn't a lie. I didn't need to make up anything extra about inspecting the base.

'Right.' Lynne grimaced. 'We don't need any more accidents around here.'

'No, we don't,' I agreed.

Sarah nodded. A few years back, a derelict watermill on the estate had collapsed and killed Eleanor's brother Robert. As far as everyone else was concerned, that had been an awful, tragic accident. Eleanor and I knew better. Like I said, supernatural encounters can be lethal if you don't know what you're facing.

'Mum?' Lynne's teenage daughter, Briony, appeared. She was working here for the school holidays, so she wore a Blithehurst House staff polo shirt and jeans like the rest of us. 'Oh, hi Dan.'

She gave me a hopeful smile. I nodded without making eye contact, doing my best to look uninterested. Mortal men find dryads incredibly alluring. Dryads are happy to use that to get their own way. I'd inherited a fair amount of my mother's charm, but the days when I'd use it to get girls into bed for a one-night stand were long gone. Besides, Briony's about half my age, so hell no, not a chance. The sooner she gets that message, the happier I will be.

'Go and ring Eleanor on the house phone, will you, love?' Lynne asked her. 'Tell her Dan's found something – well, I don't know what, exactly.'

Briony stared at the box, wide-eyed, and then looked at me. 'Aren't you going to open it?'

'Best wait for Eleanor, don't you think?' But Sarah sounded as if she wouldn't take much persuading.

'No harm in us taking a look.' I could just get the tips of my fingers into the gap between the wood and the stone. The hollow was a snug fit with a lip on the stones around it. The slab could rest on those rather than on the top of the box and still be flush with the top of the plinth. This was a skilled mason's work.

I had no idea what was inside, but I guessed Eleanor did. So I was pretty sure something unpleasant wasn't going to leap out and bite off my face when I opened the lid. Whatever it was, I wanted everyone here to see it first. Otherwise, someone would be watching Eleanor while she tried to pretend this was some great surprise. Like I said, she's not much better at telling lies than I am. I reached for the box.

'Wait a minute.' Sarah held out her phone again. 'Let's get this on video.'

'Okay. Ready?' As she nodded, I knelt down and lifted the box out of the hollow. As I put it down on the plinth, I saw it wasn't locked, just closed with a simple brass hook caught on a matching stud. I eased that open with a fingernail and lifted the lid. We saw crumpled blue velvet. I wondered how old that material was as I carefully moved the top fold aside.

'Fucking hell.'

We stared at an ornate silver cross, two candlesticks, a silver cup like something out of a movie, a round box and a shallow plate.

'Language, Dan.' But Sarah didn't sound as if she meant it.

'What's that then?' Briony came closer to see better.

'This must have something to do with the chapel.'

I glanced up to see Lynne looking over her shoulder, towards the manor house.

'I think you're right.'

Everyone who works at Blithehurst, and any visitors who take the guided tour, learns about the secret chapel hidden in some discreet rebuilding in the days when Catholicism was banned. There's a priest hole as well, and the Beauchenes stayed defiantly Catholic until – actually, I didn't know if they'd ever stopped. Eleanor wasn't a churchgoer as far as I knew, and I certainly wasn't, so the subject had never come up.

But Lynne was right. This silver belonged on an altar. Why was it here? It made sense not to hide it in the house. The guidebook mentions Blithehurst being searched for fugitive priests several times. Thankfully none were ever caught here. If they had been, they'd have been dragged away to be tortured and executed. The Beauchenes would have been in a world of trouble. They could easily have lost everything.

But they hadn't. So why had this treasure been left and forgotten in this hidey-hole? I ran my fingertips along the sides and the edges of the box. I wondered if the craftsman who had made this was the man who'd built the priest hole and the chapel, and the house's secret stair. Whoever had done that work had really understood and enjoyed working with wood.

'Run up to the office and get Eleanor, there's a love,' Sarah said to Briony.

'Hang on.' I covered the treasures with the velvet, closed the box and stood up. 'Let's just take this up to the house.' I nodded at the phone in Sarah's hand. 'Don't put that video online.'

She gave me exactly the look I deserved for that. 'You think I was born yesterday?'

'Right, sorry.' Once she'd put her phone away, I handed her the box. 'Let me put everything straight here first.'

I covered the hollow in the plinth with the slab and the three of them watched me shove the kennel back into place. Now there was nothing to show anything had been disturbed, not unless you knew what you were looking for.

We headed up the path to the house. I came last, carrying my toolbox. I had a good look around for any sign of Blithehurst's resident dryads. I wanted to know if they had known that box was there. I wondered if they had any idea who had hidden it, and when.

I did see a black, dog-shaped shadow slinking through the trees, though I don't know any dogs that stand around five foot tall at the shoulder and have eyes like burning pits of flame. I still didn't know if this particular black shuck was the one I'd seen elsewhere. If it was, I had no idea why it had followed me here. Or it might be a different spirit of darkness, one who'd lived here all along. I'd asked Asca and Frai, but they hadn't told me anything useful. Dryads may not tell lies, but they're experts at not giving a straight answer.

THE GREEN MAN'S GIFT

The shuck loped off into the shrubbery. That was a relief. Eleanor and I had been worried about what might happen when we opened up. While Blithehurst had been closed, the shuck had decided to be a watchdog. Ordinary people out for a walk who somehow decided that the house's grounds must still be open might not have been able to see a spectral black hound with fiery eyes, but their dogs sure as hell had. They couldn't get away fast enough.

So far, the shuck was behaving itself, though I was seeing it more often than I used to, especially in the mornings when I was walking over to my workshop from the estate cottage where I live in the woods.

We went around to the side of the manor house. The grand entrance is for tourists doing the guided tours. Briony ran on ahead to open the garden door that everyone who works here uses. What used to be rooms for servants at this end of the house are a staff room and an office now. They're on either side of the stone-flagged corridor that runs past the huge old kitchen with its black-leaded range and shelves of gleaming copper pots and pans.

Sarah carried the box into the library on the other side of the corridor. As she headed for the antique writing desks in the twin bay windows, Briony hung back. 'I'll get Eleanor.'

She ran off through the great hall and the dining room, heading for the main staircase. Eleanor has her own en-suite bedroom and a sitting room where she works upstairs. I heard other staff asking Briony if something was wrong. There were quite a few people about, dusting and checking the little posts holding the velvet ropes were still where they should be. They'd also be making sure the discreetly concealed alarms were in place to raise a racket if any of the antiques were moved, either by accident or by someone thinking something small and valuable like a snuff box could be quietly nicked.

I didn't hear what Briony said, but by the time Eleanor came downstairs, there were half a dozen people in the library besides me, Sarah and Lynne. I was over by the desk in the window bay. I put my toolbox behind me by the skirting so no one could trip over it.

'Let's see what you've found.' As she came into the library, Eleanor nodded to Sarah, who was standing closest to the box on the leather-topped walnut desk.

We all watched as Sarah took out the cross. Everyone could see it was designed to stand on something. She set the candlesticks on either side and put the plate, the round box and the chalice in a line. Everything matched.

'Well, it's definitely an altar set.' Eleanor's voice shook as she walked over to the desk. Everyone else but me would put that down to her being astonished by this discovery. 'It looks like it could be eighteenth century, maybe even earlier. I'll have to see what I can find out about it in the family papers.'

Everyone nodded and murmured. I reckoned Eleanor knew exactly where to look for proof that this long-lost treasure belonged to the Beauchenes. I glanced up at the ceiling, wondering who had told her where to find it. The library's walls are lined with bookcases and panelling as you would expect, but the ceiling had been made using much older, medieval carved panels stripped out of the original chapel down in the castle. The Tudor Beauchenes got away with doing that because the carvings aren't religious as such. They are leaves and twigs, fruit and flowers and what the guidebook calls mythical creatures and foliate faces.

Those faces are images of the Green Man. He's taken an interest in me since I was a kid. From time to time I see an emerald gleam deep in the eye sockets of carvings like the ones in this library, to show me he's close by. Sometimes that means he's about to turn up because there's a problem he's decided I have to sort out. I couldn't see any sign of him now though.

Eleanor had taken the blue cloth out of the box to see if there was anything underneath it. There wasn't. 'Well,' she said briskly, 'this had better go in the safe, and I need to make some phone calls.'

She didn't feel the need to tell the staff to keep this to themselves. I hoped she was right about that, as everyone headed back to whatever they'd been doing. As Eleanor packed the silver away, I stayed where I was by the window until she closed the box.

'Shall I make some coffee and bring it up to you?'

'Oh, right, yes, okay. Thanks.' Eleanor didn't look at me as she picked up the box and headed for the door.

That meant she didn't see me grinning as I followed her out and crossed the stone-flagged corridor to go through the old kitchen. Visitors on the tour never see the modern units, cooker and dishwasher tucked away in what used to be a scullery. I put the kettle on, found mugs, milk and a tray and sorted out a two-person cafetière. I'm happy enough with instant, or tea for preference, but Eleanor likes proper coffee. The kettle boiled. I made the coffee and carried everything upstairs.

There are two suites of three rooms on the upper floor of the house, as well as various guest bedrooms. Tourists see what's called the King Charles Bedroom, complete with a four-poster canopied bed and a black oak clothes press. The best of the house's Jacobean and Stuart furniture is in the adjoining sitting room and dressing room. The other suite is Eleanor's, where she has a bedroom, a bathroom with modern plumbing, and a solid lock on her sitting room to keep nosy visitors out. You wouldn't believe how many people see a door with a 'Private' sign and immediately try the handle to open it.

At the moment, the door was ajar. I nudged it wider with my shoulder and went in to put the tray on the table. Eleanor was putting the altar silver in the safe. She closed the door and worked the handle before spinning the dial to obscure the combination. Then she closed the hinged wooden panel that hid it, like the door to the priest hole or the hidden chapel stair. You'd have to know there was a safe to go looking for it. Before you could do that, you'd need to get through the alarm system on Blithehurst's doors and windows, and through Eleanor's locked door as well.

I reckoned the silver was safe enough, as long as the staff who'd seen it kept their mouths shut. I don't mean anyone would try to steal it for themselves. Everyone who worked here, or their families, had been involved with Blithehurst for years, even generations in some cases. Even so, someone might let something slip by accident.

'So that was a surprise.' I was about to ask Eleanor what she really knew about the hidey-hole when the phone on her desk rang. She snatched it up and turned away as she listened to whoever it was speaking.

'Yes, that's fine. Put them through.'

That told me someone had rung the main number on the Blithehurst website. Those calls come through to the main office in the garden centre. I pressed the cafetière plunger and poured the coffee, expecting her to be on the phone for a while. So I was surprised when I took her mug over and she offered me the handset.

'It's for you.'

Chapter Three

I took the phone. 'Hello?'

'Daniel Mackmain?' An unfamiliar voice didn't wait for me to answer. 'I did try your mobile, but that went straight to voicemail.'

'The signal's patchy round here.' That had to be better than saying 'Who are you and why are you ringing me?'

'My name's Gillian Adams. I got your numbers from Hazel Spinner.'

That got my attention. I said I'd spent most of my life without having anyone besides my mum and dad to talk to about the unseen world I'd been born into. That changed when I met Eleanor, and everything changed for us both last year. Hazel Spinner is what used to be called a wise woman, and she can shapeshift into a hare.

I'd met her down in Wiltshire, when the Green Man had sent me to sort out what threatened to become a hideous mess. Hazel had helped stop assorted mayhem, and I'd learned she was in touch with other wise women in different parts of the country. Their network did what they could to stop unsuspecting people stumbling across dangerous things lurking in the wildwoods and shadows. People who did that easily ended up dead in what inquests called freak accidents, like the one that killed Eleanor's brother.

A group of us had got together online and agreed to talk to each other when we came across something odd. The Green Man had a tendency to only get me involved when a situation had already gone seriously tits up. I'd found out the hard way that could be fucking dangerous. But this was the first time someone I didn't know had got in touch with me.

'Okay,' I said cautiously.

'I'm a psychiatric nurse. I work with community mental health services in Cheshire,' Gillian said briskly. 'I've been dealing with a patient who's had a pretty bad experience. He's a young man in his late teens who went missing for over a month. He finally turned up miles from home, dehydrated and drugged. I think there's a whole lot more to whatever happened than he's telling me. If this is what I think it is, we could have a real problem on our hands.'

She didn't go into any more details, so I guessed she didn't want to risk being overheard.

'You think he'll open up to me?' I tried not to sound too dubious.

'I've tried the motherly approach, and Iris Wicken tried charm, but he got hysterical after two minutes talking to her.' She sounded guilty about that for some reason. 'We're hoping he'll react better to a man. We can't think what else to try.'

So I was their last resort, not their first choice. 'Iris is there?'

Eleanor was drinking her coffee. I saw that get her attention.

'Is that a problem?' Gillian wanted to know.

'No, of course not. I just wasn't expecting – I don't know what I expected. Forget it. What do you want me to do?'

'Can you get up here in the next day or so? He's a voluntary patient at the moment, but if he signs himself out, I'm concerned we'll lose him for good. Until he turns up dead.' She sounded so worried about that, I guessed it must be a serious possibility.

'Okay. I'll see what I can do. Let me know how to find you.'

'Of course. I'll text you the details.'

Now she sounded so relieved that I felt apprehensive.

'I'll see you as soon as I can.'

'Thanks.' She rang off.

I put the handset down on the table and drank some coffee.

'She said something about Iris?' Eleanor put her mug down. 'Fin's sister, Iris?'

I nodded. 'It makes sense, if whatever's happened is in Cheshire. She lives somewhere Manchester way.' I told her everything Gillian had told me, which was pretty much sod all. 'Is it okay if I take a couple of days off? There's plenty of stock in the workshop if the garden centre needs more.'

'Fine.' Eleanor nodded, but she wasn't thinking about that. 'Why do you suppose this boy got hysterical talking to Iris?'

'I've no idea. People – ordinary people – don't usually even notice when one of them turns on the charm.' If nothing else, I'd go to Cheshire to get an answer to that.

Eleanor looked thoughtful. 'So we have two questions. How come he realised what she was doing, and why did that freak him out? Has anything like that ever happened to Fin?'

I shook my head. 'Not that she's said. I'll ask her though.'

Iris is my girlfriend Fin's eldest sister. I'd met her a couple of times, but I couldn't really say I knew her. I met Fin – Finele on her driving licence – a few years ago when the Green Man sent me to sort out something nasty living in a lake. Fin's a freshwater ecologist, so her advice about drainage had been useful, but the real reason the dryads decided to get her involved is she's a swan maiden.

All three sisters, their mum, their aunts and various cousins can shapeshift and become swans. They can see the same supernatural creatures and people as I can. We have other things in common too. Ordinary men find swan maidens alluring without ever stopping to wonder why. As Fin had explained to me in no uncertain terms, she found that an absolute pain in the arse. Enough creepy men think they're entitled to a woman's attention, and more if they can get it, without her more-than-human side giving them a hard-on. That's why I was surprised to hear Iris had turned on her charm deliberately.

Eleanor's thoughts had moved on. 'How is Fin? Have you spoken to her lately?'

'A couple of days ago.' I finished my coffee. 'She and Blanche are still as busy as blue-arsed flies. Apart from anything else, they're having to deal with some extremely pissed-off naiads.'

'I can imagine.' Eleanor grimaced.

Fin and her other sister run their own consultancy business, based down near Bristol. A while back, some government genius decided the answer to a shortage of water-treatment chemicals was lowering the standards for sewage plants. That was happening alongside a massive increase in supposedly unavoidable, unforeseen discharges from sewers into rivers. A lot of people were getting very unhappy. They wanted water tests and ecological impact surveys done, so they had all the facts and figures when they confronted their MPs and the water companies, to demand somebody do something to quite literally sort out this shit.

Fin and Blanche had more offers of work than they knew what to do with. They were getting as much done as they could. When you're self-employed, you don't turn down chances to put money in the bank. They were also trying to keep the peace with the river spirits they encountered. Several naiads had been threatening to take matters into their own hands. As far as I was concerned, that would be fine if they could guarantee they only flooded water company executives' houses. Ordinary people who weren't responsible for this crap didn't deserve to have their houses filled with filth, or having their chances of ever getting affordable flood insurance comprehensively screwed.

'What does Iris do?' Eleanor asked. 'I know you did say.'

'She's a commercial meteorologist. Works for a company that does detailed weather forecasts for shipping companies and airlines.'

That had given us something to talk about when we'd first met. I hadn't got around to asking her if being able to turn into a swan and fly gave her any particular insights into the weather.

'It's interesting this Gillian Adams is a psychiatric nurse,' Eleanor remarked. 'That's a good line of work to be in if she's friends with Hazel Spinner.'

She didn't have to explain what she meant. The wise women are determined to keep the unsuspecting public in the dark about the things that really do go bump in the night. Hazel's a cryptozoologist. Most of her time she's working out if some particular animal is extinct or not, or if some little brown bird on a remote island is the same species as the little brown birds on the next rock along. She also runs a website where people can report seeing the Beast of Bodmin and things like that. It gives her an excellent excuse to investigate what's really going on. If she finds a real threat, the wise women deal with it. Then Hazel convinces whoever got in touch that they really shouldn't believe their own eyes. That's how her path had crossed mine and Fin's down in Wiltshire last year. Eleanor was right. Someone who worked in mental healthcare would be very well placed to hear stories that sounded insane but were possible threats that needed checking out.

'Right.' My phone buzzed in my pocket. I checked Gillian's message and took a quick look at Google maps. 'Okay, now I know where I'm going.'

'You might as well get on your way.' Eleanor wasn't taking any chances when a delay might mean somebody ending up dead. Not after what happened to Robert. 'I'll rework the rota for tomorrow. Let me know if you're going to be away any longer than that, so I can make arrangements.'

'I'll pack a bag and hit the road.' I replied to Gillian's text as I left the room, telling her to expect me around noon.

I was halfway down the stairs when I remembered I hadn't asked Eleanor what she knew about that hidden box full of silver. Well, that could wait, unlike this teenager in Chester, assuming Gillian Adams was right. I wasn't going to bet against a wise woman.

I collected my toolbox from the library and took that back to my workshop in the old dairy yard. I checked that there were enough carved animals, honey dippers and ornamental spoons boxed up and ready to restock the shop, along with plenty of finished and polished bowls, plates, candlesticks and light pulls. I'd spent a lot of the winter wood turning on my new lathe while the house was shut. I locked up and cut through the woods to the cottage I've been renovating since I came to live at Blithehurst.

I swapped my jeans for combat trousers, which are a damn sight more comfortable to drive in and have far more useful pockets. I changed my Blithehurst polo shirt for a plain blue T-shirt and threw everything I should need for the next few days into the overnight bag Fin had bought me for Christmas. When I grabbed my car keys and headed out, Asca was standing a few paces from the front door.

'Where are you going?' she demanded.

There are two dryads at Blithehurst these days. Frai was here when Sir Graelent and his Normans arrived, and Asca is her daughter. I've no idea how old she is, but she looks like an elegant woman in her late forties. Two hundred and twenty-odd years ago she gave Eleanor's ancestor Edmund the son he needed to save the estate for his five daughters. They would have been evicted when he died and some distant cousin inherited. Though Asca wouldn't have borne any man a child if she hadn't truly loved him, according to my mum anyway.

Since she wouldn't be visible to anyone else apart from Eleanor, she was dressed in the sort of draperies Greek goddesses wear on vases. She can easily pass for human and appear in modern clothing when she wants to, but if it's just us, she rarely bothers.

'I'm off to Cheshire.' I waited for her to say something, or maybe to ask another question.

'Go carefully.' She disappeared before I could ask what she meant by that.

I wondered if it had anything to do with Eleanor finding that hidden silver. The dryads are determined to keep the estate in the Beauchene family. For a long time that had been easy enough. Several family members in each generation would be able to see them, and they could be bullied into doing whatever might be necessary. But now Eleanor is the last of her family who can see the dryads. So far, neither of her brothers, her sister or any of their cousins had any kids who had inherited that double-edged gift. Besides, none of that would matter if the business went bankrupt. Eleanor had explained that to Asca and Frai in no uncertain terms when they complained about opening up on Tuesdays.

Eleanor could deal with the dryads. I slung my bag into the back of my Land Rover and got in. Checking Gillian Adams's message on my phone, I set up the satnav to take me where I needed to go and followed the narrow estate road towards the back gate.

I tested the feel of the steering. I still couldn't decide if it was exactly the same as it had been before. The driver's seat was definitely different, and I had to admit, it was definitely more comfortable. Most importantly though, this was still my Landy. There had been times when I'd thought I'd never get it back on the road, not after it had been swamped in a storm by three-foot waves of sand and seawater. That happened when Fin and I had been trying to stop an arrogant bastard stirring up trouble he didn't understand in the East Anglian fens, where most of her family live.

THE GREEN MAN'S GIFT

Chapter Four

I reached the estate back gate, got out to unlock it and drove through. I stopped again, got out and relocked the gate behind me. A mile or so further on, I reached the main road that would take me towards the M6. I reminded myself to give Fin's dad, Simon, a call when whatever was happening in Cheshire was sorted. He'd be interested to know how the Landy handled on a decent run.

He'd let me put the salvaged vehicle in an empty building on his Cambridgeshire farm. I'd been ready to give up, but he'd persuaded me I might as well strip out the stuff that would have to be replaced and let everything else take its time drying out before I scrapped it. What did I have to lose? He had the space to spare, and it wasn't as if the insurance would pay out anything close to what the vehicle was worth to me.

He was right. It took us over a year, with me heading over to Cambridgeshire as often as I could, but we got it running again. We'd had to take the engine apart completely, as well as replace the wiring loom, but Simon did most of his own maintenance on his farm vehicles and I knew every inch of the Landy, so between us we had the necessary skills. Refitting the interior hadn't been cheap, but we'd managed to source what we needed by scouring eBay and some specialist Land Rover–enthusiast websites. Farmers Simon knew had been useful as well. His network seemed to cover the east coast of England from the Humber down to the Thames.

I reached the motorway and hit the play button on the CD player as I headed northwards. Simon had insisted on fitting that, and he'd given me a couple of Fleetwood Mac and REM CDs. That was the music he played while we were working on the Landy. It was going to be a long time before I heard any of those tracks without a vivid memory of the smell and feel of cold metal in my oily hands.

One good thing about Simon playing music while we worked was he wasn't inclined to chat. Apart from weekends when Norwich City were playing, when I could let him do all the talking. At first, I'd been a bit wary about us working together. I didn't know what might happen if Simon asked me a question I could only answer with a lie. He would be shrewd enough to spot that, even if he had no idea that his ex-wife and his three daughters could turn into swans. Unsurprisingly, his marriage to Helen hadn't lasted with her keeping a secret like that. But they had stayed on good terms and Simon loved his girls. One thing he made very clear to me was if I ever mistreated Fin I'd answer to him, even if he had to find a box to stand on to punch me in the face.

The drive didn't take much more than an hour. There was a fair bit of traffic on the motorway, but it was moving freely. I was soon seeing signs for Chester as the satnav took me around to the north side of the city via the M56. Tourist attractions included a zoo, and apparently the city walls were worth seeing. Maybe Fin and I could have a weekend break here sometime and take a look. Then the satnav took me off the main road and I switched off the music to make sure I didn't miss a turn.

Gillian had told me to go to a pub called The Grosvenor Arms. It was a mock-Tudor building in one of those suburbs with nothing distinctive about it. I wasn't complaining. The car park was well maintained, and this didn't look like a place where I'd come back to find the Landy with a smashed window. I still unplugged the satnav and put it out of sight with my bag in the back. There's no point taking chances.

Inside, the bar was clean and airy with dark-wood tables and red velour upholstery on the chairs and bench seats. A sign on the door said that masks were to be worn at each customer's discretion. The barman looked my way and I saw he was wearing one, so I fished one out of my pocket. Thanks to my mother's blood, I hardly ever catch anything that's going around, but that's not the point. I put the mask on.

'What can I get you?' The barman put down the glass he'd been polishing.

'A pint of Coke, please.' I could see Iris and another woman sitting at a table by a window with coffee cups between them. Iris looked over and recognised me, so I raised a hand to say I'd be with them in a minute. They weren't the only customers, though the place wasn't crowded.

I found my wallet and tapped my card on the terminal to pay for my drink. 'Thanks.'

The barman nodded. 'I'll bring some menus over in a minute.'

So I guessed we were staying for lunch. Fine with me. I carried my Coke over to the table by the window.

'Hello. You must be Dan.' The woman who had to be Gillian held out her hand out of habit. She pulled it back before I had to decide whether or not to shake it. 'Nice to meet you.'

'You too.' I sat down.

Gillian was a solidly built woman in her late fifties, maybe, medium height with long steel-grey hair drawn back into a ponytail. She wore glasses, and while her smile was friendly, her pale blue eyes were sharp enough to warn anyone with any sense not to mess her about. She wore dark blue trousers and a long, loose yellow-and-blue flowery shirt. Nothing about her appearance would tell you she was any kind of nurse.

If you'd ever met Fin, you'd guess Iris was her sister. She's tall and slim with the same white-blonde hair, which she keeps cut around collar length. I've never seen her without make-up, which is something Fin hardly ever bothers with. Today, Iris wore jeans and a short-sleeved maroon top that showed she was spending plenty of time in the gym. She's the oldest sister, so she's a couple of years older than me.

'Hi, Dan.'

'Good to see you.' I took off my mask and took a long drink of my Coke. It was a hot day and my Landy was far too old for me and Simon to even think about fitting air conditioning.

Gillian checked the barman was nowhere near enough to overhear us. Even so, she kept her voice down. 'I'm working in a unit for young people with mental health problems. It's mostly depression, anxiety, some borderline personality disorders. You know the sort of thing.'

I didn't, but I kept quiet. I did know that life was hard and getting harder for anyone leaving school or uni without a supportive family or someone else taking an interest. Before I lived at Blithehurst, I'd moved around a lot. I'd come across teenage runaways and kids struggling to cope on their own.

'Quite a few of our clients have been looked-after children,' Gillian went on. 'Tom is one of those. Not that anyone expected him to go off the rails. He'd been in a decent foster placement, and he got a room in a shared house when he started at the local college. He had his issues, but everyone I've spoken to thought he was coping well, even with the lockdowns and remote learning. Then he disappeared. Of course, the police decided he'd just got fed up and gone off of his own free will. They did a check for any sign of him on bus cameras and local CCTV, in case they saw him getting into a fight, but he was over eighteen. It was hard to make a case that he was a vulnerable adult. Compared to everything else they're having to deal with, he wasn't a priority.'

She was doing her best to be fair, but she was clearly annoyed. 'He turned up six weeks later, halfway up a mountain in North Wales. He was barely coherent, filthy dirty, half-starved and dehydrated, and his pockets were full of mushrooms.'

She broke off as the barman came over with the lunch menus. I took a quick look and handed mine back.

'I'll have the cheeseburger and chips, thanks, and another Coke.'

Iris made up her mind just as fast. 'Vegan burger, please, and a lemonade.'

Gillian took a moment or two longer, studying the options. 'I'll have the bean and lentil chilli, please, and a sparkling water with lemon and ice.'

'Right you are.' He wrote everything on his pad, gathered up the menus and left us to our conversation.

'Were those magic mushrooms in his pocket?' I asked quietly. The bar was starting to fill up with other people looking for lunch.

'Some were, some weren't.' Gillian shook her head. 'He swore he didn't know where they had come from, and insisted he hadn't taken anything. Of course, the police didn't believe him, even though there was no evidence on record that he'd ever used drugs before. He doesn't even drink. Both his parents were alcoholics. That's how he ended up in care.'

'Did they do a blood test?' I asked.

'No, but there was no point. By the time the police got involved, there wouldn't have been any traces left in his system. He was found by some hikers. Since he was just about able to walk, they got him down to the nearest village instead of calling out mountain rescue. That's when they called the emergency services. By the time the ambulance arrived, they'd got some hot, sweet tea into him, and he was able to tell the paramedics his name.'

'What else could he tell them?' I was still wondering why Gillian thought this was our kind of problem.

Iris answered. 'Nothing. He has absolutely no idea what happened, or how he got into Wales.'

'Which the police put down to the drugs they're still convinced he'd taken.' Gillian shook her head, exasperated. 'He was admitted to hospital for a few days, which was a minor miracle. That's when one of my colleagues was called in.'

I wondered if she meant another wise woman or a psychiatrist, or someone who was both.

'He was terrified of the dark, even though that had never been an issue before. When he finally fell asleep, he woke up screaming. They had to sedate him several times. Of course, that went on his notes as some sort of flashback to a bad trip on those bloody mushrooms. After a few days, he calmed down, but by then he had turned in on himself. He's barely speaking. He's still having nightmares, and he only goes to sleep when he can't stay awake any longer. But he's refusing to talk. He says there's no point, because no one will believe him.'

Gillian heaved a sigh. 'He's with us for the moment because after a month when no one knew where he was, his stuff was packed up and put into storage. His room had to be given to someone else. There's such a demand and nowhere near enough accommodation. I'm trying to find him another place, but that's not going to be easy when the official version is he went off of his own accord, spent six weeks doing drugs in Wales, and he's refusing to cooperate to get whoever's responsible arrested.'

'How do you know he didn't do that?' I asked bluntly.

Gillian didn't take offence. 'Because when he woke up screaming, my colleague made some notes. He was terrified of a beautiful woman who'd taken him somewhere full of strange people and music and dancing. The woman fed him strange food and took him to bed and who knows what else happened until he ran away. He didn't want to go back, but he was convinced this woman was coming to get him. If she did – when she did – no one would be able to stop her. No one would be able to even see her. He was absolutely frantic.'

'Right.' I could see why that would make a wise woman's ears prick up. Stories of ordinary people lured away to enjoy fantastical feasts crop up all over the country, and they go back centuries. 'So you think he was off with the fairies, quite literally?'

Gillian nodded. 'Doesn't it sound like that to you?'

'How do you think I can help him?' I hoped I sounded as if I wanted to help. To be honest, I had no clue.

'Getting him to open up to someone who can convince him they believe him would be a start.' Gillian sounded desperate. 'Someone who can convince him this woman can be beaten. At the moment he's in no fit state to go back to college, or anywhere else. He sits staring into space and shivering in the corner of the TV room all day. When it's getting dark, he starts looking over his shoulder. He watches every shadow as if he's expecting something to leap out and grab him.'

I was convinced. He'd met something powerful and dangerous. I looked at Iris. 'But he wouldn't open up to you?'

She shook her head. 'When I tried a little, you know, *persuasion*, he went completely ape-shit. Said I was one of them, that she had sent me. I had to leave the room. It was a toss-up whether he was going to attack me or jump out of the window, right through the glass.'

She managed a smile, but the experience had shaken her. I wasn't surprised.

Gillian looked apologetic. 'We had no idea that your sort of *persuasion* would feel so similar to whatever charm he's been subjected to already.'

That must be the conclusion the wise women had come to when they discussed it between themselves.

'There's more.' Iris reached into her back pocket for her phone. 'I went online to see what I could find, in case anything rang alarm bells. I've got five missing persons cases so far where a young man in his late teens or early twenties vanished. That's going back ten years across Merseyside and Greater Manchester. Lads like Tom from broken homes or leaving care, with no one looking out for them, or at least no one who could make the police take their case seriously.'

'Did any of them ever turn up?' Seeing her expression, I wasn't optimistic.

'Two were found dead at the bottom of rock faces in Snowdonia. Their inquests couldn't decide between suicide or accident, so the coroners recorded open verdicts.'

She offered to show me a news website on her phone. I waved it away. She put down her phone and went on. 'One was found half-dead of exposure. He seemed to recover okay, but as soon as he was released from hospital, he drowned himself in a lake the very next day. The one after that had a complete psychotic break. He's in a secure unit somewhere.'

'I'm trying to get access to his records.' Gillian didn't sound hopeful.

'That's four.' I looked at them both.

'We can't find any trace of the last one.' Iris shook her head.

'So this mysterious beautiful lady still has him trapped in fairyland, or the poor bastard has killed himself somewhere so remote that his body won't be found for years, if at all.' Either option was grim.

'Assuming these disappearances are connected.' Iris wrinkled her nose in a way that really reminded me of Fin. 'This could just be coincidence.'

'Does that really matter, just at the moment?' Gillian asked sharply. 'We need to help Tom.'

I nodded, though I still wasn't sure how we were going to do that. 'If you can get me in to meet him, I'll see what I can find out.'

Then our lunch arrived. We stopped talking and ate.

Chapter Five

Lunch was good. When we finished eating, we paid our separate bills and waited for the waitress to load our plates onto her tray and move away.

'They're going to want this table.' Iris was right. The bar was getting busy. Still, that meant plenty of voices covered our conversation.

I looked at Gillian. 'What do we do now?'

She picked up her handbag. 'You come with me to the unit. I'll chivvy Tom out into the garden to get some fresh air. See if you can get him talking.' She looked at Iris. 'Are you okay making those phone calls? I've got to catch up with some work this afternoon.'

'Yes, no problem. I can do that from the travel inn. I'm staying at one of those chain places,' Iris explained to me. 'Shall I book you a room for tonight?'

'Might as well.' I didn't think I'd be heading back to Blithehurst today. Where we might be heading tomorrow was another question.

We stood up, and a couple who'd been sitting on stools at the bar took our table before we were through the door. Out in the car park, Gillian walked with me to the Landy while Iris headed off in a newish electric Mini with shiny black paint. Commercial meteorology must pay better than freelance freshwater ecology.

We got into the Land Rover. 'Tell me where to go.'

Gillian settled her seatbelt more comfortably. 'Turn right out of the car park.'

I did as I was told. As I checked both ways for traffic, I saw Gillian frowning.

'What can I smell in here? Not a threat, but something fishy?'

I couldn't smell anything. 'Merman?' I had the sea folk to thank for salvaging the Landy, though arguably they were responsible for getting it swamped in the first place.

'Oh.' Gillian didn't ask for any details, but I could see her filing that away for future reference. If the wise women have a motto, it'll be something like 'Knowledge is power'.

She raised a hand and pointed. 'Straight through these lights and go left at the next junction.'

She was good at giving directions, giving plenty of warning before I needed to make a turn or change lanes. We soon arrived at an open area in the middle of a weary-looking red-brick estate. A convenience store, a chippy, a hairdresser's and a laundrette looked across the road at a kids' playground surrounded by a low fence.

'Over there.' Gillian pointed past the strip of shops to one of those flat-roofed buildings the NHS was so fond of about fifty years ago, with breeze-block walls and wooden panelling under the windows. Whatever the place had originally been, it was long overdue a new coat of white paint. A square of tarmac at the front had ten marked-out spaces with seven cars in them, and a stern notice saying 'Staff Parking Only'. Anyone else would be clamped.

'Stop on the street somewhere here, and you can walk around to the back,' Gillian told me. 'The gate to the garden's unlocked.'

I pulled the Landy into a convenient space and wondered why she didn't want me parking in front of the little supermarket.

Gillian opened her handbag and took out a lanyard which she hung around her neck. Then she offered me a battered pack of cigarettes, half full, with a cheap plastic lighter tucked inside. 'Take these with you.'

'I don't smoke.'

'Tom does, and he ran out of fags this morning. He can't face going to the shops himself yet, so I said I'd pick up a pack while I was out at lunch. I'll tell him I forgot and promise to do it later. He'll be gagging for a nicotine hit by now.'

'Right.' I reminded myself that these wise women could be pretty ruthless. They also had no problem telling lies. 'What do I say if someone sees me and asks what I'm doing? Apart from Tom, obviously.' Who must be in a pretty bad way if he couldn't get himself to the shop that was virtually next door.

'They won't.' Gillian was certain.

I wondered how she could be so sure, but I didn't ask. I reminded myself that wise women had been called witches in days gone by. 'Okay.'

'Don't say anything about Iris, and don't mention my name.' She got out of the passenger seat and headed for the main entrance of the grimy white building. The blue-and-white sign said this was Smith House. When she swiped the card on her lanyard, the door opened up.

I counted slowly to one hundred after Gillian went inside. Then I got out of the Land Rover. I tried not to look too conspicuous, which isn't easy when you're my height and build with a number-two haircut.

I followed a narrow tarmac path past the staff car park and along the side of the building. The regularly spaced windows had those slatted vertical blinds. They were closed, so I couldn't see inside. When I got to the back, I found more open space with a cycle path running along behind the back gardens of the closest houses.

THE GREEN MAN'S GIFT

Behind Smith House, a patch of grass about the same size as the car park had been fenced off with those lengths of angled iron that split into three sharp points at the top. If the gate wasn't unlocked, there was no way I was getting in there.

But the gate opened easily. I went into the garden. That was a flattering description for a scabby lawn yellowing in the dry weather and a few self-seeded buddleias lurking along the fence line. On one side a square of uneven paving slabs offered three wooden park benches set at right angles to each other. Feeling more conspicuous than ever, I sat on the one that faced the back door.

I put the cigarettes down beside me and got out my phone. After I'd checked for new messages and there weren't any, I carried on looking at the screen. I didn't react when I heard the back door open and close. After I'd counted to twenty, I glanced up and saw a thin-faced, scrawny lad. His ragged black hair was long enough to half cover his eyes. He wore black jeans that were ripped at the knees, not to make some fashion statement but because cheap shit was all he could afford. His black T-shirt had been washed so often it was turning grey, with barely a ghostly trace left of whatever design had been on the front.

He stood by the bench opposite, hesitating. I went back to looking at my phone, leaning back, relaxed, with my legs stretched out. Hopefully my body language was saying no threat here, honest.

'Got a fag to spare?'

I looked up and tossed him the packet. 'Help yourself.' I went back to looking at my phone.

'Cheers.' He lit one and sat down on the other bench. 'Sorry, here you go,' he said a moment later.

I looked up and caught the cigarettes as he threw them back. I put the packet on the bench beside me again. I hoped Gillian wasn't expecting me to smoke one to establish some sort of bond. I wouldn't get Tom to share his deepest, darkest secrets while I was coughing up a lung.

After another quick glance, I decided that wasn't an issue. He was staring blindly into the distance and sucking on that cigarette as if his life depended on it. I remembered hearing somewhere that teenagers and students took up smoking despite the cost and the health risks as a way to self-medicate for stress, in a world where jobs and housing and cars cost a fortune or were out of reach. That made a grim sort of sense, but this lad was taking it to a whole other level.

I wondered how long I could keep looking at my phone. It was all very well Gillian and Iris thinking he might find it easier to talk to me, but I didn't know how to start a conversation. 'Seen any good fairies lately? By good, I mean the ones who drag you away from your friends and family and wreck your life.' Because there are plenty of those in the stories that ordinary people think are myths.

'Why are you here?' Tom said suddenly.

That wasn't a challenge, but he was definitely on edge, wary of anything unusual.

'Some mix-up.' I aimed to sound more bored than pissed off. 'I was told a mate of mine was staying here. I thought I'd visit. Someone's got their wires crossed. I'm waiting for someone to find out where he has gone.'

I really hoped that whatever made Tom suspicious of Iris wouldn't mean he could tell I was lying.

'Right.' He sounded dubious.

He carried on smoking. Down to the last few millimetres of tobacco, he dropped the dog-end onto the paving and ground it under his trainer. That had a big split where the upper met the sole, and the one on his other foot had been mended with gaffer tape.

I looked up and saw him staring at the cigarettes beside me. 'You can have these if you want. My mate left them in my car.'

'Cheers.' He might not trust me, but he didn't wait for me to offer twice. Coming over, he snatched up the packet and quickly lit up another smoke. This time he sat on the other end of my bench. A few moments later, he remembered a few manners someone had taught him. 'I'm Tom.'

'Dan.'

He sucked in a lungful of smoke. 'So why's your mate s'posed to be in here then?'

I put my phone away and folded my arms, looking at the bench opposite. 'Honestly, you wouldn't believe me if I told you.'

Tom looked at me. He didn't say anything, but I could see he was curious.

I kept looking across the garden. 'He's been having some sort of assessment because he swears a fuck-off enormous black dog chased him down the high street where we live. Only no one else could see it. And it wasn't just big, it was massive, and it had these glowing red eyes, like something out of a horror movie.'

I pictured the shuck. I remembered how terrified I had been the first time I had realised one was following me through some woods. Hopefully that would give this fairy tale I was spinning some ring of truth. I really hoped Tom wouldn't ask me where this had happened, because there was no way I could invent enough detail to be convincing.

'He damn near shat himself, but no one else could see the fucking thing. They said he must be on drugs, but he doesn't do that shit.'

Tom was staring straight ahead again, sucking in smoke. He let it trickle out through his nostrils. At the moment his whole world was whatever was going on in his own head.

'But you believe him, do you?' he asked after a long moment. 'Because he's your mate?'

I silently counted to ten before I replied. 'Because I've seen the fucking thing myself.'

Tom turned his head with a sharp intake of breath. That was a mistake with his mouth full of smoke. He started coughing. By the time he managed to stop, he was red-faced and his eyes were watering. Or maybe he was crying. It was hard to tell. He stared at me with desperation, hope and fear in his face.

I looked straight at him. 'I've seen things like that since I was a kid, and I don't do drugs either. Never have, never will.'

Every word of that sentence was true. I really hoped he could hear it and see it in my eyes. Forget male bonding or any of that bollocks. If he had sensed Iris trying to persuade him with whatever charm she could use, maybe that would cut both ways. Maybe he would know I was telling the truth.

'I— I—.' He couldn't go on.

I leaned forward, resting my elbows on my thighs. 'I'm guessing something weird happened to you?'

'Fuck, yes,' he burst out. 'And no fucker believes me either.'

I looked straight at him again. 'I will.'

For a long moment, neither of us moved. A car went past on the road at the front. I could feel the summer sun on my bare arms. Tom chewed his lower lip. From the way the skin was chapped and split, he was doing that a lot.

'I don't do drugs,' he said vehemently. 'I've seen what happens when people get fucked up.'

'Right,' I agreed. 'I was working on a building site once where a brickie came to work doped over. You wouldn't believe how fast the foreman got rid of him.'

Tom looked a bit puzzled, and I couldn't blame him, because that was hardly relevant, but I wanted to keep this conversation going, and that meant telling as few lies as possible. Ideally none.

'Right,' he said a moment later. 'At college, it's more Molly and stuff, or people getting shit-faced on vodka in the park, but it all fucks up your grades. I don't do any of that.'

'But that's what they're saying?' I jerked my head towards the blank back wall of the unit.

'I had—' He scowled. 'They say I had shrooms on me when they found me. But I never bought them. I never took them. Fuck it, I wouldn't know where to start looking to buy that shit. But they say until I'm willing to admit what I did, until I'm ready to be honest with myself, I can't move on.' He mimicked somebody's patronising voice with savage sarcasm.

I realised I didn't know what the law had to say about magic mushrooms. I should have looked that up instead of pretending to check messages on my phone. I needed to ask Gillian if Tom would be charged if he admitted the shrooms were his. But I didn't need convincing that he was telling the truth.

'I believe you. Some fucker planted them on you? Someone who wanted to get you locked up?'

He looked at me, startled. That wasn't something he'd asked himself. 'I don't know.'

'So what did happen?' I prompted. Whatever Gillian had said, the longer we were sitting out here, the bigger the chances were that someone would look out of a window and want to know who I was.

Tom took another drag on the cigarette. He winced when the filter got stuck to a raw place on his lip. Dropping the smouldering dog-end, he crushed it into a black smear beside the first one. He was looking straight ahead, but this time he was searching his memories. I must have said something right, or maybe he'd had enough of bottling everything up.

'A bunch of us went to a music night. Four or five bands in a pub, you know? Someone I know from college, his brother was playing drums for one of the bands. They're actually pretty good. But they weren't all bands. There was a girl singer, blonde, just her with a guitar. She was fucking brilliant. Everyone said so. She did her set and stayed on to watch the others. We got talking at the bar.' Tom shook his head, disbelieving. 'She was gorgeous. I mean, like a supermodel or something. I told her, "You're going to be a superstar," but she wanted to know all about me. Fucked if I know why. I'm no one special.'

I heard a lifetime of pain in those four words. This poor sod had never been anyone's priority. Even people like Gillian who were trying to help him, they were just doing their job, overworked and under-resourced. He didn't have anyone who saw him as more than a case file or a reference number, alongside dozens of others who'd had an equally crap start in life.

Then this beautiful girl had wanted to talk to him, out of everyone in the pub. She didn't know his background so she couldn't have judged him. She was interested in him in a way no one else had ever been. It must have felt like a miracle. No wonder he'd been so eager to believe it.

Tom's face hardened. 'That's the last thing I remember – the last thing that's normal, anyway.'

I waited a moment before prompting him again. 'What do you remember about the weird shit?'

He looked at me, still wary.

'I told you,' I reminded him. 'I've seen shit the people here wouldn't believe. I'm not going to call you a liar.'

Tom still didn't say anything.

I got my phone out and found a website I'd bookmarked ages ago. *The North Cotswold Mercury*. 'See this? It says I saved a kid from drowning. That's true. What it doesn't say was a slimy fucking monster dragged him under when he went swimming in that lake.'

I handed over the phone so Tom could see it really was me in the photo. 'What it doesn't say, what no reporter knows, is I went back a few days later and cut the fucker to pieces with a bill hook.'

Tom recoiled. He thrust my phone at me so fast I nearly dropped it. But he didn't jump up. He didn't run off. I saw the first glint of hope in his eyes. I waited. After a few minutes, he started talking so fast I could hardly understand.

'It was like a party, you know, at someone's house? Only it was more like some sort of stately home or maybe something in a movie, all gold furniture and big silk curtains and candles, but there weren't any windows, and the rooms led into each other, and I couldn't find any doors. There was music, orchestra stuff, but I couldn't see who was playing it. Loads of people were dancing though, in one of the big rooms, and there were mirrors around the walls, but the people – their reflections – they didn't look the same. They were— they were— like animals and that, dressed up, but with human arms and legs.'

His eyes were screwed tight shut. He was trembling so hard I could feel the wooden bench vibrating. Before I could work out what to say, he started talking again.

'There was food, like a kids' party, all cakes and cream and sweet shit. It made me feel sick, but I couldn't stop wanting to eat it. There was – well, they said it wasn't wine, and it didn't get me pissed, but I wanted to drink more and more, but that didn't stop me feeling thirsty. Then... then she—' He went scarlet.

I remembered what Gillian had said. 'This girl, the supermodel one, she offered you a fuck, and you couldn't say no to that either.'

He stared at me. 'How did you know?'

Shit. Had I just given the game away? I thought quickly and showed him the pale parallel lines on my tanned forearm. 'See these scars? I got them rescuing some poor sod who'd been lured into a wood with the promise of a quick shag. What he thought was a woman? She really wasn't.'

'Fucking hell.' Tom swallowed hard. 'Who the fuck are you? Scooby Doo's big brother?'

I didn't point out that Scooby Doo is the dog. 'Someone who sees weird shit and tries to stop people getting hurt.'

I don't think he heard me. He was back remembering the living nightmare he'd been caught in.

'I thought it was just us, you know, me and her, in this big double bed with those fancy net curtains and big pillows and white sheets. But when I looked up, they were standing around the bed, the – whatever the fuck they were from the dance floor. They were watching and laughing. I wanted to stop – all right, I didn't want to, and I couldn't anyway.' He looked ready to throw up. 'I never – I mean, it was my first time.'

'Shit.' Poor bastard. It was going to take him a long time to get over that.

He scrubbed his face with shaking hands. 'When I – afterwards – they went off somewhere else and left me alone. I found my clothes and I tried to find a way out. I could barely see where I was going. I think something was chasing me. Fuck knows how I got away. I don't remember anything else until those hikers found me. One of them gave me some water and I realised I was outside, only fuck knows where.'

He looked exhausted and defeated. 'And it was six weeks later, but I only remember that one night. I can't explain it. I can't tell them what I do remember though. They'll turn me into a fucking zombie with drugs and lock me away.' Tears trickled down his hollow cheeks. 'But what the fuck do I do if she comes for me again? She said I belonged to her now that I'd been her guest. She said she'll always know where I am. She'll always be able to find me, wherever I go. Wherever they put me.'

He wouldn't have any choice about where he would be living next. He didn't have a place to go, any more than he had a family. My family might not be as big as Fin's – it's just me, my mum and my dad – but I know they will always be there for me. There have been times when Dad and I haven't got on very well, especially when I dropped out of university, but I can always go home, no matter what.

'Tell them you were roofied,' I said. 'The nurses here, I mean.'

Surprise jolted him out of his misery into confusion.

'But I was only drinking Coke.'

'You think a soft drink can't be spiked? Tell them about going to see the bands. Say someone must have put something in your drink. That's why you can't remember what happened, not much of it anyway. Give them something they can work with, then you can keep the rest to yourself. It's saying nothing that's the problem. They'll keep on at you as long as they think you've got something to hide.'

I'd learned that lesson in more than one police interview room.

'Say you think you were taken to a house somewhere. People were taking drugs, and you didn't want any part of it, but you didn't get a choice. Tell them what you think they'll believe. Say you can't remember the rest because you were drugged. You don't have to tell them about the sex, not if you don't want to.'

That was a hellish tricky one. The poor sod needed some sort of rape counselling, surely, but while I was pretty sure I could trust Gillian, I didn't know who else worked here. If someone thought one of the scummier tabloids might pay for a story about kidnaps, drugs, orgies and sex slaves, Tom could end up royally screwed.

'You do that, and I'll see what I can find out about this girl. Like I said, I don't like people getting hurt.'

'How are you going to do that?' He was desperate to believe me, while a lifetime of bad experiences was telling him that would be stupid.

I wasn't going to make any promises I might not be able to keep. That would be as good as lying to him, and enough people had done that. 'This singer, with the guitar. Do you remember her name?'

'What?'

'The girl, the supermodel one. She must have had a name. Did someone introduce her when she came on stage?'

'Oh, yeah, right. Mary?' He didn't sound certain though. Then his eyes focused. Now he had someone to blame for everything he'd been put through. 'Mary Reese.'

'Okay.' I nodded and stood up. 'I'll see if I can track her down and find out what the hell she's playing at.'

I'd seen one of the slatted blinds in the window by the back door twitch a couple of times now. It might have been Gillian trying to see how I was getting on, but maybe not. My phone had just buzzed to tell me I had a message. I wasn't going to take the chance that someone else was about to come out and ask me what I was doing in the unit's garden.

'Look after yourself.' I nodded a quick goodbye and headed for the gate.

I looked back once from the path at the side, at the last possible moment before the breeze-block building blocked my view. Tom was still sitting on the bench, watching me go with desperate eyes as he tried to light another cigarette with shaking hands.

Chapter Six

I checked my phone as I walked back to the Land Rover. That message was from Iris. She'd booked me a room and told me where to find the hotel. She said to call her once I'd checked in. I put the postcode into the satnav and started the engine.

The hotel wasn't far away. It was one of those chains that's the same wherever you go, and yes, they're clean and reliable. I was more used to B&Bs which might turn out to be crap but were half the price. I tried not to wince as I used my card to pay at the reception desk. I had been used to shabby B&Bs, I reminded myself. Back when I was moving from working on one housing development to the next place that needed a carpenter, earning my beer money, and sometimes my rent by selling carvings at weekend craft fairs. I had a proper job now. At least, I did as long as Blithehurst didn't go bust.

The smiling girl behind the Perspex screen finished whatever she was doing with two key cards. She handed them over with a printed piece of card with the room number scribbled on it. 'You're in 224, up the stairs and along the corridor. Breakfast's in the restaurant on the other side of the car park, from six till ten in the morning. Do you want a table for dinner? I can book that if you like?'

'I'm not sure yet, sorry.' The restaurant was a steak house, and if lunch was any guide, Iris didn't eat meat, like her sisters and their mum.

'You can always ring down later.' The girl behind the desk smiled and went back to doing something on her screen.

'Thanks.' I went up the stairs and found my room at the far end of the long building. Sticking one of the key cards in the slot on the wall by the door turned the lights on as I slung my overnight bag onto the double bed. That had a fake-wood surround at the head end with little shelves, light fittings and power sockets. Another fake-wood arrangement offered shelves and hanging space by the door to the en-suite bathroom. There was a TV on the wall opposite the bed, over a small desk and chair that would be no use to someone my size. The armchair by the window was a bit better. Everything was clean and tidy, and the desk had a tray with a kettle and teabags and those little pots of milk, so that was okay.

I got my charger out of my bag and plugged in my phone to top up the battery. I made a mug of tea and realised my T-shirt reeked of fag smoke, even though I'd been talking to Tom outside, so I had a quick shower and found a clean shirt. Then I rang Iris.

'I'm here.'

'I'm in 203. See you in a minute.'

Her room was at the other end of this corridor. She'd used the night lock to keep the door open, but I knocked all the same.

'Come in.'

Her room was identical to mine. She'd set up her laptop on the little desk. She looked up as I came in. 'Well?'

'I got him talking.' I edged past her to sit in the armchair by the window.

Iris angled her chair so she was looking at me instead of the door. She started typing as I started to explain.

'What are you doing?'

'Getting everything down so I can email Gillian and Hazel.'

I wasn't sure I liked that idea. 'What if—?'

'What if someone hacks my laptop or my email and reads the short story I'm working on for our creative writing group? Along with the latest chapters of the thriller and the romance novel I'm messing about with?' Iris grinned. 'Don't worry. The names have been changed to protect the innocent, or the guilty, as the case may be.'

'Fair enough.' I went back to telling her what I'd got out of Tom. 'So,' I said when I finished, 'do you know the exact date he disappeared?'

'I do.' Iris was still intent on her screen, tapping at the keys. 'I've been looking at his social media, as well as his friends' pages. Let's see what we can find out about this music night.'

She sounded confident she'd find something. I wouldn't know where to start. 'Do you do a lot of this?'

'Cyberstalking?' She grinned. 'I've been swapping notes with Hazel. She's the real expert, but I get by.'

She went back to whatever she was doing. I waited. She didn't take long. 'Tom said this singer was called Mary Reese?'

I nodded. 'Something like that.'

'I think we're looking for Mari Rhys.' She drew out the 'ah' sound in the first name, and spelled both names out. 'A couple of Tom's friends mention her in their posts, and she's definitely a singer.'

'Where can we find her?'

I waited while Iris hit more keys.

'This is odd.' She sounded as if that was a good thing, though.

'How do you mean?'

'You'd expect an up-and-coming folk-rock singer to have a website. Twitter, Instagram, TikTok, maybe a YouTube channel?'

'If you say so.' I've never seen the point of social media, certainly not for me, but I assumed Iris was right about these things.

'There's nothing like that, and I can't find a PR photo of her anywhere. How's she supposed to land a record deal and get her shot at stardom? How does she get bookings for gigs?'

My first question still stood. 'How do we find her?'

'Let's see.' A faint line deepened between her pale eyebrows as Iris concentrated.

I waited. After a while, my phone and Iris's both chimed. I checked mine and guessed she had got the same message, so I might as well save her checking. 'Gillian says she got your email, and she'll be talking to some people this evening. Can we meet in the car park here tomorrow morning at eight o'clock?'

'Fine.' Iris didn't look up.

I replied to Gillian's message and looked at the little kettle. Iris hadn't used either of the mugs today. 'Do you want a tea or a coffee?'

'Coffee, black, one sugar, thanks.' She edged her chair forward as far as she could. That gave me just enough room to squeeze past.

I made her coffee and a tea for myself. When I put down the spoon, she stood up. 'Thanks.'

I put her coffee on the desk and went back to the armchair. Iris stretched her arms above her head and then touched her toes. Something in her shoulders went click and she sat down again, reaching for her mug.

'There's not a lot to go on, but this Mari certainly makes an impression. A few people tell each other if they hear she'll be singing somewhere. She'll be part of a traditional song and story night next Saturday at the – well, it's a crafts and cultural centre over in North Wales. It's called Canolfan Meilyr, in a village called Caergynan in the Snowdonia National Park. Don't ask me if that's how you pronounce it.'

'Is that anywhere close to where Tom turned up?'

'Less than ten miles away,' she confirmed, before drinking some coffee. 'As the crow flies anyway. I guess it'll be a lot further by road. Anyway, from comments on the craft centre blog, it looks as if she's a regular performer.'

'Is there a photo? So we know who we're looking for?'

'She isn't tagged, but this might be her. Tom said she was a knock-out blonde.' She turned the laptop around so I could see the screen. She finished her coffee, watching me with a teasing glint in her eye. 'What do you think?'

The blonde girl – woman – it was hard to say how old she might be – was certainly holding a guitar. She wasn't on a stage though. She was talking to someone in a modern hall full of rows of chairs. Tom was right, if this was Mari Rhys. She was absolutely gorgeous. Her long blonde hair curled under at the ends, brushing tits that promised to fill a man's hands very nicely. She wore a dark green dress with a plunging neckline, and the man she was talking to was gazing at her cleavage. That green dress showed off her trim waist, and the calf-length flared skirt clung to her curvaceous backside. If he was about the average height for a man, I guessed she was about five foot two.

Trim waist? Who the hell uses words like curvaceous outside a sleazy tabloid? But something had sent my mind straight there. Another phrase floated through my mind when I wondered how tall she might be. All women are the same height lying down. A sparks I'd known on a building job had said that once, offering his unwanted opinion on what some passing woman might be like in bed. Why had I remembered that?

I shifted in the armchair and the pulse in my groin subsided. I drank my tea before I answered. 'I'd say she qualifies.'

Iris grinned as if I'd said something funny. 'Can you get over to this place on Saturday? To do a bit of a recce?'

I didn't know what she was finding so amusing, and I wasn't sure I wanted to ask. 'Just me?'

'I'm on shift.' She said that as if it ended any discussion.

'I'm supposed to be at work as well,' I pointed out, though it was a safe bet Eleanor would give me the time off. That wasn't my only concern. 'What happens if I disappear? Who's going to come looking for me?'

'You're thinking of trying your luck with her?' The glint in Iris's eye was a lot less friendly.

'No,' I retorted. 'But I'm still not keen on going there on my own. Hasn't Fin told you what happened in Wiltshire?' I held up my scarred forearm. I'm big, but I'm not stupid, and a hamadryad half my size had done that damage.

Iris shrugged. 'Maybe Gillian can go with you.'

I wondered if Fin might be able to come up from Dorset. If this Mari saw I was already taken, maybe she'd leave me alone. Then I could watch her and see who she went after. If she went after anyone so close to home. If that place was her home.

On the other hand, what might happen if this unknown and dangerous woman could see Fin was a swan maiden? What if she sensed my dryad blood? Would she disappear, or would she attack the pair of us? We were working with sod all reliable information yet again.

'Okay, let's see what Gillian says,' I agreed. 'Maybe one of her – her associates is free.'

I'd ask a few other people what they thought as well before agreeing to do anything. I had to do something though. I'd promised Tom.

Iris stretched her arms up over her head and her shoulders clicked again. 'What do you know about her? Gillian, I mean.'

Why was she asking me? 'Nothing. I only met her today.'

'What I mean is...' Iris ran a hand through her hair. 'These wise women, do they always work in threes?'

'The ones I've talked to seem to, but I couldn't swear to it.'

'This hare thing, how does that work? Is it a family thing, like us?' Iris was asking herself as much as me. 'If it isn't...?'

'I have no idea, and I'm not going to ask.'

'No,' Iris agreed.

I could see she was frustrated by what she didn't know, but I wondered why she expected the wise women to share their secrets. Everyone in her family spent a lifetime making sure no outsiders learned who they really were. The fenland's swan families and the ones with naiad or nereid blood went back centuries, and they had done that by staying safely unsuspected.

'So how are you getting on with Blanche these days?' Iris asked.

'Sorry, what?' This sudden change of topic caught me completely by surprise.

'Blanche. Is she still being a pain in the backside?'

The last thing I wanted to discuss with Iris was her and Fin's other sister, but I was stuck by the window. The desk chair blocked the narrow gap between the bed and the desk, and Iris wasn't going to move.

'We get on okay.' I wasn't telling a lie, exactly. To be totally honest, I found Blanche's personality as spiky as her short gelled hair. I wasn't sure if that was all her fault. Maybe I was doing something wrong. I'm an only child, so I don't know how brothers or sisters work.

'Right.' Iris paused. For a moment, I thought she was going to drop it. No such luck.

'You do realise she's jealous, don't you?'

'What? Look.' I spoke more forcefully than I intended. 'If she is, she's shit out of luck.'

'Sorry, that's the wrong word.' Iris raised her hands to stop me talking. 'Or maybe not, but I don't mean she's jealous because she wants you for herself. Don't flatter yourself. You're not her type. What Fin has with you is what gets under Blanche's skin. You and Fin can be completely open with each other. You know what we are. You see the things that we see. That's not something a lot of us ever find.'

I was ready to climb over the bed if that was the only way to reach the door and leave this conversation. I would get in the Landy and drive home, except we'd agreed to meet Gillian in the morning. I didn't want to piss off a wise woman. Let's see how Iris liked nosey questions. They say the best form of defence is attack.

'What about you? Is that how you feel?'

'It's not an issue. I'm seeing someone over in Ireland.'

But she was looking past my right ear. Fin does that, and so does Helen, their mum, when a conversation's getting too close to something they don't want to talk about.

I pushed myself up out of the armchair. 'What do you want to do for dinner? There's the steak place, or do you want to find somewhere else?'

'The steak place is easy, and they do fish.' Iris nodded at the menu stuck in a plastic holder on the desk. 'Shall I book a table for the two of us? Seven o'clock, before it gets too busy?'

She stood up as well, to let me get past. I guessed she'd said what she wanted to say. That was a relief.

'I'll see you in reception at seven.' I was out of the door before I heard her agree.

I headed back to my room and lay down on the bed, wondering how to kill the next couple of hours. I wanted to ring Fin, but she would still be working. Probably. If she wasn't, she'd ask how I was getting on, if she'd listened to my earlier message. If she hadn't, I'd have to explain what I was doing in Chester.

Either way, she'd ask what Iris had to say about everything we'd learned here. There was no way I was having that conversation. Not right now. Fin would know I was hiding something, even over the phone. That could get messy. I wasn't going to lie to her, but I really didn't want to talk about her sisters. Why couldn't Iris mind her own sodding business?

I reached for my phone and called my dad instead. He answered on the second ring. I could picture him at home, sitting with a mug of tea in his favourite chair by the fireplace. He'd bought the half-derelict cottage by the entrance to the little nature reserve where he volunteered before I was born. His friends expected him to do it up and sell it on for a profit. They'd been surprised when he sold his terraced two-bed near the factory where he worked instead. They didn't know he'd met my mum and they'd fallen in love. Properly in love. Not like Tom's nightmare. The thought of that sent a shiver down my back.

Dad's cheerful voice made me feel better. 'Hi, Dan. Got everything ready for another busy week?'

Of course. He thought I was at Blithehurst.

'Actually, I'm in Cheshire. Something's come up.' I explained about Tom, and about Gillian and Iris, though I didn't say anything about Blanche.

'I was wondering if Mum might have anything useful to suggest about this Mari woman. We have no idea who or what she is.' I was quite surprised that Mum hadn't already joined in the call. She can pick things like radio waves and phone signals out of the air when she wants to.

The silence at the other end went on for so long I looked at my screen, to check I hadn't lost my signal. 'Dad?'

'Your mother and I aren't talking at the moment.'

What the fuck? I managed not to say that out loud. But seriously, what the fuck? My parents never had rows. That happened to other kids at school. Parents argued and sometimes split up, over money, lost jobs, over a new job that would mean moving away, or because someone was shagging someone they shouldn't. My family was different. When a dryad fell in love, that was that, for the rest of her long life. My dad felt the same about my mum. He took early retirement and worked as the warden for the nature reserve full-time. We didn't have a lot of money when I was a kid, but we didn't need much. My mum kept up a convincing pretence of being human when I was at school, but that didn't cost us anything.

'Why?' I managed to ask.

Dad sighed. 'She saw my eightieth birthday cards, and she had an idea.'

I waited for him to explain.

'She suggested we go away together, so I would never get any older. Or at least, I wouldn't feel any older. Not for ages, anyway.'

My mouth was dry. I swallowed hard. 'Right.'

Dryads have a curious relationship with time. Their lives are linear, but they can choose the pace they live at. Sometimes, dryads will pass through a year so fast it means as much to them as a month means to ordinary people. Or, if they want to, they can make a week last a decade for a human. Those stories about men falling asleep on a hillside and going home to find their grandson's become an old man? That's totally believable, if you've met a dryad. Did they do that on purpose or by accident? That would depend on whether or not the sleeper had pissed them off. I had no trouble believing Tom's story about losing six weeks. I wanted to ask my mum about other people who weren't human who could do the same sort of thing.

To my astonishment, Dad laughed. 'I'm not going to do it, you daft sod. Even if you have got Fin to keep you company now.'

I managed to clear my throat. 'Right.'

Dad sounded more serious. 'Can you imagine what Dave Filkins would do if I vanished without a trace? He'd have bloodhounds searching every inch of the reserve before the sun went down.'

That made me smile. 'Yes, he would.'

Dave's a copper. Well, he's retired these days. He and my dad go back decades, even if Dave is years younger. They met when he was fresh out of police college and getting his bearings in the area. He was a good copper, and he'd had a stellar career. He wouldn't let a mystery like my dad disappearing rest until he was six feet under himself.

'I wouldn't leave you with that sort of trouble,' Dad assured me. 'Having to wait seven years before I could be declared dead, and with who knows how much other bother about wills and stuff like that? I tried to explain to your mum, but she went off in a huff.' He sighed again. 'She'll come round. It may just take a while. Don't worry about it. And don't worry about me. I'm as fit as a fiddle.'

'Right,' I said again. Dad was right. Most people thought he was barely seventy. But I didn't want to think about that.

'Anyway,' he said, bracing. 'How is Fin? What's she up to at the moment?'

'Spending most of her time in her waders.' I brought him up to date with everything she and Blanche were doing. We said our goodbyes and I ended the call.

I lay on the hotel bed, staring up at the ceiling. I really didn't want to think about what would happen when my dad died. I'd inherit the cottage, but what would that mean for my job at Blithehurst? What decisions would Fin and I have to make?

I thought about my mum. I knew she loved me. I always had. I'd never questioned it, and I never would. The thing is, though, since I'd left home, she'd had to pretend to be human less and less. She spent more and more time with her trees. Was she forgetting what it was like to be mortal? Did she really think I'd be okay with my dad disappearing, now that Fin and I were together?

I needed to remember she was a dryad, not a human. I needed to realise she could do something to hurt me without ever meaning it. Of course, she'd be upset when she realised, but whatever had been done would still be done. There's no turning back the clock for any of us.

I remembered Tom's haunted face as he tried to calm his nerves with one cigarette after another. The woman who'd lured him away, whoever she was, whatever she was, she didn't care how much she hurt him. She didn't care about those other broken, lost boys who had died or disappeared. Tom said she had laughed at him.

 We had to put a stop to that.

Chapter Seven

We met Gillian the following morning in the hotel car park. We told her everything we had found about Mari Rhys. She said she'd see what the wise women could turn up that might be useful. So far they hadn't found anything that might explain Tom's story. Gillian wasn't concerned. She said it was early days. She agreed to try to find someone to go to Wales with me on Saturday. I told her to text me if she did.

Iris didn't ask any nosy questions about shifting into hares. She said she'd ring her mum and see if their family grapevine had anything to add. I didn't think the hobs and sylphs in the fens would know much about whatever went on in North Wales. I said I'd ask the dryads. My mum might not be around, but Frai and Asca would want to know what I was doing.

'What about the Green Man?' Gillian looked at me, intent.

'If he has something to tell me, he turns up in my dreams. I never know when I'll see him though.'

'Let me know if you do.' Gillian was ordering, not asking.

I just shrugged. Since there was no more to say and Gillian had to get to work, we went our separate ways. I made a quick call to tell Eleanor I was coming back today. That was good news as far as she was concerned. I was soon back on the motorway, and I had a straight run back to Blithehurst.

I went in the back way and parked the Landy at my cottage. I dumped my bag and had a pee, and put on my staff polo shirt and jeans. Yesterday's T-shirt still smelled of fag smoke, so I threw that and a few other things into the washing machine, then walked up to the house. Eleanor would be on the rota doing the guided tours today. She was good at it, and she enjoyed it. The tourists almost never realised she was one of the family who still owned the house.

It was gone mid-morning and the gardens were busy. I put on my mask as I eased through the crowds, heading for the front entrance. The garden door's kept locked when the house is open. As I did my best to get past people on the narrow paths between the geometric beds of fragrant herbs, I heard a familiar voice.

'The knot garden was replanted in the 1920s. The family wanted to recall the house's Tudor heyday after the horrors of the Great War.'

I saw a couple of people wondering who this old lady standing by the sundial might be. How come she knew so much about Blithehurst? No one was going to ask. Frai has that effect on people, even when she's pretending to be a sweet little white-haired old lady in a shapeless dress. Asca was talking to a different group of visitors. She looked as if she'd strolled out of some glossy magazine's feature on contemporary country life.

'It really is a fascinating place. Once you've done the house tour, do walk through the park. The shop's well worth a visit on your way out as well.'

No one else would notice, but to my eye, the people she was talking to had that slightly glazed expression which meant she was *persuading* them to spend more time and money here. By the time they left, she'd have convinced them to tell their friends to make a trip to Blithehurst. This year's increased visitor numbers weren't only down to tourists giving Devon and Cornwall a miss.

Both dryads saw me. I caught the flash of their true gaze, which only people like me, Eleanor and Fin can see. A dryad's eyes are one solid colour, without white or pupil. Asca's are as green as summer leaves. Frai's gaze is the bright copper of autumn.

I nodded to acknowledge them both. We could talk later, when there were no tourists around. I l went into the house, where the current tour group had finished admiring the great hall, so I headed upstairs. Following the sound of Eleanor's voice, I found her and the punters in the long gallery.

'This is a new addition to our pictures. Anthony Hackshott was the master craftsman who built the priest's hole, the chapel and the secret stair. His name's only recently come to light in the family papers. I'm pleased to say that meant this small portrait from the family collection could be identified and restored. No one knows where Anthony was born, but he lived a long and happy life locally. His work undoubtedly saved many travelling Catholic priests from being martyred in the reign of Elizabeth the First.'

This was news to me. I'm not often in the house during opening hours, and I couldn't remember the last time I'd needed to repair any woodwork in the gallery.

Eleanor had seen me over the heads of the tour group. Since no one could see her smile through her mask, she spread out her hands in a polite gesture. 'This concludes our tour, so thank you everyone very much for your interest, and please, enjoy the rest of your day. Do visit our restaurant and garden centre, and there's a cafe in the old manor ruins if you want a drink and a sit-down after visiting the park.'

She stayed where she was as the punters wandered out onto the landing or went for a closer look at the family portraits. I waited by the door until I wouldn't get in anyone's way, and then walked over to join her.

She checked her watch and looked at the room steward, who was sitting on a chair halfway down the gallery. That way, he could see who might be taking a bit too much interest in the ornaments on the Georgian side table, or who might be about to poke a valuable painting with a sticky finger.

'Brian? Okay if I take my break?'

He nodded. 'Go ahead.'

We didn't go into Eleanor's sitting room. Visitors were bound to try to follow us if they saw her unlocking the door. We walked down to the ruins and got a tray of tea and coffee and some biscuits from the cafe. I carried the tray past the tables and chairs set out in the courtyard for the tourists as it was a nice sunny day. Eleanor sat on a low bit of long-demolished wall where we could talk and see anyone getting near enough to overhear us.

I poured my tea. 'Did Anthony Hackshott have anything to do with yesterday's discovery?'

Eleanor pressed the plunger on her coffee. 'His ghost did,' she said quietly as she took off her mask.

'Seriously?' I've seen ghosts in another old house, but as far as I knew, the spooky stories at Blithehurst were invented by bored Victorians.

'Take a closer look at that picture when you get a chance.' Eleanor added milk to her cup. 'I'm wondering if he had dryad blood.'

'Have you asked—?'

'I can't get a straight answer, beyond Asca and Frai saying he's not their descendant.' Eleanor's wry glance told me she wasn't surprised. To be honest, nor was I. It's not just people like us who are careful to keep our friends' and families' secrets. 'How did you get on in Chester?'

Keeping an eye out for anyone wandering too close, I told her Tom's story, and the little we'd found out about this singer, Mari Rhys.

'So you'll want Saturday off?'

'Sunday as well, to be on the safe side,' I said, apologetic.

Eleanor stared into the distance as she mentally consulted the staff timetable. She would have to work out who could cover my shifts on the gate by the main road. Blithehurst doesn't charge for parking, but someone needs to encourage drivers with no idea how long or how wide their car is to get it between the clearly marked-out lines. If I remember not to smile when I ask them, people generally take the hint. At weekends, I help out with stewarding the ornamental temple on the other side of the valley as well.

'We can't say you're taking holiday without everyone else complaining, and I could hardly blame them.' She grimaced. 'We'll have to invent some family emergency that's called you away.'

'Right.' I didn't like the idea of lying and neither did Eleanor, but I didn't see we had any choice.

'Will you be going on your own?'

'I'm not sure.' I explained what Gillian had said. 'It would help if we knew what we're dealing with.'

'Do not cross those who live in the hollow hills. Nothing good can come of it.'

Frai's voice behind us startled us both. I'd just dunked a biscuit in my tea and I nearly dropped it. Eleanor and I looked round. Both dryads stood there in their natural forms, so the tourists were oblivious to their presence. I wondered how long they had been listening. Long enough to hear Tom's story, I guessed.

'What do you know about them?' I cupped my hand under my dripping biscuit.

'Just as you have been told.' Frai looked at me as if I was an idiot. 'They entice young men and women to join in their revels. They discard them when they are no longer entertaining. None of this is your concern. Leave those who dwell in the darkness well alone.'

'They delight in cruelty.' Asca was angry. 'In days gone by, they would take infants from their cradles if they could. They would leave a changeling to fool the mother, planning to rear the stolen baby as their own. But they would soon grow bored and abandon the child to sicken and die. We put a stop to that.'

'How?' I asked through my mouthful of biscuit.

'Who's "we"?' Eleanor wanted to know.

'We taught our mortal friends to ward the doors to their houses with iron. We showed them how rings of woven rowan buried under the thresholds of their barns and byres would protect their beasts and harvests,' Asca said with savage satisfaction. 'A scattering of soil from a yew grove keeps the spiteful creatures away from a pasture or a growing crop.'

'That's good to know.' I've seen iron over doors and windows deter boggarts and other unwanted intruders. I hadn't come across those other ways to keep eerie enemies out. 'Thank you.'

As a rule, I'm very careful about owing favours to a dryad. They always collect, and somehow they always seem to come out ahead. Just at the moment, I'd take whatever advice Asca was willing to offer. We could balance the books later on.

'Little by little, we drove them out of the woods and meadows,' the dryad went on. 'They took refuge in the high places and under the broken ground. As the years passed, the tales told of them faded as humanity forged their new age with iron, fire and steam. Men constructed new philosophies that had no place for the unseen. That diminished their influence. Much of their power came from fear.'

'You should still leave well alone,' Frai insisted. 'These waifs and strays are no kin to you, or to the swan maidens.'

Before I could ask what she meant by that, the old dryad disappeared.

'Daniel.' Asca raised a hand to get my attention. '*Never* set foot in a fairy ring.'

From her expression, that was advice to equal 'Never start a land war in Asia'. Then she disappeared as well.

'Fairy rings.' I looked at Eleanor. 'More mushrooms.'

I tried to think if I'd ever seen a fairy ring in the pastures around Blithehurst, where the rare-breed cattle graze. I didn't think I had. I'd never thought about that before.

Eleanor looked startled. 'Frai really doesn't want us tangling with whoever these people are, does she?'

I had to admit that was unnerving. There couldn't be much that scared the old dryad. 'We know iron keeps us safe most of the time. Nothing can get at me when I'm inside the Land Rover. I know where to find rowan trees around here, and there are yew trees in the churchyard in the village. I can follow Asca's advice and take some more protection with me.'

Eleanor didn't look convinced.

'I'm only going to take a look at this Mari woman,' I reminded her. 'I won't do anything until we know a whole lot more about what we're facing.'

'Make sure you don't.' She sounded almost as stern as the dryads.

Briony came out of the cafe kitchen to clear cups and plates from the tables in the courtyard. Eleanor checked her watch.

'Time to get back to it.'

We finished our tea and coffee. I took the tray back to Sarah while Eleanor headed for the manor house. Since no one was expecting me to be working today, I went to my workshop in the old dairy yard. I could get a phone signal there, so I read up on rowan hoops as a symbol of protection. Making one was as simple as finding a thin, whippy twig and looping the two ends under each other to make a circle. I went out into the woods to find a rowan tree, cut some suitable twigs and made a handful of the circles, sized to fit into the side pockets of my combat trousers. Combats are so much more useful than jeans. I kept an eye out for the dryads, but I didn't see them, or the black shuck.

Getting some soil from under a yew tree wasn't so straightforward. I thought about fetching that after dark, after the pub had shut. I decided being caught in the graveyard around midnight would be even harder to explain. I drove the Landy to the village and parked near the church. I had a story ready, about checking dates on one of the Beauchene headstones, but no one asked what I was doing there. If anyone saw me crouch down to scoop up dirt from the bare patch under the yew trees, they didn't come up to say anything.

It wasn't so much soil as a thick mulch of the needles the yew tree had dropped, slowly disintegrating to return to the earth. As I clipped the lid on the takeaway container I'd half filled, I looked into the tree's dark green, feathery branches. I didn't expect to see the Green Man, but I wondered how old this yew might be. I had a sneaking suspicion that Asca had been talking about using earth from an age-old grove, not some random yew tree planted by a vicar in the last couple of centuries.

Fin and I, along with Hazel Spinner, encountered a truly ancient yew grove last year. Those trees held memories going back aeons. Back to the days when humans were tormented by – well, I suppose I had to call them fairies. I felt stupid doing that, even if I wasn't saying the word out loud. But I had no idea how to find any of those ancestral trees, so this was the best I could do.

I went back to Blithehurst and spent the rest of the day helping out in the restaurant and the shop. There's no Internet out in the woods where my cottage is, and the phone signal comes and goes. I wanted to be somewhere where I'd get any call or text from Gillian, or from Iris. I checked my email at the end of the day. As it turned out, I didn't hear from either of them.

I did see the Green Man that night. I went to bed pretty early and fell asleep straight away. I generally do, and I'll sleep through till dawn. Not this time. I woke up in pitch darkness, breathless and sweating. My heart was racing, though not because I was scared. I could feel the reassuring presence of the trees that surround the cottage. I lay there and tried to make sense of what I had just seen.

Normally, when the Green Man turns up in my dreams, what he wants is as clear as if I'm wide awake. Not tonight. All I could piece together was a confused recollection of running alongside him. That's why I woke up out of breath. Other people were running with us, but I didn't know who they were.

I couldn't see who we were chasing. Who or what? That was hard to say. We were running through the summer night, through an old, dense wood. An oak wood. I knew that in my bones. The moon was full overhead, but clouds kept scudding across it. Between that and the shadows cast by the leafy branches, I only ever caught glimpses of whatever we were chasing. Whatever we were chasing away, they had no place in this forest.

They ran on two feet and they had two arms, I was sure of that much at least. When I caught glimpses of their faces, some looked like cats and others looked like foxes. A couple had horns like goats, and a blunt, furred face had me baffled until I remembered seeing an otter when I was out on a riverside walk with Fin. They came and went in the shadows, changing wherever I looked. I might be seeing different creatures, or they might be shifting from one form to another. As I tried to decide, the little I could remember faded like smoke blown away on the wind.

I sat up in bed when I remembered something else with brutal clarity. I had been standing on a shifting pile of shattered stones. There was a neck-breaking drop below me, down to a stretch of woodland beside a lake in a deep valley between two barren peaks.

Scree. I remembered that's what these sloping heaps are called. This particular scree was at the bottom of a sheer cliff that shone dull as lead in the moonlight. I remembered something else about screes. They are fucking dangerous. I didn't dare move in case the whole lot gave way, cascading down the mountainside to bury me beneath tonnes of broken slate. I would be cut to pieces by the razor-sharp edges of the stone.

I looked down at my feet and saw a dead body. A kid about Tom's age lay there. Every bone in his body must be broken for him to be so sickeningly twisted. I was only glad he was lying face down. As it was, I could see his skull was smashed. His head couldn't be that shape and still be whole. He must be one of those lads who'd disappeared, whose story Iris had found online.

The Green Man wanted me to go after whatever cruel bastards were killing these boys because they thought no one would miss them.

Chapter Eight

I spent the rest of the week at work. Mike and Mark, who'd have to cover me at the weekend, each got an unexpected day off. I don't know what Eleanor told them, but they didn't ask me anything, so I didn't have to try to explain.

I heard from Iris on Thursday. She didn't have anything new to tell me, and she sounded genuinely frustrated when she explained she couldn't get over to Wales on Saturday.

'Text me with regular updates, and I'll keep looking online for anything useful. I'm really sorry, Dan. There's just no way I can swap my shift this weekend. Phil's had the week booked off for months, and he's got kids, and you know what the school holidays are like.'

I wasn't really listening as she went on with her complicated explanation. Then I realised she was talking about something else.

'You should book in advance for the story and music evening. The website says it's very popular, and they can't guarantee there'll be tickets available on the door.'

'I'll do that right now.'

Iris took the hint and said goodbye.

I was more disappointed when Fin rang a bit later to tell me she couldn't get away either.

'We thought we were about ready to wrap things up, but there's been another unauthorised discharge, and we're up to our knees in a river pollution crisis.'

'Not literally, I hope?'

'Quite literally,' she said grimly, 'and believe me, that's no fun in this weather.'

It sounded revolting. 'Any pissed-off local naiads to deal with?'

'Just one, but she's really furious.'

'I can imagine. Well, take care, best of luck with the naiad, and say hi to Blanche for me.'

'Will do. Watch your step in Wales. Give me a call when you get back, and hopefully we can get together soon.'

'I hope so. Have you ever been to Chester? I thought that might be a nice place for a weekend?'

'No, I haven't, and yes, that's a great idea.'

We said our goodbyes. I would have liked to have Fin with me this weekend, but it sounded as if she was needed where she was. Add to that, she wouldn't be coming with me into a situation that Frai clearly thought could be dangerous. Fin's no fool, and she knows the risks that come with being people like us, but honestly, I was okay with only having myself to worry about.

I would have liked to ask the dryads about the weird creatures in my dream, but I didn't see either of them all week. Not even up at the ornamental temple where Eleanor's ancestor had installed a statue of Venus modelled on his sketches of Asca.

Gillian called me on Friday. She was brisk and to the point. 'Sorry, Dan, I'm going to be busy this weekend. I've found Tom a place in a shared house with on-site support workers over near Oldham. We'll be getting his stuff out of store and I'm driving him there on Saturday. I'll have to stay over to help get him settled.'

That was clearly not up for debate, so I didn't bother. 'How is he?'

'The fact that he's talking has made a massive difference. Even if you and I know he isn't telling the whole story, he is getting some of the help he needs if he's going to get back on his own feet.'

'What are his chances, do you reckon?'

'Fair,' she said after a moment's thought. 'He's got a new case worker, and they've been talking about Tom's going back to college in September. Personally, I think he'll need a longer break, but he's looking forward now, which is progress.'

'Fingers crossed.' I hoped she was right.

'I'm still trying to find someone to back you up at this story and song evening. I'm sure someone can come. As soon as I have a name, I'll send you a text.'

'Thanks.' I was pretty sure I'd be okay either way. Like I told Eleanor, I was only going to take a look at this mysterious singer.

By Saturday morning, I'd checked out the different routes I could take. I opted for faster roads even if that meant a slightly longer drive. I had another problem though. There were no convenient chain hotels anywhere around Caergynan, and the guest houses in the village were fully booked. Well, it was peak season, and their rooms were bloody expensive even if that did include a full Welsh breakfast. I could hardly blame Mrs Morgan, Mrs Williams and Mrs Jones. Their businesses must have taken the same sort of hit as Blithehurst over the past year or so.

THE GREEN MAN'S GIFT

I was putting my overnight bag in the Land Rover when Eleanor turned up at my cottage.

'Are you all set?'

'I might end up sleeping in the Landy if I can't find a room. I've done it before. That's not a problem for one night.'

'What about a campsite?'

'I haven't looked.' That hadn't occurred to me.

Eleanor got out her phone and found there was no hope of a signal. 'Let me go up to the house and check. I'll meet you in the main car park. Give me ten minutes.'

'Okay.' I could see Eleanor wanted to do something to feel involved. What had happened to Tom and those other boys really bothered her.

She headed off through the woods and I drove around to the main car park. I got a cup of tea from the restaurant and waited. Eleanor took a fair bit longer than ten minutes. She turned up carrying a red plastic crate with a long green bag and a rolled-up foam mat, and a sleeping bag balanced across it.

'There is a campsite on the edge of the village. I've printed off the details and stuck them in here.' She nodded at the crate she was carrying. 'This is a two-man tent, and there's cooking gear and a meths-burning stove in there, as well as a few other things.'

'Thanks.' I put everything in the back of the Landy. I still reckoned I'd be sleeping in there, but it never hurts to have options.

'Drive safely, and, well, watch your back.' Eleanor picked up my tea mug to take it back to the restaurant. I saw her watching me leave as I headed out.

First things first. I hit the closest supermarket for some food that didn't need a fridge and picked up other stuff that might be useful, like matches and the makings of a cup of tea. Even if I wasn't camping, being able to stop for a brew could be good. I filled up the Land Rover with diesel and headed for the motorway. I didn't hang about in the slow lane with the lorries this time. I wanted to check out Caergynan and whatever might be around it before the story and music evening got going. Yes, I had booked a ticket through the Canolfan Meilyr Centre website.

There was a lot more traffic at the weekend, but apart from that, I followed the same route. As I passed Chester, I thought about a weekend there with Fin again.

Wondering how Tom and Gillian were getting on as I ignored the signs for Manchester, I followed the road to North Wales. Road signs became bilingual. Some were virtually the same. No one was going to get Wrexham and Wrecsam confused. How Mold ended up as Yr Wyddgrug – or maybe it was the other way round – must be a whole different conversation.

The expressway followed the coast. I left the flat expanse of Cheshire and drove though gentle wooded hills and farmland. Brown signs to tourist attractions offered sandcastles and seaside promenades on my right-hand side. The signs on the left turns suggested visiting actual castles. The hills got steadily steeper and the high ground marched closer to the sea. The road ended up doggedly claiming a narrow strip between the water and the steep, rocky slopes.

That was deep water, judging by its colour. I passed a battered jetty with loading docks on either side. A dust-covered conveyor emerged from industrial buildings built into the hill on my left. The conveyor passed right under the road and ran the length of the jetty to those moorings. Sizeable ships must have been filled with whatever the moving belt had carried down from the heights. Maybe boats were still carrying those cargoes away. I realised I didn't have any idea what people did for jobs in North Wales. They couldn't all run guest houses or sell ice creams on the beach.

Not much further on, the road builders had been forced to resort to tunnels as the grey crags plunged into the sea. Before I saw what happened after that, the satnav told me to take a left turn and head inland. There was a whole lot more traffic than I expected, and I turned off the CD player. I didn't need any distractions as the winding roads through the steep-sided valleys became clogged with cars. Narrow lanes between fields were edged with solid stone walls, and sharp bends offered sod all chances to overtake. There was absolutely no way to get past the SUVs towing caravans. I supposed bringing your own accommodation avoided the hassles of finding somewhere to stay.

I'm sure the mountain scenery on all sides was striking, but I was concentrating straight ahead. I also kept an eye on my wing mirrors for the bikers who had been belting along the coast road. A few of them came weaving through the slow-moving cars. As soon as they got the chance, they accelerated away with a roar of exhaust.

I passed a couple of scenic viewpoints as well as a car park with big boards showing what I guessed were popular walking routes. Lines of people snaked up the steep green slopes dotted with sheep and thickets of stubby trees. Every parking spot was taken, and more cars were parked wherever a grass verge looked wide enough for someone to stop. A few drivers had been very optimistic about that, leaving two wheels on the tarmac. People in walking gear on the road slowed the traffic even more.

The satnav took me through small villages where the hills rose so steeply there was only room for a single terrace on either side of the road. Narrow houses with slate roofs had one front window and a door that opened straight onto the pavement. Some had been rendered and painted in bright colours. Others were stripped back to the dark stone they were built from. Most were covered in pebble-dash in unattractive shades of grey and brown. Every one had a satellite dish facing in the same direction to catch a TV signal. On the outskirts, modern primary schools and playgrounds painted with bright colours offered a sudden contrast as I drove past. There must be jobs somewhere, if there were young families around.

I reached a bigger village, or maybe what counted as a small town. The hills weren't quite so close together and more people had claimed the flatter land. Dark stone houses in the centre were double-fronted, with bay windows and white-painted wooden porches decorated with Victorian-style fretwork. At the crossroads in the middle, I stopped for a red light. A butcher and a baker faced each other, and I could see a supermarket a little way further on, if I went straight ahead. The left-hand turn headed for a bridge over the river that had been running alongside the road and taken this chance to go its own way for a while.

The lights changed and the satnav told me to take the right-hand turn if I wanted to find Caergynan. Bright new road signs announced there was no through route and added a whole load of vehicle size and weight restrictions for anyone thinking of going that way. No HGVs? No shit. I guessed over-ambitious satnavs sent heavy lorries up there from time to time. 'Once a highway, always a highway' might be an ancient legal principle, but it doesn't necessarily work in practice.

This road was even narrower as it wound up the hillside. Even so, it was easier going, with hardly any traffic and passing places where there was room. Since I didn't have to worry about rear-ending someone who'd braked for a sheep or a hiker, I could look at the scenery. It wasn't particularly scenic. I guessed the heaps of broken stone on either side of the road were spoil from the quarrying that had gone on here. Vertical rock faces and angular ledges further away from the road were so sharp-edged and regular they could only be man-made. Whatever had been dug out here, those jobs were long gone. Brambles, thorns and wildflowers had been encroaching on the spoil heaps as well as the abandoned diggings for years.

I soon reached Caergynan. The village was in a shallow hollow high on the hillside, surrounded by fields of sheep. The first thing I saw was the sign for the campsite Eleanor had found online. It must have originally been a sizeable paddock belonging to a big square Georgian house called Plas Brynwen, according to the neat slate nameplate fixed to the stone wall surrounding the colourful garden.

I carried on driving, following the main street through the village. It didn't take long to see what Caergynan had to offer. Those narrow terraced houses I'd seen elsewhere flanked the road, interrupted about halfway up by four double-fronted houses, two on either side. Three of those were now guest houses saying sorry, they had no vacancies. Each pair bracketed a gravelled lane that headed off at right angles to the road, up to the stone walls where the fields around the village began. I guessed the lane went left and right from there, giving access to the terraces' back gardens and wherever people kept their bins. At the top end of the village, on the highest point, the tarmac stopped at the Canolfan Meilyr Centre. Only a rough track carried on down a gentle slope, flanked by stone walls that divided up the grazing. A battered and faded signpost at the head of the track pointed to somewhere called Cerrigwen, but that was all.

The crafts and cultural centre was a long low modern building built from local stone and slate. It had a sizeable car park, but a lot of people had decided to come for a Saturday out. I couldn't find a space, and I wouldn't risk parking on the road outside. Double yellow lines had been freshly painted for peak tourist season and spaces outside the houses were reserved for residents with permits only. More signs clearly stated that. There was nowhere inconspicuous to park the Land Rover and hope for an undisturbed night.

It looked like I would be camping after all. I only hoped I could find somewhere nearby. I turned the Landy around in the Canolfan Meilyr Centre car park and headed for Plas Brynwen. The short-term space right outside must have been the only empty bit of parking in North Wales. I got out and followed the sign to the old wooden conservatory on the side of the house. Clearly this was now the campsite office. A fridge offered local milk and free-range eggs for sale, and a basket on top had lettuce, radishes and tubs of raspberries from someone's garden.

'Can I help you?' The stocky middle-aged man behind the table didn't look particularly welcoming. I guessed he was the proprietor mentioned on the sign. Mr J P Williams. I wondered if he was related to Mrs Guesthouse Williams. On the other hand, I've watched rugby matches where the Welsh team only seem to have five surnames between them.

'Do you have room for a single tent and a Land Rover?' I wasn't sure he would. The paddock was pretty well filled with caravans and tents the size of rip-stop nylon bungalows.

'Just you, is it? Not expecting anyone else?'

'No. I mean, I'm on my own.' I had no idea what his problem was, but I really wished Fin had been able to come. No one would give a couple having a weekend away a second look.

He must have seen I was confused. He grinned, and now he was my friend. 'It's just we do get stag parties turn up sometimes. They can make a right nuisance of themselves, see? If it's only you, I reckon we can squeeze you in. Just the one night, is it?'

'I'm not sure. I've got a few days off work. Can we say two nights to begin with, and then I'll let you know? Is that okay?'

'Fine by me.' He pointed at the list of prices taped to the tabletop and handed me a form to fill out with my name, home address and vehicle registration.

Once his machine had accepted my bank card, he gave me a sheet of the campsite's rules and regulations. Those were basically common sense. There was a map of the site on the other side of the paper, and he circled my pitch, right at the far side of the space reserved for tents. Caravans had their own spots nearer the house with electricity hookups and a chemical toilet disposal facility. The map also showed a tin-roofed block with toilets, showers and outside taps tucked behind a tangle of rhododendrons.

'Thanks.'

'Give me a shout if there's anything you need, once you're settled in.'

'I will. Thanks.' I went back to the Landy and drove slowly through the gate.

I crossed the site at a crawl, alert for random children, dogs or footballs appearing in front of me. Their families had basically set up homes away from home on the mown grass with tables, chairs and gas-bottle cooking stoves. Everyone seemed to be having a good time.

I found my spot and worked out how to put up Eleanor's ridge tent. It had a creamy cotton and nylon mesh inner and a heavier pale green layer to go over the top. It took me a while to figure out what to do with the guy ropes and tent pegs to pull the outer sheet taut, and I was glad I had a rubber mallet in the back of the Landy. When I was finished, it looked very old-fashioned compared to these other hi-tech tents. It also looked very small. If it was supposed to sleep two, they weren't men my size. But it would keep the rain off, though there wasn't much danger of that tonight. I threw the sleeping bag and mat inside, zipped it up and left everything else locked up in the Land Rover. Then I walked back up through the village. The cooling breeze when I reached the crest of the hill was very welcome. It was a warm day.

The Canolfan Meilyr Centre turned out to be a hollow rectangle with an arched entrance. A whole load of plaques on both walls thanked the various organisations who had helped fund the building, and doors labelled Merched/Ladies and Dynion/Gents faced each other. Through the arch, a dozen units on three sides looked out onto the central courtyard, where tables and chairs ringed a circular counter selling tea, coffee, soft drinks and cakes and sandwiches. One of the units was a bakery, and another was a coffee roaster, which was a bit unexpected.

The fourth side was a hall with a higher roof than the rest of the building and a wall of windows that faced the courtyard. I couldn't see inside as the curtains were drawn and the double doors in the middle were firmly shut. I was in the right place though. Posters on the glass promoted today's traditional Welsh song and story evening from 6 p.m. to 9 p.m., with the caffi staying open for refreshments. That was clearly Welsh for 'cafe'.

I checked my phone and found it was later than I thought. I still had a few hours to kill though, so I queued to buy a ham salad baguette and a Coke. Before I reached the till, I picked up a bottle of water as well. The courtyard was sheltered from the wind, and I was getting hot. I took my time eating my baguette at one of the small tables, watching the steady stream of visitors moving slowly from window to window as they saw what local crafts were on offer besides bara brith and Guatemalan Blend. When I finished eating, I went to see for myself.

Each of the craft units was big enough to have a fair-sized workshop at the back and retail space at the front. Some of the workshops were behind internal walls and windows, for safety reasons, I guessed. Others were more open plan, presumably so potential customers could be fascinated by seeing skilled artisans at work and hopefully were more likely to buy things. I was glad no one had ever suggested a set-up like this at Blithehurst. I'd hate to be watched as I worked.

The glassmaker had some beautiful vases as well as paperweights and ornaments including, inevitably, spiky red dragons. The artist in the next unit offered attractive paintings of what I guessed were the local mountains in all weathers and all seasons. I wasn't much interested in the candle-maker, though I'm sure she was very skilled. The weaver was busy at her clacking loom while her partner sold everything from brightly coloured pieces big enough to cover a bed to twisted skeins of knitting wool.

The next craftsman made jewellery. I spent a lot of time looking in his window. He had real talent. Before I met Fin, when I was still going out with girls who had no idea who I was, I'd had a girlfriend who was a jewellery designer. We'd met at several craft fairs and enjoyed each other's company, and after a while we ended up in bed. She was long gone out of my life, but I know real craftsmanship thanks to her.

The rings on offer included Welsh gold complete with certificates of authenticity. A helpful card explained very little Welsh gold is mined these days, and I guessed the steep prices reflected that. Silver rings set with semi-precious stones or decorated with enamelled designs were a lot more affordable. But buying Fin any sort of ring would mean a conversation I didn't think either of us was ready for.

Earrings, on the other hand, didn't come with any particular baggage. Silver feathers dangling from studs caught my eye. Those were within my price range. I went through the door. Since other people were waiting to be served, I took a look around. The shop took up the front third of the space. There was a glass-topped counter opposite the door that ran across to meet a partition wall in the middle of the unit.

Sculptures in various sizes and made from different metals hung on the wall in Perspex cases. Some were foxes and squirrels and birds, but a couple were like nothing I'd ever seen. I went over for a closer look. One was made of copper wire of different lengths and thicknesses. The strands had been braided in places and twisted around two or three others elsewhere. Some of the wires had been hammered flat while others were pointed enough to draw blood. You couldn't say the figure was a man, or a woman come to that, but it was definitely human-shaped, with legs that ended in fan-shaped feet and arms holding up clawed hands. It didn't have a face, but two glittering red eyes caught the light. Were those faceted stones rubies or garnets? I didn't know, and it didn't matter. I didn't bother checking the price. I wouldn't be buying it. It made me think of fire in a way that made me very uneasy.

I glanced at the counter to see if the purple-haired girl in the mask at the till was free to sell me those earrings. I saw something else. A dark-haired and bearded craftsman had been working at a bench not far behind the counter. When I had come in, he had seemed oblivious to the conversations at the till. Not any more. Now he was watching me, sitting motionless and tense. Somehow, I didn't think it was because I was the tallest person in the room.

I stared back, silently challenging him. He was sitting down, but I didn't think he could be more than five foot six. While he was muscular enough, I'd back myself in a fight. Well, I would if he was just an ordinary silversmith. If he was something more than human, I might be in trouble. I realised I had left those pocket-sized twists of rowan twigs in the Land Rover. I'd stuck the box of yew dirt in the top of Eleanor's plastic crate of camping gear. Bugger.

I breathed a bit more easily when he finally had to blink. His dark brown eyes stayed normal. So he wasn't something like a dryad or a wose or a naiad, able to masquerade as an ordinary person. That didn't mean he wasn't a shape-shifter or something else. Frai and Asca would know. They had sensed my greenwood blood immediately, and seen Fin for what she was when she first came to Blithehurst. I'd put money on them picking one of the wise women out of a crowd too. Unfortunately, those of us who are only a little bit more than ordinarily human have no such talent for spotting each other.

The jewellery maker was still looking at me. Did he expect me to smash a display case, fill a bag marked 'Loot' and run? Sticking my hands in my pockets, I walked slowly out of the shop. I didn't look back, but I kept my ears open for any hint of anyone following me. All I heard was a woman asking for a closer look at an enamelled flower pendant. I took a card from the pottery dish on the shelf by the door. Aled James. That was the silversmith's name.

Outside in the courtyard, couples and families were idling away the last little while before the hall opened its doors. The curtains had been drawn back from the windows and people were moving about inside. I bought an iced tea and found a bit of wall to lean against on the shady side of the courtyard. Half the people out here were using the free Wi-Fi to look at their phones.

The Internet didn't tell me anything useful or curious about Aled James. He had a website that gave his address as the workshop here. The site offered to sell me a range of pieces similar to the ones I'd seen by mail order, and that was that.

What else could I learn about Caergynan? I soon found a long and unexpectedly interesting article about scammers in the 1860s persuading Londoners to invest in near-worthless slate quarries at Cerrigwen. They conned visitors into becoming shareholders by showing them stacks of slates carted in from the best quarries in Snowdonia. I was reading about that when a flurry of activity made me look up. The hall doors were open. The artisans and craftspeople were putting up their closed signs and pulling down their shutters.

Chapter Nine

I found my e-ticket on my phone and joined the slow-moving queue. I noticed the wrought-iron gates under the arch had been closed. I guessed the man gesturing as he talked to someone was explaining the evening was sold out. Iris had been right to remind me to book in advance.

The tickets didn't have seat numbers. Inside the hall, everyone was sitting wherever they liked. Cheerful ushers handed out free programmes and prompted people to move up close.

'We've got a full house tonight. Let's not leave empty seats in the middles of the rows, thank you.' The no-nonsense woman smiled at me. 'How many?'

'It's just me, thanks.'

'Oh right. There's one on the end by there. That okay?'

'That's fine, thanks.' I took the programme she offered and headed for the vacant seat on the outer end of a row well towards the back. That definitely suited me.

The hall got crowded and noisy. About half the people coming in wore masks, so I put mine on. Hopefully that would make it harder for Mari Rhys to recognise me if she saw me again without it. I'd also prefer not to catch anything swirling through the hall.

Thankfully, whoever had designed this place had understood the importance of decent ventilation. The hall didn't get too hot or stuffy. While we waited, the audience could enjoy the murals on the walls. Scenes of slate-quarrying and steam-trains were interspersed with hillsides dotted with sheep and creatively imagined historical events. A man in generic robes sat with a harp in a hall full of people. I guessed he was entertaining them with a song. Elsewhere, swordsmen on horseback in chain mail and wearing pointed helmets looked suitably horrified as a tall wooden building was struck by lightning and set alight.

I glanced idly over my shoulder to see if the jeweller was in here. He wasn't, but someone else was watching me. The woman a few rows back realised I had noticed her. She looked away, sweeping her thick plait of long black hair forward over her shoulder. She must be whoever Gillian had sent to back me up. That was a relief.

I settled myself as comfortably as I could given the lack of leg room and waited for the show to begin. A flowery perfume mingled with the faint scents of hot bodies and packets of coffee in paper carrier bags. I saw people opening jars they must have bought from the shop selling handmade soaps and the like.

As one girl rubbed lotion on her sunburn, I realised my own forearm was itching. I usually tan without any problems, but the skin around those scars must be sensitive.

Soon the curtains on the stage were drawn back, and the evening's entertainment began. A sturdy man with a booming voice and a long list of credits in the sort of TV shows I never watch kicked things off.

'Let me tell you the tale of Owain Glyndwr.'

That turned out to be a story of the Welsh fighting for independence, provoked by the English and their kings encroaching on Welsh rights and lands. Henry IV and his son took exception to Glyndwr declaring himself Prince of Wales and tried to hunt him down. The Welsh fought back, the English retaliated, and that sparked full-scale rebellion. This was no dull history lesson. The actor's performance was full of movement and drama, and his story had hints of magic that caught my attention. At least one of Glyndwr's victories was said to show his ability to influence the weather, when a whirlwind ripped through the English army's camp and Henry IV was nearly crushed by a tent pole.

Eventually, Glyndwr's wife and children were captured and imprisoned when Harlech Castle fell after a long siege. Glyndwr escaped thanks to his uncanny ability to go unnoticed and slip through the English ranks. Regardless, he was still hunted. He ended up trapped high in the mountains with his last few loyal men. They were caught between two pursuing forces with their backs to a sheer cliff. Glyndwr was able to climb the rock face, to escape and... to disappear, never to be seen again. According to legend, the actor told us in hushed tones, the greatest hero of the Welsh will reappear when his people have most need of him. There was a moment's appreciative silence followed by a well-deserved round of applause.

Dancers came on after that, with a fiddler playing their music. Men in black knee breeches, white shirts and red waistcoats paired off with women wearing white caps and aprons over long red skirts worn under long black shirts or maybe short black dresses – don't ask me. Anyway, they did the sort of country dancing I'd seen at fairs and fetes all over. I couldn't see anything particularly Welsh about it. Possibly because I was watching for uncanny shadows joining the dancers. I've seen that happen in other places, and I hadn't forgotten why I was here.

After the whole group had done their thing and I hadn't seen anything odd, several individuals showed off their footwork. Apparently, the Welsh dance around a bottle instead of crossed swords like the Scots. I'm not sure what that says about anything, but the solo dancers were impressive.

The next act was a wiry man with a bald head and a full red beard. He grinned at the audience. 'Well now, you know how the English say William

Shakespeare is the greatest writer who ever lived. I say he got his best ideas from Welsh stories!'

He told the story of a king who had been born with horse's ears. The only person who knew it was the king's barber. Unsurprisingly, he was sworn to secrecy on pain of death. Equally predictably, the secret got out and he was in the shit, but everything ended up okay. The programme said this storyteller was a stand-up comedian, and he played for laughs very well. I'd look him up online when I got the chance. All the same, I was getting impatient. According to the programme, Mari Rhys was on next. She was the last act before the first interval of the evening.

The comedian walked off and she came on stage, carrying a guitar. She was the woman in that photo online. That was a relief. This trip hadn't been a waste of time. She was even more gorgeous in real life. Tonight she wore a long floaty white dress with a low neckline and pearl buttons down the front. The skirt wasn't sewn together at the sides. As she walked across the stage in sparkly silver flip-flops, cloth parted to tempt the audience with flashes of thigh.

Her hair hung in blonde ringlets loosely tied back with a length of white lace. I took a quick look around the hall, and reckoned every straight man and boy with hair on his balls was imagining untying that bow and unbuttoning that dress, maybe sliding a hand under that skirt to find out if she was wearing any knickers. She sure as hell wasn't wearing a bra. More than a few women were probably thinking about that as well.

I wasn't tempted. Forewarned is forearmed. I might not have had those rowan rings in my pocket, but I could picture Fin lying in my bed, naked apart from the downy swan feathers that cling to her skin. I could hear her voice in my head any time I chose to. Mari Rhys couldn't compete with that, whatever she might be. Because she certainly wasn't human. As soon as she blinked, I saw her eyes turn vivid yellow without a hint of white or pupil.

The lights dimmed and she stood in a single spotlight. As soon as she played her first chord, everyone else in the audience was – well, spellbound. That's the only word for it. Even the ones who weren't thinking about how to get her into bed or the nearest dark corner for a snog and a grope. The only sound in the hall was her clear, pure voice and the soft music of the guitar as she sung a ballad. She was singing in Welsh, but that didn't seem to be a problem for visitors who didn't speak the language. Everyone sat staring at her like rabbits in the Land Rover's headlights.

I slumped down in my seat and hoped the darkness meant she couldn't see I wasn't enthralled. The programme had translated her lyrics, so I read that as discreetly as I could. Thanks to my mother's blood, dim light doesn't bother me.

To summarise, a farmer called Evan was poor but honest. He had a beautiful daughter called Olwen and they had a dappled brown cow. They made their living milking the cow and selling butter and cheese. One day, the cow went missing, so Evan and Olwen went looking for her. They couldn't find her anywhere, so they headed home at twilight.

On their way home, they saw a band of the Tylwyth Teg. That's pronounced 't-uh-l-oo-i-th t-eh-g', according to the helpful programme notes. I wasn't going to try saying that anywhere close to anyone Welsh. I guessed whoever wrote this translation didn't want to give anyone the wrong idea by calling them fairies. This wasn't a kid's bedtime story, unless you wanted to give some brat nightmares.

These Tylwyth Teg were riding mountain ponies in a circle in a field. Olwen went for a closer look. More fool her. They grabbed the girl and disappeared. Unsurprisingly, Evan was frantic. He looked everywhere, but he couldn't find any sign of the ponies, their riders or Olwen. It turned out their cow had made her own way home, but that was no consolation. Every day, he searched for his daughter, but he never found her.

Finally, an old wise man told him what to do. After waiting for a year to the day, Evan and four trusted friends went back to the place where Olwen had vanished. The Tylwyth Teg reappeared at the exact same time, riding their ponies in the same circle. Olwen was with them, riding a pony of her own. Evan tied a rope around his waist and told his friends to hang on to the other end as if their lives depended on it, because his surely did. He crept on his belly through the long grass towards the fairy ring.

As soon as he got close enough, he sprang up and dragged Olwen off her pony. The Tylwyth Teg tried to snatch her back, but Evan's mates hauled on the rope. They dragged him and Olwen out of the circle and the riders vanished. Olwen thought she'd only been enjoying herself for an hour or so.

Was that a happy ending? Maybe in some versions of the story. This ballad was something different. I didn't need to speak Welsh, and I didn't need to be caught up in whatever was *persuading* everyone in this hall to heed Mari Rhys's message. The Tylwyth Teg were powerful and puny humans should leave them alone. Correction. The Tylwyth Teg *are* powerful. Stay away from their mountains and valleys if you don't want trouble. You won't be as lucky as Evan and Olwen.

She clearly hadn't got the memo about tourism being vital to regenerate the rural economy. Whoever – whatever – these Tylwyth Teg might be, they weren't interested in living alongside humans like the dryads back at Blithehurst. Was that why Mari was dumping dead bodies on local mountainsides? Come hiking in Wales and try not to trip over the corpses? That would hardly be enticing publicity.

That was it. Just the one ballad. She ended with a muted guitar chord and walked off stage into the wings. She didn't wait for applause or offer any encore. The hall lights came up, and I was surrounded by people who looked as if they'd been startled awake from an unexpected nap. A moment later and they had shaken that off. If I hadn't known better, I'd have said they'd been alert and bright-eyed through Mari's whole song.

The hall doors opened. People smelled coffee and surged towards the courtyard for something to drink, or they joined the queues for the loo. They were talking about Owain Glyndwr and laughing at the thought of King March with his horse's ears. They told each other how much they'd enjoyed the traditional Welsh dancing. No one was even looking to see where Mari Rhys had gone. Five minutes ago, they couldn't take their eyes off her.

I looked around for Gillian's friend, but I couldn't see her either. Had she worked out some way to get backstage? I wanted to go after Mari myself, but I couldn't see how to do that, short of climbing up onto the stage. I was pretty sure that would get me thrown out. It would definitely draw attention, and I didn't want that. The longer Mari Rhys had no idea that anyone was on to her, the better.

I headed into the courtyard. I needed a cold drink. As I joined the queue, I looked around for Gillian's friend. There was still no sign of her, but I did see Mari Rhys. She was heading for the exit through the archway. She passed through the crowd like a breeze through a cornfield. No one stopped her to say they'd enjoyed her song, or to ask her to sign their programme.

I followed. I'd have to be careful to keep my distance, but we needed to know where she went. Once we knew where to find her, we could decide what to do next. I'd just have to hope Gillian's friend noticed me leaving. If I couldn't see her in this crowd, with luck, she could see me. I was the tallest person there.

The iron gates under the arch stood open for anyone who wanted to leave, or to get something from their car. A man was making sure no one came back in without showing a ticket. His eyes didn't so much as flicker as Mari walked past. He did notice me as soon as I approached.

'Good evening. Just getting some fresh air, are you?' He grinned and nodded towards a handful of smokers gathered around a rubbish bin on the far side of the car park. 'Tell them the show starts again in ten minutes, will you?'

'Thanks.' I walked in that general direction, but the smokers weren't my concern. I was looking for Mari Rhys. The good news was I could see she wasn't luring some nicotine addict to his doom. The bad news? She was walking down that track signposted to Cerrigwen. Those stone walls on either side wouldn't do much to hide me if I followed her. There was another couple of hours of daylight left at least, and after sunset the first quarter of the moon would be bright in a clear sky. This summer night wouldn't be really dark until moonset followed midnight by half an hour or so. Even then, anyone with night vision as good as mine or better wouldn't have any problems. She would easily see me coming after her.

She would if she looked back, but I hadn't seen her do that, not once. Why should she, if she was confident in her ability to go unnoticed whenever she wanted. I crossed the car park, walking towards the track. As long as I kept plenty of distance between us, she wouldn't sense my greenwood blood.

Okay, she still might see me, but with luck, as long as I stayed well back, I could just be some tourist wondering where that track might lead. Even if she did get suspicious, I should be okay. Her song in the hall hadn't worked on me. She wouldn't be able to *persuade* me to follow her into some trap.

True, but I didn't know what else she could do. I decided if I saw her turn around, I'd leg it back to the car park without waiting to find out. 'Leg' being the key word. Mari Rhys, whoever or whatever she was, might have unknown, uncanny powers, but I was still over a foot taller. My stride was a lot longer than hers, and it would be even longer if I was running away. I would have no problem doing that after some of the things I've tangled with in the past few years. I rubbed the itching scars on my arm that were a permanent reminder not to take stupid risks.

The dusty track headed down the hillside between dark stone walls. As I left the tarmac, I looked down, but I couldn't tell when a vehicle had last been along here. Even the Land Rover wouldn't leave a trace on the hard-packed flakes of slate underfoot. If I was prepared to bring the Landy down here. The track was wide enough, but anyone in the front seats could open their windows and reach the stone walls on either side. If I met a car coming the other way, I'd be royally screwed because there were no passing places. Someone would have to reverse back the way they had come. Whoever was going uphill had right of way, in theory at least.

Where was Mari Rhys going? I walked slower and stopped when I reached a gap in a wall with a five-barred galvanised metal gate. I crouched down. Now I wasn't sticking up like a church spire on the skyline, I assessed what lay ahead.

The track led to a sprawling cluster of buildings. I guessed the largest was the original farmhouse, with a fenced-off square of grass in front of it that might once have been a garden. Now it was thick with gorse bushes. There was a yard to the side and the back, and what looked like sheds or workshops. Was anyone still living there? No lights shone at the windows, and I couldn't see obvious signs like a car outside or modern repairs to those tumbledown stone sheds. Quite the opposite, in fact. One of the long low outbuildings had lost half its roofing slates, leaving the rafters bare. A sheet of corrugated iron would have sorted that out in an afternoon.

Was that where Mari Rhys was headed? I couldn't see where else she might go. Beyond the run-down farm, the land fell away steeply. There were no more stone walls to mark out pastures, just ragged turf and clumps of undergrowth. Further on, the greenery gave up completely. Where the land rose up again some distance behind the farm, someone had stripped the topsoil off the steep hillside to get at the bedrock. I knew from what I'd read earlier in the evening that had been a long time ago. The decades since hadn't done much to soften the deep scars and the ugly spoil heaps.

Mari Rhys was easy to see in her white dress and sparkly silver flip-flops. She went striding past the run-down farmhouse without giving it a glance. I thought I saw a curtain twitch, but that might have been my imagination. I lost sight of her for a few minutes as she went down the steep slope, but she reappeared soon enough. She crossed the uneven, rocky expanse in front of the quarry and disappeared behind a spoil heap.

I waited, but I didn't see her again. I waited some more. Still no sign. Wherever she had gone, Mari was gone, for the moment at least. There was no sodding way I was going after her, not on my own, not tonight. I'd text Iris with an update, and I'd tell Fin and Gillian as well. I'd see what they thought in the morning, and I'd let Gillian know where her friend could find me.

I headed back. The evening's entertainment was still going on at the Canolfan Meilyr Centre, but I didn't go back into the courtyard. I was bloody hungry. I'd had a good breakfast before I set out from Blithehurst, but that ham salad baguette was the only thing I'd eaten since.

As I walked down the main street, I saw Caergynan differently. Those two-up, two-down terraces must have been the quarry men's homes. The bigger, bay-windowed houses were surely for the foremen and bookkeepers or whatever else passed for white-collar work. Plas Brynwen? Perhaps the quarry owner had lived there, or whoever was in overall charge of managing the operation.

I realised something else. Caergynan had two chapels, even if one of them looked permanently shut up, but there was no sign of a pub where I could get a pint and something to eat. I was pretty sure I'd passed a pub in the bigger village in the valley, but that would mean taking the Landy out. As I crossed the campsite, there were still kids and dogs about. Families sitting around their folding tables, relaxing with a glass of wine in hand. I didn't fancy disturbing everyone and doing it again when I came back later. It was a good thing I'd brought some supplies.

I sat in the Landy's driving seat and turned the ignition key one click so I could plug in my phone to charge. You can't do that in a tent, and I'd used up more battery than I realised looking up things online before the hall doors opened earlier. After I'd sent those text messages, I left the phone charging on the dash and took the camping gear out of the back as well as my bag of shopping from the supermarket.

As I assessed what I had to work with, I guessed Eleanor had been a Girl Guide. I found a set of steel cutlery that clipped together, a blue plastic bowl, a dinner plate and a mug, as well as a small chopping board, a sharp knife and a battered wooden spoon and spatula. Everything had her name on it, neatly painted with white enamel, and was stacked inside a bigger bowl that would do for washing up. There was a battery-powered lantern, though when I switched that on, it was dim enough to tell me I'd better buy more batteries soon. Something solid and round in a drawstring bag turned out to be the camping stove.

It was a neat piece of kit. At first glance it looked like a lidded nest of aluminium bowls with some sort of colander on the outside. When I unpacked it and found the creased and grubby instructions in the bottom of the bag, I saw the perforated layer and the one inside it fitted together to make a windproof support for the spirit burner. There were two pans for cooking and the lid was a frying pan with a handle that clipped on. Best of all, there was a little kettle. I was glad I'd bought those matches as well as teabags and a tin of coffee whitener that would do instead of milk.

I filled the kettle from the tap outside the wash block and set up the stove a safe distance from the tent. While I waited for the water to boil, I ate a Cornish pasty. Then I ate an apple, because that little kettle was a whole lot slower to heat up than an electric one. Once my tea was finally brewing, I warmed up a tin of beans and ate those with some bread. Then I had to wait to drink my tea because powdered milk doesn't cool a drink down like milk from a fridge. When I could drink it without scalding my tongue, I had a couple of fruit scones to go with it.

Once I'd finished eating, I left the stove to get cold and carried my washing up over to the big sink in the wash block. I made a mental note to buy washing-up liquid and a scouring sponge before I tried to cook anything ambitious like scrambled eggs. For the moment, I used a well-worn tea towel I'd found folded in the bottom of the crate to get everything clean enough. I'd need to find somewhere to buy a bigger towel to dry myself if I wanted a shower, though. I should have taken the possibility that I'd end up camping more seriously.

Other people were settling down in their tents and caravans. The daylight was dimming and the kids around the campsite had finally worn themselves out. I decided I might as well call it a day. I packed everything away and put the cooking crate back in the Landy rather than sleep with the faint smell of meths. Taking my phone and my overnight bag into the tent, I didn't bother with the battery lamp as I unrolled the foam mat and got undressed. I've seen enough so-called comedies with people embarrassingly silhouetted inside lit tents.

The sleeping bag was the sort that makes you look like a giant slug rather than one with a zip. I didn't have a lot of room to manoeuvre, but I managed to get into it without wrecking anything. My feet found something rolled up in the bottom that turned out to be a small pillow. So I was pretty much set. Camping wasn't so bad, even if I had to do everything on my knees inside this Eleanor-sized tent.

Then I realised I hadn't cleaned my teeth. Forget that. I couldn't be arsed to get up, get dressed and go over to the wash block. My teeth wouldn't rot and fall out overnight. I went to sleep pretty quickly, no surprise there. I woke up later in the pitch darkness and realised I was going to have to go for a pee. Sod it.

Chapter Ten

I struggled out of the sleeping bag and pulled my combats over my pyjama shorts. I didn't bother with a shirt. It wasn't chilly and I didn't think anyone would be around to be shocked by my bare chest. I shoved my feet into my trainers and laced them loosely.

The noise I made unzipping the inner and outer layers of the tent was startlingly loud in the silence. I eased myself out and saw no other tent or caravan was showing a light, so I guessed I hadn't woken anyone up. The summer night was pleasantly cool and fragrant with the dewy scent of grass and shrubs. Up overhead, the sky was brilliant with stars in that astonishing 3D way you never see in a town.

The only man-made light around was a single dim bulb over the door to the wash block. Since getting up and moving about meant I really, really needed a piss, I headed for the toilets. Astronomy could wait.

When I came out again, movement caught my eye. It wasn't someone needing the loo. Two dogs were circling the little green tent with their blunt muzzles close to the ground. Their heads swung to and fro as if they were trying to pick up a scent. These weren't any of the dogs I had seen around the campsite. They were a lot more hound-shaped for a start. Apart from darker ears, their coats were white and smooth-haired, and they were bigger than any of the pets here on holiday. Not shuck-sized, but any dog smaller than a German Shepherd should think twice before taking one on. Actually, forget that. I've come across Jack Russell terriers that will go for anything, no matter how big it is. Let's say any dog with any sense would think twice before challenging one of these hounds.

Had they come from the village, sniffing around for food scraps? I didn't think so. I'd put my rubbish in the bins and the recycling, following Mr Williams's campsite rules. A sudden thought made me shiver, even though I wasn't cold. Were they even dogs? The problem was, I couldn't tell.

Normally it's easy to work out if I'm seeing something that no one else can. Mostly it's blindingly obvious, when I'm looking at something like a boggart or a sprite. If it could possibly be real, like the ghosts I've seen, other people looking straight through them is a bit of a clue. I could have done with someone else around to say something helpful like, 'What do you suppose those stray dogs are doing?' I mean, I was hardly going to ask a stranger straight out if he could see the damn things or not.

I waited until both dogs – if they were dogs – went around to the far side of the tent. I moved quickly and quietly out of the pool of dim light by the door.

Standing in the shadows at the side of the wash block might not do me much good if these hounds did follow my trail, but the illusion of being hidden made me feel safer.

The dogs reappeared. One sat on its haunches and threw back its head to howl with frustration. The raw noise was deafening. I expected every other dog within half a mile to start barking. That would surely be followed by shouts from people startled awake and wanting to know what was going on.

The echoes died away. Silence returned. No one was stirring. No lights came on anywhere. That answered one question, and this wasn't the first time I'd heard something that more ordinary people couldn't. That had been a threat as well.

The dog who'd stayed silent looked at the noisy one with what I'd swear was irritation. Then they both turned to look at the road, pricking up their dark, floppy ears. Whatever they had heard, I'd missed it, or maybe the noise was only meant for them. Either way, they loped away into the darkness. I breathed a bit easier.

Not much easier. I stood in the shadows for as long as I could. Eventually, I heard a tent zip open somewhere. There was no sign of those dogs coming back, and I didn't want to try explaining why I was lurking by the wash block in the middle of the night. I gritted my teeth and headed back to my tent.

I'd left the front unzipped, but there was no sign that the creepy hounds had stuck their heads inside. What normal dog wouldn't take that as an open invitation? There was something else. When I kicked off my trainers and crawled inside on my hands and knees, I felt something hard and round lying on the rucked-up sleeping bag.

I could easily tell what it was. One of the rowan circles. The thing was, though, I'd stuck those in the side pocket of my overnight bag. That was up at the far end of the tent, in the space beyond the pole. I crawled up and checked, and my bag was still there. The side pocket was still zipped shut.

I opened it up and took out the other rowan rings. I put one in the side pocket of my combats once I took them off and one at each end of the tent. Then I tried to get back to sleep. Not a fucking chance. An outer layer of nylon and an inner of thin cotton and mesh didn't feel like any kind of protection. After a while I gave up. I'd sleep in the Landy after all, no matter how uncomfortable that might be.

As I was threading my feet into my trousers yet again, wishing I had enough bloody room to stand up, I remembered something else. I cautiously left the tent, alert for any movement in the darkness. I had my keys between my fingers like some improvised martial arts tiger claw. Any dark-eared dog that attacked me would get a faceful of pointed metal.

There was no sign of the hounds or anything else. I went around to the back of the Landy. Thankfully, Simon and I had decided against installing upgraded central locking that would flash the lights and beep. I opened up without causing any disturbance and found that tub of earth I'd scraped up from under the churchyard yew tree. I took Eleanor's food prep knife out of the red crate as well.

Going back to the tent, I trickled a thin line of decaying yew needles under the outer edge of the green flysheet. I had no idea what Mr Williams would make of that, but that wasn't my concern. I'd be gone before he saw it. Meantime, I should be as safe as possible.

I got back into the tent and lay down on the sleeping bag. I kept my trousers on, and I had my keys and that knife to hand. If anything came for me, if I had time, I'd get my trainers on, but I would manage barefoot if I had to. The campsite grass was mowed short and smooth.

Whether the yew needles really did something or my subconscious just thought they worked, I fell asleep before I realised it. When I woke up, the sun was bright outside and I could hear kids' voices. Given the lack of screams and snarling, I guessed uncanny hounds weren't eating them.

I checked my phone and was surprised to see it was only just after 6 a.m. I was also surprised to find a text from Gillian telling me to ring her AT ONCE. She'd sent that at 5.40 a.m. If she'd sent it last night, I would have waited. Since she was already up, I called her.

She answered immediately. 'Hello, Dan?'

'Yes.' I kept my voice low. I wouldn't know if someone approached the tent, and I didn't want to be overheard.

'Whoever you thought you saw yesterday, she wasn't—' Gillian hesitated '—a colleague of mine. I couldn't find anyone free to join you.'

'Oh, okay.' Had the woman with the dark plait just been particularly sensitive to my greenwood allure? Or perhaps I'd imagined the whole thing. But I hadn't imagined Mari Rhys and her ballad.

That was Gillian's concern. 'This singer is definitely a threat. We're seeing what we can find out about what she might be. Sit tight until one of us can get over there.'

'How long's that going to take?' I objected. 'I have a job to get back to.'

'You said Blithehurst is closed on Mondays,' Gillian countered. 'You can give us until tomorrow night at least.'

I couldn't argue with that, unfortunately, and I guessed Eleanor would say the same. 'There's something else. A couple of white dogs came sniffing around my tent in the middle of the night. The thing is, they weren't—'

'Hounds with red ears?' Gillian interrupted.

'They had dark ears, but I couldn't see what colour. It was the middle of the night.'

Gillian didn't reply, which made me very uneasy.

'What do you think they were?'

'From that description, and given where you are,' she said slowly, 'they could be hounds of the otherworld.'

'That can't be good.'

'They're not necessarily a threat.' She didn't sound convinced.

'What do I do about them?' I patted my pocket to feel the rowan circle.

'Steer well clear, if you possibly can.' Gillian clearly realised that might not be an option. 'I have to talk to some people. Sit tight till I call you back.'

'Okay.' I couldn't see I had any other option.

She ended the call. I stared at my phone and thought about ringing her back. I wanted to ask how Tom was. If she was already making other calls, though, I'd just get her voicemail.

It was far too early for me to ring anyone else. What was I going to do now? I really, really wanted a shower after sleeping in my trousers. Maybe that supermarket down in the valley could sell me a decent-sized towel. I'd head down there as soon as they opened, but that wouldn't be for hours yet. Sunday meant limited opening times.

Since I was awake, I might as well have breakfast. I set up the camping stove, made some tea and ate the rest of the scones. The sun was rising higher in the cloudless sky, and I reckoned this was going to be another hot day. I cleaned my teeth and decided not to bother with a shave until I could have a shower. I was supposed to be on holiday, after all.

Once I'd tidied everything away, I sat in the Landy and put my phone on charge again. I hadn't used much battery, but I hadn't fully recharged it yesterday. I'd better top it up whenever I could.

It didn't take me long on the Internet to find out what Gillian had been talking about. The Cŵn Annwn are an old, old Welsh myth. 'Cŵn' meaning dogs and Annwn being the otherworld, or possibly the underworld. Depending on who was telling the story, that realm is ruled by Arawn, or by Gwynn ap Nudd. According to some tales, he's king of the Tylwyth Teg. Oh, great. That was the second time I'd come across the Tylwyth Teg in as many days.

What's that saying? The first time is happenstance, the second time is coincidence, the third time is enemy action. Still, at least I was getting used to hearing an 'oo' sound in my head when my eyes read 'w' in a Welsh word.

I looked at a Wikipedia entry that was at least fifty per cent links to other pages. Was there any point in trying to untangle all these different strands of myth and folklore, hoping to find something I could use? I could already see King Arthur was getting mentions. That never helps a folk tale make sense.

The phone vibrated in my hand. Iris was calling.

I pressed the screen. 'Hello?'

'Dan? Are you okay?' Her voice was taut with concern.

'I'm fine.' But now I was worried. 'What's the matter? Has something happened?'

'Yes. I mean, no, not to any of us. But I've found something online.'

I waited for my pulse to slow as the sickening shock of thinking something had happened to Fin faded. 'What?'

'Another boy has gone missing, from the Wirral.' Iris spoke fast, as if that could help. 'Tyler Pensby, seventeen years old, lived with his grandparents. A good kid, apparently, not that it makes any difference.'

I wondered about that. I don't mean it wouldn't matter as much if whoever went missing was some thieving, foul-mouthed lowlife. No one should go through what Tom had suffered, whoever they might be. I could tell that's what Iris meant. But would a lad who was falling through the cracks in the system, maybe already into petty crime, be more or less suspicious of this glamorous blonde who'd turned up out of nowhere? I wasn't sure, but either way, he'd be a lot less likely to be missed.

Iris was still talking. 'He went out for a music night at a local pub and never came home.'

I didn't understand. 'That has to be a coincidence. Mari Rhys was on stage here last night. I saw her.'

'He went missing a fortnight ago. His friends have only just started a social media campaign, trying to find someone who's seen him.'

'Right, sorry.'

'Mari Rhys isn't listed as one of the acts performing that night at the pub, which is odd, but I can definitely see her in the background of some of the photos people have posted.'

'Right.' It was good to know this woman's ability to make people forget her had some limits.

'Is that all you can say?' Iris was annoyed.

'What do you want me to do?' I retorted. 'I'm still here on my own. I'm waiting for Gillian to call me back, to tell me back-up's on its way. Have you told her about this missing boy?'

'No, not yet.' Iris took a moment. She went on, calmer. 'Okay, I'll ring her and see what she has to say. One of us will call you back.'

'I can have a look around here. In case I see something odd.'

'Thanks. And I'm sorry if I snapped. It's just...'

'I know.' The thought of another boy ending up dead or as broken as Tom made my skin crawl too. 'Talk to you later.'

'Bye.'

Iris was gone before I realised I hadn't told her about those red-eared dogs. Oh well, Gillian would update her. I switched off my phone and looked up at the sky through the Land Rover windscreen. It was broad daylight, and I was pretty sure fairies – yes, I still felt stupid using that word – preferred darkness or twilight. I could walk up to the Canolfan Meilyr Centre and go on to take a look at that old quarry beyond the derelict farm. Just a quick look. I might find something to give us some idea where Mari Rhys might have gone.

Who was I kidding? That had to be as likely as winning the lottery. Maybe so, but the alternative was sitting here on my arse until the supermarket down in the valley opened. While I was doing that, what might be happening to that poor kid from the Wirral? Would he be found dead, suicidal or out of his mind on magic mushrooms? Would he ever be found at all?

I got out of the Landy and checked I had that rowan ring safe in the pocket of my combats. I couldn't take the kitchen knife with me, though, or anything else that could be classed as an offensive weapon. That's asking for trouble, especially when you look like me. Besides, whatever explanation I made up, the police would see I was lying from a mile off.

If I told the truth, no one would believe me either. 'It's like this, officer. I'm trying to find a fairy folk-singer who lures vulnerable young men away from pubs to shag them senseless in some hidden sex lair.' If they decided I really believed it, I'd probably end up sectioned.

But there are no laws against carrying a penknife with a blade up to three inches long. I had one of those. So I would go and take a look in that quarry. I stuck everything from the tent into the back of the Landy. I have no idea how honest people on campsites might be, and I didn't want to come back and find everything had been nicked.

I put my keys and phone into a zip pocket with my wallet and my penknife. If I had to fight something, I could use the keys in one hand and the penknife in the other. As long as I had time to unzip my pocket and get them out. It would probably be better to steer clear of any fight.

I started walking up the hill. There were quite a few people about, and the chapel that was still being used had its doors open for Sunday services. When I reached the Canolfan Meilyr Centre, the car park was half full and the gates to the courtyard were wide open. Not everyone was here to buy crafts or a morning coffee. People with day packs and hiking boots were getting ready to go hill walking. I saw a footpath that I hadn't noticed yesterday, leading away from the car park on the far side of the building. A couple of groups had already set off down the track signposted to Cerrigwen.

I watched them for a bit, and saw something interesting. When the walkers reached that fence and the overgrown garden at the front of the farmhouse, they veered off to the left. I realised there must be another footpath down there, following the last of the stone walls that penned the sheep in their hillside pastures. It had to be an official right of way. When the next group reached the fence, I saw the woman I guessed was in charge had a map case hung around her neck. She lifted it up to check the route. Everyone headed away from the farm.

I might not look like a serious hiker in a T-shirt and trainers, but I wouldn't seem too out of place. I started walking down the track and soon passed the gateway where I'd lurked last night. I walked more slowly as I approached that fenced-off land in front of the farmhouse.

The farm and outbuildings were on a roughly rectangular plot with the two-storey house at the front and the right-hand side as I was looking. The other buildings made an L shape down the left-hand side of the sizeable yard and across the back. Once upon a time, the garden at the front had supplied the farmhouse with vegetables and flowers. Now it was a wilderness of unkempt grass and gorse.

There was still no sign of anyone living there. The farmhouse looked as if it had been deserted for years. The curtains were still drawn at every filthy window, and the paint on the window frames was peeling and stained. Gorse was growing in such thick clumps around the steps to the fretwork porch that I didn't think the front door had been opened in decades.

The track to the quarry went straight past the right-hand side of the house and the buildings behind it. There was no sign saying 'no access', 'private property' or 'no right of way'. There was no gate or anything else to stop someone from walking straight on down the track instead of turning left to follow the footpath. But no one was remotely interested in following that route. People didn't even seem to be looking at the farmhouse.

Why was the place being left to fall apart? The farmhouse and those outbuildings could surely be converted to profitable holiday lets or a guest house. There was clearly plenty of demand around here. The property presumably came with the land I could see beyond the stone-walled pastures. The boundary at the back might go as far as the quarry. Land could be built on or used for a campsite to give Mr Williams of Plas Brynwen some competition.

Unless I was the only person who could see the buildings. Shit. That hadn't occurred to me. For the second time in twenty-four hours, I wondered how to find out what was real and what wasn't. Then I saw a hiker pause where the track met the footpath. He put his boot on the lowest rung of the wooden fence so he could retie his laces. So that was solid enough. Hopefully, so was everything else.

I walked on more quickly. I didn't slow down when I reached the way-marked turn. I carried on striding past the farm as if I knew exactly where I was going and I had every right to be there. The back of my neck was prickling regardless. I half expected to hear a cross Welsh bellow telling me to stop right there and demanding to know what I thought I was doing.

No one shouted. To be fair, my size does stop most people from challenging me. Apart from middle-aged men who can't park their cars straight and who have the same mindset as a Jack Russell terrier.

A metal gate behind the farmhouse barred entry to the empty yard. I didn't stop to look any closer. If there was anyone inside, I didn't want them thinking I had any interest in their hovel. I waited until I was past the outbuildings and hidden from view before I picked up a broken scrap of the slate crunching under my trainers. There was something I had to do before I went any further. I chucked the slate as hard as I could at the closest wall at the back of the yard. The dark lump hit with a resounding crack and bounced off into a clump of nettles. So those buildings did exist. That was a relief.

Now I felt like an idiot. The property might be tied up in probate. There could be major planning permission issues. Those could sometimes be got around by letting a house decay past saving. It would cost a fortune to renovate this place in its current condition. What if it needed a new septic tank or if it wasn't on mains electricity? Getting the basics sorted out could cost thousands before any work could start on the buildings. I was letting my imagination get the better of me when I should be looking for some sign of the missing boy Iris had told me about.

Mari Rhys had gone to the quarry. I put the farmhouse out of my mind and carried on walking, careful as the hillside facing the quarry site got steeper and the track got fainter until it had all but disappeared. Once upon a time, a little stream searching for a way down to the river had cut a gully here. In this dry weather, there was barely a trickle when I got to the bottom of the slope. Only a line of tussocks of thicker, darker grass hid the risk of a twisted or broken ankle for anyone not paying attention.

Before I crossed the dry rivulet, I took a good long look at the abandoned quarry. It was impossible to work out what the original profile of this hillside might have been. Thousands of tonnes of rock must have been dug out or blasted loose to leave this great grey half-circle of bare stone looming above a rocky floor. I studied the irregular steps and ledges cut back into the hill and tried to work out how high the top was. Six storeys, maybe, so twenty metres give or take. High enough to make falling off the ragged turf edging the stone a really bad idea.

Now I was closer, and seeing it in broad daylight, my eyes picked out regular angles and straight lines in the flatter areas beside the spoil heaps. Those marked out footings for whatever buildings had once been here. Thinking back to the local history I had read online, that must have been where blocks of slate were split and shaped into thin sheets for roofing. I also reckoned I knew where the local farmers had come to find the regular, worked stone to build those walls around their fields after the quarry had closed. Waste not, want not.

Watching where I put my feet, I approached the quarry. Now I saw something else. Mine workings had been driven deep into the exposed rock. I counted four rectangular entrances as black as night in the grey stone. I wondered what had been so particularly valuable to make the extra effort worthwhile. As I went to take a look into the nearest one, I wondered why there wasn't a metal gate to stop idiot tourists or stray sheep getting inside and coming to grief.

Perhaps a barrier had been fixed to the walls a bit further inside. I walked a little way into the tunnel, careful not to bang my head. Welsh slate miners had clearly been short-arses, and I hadn't thought I'd need to bring a hard hat. I don't keep one in the Landy these days.

The rocky passage went straight on ahead as far as I could see. There was still nothing to stop me going further in. I went on a little way. Not much deeper. It was surprising how quickly the daylight dimmed. I shivered, and not only because the temperature drop was noticeable after the hot sun outside. I would never have said I was claustrophobic, but I haven't been keen on underground places since a naiad took me through some old lead workings in the Lake District.

Besides, I didn't have a torch, apart from the light on my phone. I wasn't about to use that and drain the battery. Also, I wouldn't have any sort of signal here, and I was waiting for Gillian to ring me, so staying where she couldn't reach me was a dumb move. I turned around and headed back to the sunshine.

I decided I'd go back to the campsite and take the Landy to the supermarket. That would only be a short run, so I'd have a bit of a drive around afterwards to get the lay of the land while my phone charged properly. Okay, so I'd probably end up stuck in traffic, but I wanted to get a better feel for this place. I wondered where I'd be able to buy a large-scale Ordnance Survey map. There had to be a shop somewhere around selling things like that to hikers.

Blinking as I stepped into bright sunlight, I shaded my eyes with a hand. I caught a glimpse of movement and a flash of white. I instinctively stepped back into the tunnel. Better safe than sorry. It was probably an adventurous sheep, but it might not be. I hadn't forgotten those dark-eared dogs. After a moment, I edged slowly forward, trying to look around the rough, rocky edge without being seen or sniffed out. If those dogs were here in the daylight, I might be able to see if their ears were red. That would be something to tell Gillian.

Mari Rhys was walking past the spoil heap on the far side of the quarry. She wasn't looking in my direction. Still wearing that floaty white dress and silvery flip-flops, she headed for the entrance to the furthest mine. I watched her go inside and out of sight.

Chapter Eleven

What was I going to do? Follow Mari Rhys into the slate mine like some idiot teenager in a horror movie? Since this wasn't a movie, if I got into trouble, no random hiker was going to turn up and save me in the nick of time. I was here on my own and no one knew where I was. I still didn't have a torch, and even my excellent night vision is useless where there's no light whatsoever. The sensible thing to do was head back to Plas Brynwen.

On the other hand, there was definitely something going on here. I reckoned whatever deterred walkers who might have followed the track past the farmhouse was keeping ordinary people out of this quarry as well. Maybe it even worked on sheep. Regardless, I guessed that's why no safety gates blocked access to these mines.

So I'd ring Gillian and tell her where Mari Rhys was lurking. Maybe the wise women could tell me what the so-called folk-singer really was by now. We could come up with a plan to... to do what? Trap her? Force her to hand back her latest victim? Persuade her to stop doing whatever she was playing at, kidnapping these boys? Right. Sure. The wise women would have to come up with something pretty spectacular for that to happen.

Meantime, the boy Iris had read about online was presumably having who knew what mind-wrecking experiences. If the poor bastard was even still alive. Though Tom had been missing for six weeks and he had survived. Granted, he'd been half-starved and dehydrated, but fairy food and drink must have kept him from death's door. The chances had to be fairly good that Tyler Whatsisname could be rescued.

So the best thing I could do was leave here as fast as I could. Mari Rhys hadn't seen me, but those hounds could be somewhere around. So I should find somewhere with a phone signal. I should come back later with back-up from Gillian or her friends. Hell, as many of the wise women who were available would be welcome to tag along.

Meantime, that boy Tyler could be somewhere in that hillside being fucked literally and mentally while I was right outside. How could I leave until I knew, one way or the other? I was already walking across the quarry floor. I unzipped my pocket and got out my penknife and keys. I unfolded the biggest knife blade, thankful I hadn't cut my nails too recently. Threading my keys between the fingers of my left hand, I clenched my fist around the Landy's ignition fob.

Taking a deep breath, I went into the mine working. It was bigger than the first one I had explored. That was a relief, though I still watched my head. As my eyes adjusted to the dimness, I halted. It looked as if this tunnel dead-ended not far ahead. I'm not going to lie. For a moment, that was a relief. If Mari Rhys could pass through solid rock, there was no way I could follow her. I'd done all I could and now I could leave.

I had to be sure though. As I went on a bit further, I realised the tunnel actually turned sharply to the left. I walked slowly to the corner, listening hard for any sound of something lurking ahead. The further I went into this cool darkness, the more I felt this was a bad idea.

I looked cautiously around the corner. I came face to face with Mari Rhys, and I mean absolutely face to face. My trainers stubbed her bare toes in those sparkly flip-flops. Her fluttering white dress brushed my trousers, and I was close enough to smell her perfume. I realised I knew that alluring, sensual, intriguing blend of flowers. I remembered it from last night, in the Canolfan Meilyr Centre. I'd thought it was body lotion people were putting on sunburn.

I raised my hand to ward her off. That's all I wanted to do, I swear. If I showed her the penknife, I thought she would step back from the threat of the steel. She reached for me in the same moment. I have no idea what she was going to do, but the penknife sliced into her arm.

In the blink of an eye, she was gone. Wilted blossoms and leaves tumbled through the air to pile up at my feet. Her perfume was gone. Now I smelled something like water emptied out of a vase when the last flowers in a bunch have died. My stomach heaved as I looked down. I saw what looked like broom stems and meadowsweet. There were oak twigs there too, which confused me. Whatever Mari Rhys had been, she had nothing to do with the greenwood. Don't ask me how I knew that. I just did. I felt sick, and not because of the stink of decay. I hadn't meant to kill her. How was I supposed to know it would be so easy?

What was I going to do now? I looked down the tunnel. Frowning, I licked a finger and held it up in front of me. The chill on my skin was faint, but a breeze was definitely coming towards me. I remembered the way Mari Rhys's dress had brushed against my legs. The air in that first mine I had explored had been completely still. Was I seeing something ahead, or was that my imagination? I took a step forward. That wasn't close enough. I needed to get out of the light coming from the entrance. I really didn't want to.

I looked at the twigs and flowers scattered across the uneven floor. Was Mari Rhys really heading for compost or only gone for a while? Well, I knew how to deal with her if she showed up like some plant-based zombie. I took the biggest stride I could to step over the remains. Thank fuck I've got long legs. It wasn't enough though. Something crunched under my heel, and I remembered the horrible sound when I'd run over a scurrying rat in the Landy. It had darted across the road. I couldn't even swerve to avoid it.

Trying not to throw up, I took another few steps into the gloom to get away from the dead flowers. Because this was gloom, not the absolute darkness of that other tunnel. A bit further on and I was certain there was light ahead. I could feel that breeze on my face and my bare arms now. My scars were really feeling the chill, and I made a mental note to buy some sunscreen in the supermarket.

That was something for later. Right now, I thought about the landscape outside. This tunnel had turned a corner, so it wasn't leading straight into the hillside any more. It was running parallel to the quarry face. If it went on far enough, it would go under the untouched grassy slope off to the side of the quarry. I tried to picture the undulating landscape. I couldn't do it. I had been focused on the quarry. Never mind. That glimmer of light and the breeze could mean there was another entrance, or as far as I was concerned, an exit, somewhere up ahead.

Or the light could be the proverbial oncoming train or something equally dangerous. What about those dark-eared dogs? Well, I hadn't seen or heard a trace of them so far. I had my penknife and I had the rowan ring with me. I was pretty sure that kept them away.

I was walking faster. If Mari Rhys was really dead, Tyler Whatsisname was fucked if she'd dumped him in these diggings. She wouldn't be bringing him anything to eat or drink. Even if he wasn't out of his skull on mushrooms, he would have no idea where he was, or how to get out. I had to see if he was in here.

My eyes adjusted as the tunnel opened into a bigger space. I couldn't tell if it was a natural cave or something slate miners had dug out. I could see it because water had pooled in a shallow hollow in the rocky floor. It shone with a cold blue-grey light that was as reassuring as the glow from a pond housing nuclear waste.

I stepped out of the passage. The body sprawled on the rocky floor beside the pool had to be the missing kid. He had light hair, though I couldn't say exactly what colour it was in this weird light. He wore a leather jacket over a pale shirt and dark jeans and trainers. He wasn't dead, because he was moving his hands and feet like a cat or a dog having a dream. A second look told me he was as high as a kite. I don't do drugs, but I've seen people out of their skulls. His eyes were open, but he wasn't seeing anything, or at least, not anything that was really here. I couldn't tell if he was whimpering or giggling. Maybe he was doing both.

That wasn't my main concern. A couple of metres from Tyler, where the light coming from the pool met the shadows that filled the rest of the cave, a woman sat on an ornate golden chair. It looked like something from a stately home where the owners had more money than taste. She was the woman with the long black plait who'd been watching me in the hall while Mari Rhys was playing. She wasn't masquerading as a tourist today. This was her domain and she was its queen. Her skin was as pale as milk and her lips were as red as blood. She smiled at me, and I saw her eyes were as black as onyx, without any white at all. A very scary fairy.

'At last,' she said, satisfied. 'I was starting to think you would never get here.'

She leaned back in her chair. Her pale, long-fingered hands had nails like icy talons resting on the dark velvet that cushioned the arms. Her unbound hair flowed down to her elbows, and she wore a deep red dress that would trail on the ground when she stood up. The dress had long sleeves and a high neck, like something from a history book. She didn't need to tempt anyone with the allure of her tits or thighs. She had Mari Rhys for that. Well, she had done until just now.

'Welcome to my realm.' Her voice was more mocking than friendly. 'You are a hard-headed forest boy. I saw how resistant you were to my flower maiden's charms, and not only when she was singing. Every time I put a thought in your head, to convince you to come and meet me, you found some reason to delay. I suppose that is only to be expected. Your kind are always so foolishly stubborn.'

I didn't say a word. I was assessing the distance between me and Tyler. He was as skinny as Tom, so I should be able to scoop him up easily enough. That was the only good news. He was on the other side of that glowing pool on the rocky floor between me and the woman on the throne. I'd have to go around the water. I sure as hell wasn't splashing through it. Unfortunately, I didn't think I would reach him before whatever the fuck lurked in those shadows sprang out to stop me – or to rip me to pieces.

Dark shapes prowled in the darkness behind the scary fairy's throne. I couldn't make them out at first. Then I remembered that dream the Green Man had sent me. They were those fox-cat-goat-faced things, I was sure of it. I didn't have a hope of counting how many there were, but that didn't matter. There were far too many for me to take on with a penknife and a bunch of keys.

Sorry, Tyler. It was every man for himself. If I could get out of here, maybe I could come back with the wise women and rescue the poor kid. If I could get out of here in one piece. I tried to estimate the distance back to the tunnel without turning my head. I didn't dare look away from the scary fairy in case something jumped me.

If I could reach the tunnel before those shadowy monsters reached me, they could only attack me a few at a time in that narrow space. I'd have to turn my unprotected back to them though, and I had no idea how much damage they could do. I didn't just need a hard hat. I needed sodding body armour, and I couldn't buy that in a supermarket. The scars on my arm were burning, as if those wounds were still fresh.

Then the woman on the throne waved a hand and the shadows stopped roaming around. The pain in my forearm dulled. That was a relief. It had been getting hard to think straight.

'What brings you here?' She laughed, as if we were having a normal conversation. 'Not *here* here, obviously. I mean, what brings you to Cerrigwen? You're a long way from home.'

That had the unmistakeable ring of truth. What did that mean? What did anything this scary fairy queen said mean? I thought fast. Whoever she was, she could tell who and what I was, but I didn't think she could read my mind, even if she was claiming she could put ideas in my head. She thought she had lured me into her cave, but she had no idea why I had been in the hall to hear Mari Rhys sing.

On the other hand, she'd know at once if I told her a lie here and now.

I cleared my throat. 'My girlfriend and I – I'm not sure where we're going. I mean, I don't know if we should talk about moving in together. That wouldn't be easy. We both work. I don't know what her sisters think—'

'Enough!' she snapped, with a flick of her hand like someone getting rid of a fly. 'You mortals with your pathetic love affairs. You thought clear mountain air might clear your head, did you, poor forest boy?'

No question, she was mocking me. The things in the shadows sniggered. I felt myself going red. Pricks. Whatever else those things might be, they were pricks. But that didn't matter. I had been telling the truth and the scary fairy had taken what I said at face value. Now I was convinced she had no idea I had come looking for Tyler. Why should she? She had kidnapped the boy before she even knew I existed. She couldn't have any idea that I knew what had happened to Tom.

I pointed at Tyler. 'Why is he here?'

'Who?'

For an instant I was convinced she had forgotten the boy was even there. Then she looked over at him with a cruel smile. 'Our plaything, you mean? What of it?'

'What do you want with him?'

'Amusement.' The scary fairy cocked her head like a bird. 'What amuses you, forest boy? How do you like to have fun? If I made another flower maiden, she could show you undreamed-of delights. That could help you decide if you truly love this girl of yours?'

'No thanks.'

She pursed her lips, irritated. She might not be able to read my mind, but she could see there was no way I'd take up any invitation from her. The things in the shadows behind her grumbled too.

I waited. If she had set out to lure me here, and not because she had realised I was on to her kidnapping scheme, she wanted something from me. She could tell I had greenwood blood, so that must have something to do with it. Hopefully my chances of getting out of here alive had just improved. How was I going to get out of here with Tyler though?

She smiled at me, sly. 'If you're looking to a future with this girl at your side, you will need money. Mortals always do. I will pay handsomely if you do something for me.'

Now I was over the first shock of meeting her, I was starting to notice how often her face betrayed her. She had never had to learn to hide what she was really thinking. When she was dealing with her own kind – or mine – she couldn't tell lies. When she was dealing with ordinary people, she could overwhelm them with her charm or her glamour or whatever the wise women would call her power.

Whatever she wanted must be important. That might give me some advantage. I chose my next words very carefully. I wanted to get out of here before I committed myself to anything, so I could talk to Gillian and Iris. On the other hand, if I turned her down flat, Tyler was probably screwed.

'What might you want doing by someone like me?'

She leaned forward in her chair. Lacing her fingers together, she rested her elbows on the velvet-padded arms. She studied my face intently. That was unnerving. Nothing moved behind her and the silence was absolute. I stood as still as I could and stared back at her. I tried not to blink first, making sure I could describe her in detail when I got out of here. I noticed she had a silvery scar on her left hand between her forefinger and thumb.

'I want some property retrieving.' She looked away as she leaned back in her chair and crossed her legs.

I could tell that wasn't a lie, but it wasn't the whole truth either. Whose property were we talking about, just for a start? She hadn't said it was her own. I decided not to ask that just yet, or anything else that might piss her off.

'How did this property go astray?'

'Methodists,' she hissed. The shadows behind her stirred and growled.

That was undeniably true, but it made absolutely no sense to me. 'Sorry, what?'

Glowering, the scary fairy looked past me towards the outside world. 'You have no idea, with your mayfly lives. We lived happily alongside mortal folk since time out of mind. Favours were traded on either side and payment made for services rendered. The scales balanced, more or less. Then dull little men with narrow minds came to plague our mountains. They dug and despoiled the land. They blocked the rivers and fouled the waters. They drowned whole valleys eventually, never caring what they destroyed.'

She glared at me, ferocious enough to send a chill down my spine, even though I wasn't who she was angry with. 'They convinced the mortals who had been our friends to abandon us for good, to forswear us completely. All for the promise of unseen rewards in some imagined life to come. What's wrong with enjoying life in the moment? What do mortals think they will gain when they are dead if they deny themselves the pleasures of eating and coupling, of music and dance, while they live?'

I shook my head. She could read whatever she liked into that. I wanted to get back to the point of this conversation.

'What might this property be, exactly?'

She smiled suddenly, as if I'd just agreed to something. 'It is a harp.'

'A harp?' That was unexpected. 'Where is – where might it be?'

She looked at me through narrowed eyes. 'You don't think you can do this?'

'I haven't said I'm going to do anything,' I said quickly. 'We have made no agreement.'

The shadows stirred, dissatisfied, but the scary fairy couldn't say different.

'Why might you find this trivial task such a daunting challenge?' she asked me, trying to provoke me with a hint of mockery.

'Because a harp is sodding enormous,' I said bluntly. 'They're, what, about as tall as I am and half as wide?' I was guessing, mostly. I hadn't seen an orchestra in real life since I'd been on a school trip to see the City of Birmingham Symphony. I didn't think I was too far off though.

'That's not something I – not something anyone could just stick under an arm and sneak off with, hoping no one's going to notice. You might as well ask me to try nicking a piano.'

'What are you talking about?' She stared at me, genuinely confused. I heard baffled murmurs from the shadow creatures.

'What are you talking about?' I countered.

She turned and snapped her fingers at the darkness. One of the creatures walked into the light. It had a fox's head, but before I got a proper look, it transformed itself into a person. A man with long dark hair and a beard sat on a three-legged stool. He wore dark generic historical drama robes and held a harp small enough to balance on one thigh. A moment later, I recognised the pose from the mural in the Canolfan Meilyr Centre.

He rested the harp against his chest, and the carved top jutted a few inches above his shoulder. He held the curved front steady and used his free hand to sweep a chord from the strings. The sound echoed and reverberated inside the hollow hill.

Tyler shrieked and writhed. He looked like he was having a seizure. I clapped my hands over my ears, partly to muffle the sound and partly to stop my skull from coming apart. I had an instant, blinding headache. The hellish music faded away. I blinked away tears and looked at the harpist. He – it – whatever – was looking at me and grinning viciously. His hand was poised to brush the strings and his dark eyes dared me to try and stop him.

I didn't believe for a minute that these creatures, whatever they were, had lived peacefully alongside ordinary mortals, not if they could do things like this. I looked over at Tyler. Still barely conscious, he was throwing up. If the kid breathed in that vomit, he could easily choke to death. The thought of trying to do CPR to save him made me want to throw up as well.

I forced myself to lower my hands and looked at the scary fairy queen. 'So you're talking about something smaller than I thought. It's still big enough to be noticed, and you still haven't told me where it is.'

She shrugged as if that should be obvious. 'Cerrigwen.'

'In the farmhouse?' I glanced in that direction before I could stop myself.

When I looked back, she nodded as if we'd come to an agreement. 'Name your price, forest boy. It is worth a king's ransom in gold to me.'

I tried to work out where I'd lost control of this conversation. I still had no idea what Methodists had to do with anything, and she hadn't given me a single hint to explain why she wanted this sodding harp. I decided that didn't matter, not at the moment. Right here and now, I had to make a deal if I was going to save Tyler.

'Your gold will turn into what, autumn leaves, the following day? No thank you, all the same.'

She laughed. 'Your mother taught you some things at least. Very well. What payment will you take?'

'Him.' I pointed at Tyler. 'He has no place here, and you know it as well as I do.'

She pouted, but only for a moment. She couldn't hold back a gleeful grin. 'Very well.'

Shit. Somehow, she thought she had won. Where had I screwed up and how badly?

The creatures behind her throne stirred, dissatisfied as well as confused.

'Enough,' she snapped. 'You've had your fun for now.'

She broke off as I walked around the glowing water, staying as far away from the evil harpist as I possibly could.

'What are you doing?' she demanded, indignant.

'Taking my payment.' I pointed at Tyler.

'Payment on delivery, forest boy.'

'No deal if he isn't still breathing by then.'

'How do I know you will keep your word,' she protested with fake indignation, 'if I let you take him now?'

'Because you'll know if I'm lying when I promise we have a deal.'

She shook her head. 'I can hear other things in your voice besides the truth, forest boy. I don't know what tricks your mother or your master may have taught you. No, the plaything stays here until I have the harp in my hands.'

I could see from her face that wasn't up for discussion. I had to make the best of whatever else I could get out of her then.

'I need to clean him up and make sure he's going to be okay. Once I'm gone, you must keep him safe and alive. Safe, alive and not driven mad by whatever you've been feeding him. Keep him asleep and not dreaming. I want your word on that.'

She pursed her lips for so long I thought she was going to refuse. I had no idea what I was going to do if she did. I'd have to cross that bridge if we came to it. I used the time to work out what I was going to say if she agreed to my terms very carefully.

'Very well,' she said at last, grudging. 'As long as you promise to bring me the harp.'

'I will bring it here for you to see, as a show of good faith. Then I will take the boy and the harp out of here.' I looked her in the eye. 'As soon as I am certain he is safe and well cared for, I will give you the harp myself. I promise.'

She took another long, long moment to think that through. Finally, she scowled. 'Agreed.'

She must really want this harp. That couldn't be good, but it was something I had to think about later. She leaned back on her throne, and her gesture told me I could go to Tyler. I didn't waste any time, sticking my penknife and keys in my pocket. I was going to need both hands. I looked warily at the harpist, but he didn't move.

I found my handkerchief in a pocket and forced myself to dip it in the shimmering pool. That was the only water around. I was ready to snatch my hand back if I felt any threat. I didn't. I clenched my jaw and focused on wiping puke off Tyler's face. I swallowed hard. Dealing with someone else's vomit makes me want to hurl. I knew from first aid lessons at Blithehurst that I should stick a finger in his mouth, to clear out any remaining sick, but that wasn't going to happen. Not if I was going to keep my breakfast down.

'Sorry, kid,' I said through gritted teeth.

I made sure he was lying in the recovery position. His breathing was steady and regular, even if his skin was a weird colour in this eerie light. He was warm to the touch, which was reassuring. Don't ask me why, but I expected him to feel cold and clammy. I chucked the foul handkerchief into the darkness and looked up at the scary fairy queen on her throne.

'If he's not alive and well when I get back, I will smash the harp in front of you. Your—' I nearly said minions, but this was no kids' story '—your people won't be able to stop me.'

As I spoke, I heard the distant rush of a strong wind tearing through a forest. The scary fairy obviously heard it too. She looked at me, suddenly furious.

'You think you can challenge my power in this place, foolish forest boy? Let's see how brave you truly are. Learn some humility and we have an agreement. Fail and you will never walk your woods again.'

She waved a hand and the cave vanished. I was surrounded by thick mist. It was cold and wet enough to make me shiver. I looked down. I was standing on a knife edge of slick grey rock that fell away damn near vertically on both sides. Even though I couldn't see more than a few metres, I sensed vast emptiness around me. I realised this wasn't mist. I was standing in the middle of a fucking cloud.

Chapter Twelve

I really had better remember that pissing off the scary fairy was a seriously bad idea. As far as I could tell, I was somewhere on a mountain top. I don't particularly like being underground these days, but I'd take that over this any time. I didn't dare move an inch. If I slipped, I had no idea how far I would fall. I remembered that dead boy in my dream, smashed to pulp on a scree below a sheer rock face.

Cold wind buffeted me. It carried the distant sound of mocking laughter. The scary fairy wanted me to know that she had done this. She wanted to see what I was made of. One false step and she'd be seeing that literally. I'd be splattered down this mountainside, leaving smears of blood on the rocks until I landed like a torn bag of broken bones.

The wind pushed me harder and I heard that hateful laughter again. The scary fairy and her creatures were enjoying this. I had to move or I was going to be shoved off. She would find someone else to steal her harp.

And Tyler would die. My life wasn't the only one at stake. Very, very carefully, I lowered myself down. When I was sitting on the uneven, shattered stone, I could breathe a bit easier. Do the job that's in front of you. That's what my dad always says. The first thing I had to do was get off this sodding mountain in one piece.

I tried to focus. That wasn't easy as I was getting colder and colder, and I couldn't stop thinking about the drops on either side. This narrow crest of rock wasn't even a fucking path. I must be on the very top of a ridge between two valleys. Which valleys? I didn't know, and I didn't care. What I needed to know was which way was down. At the moment, I simply couldn't tell.

Feeling around very carefully, I found a loose stone. I tossed it away. Watching it roll and bounce across the rocks gave me some sense of my bearings. The way ahead of me was going upwards ever so slightly. That must be the scary fairy's idea of a joke. Bitch.

Slowly, ever so slowly, and trying to keep hold of the ridge with both hands, I turned around inch by inch. My mouth was dry and my stomach was hollow. My heart pounded and my breath came shallow and ragged. Once I was facing the other way, I stayed sitting with my feet on either side of the ridge until I calmed down a bit.

Just the thought of trying to stand up made me dizzy. Okay, I'd go down on my hands and knees if that kept me closer to the ground. If this could even be called solid ground. I studied the fractured rocks ahead. After a bit of thought,

I shifted both of my feet over to the slope on my left-hand side. I didn't particularly like doing that, but if I didn't, I was going to have to bend right over to keep both hands on the mountain. That would do nothing good for my balance. I really didn't fancy falling head first down the mountainside, seeing the rocks coming up to kill me.

I started moving, only shifting one foot or one hand at a time. I tested my footing every time I moved an inch before I trusted my weight to whatever was under my trainers. It was agonisingly slow going. My back was soon aching and my fingertips grew steadily more and more sore as I tried to cling to the gritty grey rock. Wondering how more much of this ball-ache was ahead of me, I might have been tempted to hurry until my right toes slipped.

Whatever I had thought was solid was gone. There was nothing under my foot at all. I threw myself against the mountainside, bruising my knees and my chest. My muscles locked solid as I heard rocks crashing into the emptiness below me.

I listened for shouts of outrage or surprise as I clung to the uncomfortable stones. I wasn't too proud to be rescued if there were rock climbers around. I'd struggle to explain how the hell I'd got up here in the first place, but I'd play the dumb tourist if I had to.

No such luck. I was up here on my own.

My pulse eventually slowed and I gradually untensed my arms and my legs, one at a time. My trainer was still waving around in thin air. Taking a deep breath, I tried to find somewhere solid to put my foot. It took me several goes. Each time I thought I was secure, another rock went bouncing down the mountain. I had to fight a surge of panic before I could force myself to try again. Eventually my toe found something that held. I drew back my foot and kicked at whatever it was. Nothing moved. Clenching my teeth so hard my jaw ached, I put my weight on it.

It held. I started moving again. This time it was even harder to trust to each hesitant step. My trainers weren't made for this. I could feel the lack of grip from their soles. But going on was the only way I was getting out of this mess, so that's what I had to do. One step at a time, swearing under my breath all the way.

The chilly cloud swirled around me, but I was sweating like a pig. I had to keep stopping to wipe my hands dry on my combats, one at a time. Between the rasping grit and my own salty sweat, my fingertips were stinging like a son of a bitch. I couldn't let that distract me. I had to concentrate. One hand. Next hand. Next foot. Last foot. One hand. Next hand. Next foot. Last foot. Rinse and fucking repeat for what felt like half a sodding lifetime.

I was concentrating so hard that it took me a while to notice the knife edge of the ridge was broadening out into something that a mountain goat might call a path. I only realised when a splash of colour caught my eye. I'd been looking at rocks in every shade of grey for so long that a twist of blue and red seemed ridiculously out of place. An energy bar wrapper was wedged in a crevice. Some lazy sod had carried his snack all the way up here but couldn't be arsed to stick the litter in a pocket and take it back down again. Tosser.

Of course, now that I'd found it, I'd have to take it with me until I found a bin. Still, it proved that people did come up here, even if I thought they must be mad. I picked the wrapper out of the crack and shoved it in my back pocket. Then I got carefully to my feet.

I started walking. Bizarrely, this was almost worse. The slope I'd been working my way down had been gradual. This path was steep, and it soon got a hell of a lot steeper. I would have been okay going uphill, but with the whiteness all around me, my balance felt off walking downwards. I could have done with one of those hiking poles I'd seen the hill walkers setting off with.

The path eventually got wider, and to my immense relief, it levelled out a bit. That didn't mean I was anywhere near level ground. As the cloud thinned to mist, the steep drops on either side became visible. Now I could see how far I would fall, and that was scary. When the breeze blew the last wisps away, I was still more than halfway up a mountain.

At least the summer sunshine warmed me up and dried me off. I got my phone out of my pocket. The last time I'd had to replace my handset, I'd bought one of those folding hard cases and a screen protector. That had been money well spent. Even though I'd hit the rocks on that mountainside pretty hard, the screen was still in one piece. I even had a signal – for emergency calls only. I'd need more than that before an online map could tell me where the hell I was. I carried on walking.

I could see other hikers on the valley's lower slopes. This path was going to join a network of pale lines traced across the dusty green turf. A bit further on and I could see a car park and a darker line of tarmac that had been hidden by a shoulder of land. I remembered the parking spots I'd seen on my drive here yesterday. Hopefully the car park would have a noticeboard showing me where I was.

Once I knew that, I could work out what to do next. With luck, there'd be a bench where I could sit down for a bit. Who was I kidding? I'd sit on the side of the road if I had to. I was absolutely knackered.

Soon I was walking past proper hikers with expensive all-weather gear, hi-tech boots and backpacks. One was sucking water from a plastic tube threaded back over his shoulder to some sort of hidden bottle. I realised how thirsty I was, and starving hungry. I caught a few sideways glances at my trainers, combats and T-shirt. Some of the serious walkers were smugly superior and some were exasperated with me. I glowered, daring anyone to say a word. Nobody offered me their unwanted opinion. Sometimes being able to look a right bastard comes in useful.

I reached the car park. People and vehicles were coming and going. Hallefuckinglujah, there was a painted map on a noticeboard. No one paid me any attention as I found the You Are Here arrow. It took me a moment to find Caergynan. When I did, I felt a chill despite the hot sun. The scary fairy queen had sent me miles away with a sweep of her hand. I had a hell of a walk back ahead of me.

But I had to get back, so which way was I going? A cross-country path led to the Canolfan Meilyr Centre. That looked shorter, but it would go up and down across the steep hills. The tarmac road would be longer, but more on the level. On the other hand, there was at least as much traffic as yesterday, maybe even more. I really didn't want to get clipped by someone's wing mirror or worse.

Sod it. I'd take the road. I started walking and tried not to think about the long climb ahead, up from the bottom of the valley to Plas Brynwen. I'd stop off at that pub by the supermarket first, I decided. I had my wallet with me, so I could get something to eat and drink. Then I'd go and get the Landy and do my shopping.

I hadn't forgotten about Tyler. I'd use this time while I was walking to think about the deal I'd made. I wasn't keen on the thought of breaking and entering to steal this bloody harp. The farmhouse at Cerrigwen might be out of the way and apparently unprotected, but I'm not exactly built like a cat burglar.

I'd barely walked fifty metres when I heard an engine behind me. I looked back to see what was coming. In theory, I was walking on the right side to face oncoming traffic, but on a road this narrow that was highly theoretical.

A red Ford Fiesta van stopped a metre behind me and the driver's door opened. A man put one foot on the road and stood up, half out of the vehicle, so I could see his face. What the hell was Aled James, the jeweller from the Canolfan Meilyr Centre, doing here?

'Want a lift, mate?'

I was still trying to work out what to say when he jerked his head towards the other side of the road.

'I said, do you want a lift, mate?' He raised his eyebrows at me, clearly urging me to say yes.

Two big white hounds with russet-red ears were bounding across the turf towards us. The hikers they passed were oblivious, though a couple of dogs on leashes were going berserk.

'Thanks.' I opened the van's passenger door. I tried to get in, stopped, and reached down for the handle so I could slide the seat back on its runners. I got in and slammed the door, reaching for the seat belt.

Aled James drove off, fast. Faster than I would have dared to drive along these narrow twists and turns, but he obviously knew the road. I saw his head shifting slightly as his eyes went from the wing mirrors to the road ahead and back again. After a few minutes, Aled relaxed his grip on the steering wheel.

I checked the wing mirror on my side. I couldn't see any sign of those dogs. Hopefully the scary beasts couldn't track me now I was surrounded by metal. What now though? I was grateful for the rescue, but I had all sorts of questions, starting with how come Aled could see the red-eared hounds. How had he known where to find me in the middle of these mountains?

I cleared my throat and said something different instead. 'Are you heading back to the Canolfan Meilyr Centre? If you can drop me off at the Plas Brynwen campsite, that'll be great, thanks.'

'It's the Canolfan Meilyr or the Meilyr Centre.' He shot me a quick grin as he changed gear. '"Canolfan" means "centre" in Welsh.'

'Oh.' That explained some of the road signs I'd seen.

'Meilyr was a famous poet. The court poet for Gruffydd ap Cynan.' Aled changed gear again. 'He was the king of Gwynedd who defied the Normans. Cynan, his father, the village is named for him. Caergynan. Cynan's Stronghold. History's written in the landscape around here, if you know how to read it.'

'Right. Thanks.' I wondered if these place names could offer any help with dealing with fairies.

We drove on. I remembered the sculpture Aled had made, the one that made me think of flames. Sod it. I needed to know if I'd jumped out of a frying pan into some equally dangerous fire.

'What brought you over this way?' I asked as casually as I could.

'Litter picking.' He jerked his head towards the back of the van. 'Mate, you wouldn't believe what some dirty swines leave on the mountain paths. But no,' he went on, 'that's not all. I saw you this morning when I came to open up, when you went past Cerrigwen towards the old quarry.'

'And?' I tried and failed to not make that a challenge.

Aled didn't sound bothered. 'I told Daisy I was going to do some paperwork out the back. My office window overlooks the car park. I saw those Cŵn Annwn go haring off along the path that leads here. I told Daisy I was going out for a bit, and I came round by road. I saw the Cŵn Annwn going back and forth. It was obvious to a blind man they were waiting for someone to come down off the mountain. I did some clearing up while I kept an eye out. So anyway, what do the Tylwyth Teg want with you? How did you end up on the top of that mountain?'

So that's how those Welsh words were pronounced. I still wasn't going to try saying them. I also wasn't going to answer his questions until he answered some of mine. 'How come you can see those dogs?'

He didn't answer. Then he made an abrupt turn into the narrowest lane I'd seen yet. This wasn't the way back to Caergynan. I'd got my bearings from the map in the car park, and I knew that for certain. I reached for the door handle, ready to undo my seatbelt. If I had to jump out of a moving vehicle, there were plenty of nettles along the roadside to break my fall.

'Where are we going?'

Chapter Thirteen

'No offence, mate, but you look like crap.' Aled was amused. 'Let's get some lunch and we can talk properly.'

I still didn't like this at all. 'Don't you need to get back? If you've left what's her name, Daisy, on her own?'

'Relax. I told her to give her Jacob a ring. He can help out in the shop for a couple of hours.'

He really wasn't going to take no for an answer. He didn't seem to be a threat though. I would look a right idiot if I jumped out of the van instead of agreeing to go for some lunch. I also had no idea where we were now. It could be midnight before I found my way back to Plas Brynwen.

'Okay.' I couldn't think what else to say. Apart from telling him my name. 'I'm Daniel, by the way. Dan.'

'Aled.' He shot me another quick glance. 'But you already knew that. I saw you take a card when you came in the shop.'

I remembered him watching me like a hawk. 'Why were you so interested in me?'

He grinned again. 'The smell.'

'Sorry?' I was more baffled than offended. I hadn't been anywhere near as sweaty yesterday as I was now.

'You came into the shop, and it was like someone had opened the door to a forest.' Aled was clearly intrigued. 'All I could smell was trees and leaf mould, you know? Weird, right?'

'I guess so.'

We soon arrived in a village tucked away in a fold of the hills. A sign in English and Welsh welcomed us to somewhere beginning with Llan and asked us to drive carefully. I'd thought Caergynan was small, but this place was miniscule.On the other hand, it did have a pub. The Black Bull was a long, low, white-painted building. I knew from what I'd read online it would have started life with a cowshed at one end and a single room for the family at the other. Along with the rest of the houses, it looked as if it had been built out of whatever rocks had rolled down this particular mountainside from the towering peaks overhead.

Aled pulled up on the gravel outside. 'After you.'

I got out of the van. I could smell Sunday lunch cooking. I went in through the door in the centre of the building, careful not to brain myself on the low lintel. Thankfully the ceiling inside was just high enough for me to not have to stoop. Even so, going inside felt uncomfortably like going underground.

The hum of conversation around half a dozen or so dark oak tables was in Welsh. As soon as I came in, everyone fell silent. After a moment the barman asked me some sort of question. The men at the tables chuckled. They were all men and old enough to be drawing a pension. They didn't look or sound very friendly.

I didn't have to speak Welsh to guess what the barman had said. 'What's the weather like up there?' or maybe 'I bet you know it's raining five minutes before anyone else'.

Ha ha. Tell me one I haven't heard a hundred times. Saying that usually shuts comedians up. This time I tried for a friendly smile instead. I don't think I succeeded. At the closest table, one old boy grabbed both pint glasses while his mate reached for the box for their dominoes.

Aled appeared from behind me. He said something that prompted a ripple of laughter which was a lot more friendly. He said something else to the barman and nodded at a vacant corner table over by the window before turning to me. 'What are you drinking?'

'A pint of whatever's good around here.' I headed for the table and sat down on the bench seat. Someone had put a lot of effort into knocking a big window through the thick stone of the end wall. I was grateful to them as I looked out into a rough field where three small black cattle were grazing in the bright sunlight. If I couldn't be out in the open, this was good enough.

Aled came over with two beers. I tried not to down mine in one. I failed. Aled grinned and took the glass back to the bar. He came back and put the refill in front of me. 'Good thing you are not driving.'

'Thanks.' What else could I say?

Food arrived. Two plates of roast lamb, roast potatoes, carrots, cabbage and peas delivered by a smiling, sturdy woman with long black hair tied up in a bun. A girl who had to be her daughter followed with a tray holding cutlery, gravy and mint sauce.

'Local lamb born and reared not half a mile from here,' the smiling woman assured me.

'Thanks.' Seeing Aled wasn't hanging around, I started eating too.

Everyone else went back to their dominoes or their conversations in Welsh. Fine with me. Neither of us spoke until we'd cleared our plates.

'That was great.' I put down my knife and fork and reached for my glass. 'So what did you say when you came in?'

'What?' Aled looked blank for a moment, then grinned as he screwed up his paper napkin. 'I said, "I could hear a needle drop on a sheep's fleece in here. You lot never seen an Englishman?"' He took a swallow of beer. 'Not just an Englishman though, are you?'

I could see the eagerness in his eyes. I recognised it. He was used to being the only person he knew who could see things that no one else could. Now he'd found someone different, like him. He wanted to know what that meant.

Wetting my lips with the last of my pint, I wondered what to say. There was no point trying to bullshit him. If he could see those Cŵn Annwn, I guessed he would know if I told him some lie. Besides, he had rescued me, and brought me here for roast lamb. No one was paying us any attention, and no one was sitting at the closest tables. All the same, I replied as quietly as I could.

'My mum is, well, she's a dryad. A tree spirit.' I could still count the people I'd told that on the fingers of one hand. It still felt like some sort of betrayal.

Aled nodded, bright-eyed. 'The fair folk of the wood, we call them. That explains the breeze that followed you into my shop. I don't suppose that pays your bills though. What do you do for work?'

'Carpentry, joinery. A couple of years ago, I got a job with a landowner in the Midlands, looking after the woodland as well as doing maintenance on the property.' I could see I'd have to tell him the truth about myself if he was going to share any secrets. 'How about you?'

'You've seen what I do for a living. As for the rest, I'm as Welsh as these mountains and a bit more than most.' He looked me in the eye and his smile faded. 'Which is why I know there's something going on. Something that's not right. I reckon you know something about it.'

'Something,' I said cautiously. 'Not everything, not by a long way.'

'Let's put our heads together then. See what we can make of it.' What Aled saw in my face must have satisfied him. He went on, folding his arms comfortably.

'My old taid – my grandad – he used to tell me the stories his taid told him, back when he was a nipper. *His* dad, Elias Pritchard, so his taid always said, he was what they used to call dyn hysbys. A cunning man, you might say, one who travelled and sold cures as well as setting bones and pulling teeth. Some say the cunning men worked charms and laid curses too, but by all accounts, Elias Pritchard never did anyone any harm. He was his mother's blessing, born a year and a day after his mother's husband had died. Jeremiah, the man they called his father, he was a miner. There was a cave-in, but Jeremiah went back into the seam, swearing he wouldn't come out until he found the three men who were trapped. He got them out all right, but the pit props broke and the roof came down. They dug Jeremiah out, but his back was broken.'

Aled shook his head, as solemn as if the tragedy had happened last week.

'The way of it was back then, if a man was killed in an accident, an unwed miner who needed his meals cooking and his clothes washing, he would take on the widow and her children. Not this time. Jennet Pritchard was left well alone. If anyone saw a shadowy figure at her door after midnight on the eve of winter or St John's Day, they looked the other way. She earned her bread with laundry and sewing, and she raised her four sons and three daughters to be honest and hard-working.'

He paused for a sip of beer. 'Her youngest son grew up, and he went down the mine like his brothers and their father before them. Turned out he had a knack for finding the best seams of coal, and for knowing if a roof wasn't safe, or the air was going to turn foul. He could hear the coblynau, what the Cornish call the knockers. They're the kindest of the fair folk who live under the hills. As long as the miners treated them with courtesy, they'd repay the favour, showing the men where to find the finest coal or slate, even gold and silver ore when those were mined in Wales.'

He took another sip from his glass. 'Not all of those who live under the hills are so well disposed to miners. One time, Elias saw a red fairy, one of the creatures that spark fires underground. He got the men out just in time, before the gas exploded, but the mine owner was furious at losing half a shift's profits. He sacked Elias on the spot. Told him to pack up and leave the village and never show his face again. Elias went to tell his mother, and she told him he had nothing to be ashamed of. He was a hero for saving so many lives. More than that, he could see the red fairy because his true father was one of the coblynau. One of them had tried to save her husband, but he couldn't persuade Jeremiah to leave those trapped men to their fate. He had come to beg Jennet's forgiveness, and, well, one thing led to another, as they say. Once Elias knew the true story of his birth, he set off to make his fortune using whatever talents the fair folk of the mines had given him.'

He broke off as the girl appeared with two bowls of rhubarb crumble and custard on her tray.

I took one and reached for a spoon. 'Your grandad was a great storyteller.'

'One of many around here.' Aled ate a mouthful of crumble and nodded at the other old men in the bar. 'Time was, on a Sunday afternoon, everyone would get together in some house or other and share their stories and songs. No one needed the wireless or the telly.'

I heard another echo of his grandfather's voice when he said 'wireless'. 'So, that statuette, the one you made out of copper wire...?'

He shook his head. 'No, I've never seen one, but while I was making it, the shape felt right, you know?'

'I do.' I really did. 'I don't only do carpentry. I carve wooden animals and ornaments. Sometimes...'

I couldn't put what I wanted to say into words, but Aled nodded as if he understood.

'Why did that piece catch your eye?' He looked at me intently.

'It made me think of fire.' Now I knew why. 'Have you ever heard anything underground?'

'Sometimes.' He finished his pudding before he went on. 'I go potholing, down in the Brecon Beacons. Great caves they've got down there. Comes in very handy, me knowing when taking a particular route is a bad idea. I just call it instinct though, gut feeling. People can handle that.'

'What can you tell me about the caves in that quarry at Cerrigwen?'

'Not caves. Mines.' He shook his head. 'I don't go down there.'

'Why not?'

'Because the Cŵn Annwn show up any time I walk down that track, and they warn me off, good and proper,' he retorted. 'I can take a hint. I don't fancy getting on the wrong side of whatever's living in those diggings. Is that what you did? Is that what's going on?'

'What about Mari Rhys? Have you ever seen her down there?'

He looked at me, completely blank. 'Who?'

'The singer. From last night, at the Canolfan Meilyr?'

Aled was utterly confused. 'I don't know who you're talking about, mate.'

'The folk-singer. Young. Blonde. Drop-dead gorgeous. Sang a song in Welsh just before the first interval.'

He shook his head, still mystified. 'The only regular singers at the centre are Brian and Gwenllian, and she's sixty if she's a day. Got a great voice, mind.'

Bugger. I'd thought I'd found a useful ally. I guessed the scary fairy had some way to stop Aled from seeing or hearing things she didn't want him to see. Whatever talents he'd inherited from his underground ancestor clearly weren't a match for her.

'Are you going to tell me what you're talking about or what?' He looked at me, expectant.

I reached for my wallet. 'Let me get the bill and I'll explain in the car.'

This was a conversation I wasn't going to risk anyone overhearing.

Chapter Fourteen

After we'd talked in the car, Aled dropped me off at Plas Brynwen. I headed for the office in the conservatory and paid Mr Williams for two more nights. It was obvious I was going to be here at least that long. Walking through to the campsite, I found the tent and the Land Rover were exactly as I had left them. That was a relief.

I got into the Landy and slowly drove out to the road past the tents and caravans. There weren't nearly so many kids and dogs around. The afternoon was baking hot, and pretty much all of them had found some shade. There was no sign of the Cŵn Annwn or anything else eerie. That was even more of a relief.

I made my way down into the valley and took the right-hand turn towards the supermarket. After I'd done my shopping, I stayed in the car park and plugged my phone into the charger. The screen didn't show any missed calls from Gillian or Iris. I hesitated, wondering who I should call first. Since I was pretty sure Gillian would give me a bollocking for not doing as I was told and sitting tight until she spoke to me, I rang Iris. She would want to know about Tyler Whatsisname as soon as possible.

'Dan?' Her voice was anxious.

'Hi.' I took a swig of the cold apple juice I'd bought along with a few other things in the supermarket. 'He's still alive.'

'Tyler? Okay, but...?' She could tell from my tone this wasn't all good news.

'Are you okay to talk for a while?'

'Yes, fine. Go on.'

I told her about my eventful day.

'Bloody hell,' she said faintly. 'So this Aled, he's one of us.'

'And he's seen the news on the web about those boys who died locally, and he knows about Tom being found by hikers. He guessed the fairies had something to do with all that, from some of the stories his grandad told him. When he saw those red-eared dogs were on my trail, he reckoned I must know something. He wasn't about to try doing anything on his own though.' I couldn't blame him for that.

Iris agreed. 'That's fair enough. So what are you going to do now?'

'I've made a deal with the scary fairy.' I paused to tip my head back to get the last drops of juice from the carton. 'I've got to try to get hold of that harp, and I want to do it as soon as I can. I have to get Tyler out of there. She's already had him for a fortnight. That's bad enough.'

'I can't argue with that,' Iris agreed. 'Are you sure the harp's in that farmhouse?'

'The scary fairy seems convinced. I wouldn't bet against her.'

'What do you suppose she is? And what about those creatures you could see in the shadows?'

'Aled said she sounds like a woman of the lower world.' He'd called her something in Welsh, and even written it down for me on the back of an old petrol loyalty points voucher. Gwraig Annwn. 'Though he said they usually crop up in myths about lakes.'

'Does he have any idea what's so special about this harp?'

'He said there are a whole load of stories about those. So, no,' I clarified, 'he doesn't know anything specific.'

'Does he know who lives in the farmhouse?'

'An old woman called Annis Wynne.'

'A woman?'

'As far as he knows.' I knew what Iris was asking. Was Annis Wynne human, a bit more than human, or was she something else entirely?

When I'd asked him about her, it turned out Aled didn't know that dryads and the like would be betrayed by their eyes when they blinked, when they were masquerading as humans. He'd never seen that for himself. He hadn't seen much that was uncanny, to be honest. Just the Cŵn Annwn and occasional groups of Tylwyth Teg off in the distance at dawn and dusk. Since his grandad had told him the story of Olwen and Evan and a whole lot of others when he was a kid, Aled never went near them.

'She must be about a hundred and three.' I was exaggerating, though not by much. 'She came here sometime in the 1950s. Most of the Cerrigwen land was bought up by the investors from London who opened the quarry in the eighteen-whenevers. The Wynne family kept the house and worked a few fields that were left as a smallholding, while their surplus sons and daughters worked as labourers and servants on other farms. The last son and heir went off and got killed doing his national service. Annis Wynne was his widow, apparently, arriving from Cardiff, where they'd been married. Eventually the parents-in-law died, and she's been on her own ever since, with the place falling to bits around her.'

'He knows all this how?' Iris wasn't doubting Aled specifically. She just wanted to be sure we knew what we were dealing with. Her own family had a long tradition of concealing the truth with stories of conveniently dead husbands in other parts of the country.

I'd asked Aled the same thing. 'He has more aunts and uncles and cousins around here than you have in the Fens. Everyone knows everybody's business.'

'She still lives there on her own?' Iris sounded dubious.

'She has her shopping delivered and a home help goes in two times a week. She's still got all her marbles, apparently, and can get around with a walking frame. The house itself is weatherproof, even if it's run down. Aled says social services won't try to move her until it's clear she really can't cope. Half the village keeps an eye on her. According to Aled, there's a lot of quiet speculation about what will happen to the house and the land when she finally dies. The quarry reverted to the family by some sort of agreement when the mining company went bust.'

'I wonder if that's what's stirred up this fairy queen. She must realise things will change for her if the property is sold.' Iris moved quickly on. 'So we really need to know why she wants this harp.'

'She's up to nothing good is my guess. It must be important though, if she's willing to trade Tyler for it.'

'Why hasn't she gone and got it for herself?' Iris wondered aloud. 'Why does she need you to steal it?'

'Maybe there are old horseshoes nailed over every door and window. Whoever lived in that house in days gone by may well have known there were fairies in the hill.' Or it could be something else entirely. 'I won't know until I get a closer look.'

'You're really going to do this?'

I could hear Iris was struggling with this. I didn't blame her. So was I. I mean, breaking and entering? Seriously? On the other hand...

'If I don't, what happens to Tyler?'

Iris didn't answer for a long moment. That was okay. I knew how she felt.

She sighed. 'When are you going to check the place out?'

'I'll have to wait until well after dark.'

'You're doing this on your own?'

'Aled's going to keep watch from the Meilyr Centre car park.'

'While you burgle a helpless little old lady.'

I could hear Iris grimace. We're supposed to be the good guys, aren't we?

'While I see if I can work out the best way to burgle a helpless little old lady,' I said. 'I'm not doing anything else until we know what Gillian has found out. You did speak to her, didn't you?'

'I did. So tonight's just a recce. That makes sense.' Iris was relieved. 'What are you going to do until then?'

'Read a book. Take a nap.' I'd picked up a paperback thriller when I was going round the supermarket. 'Can you give Gillian a ring and bring her up to date?'

'I can.' Now Iris was grinning. I didn't need to see her to know that. 'You'd better not dodge her call if she rings you.'

I wasn't going to answer that. 'I'll let you know how I get on tomorrow morning.'

'Okay. Mind how you go tonight.' She ended the call.

I looked at the time on the phone screen. I had bloody hours to kill. Going online, I found the nearest bookshop, which turned out to be miles away. Well, I wasn't in any hurry. I went there and bought a large-scale Ordnance Survey map of the whole area. Then I made my way to the car park on the other side of the mountain where the scary fairy had dumped me. The traffic made both journeys slow going, but that meant my phone battery ended up fully charged.

There are easier things to wrangle than a large-scale map in the front seat of a Land Rover. After a bit of effort though, I managed to work out where I was. As I got more of a feeling for the local geography, I was even more grateful that Aled had come to find me. I'd have had a hell of a walk back to Caergynan.

As I sat in the car park, I watched hikers coming off the slopes. There wasn't a cloud in the sky now. I thought about ringing Fin and decided that could wait until tomorrow. I could tell her what I'd found at Cerrigwen, and we could discuss whatever advice Gillian had to offer. There was no point in both of us getting no sleep tonight.

Gillian still hadn't rung me. I couldn't decide if that was good news or bad. Maybe Iris hadn't been able to reach her. Maybe she had been too busy getting Tom settled to make any phone calls of her own. I tried to call Eleanor but got her voicemail. I sent a quick text instead, saying sorry, I wouldn't be back until Tuesday at the earliest. I promised I'd call her tomorrow with an update.

I headed back to Plas Brynwen. Now the sun was lower and the shadows were longer, more kids and dogs were out and about. As I got my shopping out of the Landy I heard a startled shriek and a lot of excited barking.

'Look! There's a fox!' A boy I guessed was about ten years old jabbed the air with a finger. He was so excited he was hopping from one foot to the other.

I caught a glimpse of a white-tipped, brushy red tail disappearing through the privet hedge that ringed the campsite.

A woman in a T-shirt and shorts was astonished. 'Where did that come from?'

'It was curled up over there. I only saw it when it jumped up.' The boy looked at me, mildly accusing. As far as he was concerned, the Landy had startled the animal.

I wasn't so sure. If that had really been a fox, it hadn't made a run for it when the Landy first pulled up. It had waited until I started getting things out of the back. I remembered the creatures with the ever-shifting faces lurking behind the scary fairy. I also remembered how the scars on my arm had been hurting. They were itching now. I reckoned she had sent one of her creatures to keep watch, to see when I came back. To see whether or not I came back?

I put my bags of shopping inside the tent and tried not to look too obvious as I checked around the sides for any signs of... well, I wasn't sure exactly. I couldn't see anything out of place, so that would have to do. The rowan rings were where I'd left them inside, which was some reassurance.

I'd bought a towel, so I could have a shower, which was very welcome. I stayed in the tent afterwards, only wearing clean underpants and a fresh T-shirt. Leaning against my overnight bag, I stretched out on top of the sleeping mat and read the paperback I'd bought in the supermarket. A thriller featuring exiled secret agents and rogue ex-military types fighting shadowy corporate super-villains was a definite change of pace. It was a fun read, and I decided I'd buy the sequel when I got the chance.

As the sun set, I unzipped the cold bag I'd bought this afternoon and ate a packet of sandwiches and some crisps. That would do me for an evening meal after that roast lamb lunch. A bit later, I put my trousers on and made some tea on the camping stove. These things gave me excuses to go over to the bins, and over to the tap by the wash block several times. I walked casually there and back, alert for any flicker of movement that might betray a shadowy watcher. Nothing caught my eye.

Dusk settled across the mountains, and the campsite quietened down. I'd bought fresh batteries for the lamp from Eleanor's camping crate, but I didn't switch that on, even when it got too dark to read inside the tent. I didn't want to draw any attention from whatever might be watching. Let them think I'd gone to sleep. There was no danger of that though. I was far too tense.

Of course, if I wanted any watchers to think that nothing unusual was happening, I couldn't pack everything into the back of the Land Rover for safekeeping before I headed out. Thankfully that had occurred to me earlier. I'd managed to buy a small padlock to secure the tent zip against casual human thieves. That would have to do.

A few more hours crawled by. I'd even have welcomed a phone call from Gillian. On second thoughts, no I wouldn't. There was no knowing if some creature might be listening on the other side of the thin nylon. I had no idea how much of our conversation something that lived under a mountain might understand, but I didn't want to take any risks.

Finally, at long bloody last, it was midnight and the moon was sinking. It was just about cool enough to justify wearing the hoodie I'd bought that afternoon. It was cheap supermarket gear and only just big enough for me, but it was plain dark blue, and that's what mattered. I wanted to be as hard to see as possible, as far as human eyes went anyway.

I got out of the tent as quietly as I could and looked around. No sign of movement in the shadows. I snapped the padlock onto the tent zip and went for a pee. Still nothing caught my eye. Of course, the dim light over the wash block door did my night vision no favours. I walked along the hedge line at the edge of the campsite, where the so-called fox had been. If anything was lurking anywhere, it was lying very low indeed.

I headed for the road, keeping an eye out to either side. Every few paces, I glanced behind me. Maybe I was being paranoid, but like they say, even paranoids have enemies. If the scary fairy wasn't my enemy just yet, she sure as hell wasn't my friend. For the moment though, she seemed to be leaving me alone.

Chapter Fifteen

When I got to the unlit street, I walked faster. I wanted to look like a man with a purpose rather than some oversized stranger sneaking about. Aled had said there was a neighbourhood watch, so if anyone challenged me, we had agreed on a story. I'd say he was up at the car park looking for some earrings he'd dropped earlier. He'd rung to ask me to come and help. That was a pretty crap lie, let's be honest, but no one would be able to prove any different. I had a torch in my pocket along with my penknife, but that was hardly going equipped for breaking and entering.

The stark black outlines of the terraces were silent against the starlit sky. I soon reached the Meilyr Centre. The only vehicle in the car park was Aled's van. Now our story would change if anyone came to ask what he was doing there. He'd send me a silent text as soon as he saw anyone approaching, to warn me to head straight back. He'd say we'd been searching for those earrings when we thought we saw someone on the footpath by Cerrigwen. Someone who looked suspicious. I'd come back saying I hadn't found anyone, so we must have imagined it. Even if anyone asking us thought that was a load of bollocks, they still wouldn't be able to prove it.

I really hoped no one came nosing around, however keen they were to safeguard their community. If I was going to be burgling this place tomorrow, the last thing I needed was suspicions stirred up tonight. If someone called the police, I'd be in enough trouble to make doing anything tomorrow pretty much impossible. If I was caught breaking and entering, I'd be completely screwed. A criminal record is a criminal record, even if mine was for defending my dad from a thug a bit too emphatically. Once a copper saw I'd pleaded guilty to occasioning actual bodily harm, I wouldn't get the benefit of any doubt.

I put my hood up and walked down the track towards the old farmhouse. Even with the hoodie covering my head and arms, I felt uncomfortably exposed. I wanted trees around me. I wanted to be walking on deep dark soil, enriched year upon year by autumn's falling leaves. I couldn't remember ever feeling this so strongly. This slate-riddled ground beneath my feet was all wrong. The vast emptiness above me was impossibly full of stars. I wanted the shelter of leafy oak branches overhead. A faint chill breeze brushed my face like a whisper telling me I had no place here.

Maybe I didn't. What did that matter? Neither did Tyler or Tom, or any of those other lads the scary fairy had kidnapped. I was here because I had a job to do. When that was done, I'd head for home. The breeze faded away and that uneasy feeling faded with it.

I stopped when I reached the fenced-off garden in front of the Cerrigwen farmhouse. Gripping the closest post, I gave it a good shake to see how solid it was. If I had to make a run for it, I wanted to know if the fence was safe to climb over or if it would collapse under my weight.

Two things happened. Firstly, I noticed chicken wire had been stapled along the inside of the fence. Second, my hand brushed a sprig of the gorse that was everywhere around here. It didn't scratch me with its prickles. Instead, its vanilla scent filled the air, and I felt a powerful sense of warmth and belonging. I wasn't expecting that. What did it mean?

I waited a moment to see if anything else happened. When nothing did, I walked down the track towards the house. Now I could see that the chicken wire ran all the way along the inside of the fence, right to the front of the house. Nothing growing in the abandoned garden was worth this much effort to keep rabbits out. Come to that, I hadn't seen any trace of rabbits around here.

Galvanised-steel mesh should be an effective barrier against the scary fairy and her creatures. Was that accidental good luck, or did Annis Wynne know they were out there? Was she aware they wanted to steal from her? Did she know what they wanted to steal and why? I wasn't going to hand over that harp until I had some idea why the fairy wanted it.

The farmhouse wall that overlooked the lane had no windows, so I didn't have to worry about being seen as I walked past. The scent of the gorse came with me, and that was nice. Now I was interested in what was behind the house. What I hadn't seen or heard or smelled when I passed by earlier was any sign of chickens, and they are pretty hard to miss. This time, when I reached the five-barred metal gate to the farmyard, I took my time assessing it. The latch end was solidly padlocked to a metal post coach-bolted to the stone wall of the house. The hinges were equally firmly fixed to the outbuilding at the other end. The roof of that might be sagging, but the walls were sound.

I paused and took a long look around before I went any further. Plenty of isolated rural buildings have CCTV these days. Unlikely as that might be, I had to check for cameras. I looked at the usual spots, on the corners of the house and the outbuildings, and where the downpipes from the guttering offered handy brackets. Since they're supposed to be a deterrent, cameras are usually pretty obvious, even if there isn't a big fuck-off sign from whichever company installed them. I couldn't see any sign of a security system. Besides, nothing about this run-down place hinted at valuables inside. That was probably enough to put off any passing burglar. One less thing for me to worry about.

I climbed over the gate. I wondered if the scary fairy's creatures could jump over a metal barrier, even if they wouldn't want to touch it. If they could transform into goats or cats, those animals could leap quite high, and maybe foxes had some chance, even if I reckoned otters were doubtful. Unless they met something like a science fiction force-field and bounced straight off. I grinned at the thought of that. More seriously, I needed to remember to ask Eleanor to ask the dryads. Knowing something like that could be useful.

Knowing if any of them were watching me now would be even more important. I looked around. There wasn't any sign of movement in the shadows on the other side of the gate, or beyond the outbuildings. I rubbed the scars on my arm through the sleeve of my hoodie. Those weren't itching, and I was starting to think that was significant.

Now I was inside the farmyard, I noticed dark clumps of gorse sprouting from the paler gravel. The path to the back door was clear though, and I saw one of those metal boot-scraper mats in the narrow porch. No one could go through that door without crossing that. Maybe Annis Wynne wanted to keep her floors clean. The track outside must get muddy in wet weather. Maybe a metal barrier at her threshold was more significant.

Somebody kept her well supplied with firewood. Even now, in the height of summer, I saw a good stack of chopped logs under the sloping felted roof of a store beside the porch. Someone had built that pretty recently, and they'd made a good job of it. Aled said people from the village looked out for the old lady.

How many knew the code for the grey metal key safe screwed to the stone wall of the house? It was one of the ones with four rotating wheels like a combination bike lock. That meant anywhere between five and ten thousand possibilities, so there was no point in me randomly having a go. Could Aled find out the right number? Somehow I didn't see Iris looking up family birthdays and anniversaries on Annis Wynne's social media, to give us dates and ages to try.

No, we had better forget that. Asking around would make Aled the coppers' prime suspect as soon as the old lady realised she had been robbed. I grimaced. I still hated the sound of that word, even when it was only inside my own head.

I took another look around the yard. There was no sign that these outbuildings had been used for anything since the millennium at least. I couldn't believe anything valuable was stored in there, or anything the old lady thought the scary fairy might want to get hold of. I had to get into the house.

The closest window was between the back porch and the gate. It had a roller blind which hadn't been pulled down. I cupped my hands around my eyes, getting as close as I could to the glass. I could see inside, but even my night sight was struggling to make anything out. There were no lights on inside the house at all. I could just make out this was a kitchen, which was no great surprise. A deep oblong sink was right underneath the window with plates and cups on the wooden draining board beside it. The chances of me climbing in quietly through there were pretty much zero even if I could get the window open.

Did that matter? One old lady was hardly going to force a man my size out of her house single-handed. No, but I didn't want to scare her into a heart attack or a stroke or a fall that could break her hip. If she died, I'd be on the hook for manslaughter at the very least, if I was caught. If I wasn't, I'd have to live with the knowledge that I'd killed a little old lady. I wanted to save Tyler, but that couldn't be the price.

I took another look at the back door. There wasn't a cat flap, so that was one less thing to worry about. On the other hand, Annis Wynne could have some sort of personal emergency alarm since she was living here alone. I vaguely recalled seeing adverts for accident alert systems. I hadn't bothered looking into them because my dad is still fit and active and he has my mum.

I went over to the window on the other side of the back porch. The curtains were closed tight, so I had no way to know what was in this room. I could see the brass catch inside the old-fashioned sash was fastened. Getting my penknife out, I used the small blade to scrape off some flaking white paint. The wood underneath was soft and crumbled under the slightest pressure. I should have no problem getting the big blade on my knife through the gap to force the catch open.

Then what? I assessed the whole window. There was no way to know when it had last been opened. If the decaying sash stuck instead of sliding upwards, the squeal of protesting wood would be deafening. If the sash cords had frayed and snapped, I'd have no chance of opening it. Worst-case scenario? I might undo the catch and lift the sash and the whole sodding thing would come apart in a shower of broken glass and splintered wood.

Careful not to tread on any of the gorse and leave a clear sign that someone had been prowling, I went around the corner of the house. These windows with their stubbornly closed curtains made it fairly easy to guess the layout inside. There would be two more rooms at the front, separated by an entrance hall, and the two at the back. Stubby chimney stacks on either side of the pitched roof explained the windowless side walls. I guessed each room had a fireplace and they shared a flue on either side. Exactly where the interior doors might be, and whether there were hall cupboards or things like that, would depend on where the stairs were. Those were questions for another day. Tonight I was just here for a recce.

The first front window's wooden frame was sturdier. I reckoned I'd have a better chance of getting that open, but I still had no way to know what was hidden by these sagging curtains. Taking a few steps back, I looked up at the front of the house. There was no point even thinking about trying to get in through any of the upper windows, even at the back where I'd be less visible. I wasn't going to trust my weight to the roof of either porch, or to any ladder I might find in those outbuildings, never mind if it was a wooden one or aluminium. Forget trying to force a window open while I was balancing ten feet off the ground. Even if I could get the sash up, even a little old lady would only need to give me one good shove and I'd go crashing to the ground. That would be a brutal fall for someone my size.

So how the hell was I going to get inside? I'd promised the scary fairy I'd take her the bloody harp. Tyler's life, or at the very least his sanity, depended on me doing that. The responsibility was tying my guts in knots.

I looked at the front porch. Dark stone steps led up to a broad plinth floored with, unsurprisingly, slate. The porch was quite a bit wider than the actual front door. I could see little windows on either side that must look into the hall. A wooden balustrade ran around the plinth with pillars at the corners and flanking the steps. The pillars held up a pitched roof tiled with, yes, more slate and edged with fretwork. Once upon a time, the woodwork had been painted white, but that had been decades ago.

I might as well see what I could see through those little windows. Pushing through the thick gorse blocking the steps stirred another soothing waft of vanilla scent. That made me feel a bit less stressed. Unfortunately, even cupping my hands to the glass didn't help me see a thing through those little windows.

I could barely see the front door in these shadows. I ran my hands over the wood instead, checking every square millimetre. I started at the top, and by the time I was on my knees, feeling my way along the bottom, I had the beginnings of an idea. Hallebloodylujah.

I tested the door-knob. It moved stiffly, and I could feel the latch scraping. The door itself didn't shift at all. Searching the porch floor with my fingertips, I found a stray twig blown in from somewhere. I poked it into the keyhole below the knob. The key wasn't in the lock, waiting for me to knock it onto the floor and somehow get it out through the gap under the door. That would make my life far too simple. Real life is nothing like the movies.

I didn't care. I wasn't checking for a key. I felt around for a little bit longer and tossed the twig away. I still wasn't a hundred per cent certain I could get in this way, but it was the only plan I could come up with.

It was time to leave. I checked my phone. I had dimmed the screen as far as the settings allowed and I had it set on vibrate. No, I hadn't missed a text from Aled. So far, so good. I took one last look around for any sign of the scary fairy's creatures. Nothing caught my eye. I climbed over the fence by the front of the house and walked back to the Meilyr Centre car park.

Aled reached over and shoved the passenger door open as I approached his van. 'Well?' he asked as I eased myself into the seat.

'Burglary is nowhere as easy as it looks on TV,' I said with feeling.

'You can't see a way to get in?'

'I didn't say that.' I yawned. 'Let's call it a night and discuss it tomorrow.'

'Meet you for a coffee mid-morning?' Aled nodded at the closed gates to the centre's courtyard.

I shook my head. 'We need to get well away from here. You never know who might be listening.'

'I can take an hour for lunch, but that's all the time I can spare.' He turned the key in the van's ignition and we drove away.

Chapter Sixteen

I was back in Annis Wynne's front porch twenty-four hours later. Thanks to adrenaline and caffeine, I was wide awake. I hoped that would see me through whatever lay ahead.

Last night, I'd fallen asleep soon after Aled dropped me off at the campsite. There was no sign of anything watching for me, and besides, I was knackered. Even so, I woke up just after six, partly because of the sunlight and partly because I was stiffer than I expected after getting safely down from that mountain ridge. If I'd been in a bed, I might have got back to sleep again. In a sleeping bag on a camping mat? No chance.

I went to the wash block with the towel I'd bought from the supermarket. Hopefully a shower would loosen up some of my protesting muscles. I wasn't the only one up and about so early. One of the boys from yesterday was walking along the privet hedge, coming towards me. Every couple of steps, he bent down to peer under the lowest branches.

The next time he straightened up, I waved a hand to get his attention. 'Seen any more foxes?'

He looked unsure about talking to a stranger, but he answered me anyway. 'No.'

I nodded and went on my way. That was good enough, for the moment. After breakfast, I got into the Land Rover and drove over to the coast. I found a place to park up overlooking an estuary and made a whole lot of phone calls sitting inside the Landy with the windows closed. Then I headed back to Caergynan.

Aled and I had agreed to meet at one-thirty. I walked up to the Meilyr Centre. He was waiting with a cardboard cupholder tray with takeaway coffees and baguettes from the caffi. He drove as far as we could get in twenty minutes, and I brought him up to speed while we ate.

After Aled dropped me back at Plas Brynwen and went back to work, I drove over to the bookshop. At least there was less traffic now it was Monday. I bought the sequel to that thriller I'd found in the supermarket. I needed something to take my mind off what we were planning. A story where the good guys were going to win, even if that meant them doing some shady things. All right, downright criminal things. For the greater good. I needed to keep telling myself that. I still couldn't see me convincing a North Wales copper though. I wondered if the wise women had a good solicitor in one of their trios, in case I ended up needing one.

Since this was going to be another late night, I tried to have a nap in the afternoon. Naturally, the campsite kids decided to have a noisy game of football. I ended up reading my new book. Around six, I cooked myself some tinned hot dog sausages on Eleanor's camping stove to go in a couple of buns, along with a mug of tea. I ended up throwing half of them away. I didn't have much of an appetite.

And now it was midnight, and I was outside Annis Wynne's front door. If the ends were going to justify these means, I really needed to concentrate. I had to find a very tricky balance between doing this quickly and doing it quietly. Go too fast and the noise risked waking the old lady up. Aled couldn't remember if he'd ever seen her wearing hearing aids, so I had to assume she didn't need them. Go too slowly, and every passing minute increased my chances of being seen by some insomniac hiker, even at this unholy hour, even in the porch's shadows and wearing my dark blue hoodie.

If I was asked what I was doing there, I'd have a hard time explaining away the cold chisel in my hand, or why I was wearing disposable vinyl gloves. Fingerprints, officer? I have no idea what you mean.

I knelt down and felt up and down the door frame by the keyhole. Finding the softest spot, I eased the edge of the chisel under the strip of wood nailed on as a doorstop, and to prevent wind and rain getting in through the gap. Even though the front door was sheltered by the porch, this strip of wood was rotten.

Build anything against the front of a house and you need to cover the join between the wall and the roof with flashing. That always used to be thin sheets of lead, but these days modern alternatives are quicker, self-adhesive and much less likely to be stolen. If you don't use any flashing, rain will get into that gap between the wall and the wood, I guarantee it.

I didn't know if the original lead had been stripped off this porch or if the metal had simply deteriorated after decades of expanding in hot summers and shrinking in the frosts. I didn't care. Rain had got in and this doorstop was rotten. It wasn't as bad as the window frames, but the wood was soft enough to suit me. I stripped off about ten centimetres of wood, above and below the lock. I hit a couple of nails, which would do a decent chisel no favours, but I was using a cheap one with a plastic handle that already had a few notches in the tip.

I couldn't even remember why I'd bought it, but I was glad I'd tossed it into the toolbox I keep in the back of the Landy. Just the essentials, just in case. Flathead and Phillips screwdrivers, a few wrenches and Allen keys, a claw hammer and, most recently, this cheap chisel. You never know when you might need to lever something open.

I started digging into the exposed door frame, working on the same level as the keyhole. The cracking wood sounded horribly loud as I stripped away matchstick-sized splinters. I told myself that was just my imagination. Mostly my imagination. I dug deeper, getting my shoulder into it as I hit more solid wood that the rot hadn't reached. The slate under my knees was cold and hard. I wished I could have brought something to kneel on, but the fewer things I was carrying tonight, the better.

Finally, I felt the tip of the chisel grate against something hard. Harder than wood. Something that didn't give. I pulled the chisel back and, very cautiously, used a finger to feel around in the hole, trying not to rip my thin vinyl glove on a splinter. There it was. The pointed tip of a screw. I sat back on my heels for a moment and visualised where the other one must be. Getting to work with the chisel again, I soon found the second screw. I dug out more wood, on either side of the screws and between them as well as above and below. More suddenly than I was expecting, the chisel broke through to the other side of the door frame. The screws rattled, coming loose.

I was born and brought up in an old house. The locks there aren't modern insurance-approved five-lever mortices in brass or chrome that fit inside the thickness of a door, carefully lined up with the strike plate so the bolt goes into the frame. Old-fashioned houses have old-fashioned rim locks, where the whole mechanism is screwed to the inner face of the door. Seeing the original brass catches on the Cerrigwen sash windows last night, as well as that pre-war door-knob, I'd wondered if these locks were the same sort of vintage. If something isn't broken, why fix it, especially if no one ever goes in or out of a front porch? When I'd had a feel around with that twig, the depth of the lock mechanism had convinced me I was right.

A rim lock key turns to send the deadbolt into a metal keeper fixed to the inside of the door frame. That's what I was attacking now, sweating with stress as well as exertion. As Aled had helpfully pointed out, if there were ordinary sliding bolts on this door as well, I was screwed even if I got the lock keeper loose. All this work would have been for nothing.

There weren't any extra bolts. The metal keeper dropped away into the darkness and the door swung open. Caught off guard, I fell forward, ending up on my hands and knees. The sharp bristles of the doormat pricked my hands through my thin gloves. Thankfully, I still had hold of the chisel. I stuck that in my hoodie pocket and groped around until I found the lock keeper. I put that by the skirting board so I wouldn't tread on it. Then I got to my feet.

My pulse was racing. I moved quickly, stooping to grab the biggest bits of the wood I'd stripped off the door frame. Those were enough to wedge the door closed. Obviously, anyone who came into the house in daylight would see the damage at once, but I needed to hold the door shut while I was in here sneaking around. I took my torch out of my pocket. Aled and I had discussed the pros and cons of using a light so I could search faster against going more slowly and relying on my night vision. I switched on the torch.

The hall floor was deep red tiles under a strip of faded and threadbare patterned carpet with a pale fringe along both edges. The doors to the right and left of me were closed. Halfway down the hall, a coat, hat, umbrella and everything else stand with umpteen empty hooks and a mirror faced the bottom of a staircase. That would turn back on itself to reach the landing upstairs. Past the stairs, two doors side by side must open into the kitchen and the other room at the back.

Taking care not to make a sound, I opened the door on my left. I shielded the top of the torch with my hand and took care not to shine the light directly at the windows. Hopefully these old curtains were thick enough to stop anyone outside seeing a glimmer of light.

Once upon a time, maybe this had been the farmhouse's front parlour. These days it was a sitting room set up for one person, with a big telly and a bulky armchair positioned right in front of the screen. The TV remote was on a coffee table within easy reach, along with a landline phone. The fireplace in the side wall had been fitted with a wood-burning stove cleaned out and left cold for the summer.

Apart from the space over the mantelpiece where my torch beam glanced off the glass of a picture, the walls were shelved from floor to ceiling. Every shelf was crammed full. I could see hefty leather-bound books, old-fashioned cloth-covered hardbacks and paperbacks from what looked like every decade from the last century. Where there was no more space on a shelf, more books had been slotted sideways into the gaps on top of the others.

There wasn't any sign of a harp or any cupboard or box where one might be hiding. I closed the door and moved silently past the enormous hall stand. The next room, the one at the back of the house, must have once been a dining room. There was a mahogany table with six chairs as well as a tall dresser against the wall that had a connecting door into the kitchen. The table and the dresser were covered with piles of crockery and clusters of glassware. More books and dust-covered cardboard boxes were stacked on the chairs and the floor. Random bits of furniture filled any available gaps. The fireplace in the side wall was full of boxes too. No wonder no one ever opened the curtains. It wasn't quite a TV documentary hoarder situation, since I guessed that would be a red flag for social services when they came to check how the old lady was managing, but it was still a lot of clutter.

I stood in the doorway and searched the room with my torch as methodically as I could. Nothing that looked like a harp or a box big enough to keep one in. Of course, that didn't mean it wasn't shoved under the dining table or even inside the bottom cupboard of the dresser. I decided I'd check the rest of the house before trying to work out how I could possibly search in there.

Checking the kitchen didn't take long. It was as old-fashioned as I expected. A wide fireplace must have once held a coal-burning range taking up most of the wall that backed onto the lane. An antiquated electric cooker stood there now, next to a fridge that belonged in a museum. Given the lack of radiators, it was clear there was no mains gas, even if there was electricity.

I didn't think a harp would be stashed in either of the two free-standing cupboards, but since I'd look a right idiot if that's where the bloody thing was, I opened the doors to be sure. The shelves behind the glass panels at the top held assorted cans and packets that I didn't bother identifying. I found saucepans and mixing bowls in the bottom of one and crockery in the other.

Leaving the kitchen and the faint smell of a bin that definitely needed emptying in this hot weather, I continued my clockwise circuit of the hall doors. I expected to find a spacious walk-in cupboard under the stairs. That had to be a good place to look, right? Wrong. It had been converted into the world's smallest wet room. Opposite a modern toilet bracketed with grab-rails, I saw a sit-down shower. No one would be keeping an antique musical instrument in there.

I should have thought a bit more about that wet room. If I had, maybe I wouldn't have been so startled when I opened the last door, into the other room at the front of the house. The torch beam showed me a couple of crammed bookcases and pictures hung on the walls. No great surprise. I wasn't expecting to see a low-level single bed in front of the empty fireplace. A little three-drawer unit stood by the headboard, and one of those three-wheeled folded walkers with handlebars and brakes was ready and waiting by the foot. A little old lady was fast asleep under a flower-patterned duvet, with her false teeth in a glass on the nightstand.

I switched off the torch so fast I almost dropped it. Stepping back, I only stopped myself from slamming the door at the last second. I eased the handle softly and silently up, listening for the soft click of the latch. My heart was pounding and I was sweating again. Shit. Why hadn't it occurred to me that Annis Wynne might not be able to manage the sodding stairs?

Leaning against the wall, I waited until I got my breath back. I did my best to picture what I had just seen. For a start, Annis Wynne really was a *little* little old lady. She'd looked barely bigger than one of the kids from the campsite as she lay in that bed, snoring softly.

I listened. She didn't miss a breath as the snoring continued. If she wasn't deaf, she was a very sound sleeper, and thank fuck for that. What else had been in that room though? This felt like playing that game where you show a kid a tray of things, make them turn away and then get them to look again and tell you what's missing.

Two shapes I'd glimpsed had to be chairs. Belatedly, my nose recalled the faint acrid smell of piss. One was probably a commode. Either that or the old lady had wet the bed. There were a couple of chests of drawers, and the one under the front window was piled high with neatly folded clothes. I couldn't believe the harp was anywhere in there. If it was, we really had a fucking problem. I couldn't see any way of looking for it without waking up the old lady.

If the harp was in there. I reminded myself what I'd decided when I'd seen the state of the dining room. I'd look everywhere else first. It was time to go up the stairs. The first step gave a horrendous creak. Shit. I lifted my foot and tried putting my weight on the side of the tread, on the bare wood between the wall and stair carpet that matched the runner in the hall. The step still creaked, but nowhere near as loudly. I went slowly up the stairs, keeping my feet as close to the walls on either side as I could. Long legs come in useful for the strangest things.

At least I didn't have to worry about disturbing anyone in the bedrooms. Like downstairs, there were four doors off the landing. Unsurprisingly, the one right above the kitchen had been converted into a bathroom ages ago. A sizeable claw-footed metal tub was underneath the window, beside an equally substantial ceramic pedestal basin with angular taps. None of the taps dripped, but I saw old stains in the basin and the bath. Checking the big cupboard built into the corner opposite the door, I found an immersion heater underneath shelves of old towels and bed linen. No harp.

I tried the next room, going anti-clockwise this time. I wanted to stay as far away from the floor over the old lady's head for as long as I could. There were no carpets, so I tested the boards at every step to keep creaks to a minimum. The iron bedstead by the back window was stripped to the mattress and piled high with cardboard boxes. I wasn't interested in those. As three angled mirrors in the corner reflected torchlight back at me, I saw the harp standing on a dressing table.

The harp? A harp. I took a quick look through the other two doors. Beds with bare mattresses were heaped with more boxes and flanked by random furniture. No more harps, or anything big enough to hide one. Okay then.

I went back to the back bedroom and walked over to the dressing table. The harp was somewhere around seventy-five centimetres tall. Call it thirty inches in old money, as my dad would say. At its broadest point, it was two thirds as wide as it was tall, maybe a little bit more. I used the torch to get a good look before I even thought about touching it. Thinking back to the scary fairy's creature and its illusion, I could see the hollow sound box would be held closest to the harpist's body. That had been skilfully carved from a single block of wood, though I'd need to see it in daylight to know what tree it had come from.

The top arm of the roughly triangular shape dipped down, concave. It was studded with metal pins on a strip of brass fastened to the wood. The harp's strings ran taut between those and identical pins on another brass strip that ran down the length of the sound box. The front pillar curved outwards, convex. That age-darkened wood was covered with incised designs that I couldn't make out. I ran my finger along the faint line to try to get a sense of their shape.

That was a mistake, even wearing gloves. The strings hummed, soft and seductive. The wood was warm and silky smooth under my fingertip. This harp longed to be played. I wanted to play it... for about thirty seconds. Every kid had been encouraged to play the recorder at primary school, and Mr Catling said I had a good singing voice. Being involved in music meant standing up at the front of the hall though, and I hated having everybody looking at me. I really liked Mr Catling, but I couldn't do that, not even for him.

As soon as I pulled my hand away, the feeling faded. So I'd found the bloody thing. Now I had to get it out of here. Since it was clearly eerily powerful, I wanted to touch it as little as possible. Unfortunately, there was no handily harp-shaped box or case anywhere in here. I crossed the landing into the bathroom as quickly and quietly as I could. I took an old woollen blanket from the shelf above the hot water tank and wound that around the harp. The strings thrummed in protest. The bloody thing was really giving me the creeps. I hated to think what the scary fairy might do with it.

I had to carry it in both hands. That meant putting my torch and the chisel in my trouser pockets. That meant I had to stand and wait for my night vision to return. That took fucking ages. At least, that's what it felt like. I could feel the harp vibrating through the blanket. It made my skin crawl.

When I couldn't stand it any longer, I made my way cautiously out of the room and down the stairs. I didn't dare put the harp down in case it made another noise, so I had to use my foot to find the bits of wood I'd wedged under the front door. Dragging them free with my trainer wasn't easy. I was right outside the old lady's bedroom, so I couldn't even vent my frustration with a few well-chosen swear words.

At long last, the front door swung open towards me. I could get out of here. I went out into the porch and stopped. Was I going to leave this house wide open with an old lady asleep in her bed? Was I fuck.

Carefully, I put down the blanket-wrapped harp, leaning it against the porch's wooden balustrade. The strings murmured sulkily. I ignored it as I knelt down and took hold of the nearest and smallest gorse bush as close to the roots as possible. I could feel pinpricks from its spines on my face and that vanilla scent surrounded me. It was unexpectedly soothing.

I offered the plant a mental apology and uprooted it with a swift jerk. I threaded the stems under the bottom edge of the door and used the handle to pull it closed as hard as I could. From the outside I couldn't wedge the door in the way I had done before, but this crushed gorse wouldn't slide across the doormat, so the door would look closed to a casual glance.

That would have to do. I had to rescue Tyler and the summer night was short. I picked up the harp and hurried around to the back of the house. I passed the harp over the metal gate and lowered it carefully to the ground. It protested with a sharp discord that made my teeth ache. I climbed over and picked it up. It felt twice as heavy, slipping inside the folds of wool. I could swear it was doing that on purpose to make itself awkward to carry. The sooner I was rid of this bloody thing, the happier I would be.

Chapter Seventeen

Outside, I headed for the abandoned quarry. I soon saw shadowy figures lurking on either side of what passed for a path. More were up on the spoil heaps. I could see them outlined against the starry sky. Some had pointed ears. Some of those had muzzles like foxes. Others were blunt-nosed and round-headed, in sharp contrast to the ones with sweeping horns. They were all waiting for me. I wished I had a hand free to get that chisel out of my trouser pocket. Steel would give the bastards something to think about.

I forced myself to slow down as I reached the bottom of the slope. If that dry stream bed tripped me up, I didn't think accidentally breaking the harp was the worst thing that could happen, not by a long shot. Menacing low growling was getting closer and the scars on my arm were itching. I didn't need that to tell me these things were hostile. If I fell flat on my face, they'd seize their chance to attack. These creatures wanted a piece of me. I wasn't sure there'd be enough to go round, seeing how many there were. I knew there were more in the shadows.

So I made damn sure I didn't trip over. Any sort of scuffle would slow me down. I had to get in and out of here as fast as I could. I reached the mine workings and headed for the entrance on the left. The rectangular hole in the rock face was as black as pitch. I wished I could get my torch out. As soon as I thought that, I saw faint radiance coming from inside the hill. The creatures on all sides snickered, as if their queen had somehow got the upper hand.

Fine. She'd switched the lights on. I sure as shit wasn't going to thank her for it. I stopped a metre or so from the entrance. The lurking creatures clustered closer, filling the air with a rank animal smell.

'Back off.' I didn't raise my voice, but I put all the threat I could into the words.

If they didn't understand me, they got the message from my tone and my expression. They retreated with a low murmur of discontent.

That was as good as it was going to get. I took a deep breath and went into the mine. Hearing the creatures following me, I had to fight the urge to hurry, to get away from them. I forced myself to walk slowly. Clutching the blanket-wrapped harp, I stooped to be sure I didn't bang my head. The last thing I needed right now was a scalp wound or concussion.

I reached the cavern with the glowing pool. At first glance, nothing had changed since yesterday. The scary fairy sat on her golden throne wearing her red velvet gown. Tyler lay on the floor by the water. As far as I could tell, he was sleeping peacefully. Someone had even washed his face and zipped up his leather jacket.

The scary fairy leaned forward. Her black eyes gleamed with anticipation in the eerie light. 'You have it?'

Before I could answer, the harp replied with a yearning chord. The unsettling harmony echoed back from the cavern walls, even muffled by the blanket. I gripped the bloody thing tighter and wished I knew how to make it shut up.

'Then our business is concluded.' The scary fairy leaned back. She waved a long-nailed hand, dismissive. 'Leave the harp and take your prize. I wish you joy of him. He has been very dull company.'

The creatures that had followed me in through the tunnel were spreading out around the cavern. They started snickering again.

'No,' I said.

That shut the fuckers up.

'What did you say?' The scary fairy's instant of confusion quickly changed to fury. 'If you break your word, forest boy, I will—'

'Our deal was clear. I take the boy out of here once you know I've got the harp. Once I know he's safe, I'll come back and give you the harp.'

The fairy's scowl told me she'd been hoping I would be too distracted or too anxious to remember the precise details of our agreement. I had no idea how exactly she had planned to screw me over, and Tyler too, but that didn't matter. She wasn't going to get the chance.

'Very well.' She tried to sound offhand. 'If you want him, come and get him.'

Of course, when I'd made those terms, I'd had no idea how big the harp was going to be, or how sodding inconvenient it was to carry. And speaking of inconvenient, Tyler was absolutely spark out. Sod it. I should have said I wanted him awake. No, sleepwalking would have been better. Too late now.

As I reached the kid, I put the harp down on the rocky floor and let the blanket fall away. I kept hold of the concave top spar with one hand, partly to stop the bloody thing toppling over, mostly to show I hadn't relinquished possession. The creatures in the shadows muttered and hissed. They would snatch it away if they got the chance, no question.

Crouching down, I used my free hand to check for a pulse in Tyler's neck. It was slow but steady. That was good. On the other hand, his clothes were rank with sweat that smelled... wrong. I had to get him away from here, and since he wasn't going to walk out on his own two feet, what was I going to do?

I glanced at the scary fairy. She was gloating, and she made no effort to hide it. If I asked her to rouse Tyler, she would insist on making some new deal in return for that favour. I could guarantee that would be bad for both of us. No chance.

I got a good grip on the collar of his leather jacket and on the shirt underneath it. I managed to haul him into a sitting position. His eyes didn't even flicker. He really was dead to the wor— right out of it. What now? If I let go of his collar, to try to slide my hand and my shoulder under his arm, he'd slump straight down onto the floor again.

Fuck it. I tightened my grip and stood up. I still had hold of the harp in my other hand. Mercifully, it stayed silent. I started walking sideways like a crab and dragged Tyler across the rocky floor. He was dead wei— completely limp, so it was sodding hard work. I hated to think how many bruises he'd have, but that didn't matter. Bruises would heal. I only hoped the scary fairy and her creatures hadn't done too much other damage. Damage that no one could see.

I hauled him around to the other side of the pool and paused to take a breather. By now I was sweating like a pig for the third time tonight. I must smell as bad as these shadowy creatures. They were pressing closer again. I warned them off with another glare. This time, I bared my teeth. Something, somewhere, snarled back.

The light from the water blinked out. The darkness was impenetrable. The air was oppressively still. I could sense the shapeshifting creatures getting closer. Their claws tick-ticked across the rocky floor. Eager panting echoed back from the cavern walls.

'I'm going to keep walking.' I managed a conversational tone. Possibly because I'd gone right through desperation and come out somewhere on the other side. 'If I trip or fall, or if I walk into a wall, I might well break this harp by accident. If anything attacks me, I *will* use it as a weapon. Trust me. I told you I'll smash this fucking thing if I have to, and I meant it. If I can't get the boy out safely, our deal's null and void.'

The harp protested with a sharp twang. I tightened my grip on the ancient polished wood. The harp made a more muted sound. I heard shuffling as the panting creatures retreated. Not far, but far enough.

I took a step through the darkness. I took another. Tyler stopped sliding across the floor. Had his clothing caught on some jagged rock, or had some sly creature got hold of his feet, now that I couldn't see? I tightened my grip and yanked harder.

'Oh shit!'

I hadn't lost my balance. Nowhere close. I sure as hell sounded as if I had though, and I thumped the base of the harp on the ground. Caught unawares, the strings jangled with alarm and the soundbox reverberated.

Sudden light from the pool filled the cavern. I saw the shapeshifting creatures were a whole lot closer than I'd imagined. That was sodding terrifying. They weren't focused on me though. Every one was looking back towards the scary fairy. I desperately wanted to see her expression now she knew that she'd been tricked. I resisted the temptation.

My only aim was getting out of here with Tyler. I dragged him along the tunnel. That was even more awkward going. With me hauling him along by his collar, Tyler's arms were forced upwards, sticking out at odd angles. I heard and felt his limp hands smacking against the tunnel walls. I gritted my teeth and told myself that broken bones would heal too.

The sullen light from the cavern grew dimmer, and the creatures crowding behind us quickly blocked out the rest, but I didn't care. The scary fairy's creatures couldn't surround us in this narrow space. Ever so faint, up ahead, I could see the shimmer of honest starlight outside this miserable fucking hole. As I rounded the corner in the tunnel, I tasted the dewy fragrance of greenery on a breath of breeze. That was where I belonged. We both belonged out under the starry sky, me and Tyler. Of course, it would have really fucking helped if that scent had woken him up, but that didn't happen.

At long last I reached the outside world. Putting in one last effort, I dragged Tyler a few metres away from the mine entrance before I stopped for another breather. My shoulders were burning as if I'd spent the evening lifting weights. Maybe I should join a gym. This wasn't the first time I'd had to carry an unconscious man away from trouble he had no idea he'd got into. At least Tyler was a lot lighter than the last fat bastard had been.

He wasn't out of danger yet. I took a deep breath and planted my feet firmly on the ground. Putting the harp between my trainers, I gripped it with my knees. It made a startled sound. I didn't care. Now that I had both hands free, I could keep Tyler sitting upright by gripping a handful of his greasy hair while I untangled my other fingers from his jacket collar. I flexed my hand several times to ward off the threat of cramp.

Now I had to get him onto my shoulder. I reached down to grab his hand and hauled him upwards as I bent at the waist. It took just about all my strength. If he'd been any bigger, I couldn't have done it. Finally, I managed to get him into something like a fireman's lift. That would have been a hell of a lot easier without having to hold some mysterious musical instrument between my knees. As it was, I had to take an unexpected step to avoid falling over.

That was a nasty moment. Losing my footing would be a seriously bad idea. I could feel the upper curve of the harp against my inner thigh, unnervingly close to my balls. I really didn't want to slip while I was straddling it. Do that, and breaking the fucking thing would be the least of my worries.

THE GREEN MAN'S GIFT

The harp slipped forward. I heard an eager yelp in the darkness. The weight of the harp was still pressing against my shin. I bent my knees very carefully and reached down with my free hand before any ambitious shapeshifter could decide the harp was up for grabs. I got a firm hold of it and straightened up. Now I had to head back up the track and get to the Meilyr Centre car park. One step at a time, like my dad always says. One fucking step at a time.

I started walking. I tried not to think about the revolting cracking sound that Tyler's arm had made when I hauled him upwards. Had I dislocated his shoulder or his elbow? At this rate, this rescue had probably done him more physical damage than the scary fairy. Injuries to his body, at least. I really hoped he wasn't going to suddenly wake up and start thrashing and screaming in agony. I couldn't possibly explain what was going on.

I was conscious of the things in my combat trouser pockets. Chisel, torch, phone. I couldn't get at any of those. If my handset buzzed with a warning text right now, I was shit out of luck. If there was some copper in the car park, answering some concerned citizen's call, I was utterly screwed. How could I possibly explain what I was doing with an unconscious teenager slung on one shoulder and an antique musical instrument in my other hand? Well, you see, it's like this, officer...

Don't go borrowing trouble. Do the job that's in front of you. Like my dad says. I kept watch on those creatures in the shadows. They were coming with me, presumably on the scary fairy's orders. I wasn't sure what they would do if they thought I was going to cheat her, but 'rip the lying forest boy to pieces' seemed a likely place for them to start.

I did see something interesting when I drew level with the Cerrigwen farmhouse. All the creatures pressed against the stone wall on the far side of the lane. Some even jumped it to run along on the field. None of them wanted to go anywhere near the five-barred galvanised-steel gate or the fence lined with chicken wire.

There were no lights on inside the house, as far as I could see. Trying to look at the front windows and the front door would have meant stopping and turning around. I didn't want to risk that, not after getting so far through tonight's insane to-do list. I had a lot ticked off, but there were still massive challenges ahead. I didn't want these vicious creatures to realise the old woman was in there asleep, defenceless behind a door that wasn't secured with an iron lock any more.

The last stretch uphill was murderous. After what felt like half a lifetime, I reached the end of the rough track. The tarmac road wound down through the village on the hillside. On the far side of the Meilyr Centre car park, a single vehicle waited. I started to trudge towards it. The driver started the engine. The car headed towards me, shockingly loud in the silence. I kept on walking. The sooner I handed Tyler over, the better.

The big old estate with a VW badge reached me and pulled up. As the passenger opened the door, the courtesy light came on. I noticed the back seats had been put down. Before I saw anything else, the driver flicked the headlights on and off, nearly fucking blinding me. I screwed my eyes tight shut and swore.

'Here, let me take him.'

I recognised Gillian's voice. I stood still while she and the Passat's driver came to lift Tyler off my shoulder. It was obvious they were both used to handling unconscious patients. That gave me a free hand to rub my stinging eyes.

'I hope he's not too badly beaten up.' If he was, I'd admit my share of responsibility for it later.

Gillian just grunted. 'Can you open the back for us?'

I walked around and pressed the catch on the tailgate. I still had firm hold of the harp, but that was a one-handed job. The two women got Tyler into the back, laying him down on a thick layer of towels. The driver unzipped his leather jacket, and between them, they managed to strip it off him. That would probably have been a bit easier if they hadn't both been wearing blue hospital gloves.

'I still say we should have used the scissors,' the driver muttered.

She unbuttoned Tyler's shirt cuff and ripped the sleeve along the seam to his armpit. She'd done that before. Paramedic? Nurse? I guessed she was something like that, when she wasn't being a wise woman. She had short red hair, a square face and a competent manner.

Gillian scanned Tyler's forehead with a digital thermometer and clipped one of those pulse oximeter things onto his forefinger. She glanced at me. 'How about you? Any cuts or scrapes?'

I realised I was scratching my arm through the sleeve of my hoodie and stopped. 'Nothing that a long hot bath won't fix.' I tried not to think how far I was from any chance of that.

'Blood pressure's low but not drastically so.' The driver was using a neat machine that pumped itself up around Tyler's skinny arm and beeped as it gave her the readings. 'Of course, we have no idea what's normal for him.'

She looked at me, and for a moment, I thought she was going to ask me about the kid's medical history. How was I supposed to bloody know? Then I realised she was looking at the harp.

'That's it then, is it?'

'Yes.' I had no idea what she might be asking.

THE GREEN MAN'S GIFT

The harp didn't make a sound.

Gillian was getting an intravenous drip needle, some tubing and a bag of clear liquid out of a grey plastic box. 'You're sure about this, Daniel?'

'I am.' I watched her tie a thick elastic band around Tyler's arm.

'Right then.' She didn't say anything else as she got the needle into a vein, first go, and started the drip. She climbed into the back of the estate car and hung the bag of liquid on one of those hooks for suit jackets. 'We'll see you later. Now we'd better get him out of here.'

'See you later.' I pulled down the tailgate.

The driver was still standing by her door. She watched as I rested the harp against my leg and sorted out the things in my pockets. 'Do you want me to scatter that lot with the lights again?'

She gestured towards the track to Cerrigwen. The shapeshifting creatures were prowling in circles at the edge of the tarmac, frustrated. I wasn't sure what was keeping them at a distance, but whatever it was, I was grateful for the breather. My night's work wasn't anywhere near over yet.

'No. Let's not let them know for certain that you can see them.'

'Okay.' Her tone said she thought I was wrong, but she got into the car and drove away. I saw her turn on the headlights once she was well down the road. So Tyler was finally safe, and out of the scary fairy's clutches.

I looked up at the night sky. It was still dark and thick with stars, but midnight was long gone and daylight came early at this time of year. I had a lot to do before then. I took a moment to stretch my aching shoulders before I started walking back to the track that led down to the quarry. I carried the harp in both hands, holding the top curve and the sound box. I was being very careful not to touch those indistinct carvings on the front spar. The strings thrummed quietly, though I could barely hear it over the slight sound of my steps on the tarmac.

The creatures drew closer as I reached the track. The harp grew louder. They quickly retreated. I heard a few soft whimpers. What was that about? I walked on, faster. The harp fell silent as we approached the Cerrigwen farmhouse. Now I was facing the porch, I couldn't see any sign that the front door had swung open. That clump of gorse I had used to wedge it was holding. That was a relief.

All the same, I wasn't kidding myself. The old lady would see someone had broken in as soon as she got out of bed. She would phone for help. The burglary would be the talk of the village before morning coffee time tomorrow. I had to hope that no one had seen me leave the campsite in the dead of night. I wondered what my chances were of making it back to my tent before dawn.

I reached the bottom of the path and crossed the gully. The quarry was dark and silent. As I approached the tunnel entrance, I could see the eerie glimmer coming around that corner. The harp stayed quiet and the creatures clustered closer. I ignored them as I headed into the darkness. They followed close behind. As soon as I stepped into the cavern, they rushed past me to huddle in the shadows behind the scary fairy's golden throne.

She rested her chin on one long-nailed hand, with her elbow propped on the padded arm of her chair. Her other talons drummed lazily on her thigh. I wasn't sure if she was mocking me or taunting me. I didn't care.

I walked around the pond. A single string on the harp sounded a penetrating note. A shiver ran through the creatures lurking in the shadows. The scary fairy was looking at the ancient instrument with an odd mix of anticipation and apprehension. She wasn't drumming her fingernails on her thigh now.

I stopped and held out the harp. 'You wanted me to give you this in return for the boy.'

'That is what we agreed.' She beckoned me forward with a casual curl of her fingers.

I stayed where I was.

She scowled. I still didn't move.

'If you want it, come and get it.'

She glared at me as she got to her feet, flicking her long black hair back over her shoulder. She can't have been much more than five foot tall. Her long velvet skirt brushed the rocky floor as she walked towards me. The shapeshifting creatures stood motionless in the shadows, not making a sound.

She took hold of the harp with both hands. I let go, and I saw the weight didn't bother her in the slightest.

'We've both kept our sides of the bargain. We have no more business with each other.' I shoved my hands into my hoodie's pockets.

Her blood-red lips curved in spiteful triumph as she studied the harp intently. 'Agreed.'

I ripped it away from her with one hand and punched her in the face with my other fist. I'd threaded my fingers through the rowan ring in my pocket, so I was wearing the twisted wood like brass knuckles.

I'd agreed to give her the harp in return for getting Tyler back. I'd done that. I never said a word about letting her keep it.

Chapter Eighteen

I'd caught her completely off guard. The scary fairy staggered backwards, astonished. The rowan wood left a raw red gash across her pale cheek. I didn't hang around to see anything else. The other thing I had put in my hoodie pocket was my torch. I ripped it out as I ran for the tunnel and switched it on just in time. The beam lit up the rock wall ahead as the radiance from the pool blinked out.

In the darkness behind me, the scary fairy screamed with incandescent rage. The shapeshifting creatures howled and gibbered. I could hear them coming after me. Too late. I'd reached the tunnel. I ran as fast as I could, raising my hand and using my torch to make sure I knew where the roof was. I skinned my knuckles on the dark rock several times, but I had to ignore the pain. The stinging in my scars that told me those creatures would do their best to kill me if they caught me made that easier.

I held the harp in my other hand, gripping it by the curved top arm. It was heavy and awkward to carry it like that, but I had the base of the instrument shoved out in front of me. Anything charging into the tunnel from the outside, hoping to trap me between two enemies, would get a faceful of creepy ancient wood.

Savage yelps made me hope the shapeshifters were getting in each other's way in the cramped space. That hope lasted until a claw snagged the back of my hoodie. I staggered and threw my weight forward. The stretchy fabric stretched. A moment later, it tore and I staggered forward. I barely saved myself from falling flat on my face by hitting the tunnel wall with the hand holding my torch. That talon scraped down my back, and I felt cold air on the skin beside my spine. So this T-shirt was going in the bin, but I couldn't tell if I was bleeding or not.

The claw reached the hem of the hoodie. It snagged on the thick band of elasticated material. That wasn't going to rip. No matter how hard I struggled, I couldn't go on. The reek of the creatures filled the tunnel and their howling deafened me. Fuck. I raised the hand holding the harp, ready to smash it against the rocky wall. I hoped I'd be left with a piece of broken wood jagged enough to use as a weapon. I could probably do some damage with those strings if I could get a safe handhold at each end.

In the split-second before I brought my hand down, the harp's strings made a sound like a knife blade scraped across a plate. It made me wince, but the creatures behind me chittered with agony. Now the one with its claw caught in my hoodie was fighting to get away.

I was nearly at the bend in the tunnel. I hurled myself forward, chucking the torch away. It smashed, leaving me in the pitch dark. It was worth it. I hooked my hand around the rocky corner. I hauled harder and managed to get around the sharp angle. Whatever was behind me was caught off balance. I felt it skid and slam into the slate wall. I threw myself backwards to crush the fucking thing between my considerable weight and the unforgiving stone. I heard cracking noises. It squealed and gurgled. Good enough. When I ran out into the night, it didn't follow.

The other creatures were still coming after me. I made a fast right turn. The ominous bulk of the spoil heap rose up on my left. I had the black outline of the ravaged hillside to my right. I ran for the gap between them. Loose scraps of slate skidded under my trainers. The harp vibrated in my hand, but it stayed silent.

A hare darted past my feet, going back the way I had just come. Another one followed it, and then a third. More of them surged up the slope. I snatched a glance over my shoulder. My eyes had readjusted to the night, and I could see cats and foxes darting this way and that. The temptation to chase the hares was too much for them to resist.

The hares knew it and they were working together. As soon as a predator focused on one of them, another darted across its path. Distracted, the predator would pursue the newcomer. Yips and yowls of frustration turned to aggressive snarls as the creatures warned off rivals chasing the same scent. The creatures were so intent on the hares that they forgot to watch where they were going. Two long, lean shapes crashed into each other as two hares criss-crossed so close that their trailing ears probably touched.

One fox had more success. Its jaws fastened on its prey's back leg. Another hare came out of nowhere. Leaping high into the air, it slammed its muscular back paws into the fox's ribs. The creature whipped its head around, yelping with startled pain. The hare it had just seized sprang free. Both long-eared shadows bounded away into the darkness.

I let them get on with it. The hares had their job and I had mine. Once I was past the spoil heap, I cut across the hillside. I desperately tried to picture where I was going. I'd studied that Ordnance Survey map for hours earlier, but even with my night vision, it wasn't necessarily easy to relate what I could see now to the picture in my head. The ground sloped away beneath my trainers. I went on as fast as I could without risking a fall. I hoped to fuck I was going the right way.

Just as I was starting to doubt myself, I saw light ahead. It wasn't anything mystical or magical but a solid white LED beam. Thank fuck for that. I hurried towards it. Aled was waiting by the entrance to another mine, wearing orange overalls. His round red helmet had a lamp fixed to the front, powered by a battery pack on his belt. I put the harp down and took the wide webbing belt he was offering me, complete with battery pack.

'This is it then, is it?' He looked down and his lamp's beam shone on the polished wood. 'Bigger than I expected.'

'Is that going to be a problem?' I tightened the belt around my waist and tugged my torn T-shirt and hoodie down at the back. I could still feel cool night air on my skin, but that was better than nothing. More importantly, I was pretty sure that whatever had shredded my clothes hadn't drawn blood. I couldn't feel any stinging or wetness.

Aled handed me a white helmet like the one he was wearing. 'I reckon we'll be okay. I mean, it should go through anywhere you can get through.' He sounded reassuringly confident as he checked the connection between my head lamp and the power pack.

The harp was making faint unhappy noises. I ignored it as I adjusted the fit of my helmet and fastened the strap under my chin. 'Ready.'

Aled reached up to turn my lamp on. He looked past me, and I saw his expression change as he spotted whatever was heading our way. 'Yes, we had better go.'

He thrust a pair of thick work gloves at me. I pulled them on and picked up the harp. We headed into the mine. Aled went first, striding ahead.

'Now, you remember what I told you?' he called back over his shoulder. 'You walk where I walk, and you only put your feet on solid rock. Step on any planks and you might not just find out they're rotten. They could be covering a drop that'll break your leg or your neck. The last thing we want to do is to have to call out cave rescue.'

'I'll be careful,' I assured him.

I heard snuffling somewhere behind us. I didn't bother looking over my shoulder or reaching for that cold chisel I still had in my combats. The scary fairy's creatures wouldn't be following us down here. We were walking between narrow iron rails that had once guided small wagons laden with slate out into the daylight. The faint vibration in the wood of the harp died away to nothing as we went on, and I wondered if being close to the metal had done that too.

Part of me still wanted to protest, to ask what the hell we were doing, going underground again. Wasn't that where the things we wanted to get away from lived? Why hadn't I simply headed for the Meilyr Centre car park and handed the harp to someone else waiting in a car? I could be watching the thing being driven away right now, carried way beyond the scary fairy's reach.

Well, for one thing, her shapeshifting creatures would most likely attack me out of sheer spite if they realised the harp would be going where they couldn't possibly follow. The scary fairy would be looking for payback, and we already knew she wasn't bothered about killing ordinary people.

We'd discussed all this yesterday for a long, long time, on the conference call that Gillian had set up, while I sat in the Landy in that car park by the coast. I'd had no idea where everyone else was calling from, or who most of them were. Wise women rarely introduce themselves unless they have a good reason. I had learned that since the previous autumn.

To start with, we agreed that I needed to hand off the harp as soon as possible. There was no way to know who might know it belonged to Annis Wynne. If I carried it back to Plas Brynwen, if anyone challenged me to explain why I had the thing out on the street in the middle of the night, I wouldn't have any sort of convincing answer.

Initially, I'd assumed I'd take it somewhere in the Landy. I reckoned I should be able to get as far as the car park in one piece. Once I'd handed it over to whoever was going to deal with it, and that was what I really wanted to discuss, I would head back to the campsite. I'd go to sleep in the little tent for whatever was left of the night, protected by the yew dirt and the rowan rings. We knew those worked as defences.

In the morning, I'd be shocked and surprised by news of a burglary at Cerrigwen. If anyone asked, no, I hadn't seen a thing as I went out for a late night look at the stars. I'd pack up sometime around lunchtime and head back to Blithehurst. Obviously, I didn't want to arouse suspicion by leaving in a hurry first thing. I could leave the Landy's doors wide open while I was putting away the tent and everything else. Anyone passing could see for themselves I couldn't possibly be hiding something as big as the harp. I'd let Mr Williams check if he didn't seem convinced. Hell, I'd let the cops take a look if they wanted. There wouldn't be anything for them to find.

The wise women didn't agree. They reckoned the chances of me reaching the car park in a fit state to drive were somewhere between zero and none. I'd be shredded by the scary fairy's creatures. As for getting down Caergynan's sloping street and back to the campsite without the harp? Forget it.

Of course, they assured me, they wouldn't leave me on my own to be injured or killed, but the uproar would surely attract attention, and not just from the neighbourhood watch. That was unacceptable. One of them actually said that. The danger of a horde of uncanny creatures biting lumps out of me was less important than the risk of some ordinary member of the public being disturbed by the noise and seeing something that got them screaming about monsters. Worse still, someone might try to film whatever was happening on a mobile phone. If the creatures turned on them, we risked the situation getting totally out of hand.

Okay, I was forced to concede that would be very bad. I also remembered seeing the Cŵn Annwn prowling around the campsite. I hadn't seen those red-eared hounds since we'd given them the slip in Aled's Fiesta, but they knew where to go looking for me. The thought of them causing carnage among the kids and pet dogs on their summer holidays made my blood run cold.

Gillian insisted I needed an alibi. What if someone had noticed me walking down to Cerrigwen? Just because I hadn't seen them, that didn't mean they hadn't seen me. What would the police think if they asked me where I'd gone on my midnight ramble and all I could give them was lies? I needed to tell them something that would ring true, even if it wasn't the whole truth.

Then there was the fact we still didn't know why the scary fairy wanted this bloody harp so badly. Iris brought that up. We had absolutely no idea what the instrument might be capable of. The various myths that she had found weren't remotely reassuring. Harps lured people away in folk tales, taking them out of their own time for a year and a day or even longer.

What would happen to someone driving a car, or their passengers, if the damn thing did something unexpected? We might be able to resist the music in our different ways, but that wasn't guaranteed. Did we want to take that chance? Concerned citizens from Caergynan's neighbourhood watch would be easy victims, and who knew what might happen to them? She reminded us that at least one of Mari Rhys's victims had never been found.

Okay, I had agreed, it was probably best if we kept the sodding harp well away from ordinary people. We didn't want anyone ending up as collateral damage, or being interviewed by the tabloids about some outbreak of mass hysteria or inexplicable disappearances. So what exactly were we going to do?

I still favoured the most direct solution, namely smashing the harp into firewood. The wise women weren't having that, certainly not until they knew more about it. I suggested driving a handful of six-inch nails into the soundbox. That would stop it doing whatever it did while they were trying to find out, but they weren't having that either.

That's when Aled spoke up. Gillian had insisted on including him in the call. I had agreed, mainly so I wouldn't feel so heavily outnumbered. Anyway, Aled had told us that while he went potholing in the Brecon Beacons with an official caving club and all the necessary safety gear and precautions, he also explored a lot of the old mine workings closer to home.

Most of the time, he didn't tell anyone what he was doing, because more often than not, he was trespassing. Occasionally he went in with another caver, especially if tourists had recently needed rescuing. Then the emergency services would want an up-to-date survey to assess the current risks. Mostly he explored on his own. He relied on his skills to stay out of trouble, and he reckoned the knockers would come to help if he ever got into a situation he struggled to get out of. That hadn't ever happened yet, he assured us with a grin, holding his crossed fingers up for the camera on his phone.

I wasn't particularly surprised. Looking at the Ordnance Survey map, I'd been struck by the number of old quarries and mines dug into the hillsides around here. Anyone thinking these empty mountains were an untouched natural wilderness was kidding themselves. This had been an industrial landscape within living memory.

The evidence surrounded me as we walked into an even bigger cavern than the scary fairy's throne room. The lamp beam from my helmet showed me rusted lumps of metal that must have once been essential equipment for whatever had gone on here. The rails underfoot split into different tracks curving away towards the cavern walls, where dark entrances opened onto deeper workings. I saw the skeletal remains of carts whose wooden sides had rotted away. Those were never going to move again. A damp, metallic tang hung in the cool air.

'Aled!' I shielded my eyes with my hand as he turned around and his lamp beam found me. 'Wasn't it worth anyone's time carting this stuff out to sell it for scrap?'

'Probably couldn't agree who should get the money, then spent so long arguing that everyone lost out. Most of these mines went bust with the owners up to their necks in debt. Means nothing nasty's going to be following us down here, mind. Told you, didn't I?' He grinned, then turned and headed for one particular tunnel.

'You certainly did.' I followed, careful where I put my feet.

Even with the possibility of falling down unexpected shafts, this was a very different experience to going into the darkness alone. For a start, our helmet lamps lit up the tunnel and left no shadows for anything to lurk in. More than that, Aled was perfectly at home. He strolled along ahead of me, as relaxed as if we were on our way to the pub. His calmness made me a lot less stressed.

The harp in my hands was as lifeless as any piece of wood I'd ever handled. Was that because we were surrounded by so much metal or because we'd got far enough away from the scary fairy and her creatures? Either way, I was relieved.

The silence wasn't total. I heard occasional splashes of water between the echoes of Aled's booted footsteps. As we walked on, I wondered about the knockers. Aled's grandad had said they were happy enough to show miners where to find seams of gold and silver ore, as well as slate or coal, but what did they make of iron and steel? Did they find those metals as off-putting as most of the non-human folk I'd encountered? If so, I wouldn't be quite so confident that they'd come to rescue him if he got stuck.

So we'd better not get stuck. 'How much further have we got to go?' I called out.

'A fair way yet.' Aled didn't sound concerned.

On we went. I resisted the temptation to start humming 'Hi ho, hi ho...'. Drips of water landed on my helmet a couple of times, and a trickle hitting my shoulder soaked through to my skin. I wouldn't have minded a set of overalls like Aled's, but he had said he didn't know where to get some in my size without having to put in a special order.

Besides, he reckoned I wouldn't have time for a wardrobe change. He'd been right about that. I still had the rowan ring on my hand. I'd pulled the glove on straight over it. I thought about taking a moment to put the ring back in my pocket. I decided not to. There was no knowing what we might still meet down here under these hills.

A bit further on and my head lamp flickered alarmingly. Thankfully, I realised I'd knocked the lead connecting it to the power pack. I told myself that Aled would know how long these batteries had to last if he knew the route we were taking. Then I realised I'd never asked him how well he could see in the dark. A moment later, I saw he had stopped at a junction up ahead.

'This is where the fun starts.' He grinned and disappeared into the side passage.

I walked up to the turning and hesitated. 'This is taking us away from these rails.'

'Don't worry about that,' he called back.

I wished I shared his certainty. How long would it take for the scary fairy to realise where we had gone? Okay, we didn't have any reason to think she could sense where we were through solid rock. The wise women had agreed on that when Aled had explained his plan. They had examined it from every conceivable angle while we sat and waited for them to make up their minds. That was all very well, but none of them had answered me when I pointed out they didn't know she couldn't keep track of us.

I realised I was gripping the harp tighter. It was still completely silent. That was something in our favour, at least. Do the job that's in front of you and worry about the rest later. I started walking. This passage was much smaller, with a lower roof and irregular sides. The roof quickly got even lower and the walls closed in. A bit further and I was stooping while both my shoulders brushed the rock on either side.

Ahead, Aled stopped. He eased himself sideways through a narrow gap that I hadn't even noticed. Seriously? I went closer for a better look. Aled startled me by reappearing, though at least he didn't blind me with his lamp this time.

'Do you want to pass that through first?' He gestured at the harp.

'Okay.' It took me a moment to work out the best angle to try. I ended up putting the top spar into Aled's waiting gloved hands. 'Got it?'

'Got it.'

He eased it through the tight zig-zag space with a scraping sound. I wondered how many of these squeezes lay ahead. I could bend myself around awkward corners, up to a point. The harp was rigidly inflexible. Had Aled taken account of that? Just how good was his spatial awareness?

I reached through the gap with one foot and one hand. I felt solid rock underfoot, and space opened up when I swung my forearm. I shifted my weight and shuffled sideways. It was a bloody tight fit. The torn cloth on my back was dragged out of the belt holding my battery pack. The rock was cool against my skin, but thankfully, I didn't scrape myself on anything sharp.

Once I was through, Aled was waiting. He stood holding the harp while I did my best to sort out my clothes.

'Okay?'

'Okay.' I took the harp back from him.

The tunnel carried on, as cramped as it had been before. I had to pass the harp to Aled through another couple of places that were nearly as tight. One section was so low that I gave up and got on my hands and knees, bumping the harp along ahead of me. I lost any sense of direction, and don't ask me how long we were walking and crawling. I wasn't wearing a watch and there didn't seem a lot of point in stopping to look at my phone. We'd get out of here when we got out of here. It was as simple as that.

If miners had dug out this route through the mountains, I had no clue what they had been looking for. I wondered if they had known themselves, or were they chasing some dream of riches that never came to anything? Then I saw Aled reach what looked like a complete dead end.

'Right, we need to do this next bit on our bellies. Wait for me to give you a shout, and you can send the harp on through.'

How could he sound so matter of fact? Before I could ask, he reached up and took hold of a ledge I hadn't even noticed. Using his feet on the walls on either side, he worked himself into a gap like someone getting a package into a post box. *Seriously?*

I watched his boots disappear. I waited, listening to scraping noises. Everything went quiet for a long moment. Then I heard Aled calling.

'Right you are then. Let me have the harp.'

Well, we'd got this far. Plus, my only other option was turning around and going back the way we'd come. I pushed the harp into the gap, shoving it as far forward as I could. At least I had the advantage of a good long reach.

'Got it,' Aled confirmed.

I saw the base of the soundbox heading away from me. I took my time going after it. The first challenge was getting my upper body into the gap. My longer legs helped, and my trainers got a decent grip on the rock walls. I took a breather when I was in up to my waist, letting my legs dangle. Then I felt for new finger and toeholds and forced myself forward, using my elbows then my knees as much as I could. Even going so slowly, it was absolutely knackering. I banged my helmet on the ceiling more than once. Each time came as a jarring shock, even if the impact didn't hurt. The chances of me ever taking up potholing as a hobby were now equal to the square root of fuck all.

This bloody tunnel seemed to go on for ever. Finally, I heard Aled's voice.

'Right, you're nearly there. Just a bit further, and I'll give you a hand.'

At least the way out of this crawl space wasn't a drop. I did come out onto a disconcertingly steep slope. I was grateful to find Aled offering me his hand. He helped me work my way sideways, so I wasn't crawling out with my feet higher than my head. Once I was all the way out, I sat down to give my brain a few minutes to decide which way was up. As I looked around, the beam from the lamp on my helmet showed me where we were.

'Bloody hell.'

'Something, isn't it?' Aled grinned.

This cave was absolutely massive. I couldn't tell if it was natural or not. Enough water to be called a lake had collected a long way down below us, at the base of the slope. I had no idea how deep that might be and no wish to find out. Apart from anything else, the water was a seriously off-putting green colour in the lamplight. That sheen might not be magical, but it certainly wasn't natural. I hated to think what had drained into the cave from the cascade of discarded domestic appliances I could see tumbling down the opposite slope. The air smelled oily and unpleasant.

'Came across this a few years back,' Aled remarked. 'Bloody fly-tippers. Reported it, obviously, but getting this rubbish out will be ten times the work of dumping it. Dangerous too.'

'I'll bet.' I picked out knackered microwaves and washing machines alongside kitchen units ripped out in some refit. An old moped had been chucked in, landing next to a couple of massive cathode-ray TVs that had to be twenty years old.

'Enough metal around to put our friends off, mind,' Aled said cheerfully.

'Right.' I tried to see the top of this avalanche of waste. 'Is that our way out? The same way that stuff came in?'

That would be a horrendous climb, even if we stuck to the rocky slope at the side of the dump. Scattered debris would be a hazard, and I reckoned there was a very real risk of us starting a trash-slide if we knocked something into the river of junk which knocked something else loose. The whole lot looked unstable.

On the other hand... I looked down at the noxious water. Suppose I chucked the harp in there and worked out a safe way to send that garbage crashing down on top of it. That would stop the scary fairy or anyone else ever getting their hands on it. Of course, the wise women would be furious.

'Oh no,' Aled assured me. 'Up top's been blocked off to stop any more stuff being dumped. I found another way out over by there.'

He pointed, and his helmet's lamp beam followed his hand. All I could see was a darker shadow against the slate-grey cavern wall. If Aled said that was the exit, that was good enough for me.

I got carefully to my feet. 'Where's the harp?'

'Here.' Aled had rested it against a convenient outcrop. 'Do you want to take it or shall I?'

I hesitated. I felt the bloody thing was my responsibility, but I'd be a lot happier working my way across this slope if I had both my hands free. 'If you don't mind.'

'No problem.' He picked it up and started walking.

I followed more slowly, half leaning so my gloved hands were never too far from the rocky slope. I was ready to throw myself down if I felt my feet slip. I'd take a few bruises over whatever injuries I might suffer in a worse fall.

At the side of the cave, Aled looked back to see how I was doing. He grinned. 'We'll make a caver of you yet.'

'Not a snowball's chance in hell.'

He laughed and waited for me. When I reached him, I caught a breath of the cool night air outside. I sucked it in. I wanted to push past Aled and fight my way out into the open. I felt as if I'd spent a lifetime under this mountain.

He held out the harp. 'Let me go first. I keep some planks wedged in here to keep the tourists out. Then there's brambles and all sorts after that.'

'Right.' I took the harp and gritted my teeth.

Aled went into the narrow cleft. I heard wood scrape on rock which wasn't the harp taking a battering for a change. The fresh scent of the night outside grew stronger. I heard rustling and a muffled curse from Aled. I guessed the brambles were fighting back. Then he yelled, startled and afraid. Something growled, low and threatening.

I forced myself through the crack in the mountainside. I smashed the brambles aside with the harp, not caring if I broke the fucking thing. I bumped into Aled. He was retreating back into the darkness. I was tall enough to see past him to realise why.

The Cŵn Annwn were waiting for us.

Chapter Nineteen

The red-eared dogs bared their long white teeth, snarling. Aled was still trying to retreat into the cave. I thought about thumping the closest one with the harp, if I could get past him. The harp was heavy enough to do some damage. If the hound dodged it, for fear of the harp's magic or just because it didn't fancy a smack in the head, that might give us enough space to get out of this narrow crevice.

What then? I still had the rowan ring on my hand under the glove. Okay, but if I shoved that down the throat of one trying to bite me, we still had to deal with its friend. I gripped the harp and lifted it up so I was looking through the strings and muttered to it, 'This would be a very good time to do whatever made her other creatures back off.'

A long-necked white shape swooped out of the luminous sky. The swan flew between us and the hounds, hissing fiercely. A second landed a few feet away with its wings spread wide and flapping loudly. Another hit the ground behind the closest dog. Its beak darted forward to stab the hound's rump. The beast spun around, baying. It wasn't interested in us any more.

More swans were landing. As soon as a hound lunged at one, the great bird sprang into the air. It didn't fly away though. The swan went straight for the attacking dog's head. Two or three others attacked its flanks and hindquarters. A swan's gaping beak might not be ideally suited to biting, but I saw one dog struck in the ribs so hard it staggered sideways.

The Cŵn Annwn fought back, snarling and snapping. They jumped up to try to catch the swans on the wing. White feathers spun away to vanish on the breeze. The sky was already pale with the first promise of dawn, but I couldn't see if those feathers had blood on them. My heart was racing and my mouth was dry, but there was nothing I could do.

Then the battle was over and our side had won. The Cŵn Annwn were racing away down the hillside. The swans in the air landed, and the ones on the ground shook out their wings with a rattling sound. I was about to count them when I remembered to put a hand over my eyes. I still registered the series of bright flashes as the swans shifted back to their human forms.

'Bloody hell!' Dazzled, Aled recoiled, banging into the harp and me.

'Sorry. I should have warned you about that.'

A familiar voice called out, 'Dan? Are you in there?'

'Yes, and I'm okay.' Now I did give Aled a shove, now that wouldn't send him straight into the Cŵn Annwn's jaws. 'Let's get out of here.'

He moved more slowly than I would have liked, but we fought our way through the tangle of brambles and out onto the side of the mountain.

'Fin?' I looked around.

'Over here.' She raised a hand to shield her eyes from my helmet's lamp.

I switched it off as Fin wrapped her arms around my waist. I closed my eyes to shut out everything else. I could smell the shampoo she liked scenting her hair as she tucked her head under my chin. I would have hugged her back properly, but I still had that bloody harp in one hand. I seriously considered chucking it away. To hell with the thing. It wasn't my problem any more.

Fin's hands found the gaping tears in the back of my hoodie and T-shirt. 'What on earth happened to you?' She was more incredulous than concerned. She could see I was walking and talking and not dripping blood onto the grass.

'This is what's causing all the mischief then?' a deep Irish voice asked, thoughtful.

I opened my eyes to see a burly man with an intense dark gaze. Standing beside Iris, he looked at least ten years older than her. Another woman and two men were there too. I didn't know any of them.

I offered the first man the harp. 'You're welcome to it.'

Fin loosened her hold on me and turned to see. 'What are you going to do with it?'

'First, we get it over the water.' The Irishman came over and took the harp. He peered at the carvings. The woman turned on the torch on her phone to see them more clearly, or maybe she was taking some video. I realised the intertwined designs showed the profiles of animal heads. Each one unravelled and flowed into the next. Goat changed into fox into otter into cat and back to goat again.

'How—?' I couldn't think how to ask the rest of my question.

The Irishman was examining the strings. He looked up. 'We pack it inside a bloody great suitcase and catch the ferry back to Dublin from Holyhead.' He grinned. 'You didn't imagine we'd be flying it back ourselves, did you?'

I wasn't going to admit that had been my first thought, and I couldn't see how they could manage, even if they used some sort of straps. Before I had to find a different answer, Fin reached for my gloved hand. 'Come on, let's get down to the car park.'

As everyone started walking, I was able to do a headcount. Blanche led the way down the path, followed by the four Irish swan shifters. As well as Fin and her two sisters, I could see their cousins, Will, Laurel and Holly. A lot of people had travelled an awfully long way in the twenty-four hours while I'd been waiting to start my new career as a burglar.

Fin squeezed my hand. 'That wasn't what we were expecting.'

'No,' I agreed. 'Do you know if the others are okay, back at the quarry?'

'Pretty much. No broken bones, anyway.'

That wasn't quite the reassurance I was looking for, but we reached an awkwardly steep bit of path. We stopped talking as we looked down to see where we were putting our feet. No one else was talking, so we walked the rest of the way to the car park in silence.

Six vehicles were parked together, so I assumed they belonged to our people, or to the Irish visitors Iris had enlisted. If they weren't, someone out for some dogging was going to be very confused. I wondered what story the others had come up with to explain why they were out here. Orienteering in the dark, navigating by the stars? We were too old to be doing some Duke of Edinburgh Award night hike.

A car door opened. The courtesy light showed me Eleanor Beauchene getting out of the driver's seat. Hazel Spinner got out of Aled's Fiesta with a young woman I didn't know. I realised she had driven the van here.

'Coffee!' Eleanor opened up her hatchback.

Hazel reached into the back seat of the van and took out a big Tupperware box. 'Flapjacks, anyone?'

'Melangell?' Aled looked at the other girl, astonished. 'Blimey.'

'Good evening to you, Aled James.' She was amused by his surprise. She took the lid off the box she was holding. 'Welsh cake? Homemade.'

Eleanor was filling travel mugs from thermos jugs standing in a crate in the back of her car. I recognised those jugs from the staff room at Blithehurst. From the smell, she had brought the good coffee. I guessed hot water had come from the same place as the home baking. Wise women are good at that sort of thing.

She looked up as Fin and I got closer. 'Tea, Dan?'

'If you've got it. Thanks.' I started passing cups of coffee out to Will, Blanche and the others.

Fin saw a smaller crate with plastic cartons of milk and a box of sugar lumps. She took it out of the boot and moved a few steps away so everyone could help themselves.

'I'm not sure how drinkable this will be.' Eleanor reached for a smaller thermos tucked at the back of the coffee jugs.

'Can someone tell me exactly happened up there?' Hazel's question was edged with impatience. 'Those weren't the creatures we saw in the quarry.'

That's what we had expected to find coming after us again, when we'd discussed how to make sure we could hand the harp over to Iris's friends from Dublin. Since we didn't know what might have happened to the hares, or how successful they would be at distracting the scary fairy's creatures a second time, the swans had volunteered to be ready and waiting when Aled and I came out of the mountain.

'Cŵn Annwn,' Aled said to no one in particular. He went on to say a whole lot more to Melangell in Welsh. She started talking to Hazel. Blanche and the others went over to listen, and to help themselves to a snack.

Eleanor waited as I stripped off my gloves. She nodded at the rowan ring as I worked it off my hand and shoved it into my pocket. 'So Asca was right about that coming in useful.'

'She certainly was.' I wondered what the dryad would say when I told her about punching the scary fairy in the face. If I told her. I was still wearing the vinyl gloves I'd worn in Annis Wynne's house. I stripped them off as well and wished I could wash my sweaty hands.

'She'll be glad to know you're still in one piece.' Eleanor handed me a mug of tea.

'And not stuck somewhere underground.' Being out on the mountainside was a good start, but I was really looking forward to being back in Blithehurst's woods.

Fin came over, and I poured milk into my tea. After a moment's thought, I added two lumps of sugar. I swirled the mug around for a minute before drinking it down. I was so thirsty I wouldn't have cared if it was so stewed it turned my teeth brown, but it was fine. Eleanor might be a coffee drinker, but someone, sometime, had told her not to leave the teabag in a thermos.

'Another?' She was ready to pour me a refill.

'In a bit, thanks.' I put the mug on the tray. 'Have you got my keys?'

Eleanor fished them out of a pocket. 'Here you go.'

'Cheers.' My Landy was at the end of the row of vehicles. I went over, opened up the back and found the bag I'd put in there earlier.

Fin handed the milk and sugar crate to Blanche and joined me. I gave her a quick kiss on the cheek. 'Everything went okay with Mr Williams?'

That was a stupid question. If it hadn't, she might not be here, and the Land Rover certainly wouldn't. Thankfully, he hadn't seemed particularly curious when I told him I was going out for the evening with some new friends. I asked if he could look after my keys, so my girlfriend could collect the Landy and pick me up later. I had shown him a picture of Fin on my phone.

'He was fine,' Fin assured me. 'I offered to show him my driving licence, but he said he was expecting me.' She grinned. 'I didn't even have to turn on the charm.'

I took off the hard hat and unclipped the belt that held the power pack. Putting everything down in the back of the Landy, I took the rowan ring, the chisel and my phone out of my pockets. I had a signal and the screen was still in one piece. That hard case had been worth every penny. I'd need to buy a new torch though. I like to keep one in the Land Rover for emergencies. I dragged the ruined hoodie and T-shirt off over my head.

'So what did that to your clothes?' Fin asked, a little bit tense.

'No idea. It was behind me in the dark. Did it leave a mark?'

She took a look at my back. 'No.'

She was relieved, and so was I. 'Good to know.'

I pulled on a fresh T-shirt. I had one more change of clothes back at the campsite, so I could wear those for the drive back to Blithehurst. I'd take a shower at Plas Brynwen before I packed away Eleanor's tent. I was really looking forward to getting back to a real bed and my own bathroom.

Fin yawned. 'Long day.'

'You're not kidding.' I hoped she'd got some rest when Eleanor had driven her, Blanche and Hazel over from Blithehurst.

'Not as long as Will's.' Fin yawned again.

I wondered if he had done all the driving over from Norfolk. Not that it really mattered. I realised I was hungry, now that everything was over.

'I could do with a bit of that flapjack.'

'Right you are.' She kissed my cheek and went to fetch some.

I took off my trainers and stripped off my combats. They weren't as filthy as I'd expected, but I might as well keep the new seats in the Landy as clean as possible. As I pulled on my spare trousers, I saw Melangell was talking to Hazel Spinner. Eleanor, Blanche and her cousins were listening with interest as they drank their coffee.

Aled and Will Saffrey were having a different conversation. Will's a photographer. His day job is brochures and PR stuff. His real love is wildlife and the countryside.

He was looking at the sharp-edged mountains against the paling sky. 'I'll have to come back here with my cameras sometime.'

'Ever been caving?' Aled grinned. 'There's plenty to see underground.'

'I live in Norfolk. Not known for its caves.' Will looked interested all the same.

Iris was over by a big Mercedes SUV with Irish plates. One of her friends lifted a large suitcase with four little wheels out of the back. There was just enough room in it for the harp. That was a relief. I rarely make a mistake measuring something by eye, but no one's infallible. This wouldn't have been a good time to be wrong. As I put my phone and my wallet into my pockets, I watched them pack the uncanny thing securely with what looked like old blankets. One of the Irishmen carefully zipped the case shut.

Fin came back with flapjack and Welsh cakes. She was looking over towards the SUV too.

'Thanks.' I took the flapjack and ate it in a couple of bites. It was good, with sultanas. 'Have you got any idea what they're going to do with it?'

'Not a clue,' she said around a mouthful of Welsh cake. 'Iris says they know what they're up to.' Her shrug said she trusted her sister's judgement.

Since we still knew next to nothing about the harp, I wasn't about to argue. 'Do you want another coffee? I wouldn't mind some more tea.'

'Okay.' Fin gathered up Aled's helmet and the belt with its battery pack so I could shut the back of the Land Rover. We walked over to join the others.

'Hiya, Dan.' Will greeted me with a grin. 'Good to see you again.'

'You too.' I nodded at Laurel, Holly and Blanche, to include them in that hello.

The SUV started its engine. We looked over and saw Iris in a clinch with the Irishman who seemed to be in charge. The others were already in the vehicle. He let Iris go and got into the front passenger seat. The SUV pulled away.

I turned to Eleanor. 'Can I have that other cup of tea now, please.'

'So are we done here now?' Blanche asked, brisk.

There was a moment of awkward silence. Eleanor went to the back of her car and came back with my refilled mug.

'Is there anything else you need us for?' she asked me.

Much as I wanted to spend more time with Fin, I couldn't lie. 'I can't think of anything. Are you heading straight back to Blithehurst? All of you?' I looked at Will. He nodded.

'I'd say so. Okay if we head off?' Eleanor looked at Hazel Spinner and Melangell.

'We're done here.' Hazel looked from Eleanor to me and back again, to make it clear she was talking to us both. 'I'll give you a ring once we've had a chance to swap notes. When I've had an update from Gillian about the boy.'

'Fair enough.' I nodded.

Everyone leaving the area had always been the plan, as long as no one was injured and needed first aid from the wise women. It was the main reason why Eleanor was driving, since she wasn't going to get involved in fighting off any shapeshifting creatures. A whole group of visitors trying to find somewhere to stay at short notice would be far too memorable if the police started making enquiries after a valuable antique was reported stolen.

'I'll see you later in the week, Aled.' Melangell grinned at him.

He took a moment to answer. 'Right you are.'

I could see it would be some while before he came to terms with what had happened tonight. He could do that on his own time. There were things we had to do first. 'We had better make sure the entrance to that cavern is blocked. So no tourists or dogs get in there.'

'What?' He looked at me blankly, then focused. 'Oh, yes. Right.'

Fin gave me a hug and a proper kiss. Letting her go was a hell of a wrench, but the others were getting into their cars. Blanche was the first to leave, driving Will's new Suzuki jeep. Eleanor stood by the open hatchback, waiting for Fin. I took Aled's caving gear from her and handed over the travel mug. 'I'll see you tomorrow at Blithehurst?'

'You will,' Fin said firmly.

I wondered if Blanche had wanted to get back to Dorset as soon as possible. If so, I didn't reckon much for my chances of persuading them to stay an extra night. Oh well. 'We should work out how to get a weekend off together. Plan that visit to Chester.'

'As soon as we can.' Fin gave me another quick kiss and ran across the car park to join Eleanor.

I went to give Aled back his caving helmet and lamp. He had been talking to Melangell and Hazel. They were both in the same car now, leaving his Fiesta van so he could get home. I watched Eleanor and Fin drive off. This tail end of the summer night felt chill and empty.

'Let's get this cave sorted,' I said to Aled, 'then we can get some sleep.' I'd got, what, ten hours' kip in the last forty-eight?

Aled was still trying to get his head around everything as the wise women drove away. 'I've known Melangell since we were kids. Well, secondary school anyway. I had no idea.' He broke off. 'Sorry. Right you are.'

I handed him the helmet and battery pack, and he put those in the back of his van. I kept the work gloves. Those brambles had been vicious. We headed back up the path as the twilight grew brighter. The climb made me realise how shatteringly tired I was. Never mind. We'd got Tyler back from the scary fairy, and she hadn't got the harp. I wondered what the Irish swans would tell us about it.

Aled was still wearing his caving overalls, so he forced his way into the brambles to find the planks he'd tossed aside. He passed the first one out to me.

'So, this sort of thing, you do it a lot, do you?'

'Hell no.' I dropped the plank onto the grass. 'Mostly my life's as normal as anyone else's. Work, bills, trying to work out how to spend time with my girlfriend. Then something weird comes up and we have to stop it becoming a problem.'

Doing that was a damn sight easier now I wasn't facing these challenges on my own.

'Right.' Aled still looked dazed.

He handed me another two planks and I stacked them with the first one. He fought his way free of the brambles, and we carried the planks into the cleft. Aled went in first and I passed him the lengths of wood. After a bit of thumping, he reappeared.

'Right. That should do it.'

Just to be sure, he dragged the tangled brambles back together to hide where we'd forced our way through. Then we walked down to the car park.

I got the Landy keys out of my pocket. 'I have no idea where we are. I hope Fin left the satnav set up.'

'You'll be better off following me.' Aled sounded pretty much back to normal. 'There are a couple of places around here where satnavs think a car can follow the same path as a sheep.'

'Right. Thanks.' I had been caught out by those artificially unintelligent routes before. Sending me down a single-track lane with grass growing along the middle to save half a mile by cutting off a corner when the main roads would have been twice as fast.

'I'll take you to the Caergynan turn,' Aled was saying, 'then I'll head off home. See you for a coffee at the centre in the morning? Say ten o'clock?'

'Sounds like a plan.' Between the birdsong and the kids in the campsite, a lie-in was something else that would have to wait until I got back to Blithehurst.

Aled got into his van in his caving overalls and boots. I headed for the Landy. As I followed him out of the car park, I wondered how far he had to drive. I realised I had no idea where he lived, or if he lived with anyone, come to that.

Maybe he'd tell me in the morning. Right now, I had to concentrate on following the Fiesta's tail lights through these twisting roads without falling asleep at the Landy's wheel. I really was knackered.

Aled must have been exhausted too. When the white shape leaped out of the hedge into the middle of the lane, instinct made him swerve hard to the right. If his reactions had been a fraction quicker, he might have made an emergency stop. Instead, he ran the Fiesta hard into a stone wall with a crash of shattered glass and mangled metal.

I slammed on my brakes. I was just able to avoid hitting the Fiesta. I saw the white thing in the road was a shaggy goat with curving yellow horns. Only, no it wasn't. It shifted into something with a goat's head and two arms and two legs and ran away beyond the next bend in the lane.

I didn't care where the fuck it had gone. We had a much bigger problem. A creature of living flame stalked through the broken glass on the tarmac, where the impact had shattered the Fiesta's side window. Aled was fighting to get the airbag out of his way as he tried to force the buckled driver's door open.

Chapter Twenty

I got out of the Landy as fast as I could. 'Hey, arsehole! Over here!'

I had no idea what I was going to do if the blazing creature came for me, but Aled was trapped. He might get that door open if I could get him a few more minutes.

The thing ignored me. I couldn't even tell if it heard me. It laid a fiery hand on the Fiesta's front wing. Smoke billowed out from the engine. I heard Aled yelling, terrified.

I raced around to the back of the Land Rover. Simon and I agreed you should always keep a fire extinguisher in a vehicle. I grabbed mine and ran towards the crash. The creature was melting the sagging, shattered windscreen, and Aled was screaming.

The fire prevention officer who does Blithehurst's annual inspection and staff training day says ABC dry powder extinguishers are good against three things: burning wood and paper, flaming liquids and electrical fires. They're a solid all-purpose choice to keep in the boot of your car. They're fuck all use against arcane creatures that make coal mines explode. I barely managed to distract it even though I emptied the extinguisher, spraying up and down its back.

Barely was better than nothing. It turned to glare at me. Don't ask how something without a face could do that. It just did. As the garnet pinpoints of its eyes fixed on me, I rammed the base of the extinguisher right between them. I felt my bare hand scorching and realised from its weight the cylinder must be made from aluminium, not steel. Fuck.

I threw it as hard as I could at the creature regardless. As I took a swift step back, the extinguisher passed straight through the blazing figure and hit the burning car with a clang. The creature took a step towards me. I backed off some more. It followed me again. Those flaming hands were reaching for me.

I couldn't see past the fucking thing, but I could see thick black smoke billowing upwards. Aled was yelling. So he wasn't dead – yet. I had to keep him that way – and me as well. The extinguisher wasn't the only thing I'd grabbed out of the back of the Landy. The rowan ring was battered and splintered, but the twig was still twisted in a circle. Backing away as fast as I could, I sent it spinning towards the fiery creature with a flick of my wrist. I had no idea if it would do any good, but I had fuck all else to try.

Another warning the fire prevention officer repeats is never throw an aerosol onto a bonfire. I'm pretty sure no one would be that stupid at Blithehurst, but I know why she says it. When a building site's been cleared, the quickest way to get rid of the trash is usually to burn it. More than once some tosser has chucked an old spray paint can into the flames.

This was like that, only more so. The fucking thing exploded. I ducked away as soon as I threw the talisman, but I still felt the sting of flash burns. I wondered if I was missing my eyebrows.

That didn't matter. What had happened to Aled? I couldn't see him in the Fiesta's driving seat, dead or alive. The whole vehicle was burning now. Had he slumped down, out of sight? Between the stink of the burning van and the horrifying thought of what I might find, I felt ready to vomit as I went as close as I dared. The heat was brutal.

Movement caught my eye on the far side of the Fiesta. I skirted the rear end of the fire, ready to strangle the scary fairy, those red-eared dogs or anything else with my bare hands. I saw Aled sprawled on his back on the ground. The passenger door hung open. He must have used both feet to kick it free, knowing getting out of there was life or death.

His face was red and blistered, but he looked up at me and opened his mouth. I couldn't hear him over the roar of the fire. That didn't matter. I hooked my hands under his armpits and dragged him down the road until the dawn chill overrode the heat from the burning car. He was muttering savagely in Welsh. That meant he was still conscious. I dragged him onto the narrow verge and propped him against a stone wall. I tried not to think of those TV medical dramas where someone gets rescued from a fire, but they die later from damage to their throat or lungs.

'You have to stay sitting up. You can't lie down.' The fire prevention officer taught us first aid for burn victims. That was one of the two things I could remember for when someone's face was hurt.

My hands shook as I got my phone out and called 999. I looked down at Aled as I answered the emergency operator's questions. His eyes were swelling shut now.

'Fire service, and an ambulance. There's a car fire and the driver's been hurt – burned.' I could see several blackened holes in Aled's overalls, but I had no idea how bad any injuries underneath might be. At least he'd been wearing his gloves, or maybe he'd dragged them on when he saw the threat heading his way. Hopefully that had saved his hands.

'Sorry, I've no idea where I am.'

The operator assured me they could get a GPS fix from my phone.

'How soon will they get here?'

She could only tell me 'as soon as possible'. She told me to stay on the phone, so I did, though I wasn't really listening as she carried on talking. I headed back to the Landy. I had a litre-and-a-half bottle of mineral water in the back. I'd bought that in the supermarket in case I got stuck in the traffic around here on a hot day. That was the other thing I remembered about burns. Get water on them as soon as you can. Just water, lots of it, and nothing else, while you wait for the ambulance. Of course, the fire prevention officer assumed we'd be dealing with someone who'd got burned in a kitchen, or at the very least within reach of a cold tap.

I knelt on one knee beside Aled and put the phone down on the road. 'I'm going to pour water on your face. I'm really sorry if this hurts, but it's the only thing I can do to help until the paramedics get here.'

He raised a shaking hand to give me a thumbs up. I unscrewed the cap on the bottle. Thank fuck I'd gone for still water instead of sparkling, or Coke. I started pouring as slowly as I could, to get the maximum benefit.

Aled's whole body went stiff. He turned his head away. He couldn't help it. I used my free hand to grab his gloved one. His grip was strong enough to crush my knuckles, but he managed to keep still as I carried on pouring the water. He couldn't help whimpering. I squeezed his hand. I hated to think how much pain he was in.

I hated this. All of this. I've had the shit beaten out of me a few times, going up against uncanny things, but this was ten times worse. Twenty times worse. A hundred. Not just because the thing had been made of fire, and yes, that had been fucking terrifying. What was worse, far far worse, was seeing someone else get hurt. Seeing Aled suffering was more painful than any flash burns on my own face or arms. I felt so fucking useless. I'd done everything I could, and that had been nowhere near enough. People talk about searing guilt. Now I knew what that meant.

The last of the water trickled down his face to soak the front of his overalls. He was breathing heavily and starting to shake.

I took hold of his hands. 'I'm going to go and see what's in my first aid kit. Stay here.'

That was a fucking stupid thing to say, because where was he going to go? My brain was struggling to keep up with my mouth. I squeezed Aled's hands one last time and got up. The van was still burning, but there was enough space for me to run past it, back to the Landy. Thank fuck I'd listened when the fire prevention officer had told us every vehicle should have a proper kit, not a plastic box with a few plasters and something for wasp stings. Why the fuck hadn't I remembered it sooner?

The Landy's back door was still swinging open. I found the green box with the white cross and opened it with shaking hands. I fumbled through a handful of sealed white packets with different-coloured writing. I'd read the list of contents when I'd bought this kit, but my mind was a total blank. Emergency foil blanket? Toss it. Adherent dressing pad. No way. Washproof plasters. No fucking use. Sterile burn dressings, two of them, ten by ten centimetres. Thank fuck for that. I took them out of the box and dropped them onto the road.

FUCK!

I slammed the Land Rover door. My stinging palm and the noise startled some sense into me. I hit the door with the flat of my hand again. That helped a bit more. I started to take a deep breath, and stopped when acrid fumes caught in the back of my throat. Coughing up a lung would waste time Aled couldn't spare. Okay, I was calmer now. I picked up the sealed dressings. There was no way I could tear them open, but there were scissors in the first aid kit. I opened the door, found those and took everything back to Aled.

'Right. I've got two proper burn dressings. We're going to use them on your eyes.' I started taking his work gloves off as I was talking to him. 'I'll put the first one on and you hold it, okay? Then we'll do the second one.'

Aled nodded jerkily. His hands looked a bit grimy, but even in this dim light, I could see they weren't burned. That was such a relief, I had to swallow hard before I could go on. My eyes weren't just stinging from the acrid fumes.

'Right, I'm cutting the first pack open. It's a pad soaked in something. Can you smell that? Does it feel all right?'

I touched as little of the dressing as I possibly could as I laid it over his red and swollen right eye. I guided his hand to hold it there, and then I did his left eye. Whatever the dressings were soaked with smelled reassuringly medical and quite nice at the same time. I vaguely remembered a whiff of something like that in Fin's bathroom once. It was a hell of a lot nicer than the reek of the fire.

'How does that feel?'

Aled managed a slight nod. All I could do was kneel there and hold his shoulders to let him know he wasn't alone.

'You're going to be okay. The ambulance will be here any moment. You're going to be okay. They'll be here soon.'

I kept repeating myself. I couldn't think what else to say. I couldn't tell if he believed me. I wasn't sure I believed it myself. But there was nothing else I could do. We could only wait. I looked down for my phone, but I couldn't see it. I had no idea what the time had been when Aled had crashed. I had no idea how long we had been waiting.

'This was merely a warning. Make amends or worse will follow.'

The goat-headed creature was back, standing a few metres up the lane. It stared straight at me. I dropped Aled's hands and sprang to my feet. Fuck. Why hadn't I grabbed that chisel when I'd had the chance?

The creature mocked me with a bleating laugh and disappeared. Then I heard diesel engines coming up behind us. I turned around to see the flicker of blue lights.

Of course, Sod's Law meant the fire engine and the ambulance arrived behind the Land Rover. There was no way I could move my vehicle to let them through in this narrow lane. I wasn't even sure if they could see past the burning Fiesta, to realise we were further up the road.

'Wait here. I'll get help.' I patted Aled's shoulder and set off towards the fire engine. Then I came back and picked up my phone. The last thing I needed was a boot crushing that.

As I skirted the car fire, firefighters were already smothering it with foam. I left them to it, passing the Landy on the other side to their hose. I met a paramedic coming the other way. He was a middle-aged bloke with a balding shaved head and a backpack slung on one shoulder. Above his mask, his eyes looked as if nothing was going to surprise him.

'The casualty's on the other side of the fire. His face got burned. I had some water, so I tried— I tried—' I couldn't think what to say.

'All right, mate, we'll get him.' The amiable Scouser took my elbow. 'You wait here, there's a good lad.'

Before I realised what was going on, he sat me down in the open back of the Landy. He shouted something to his partner, who was waiting by the fire engine. The other paramedic was younger than me, lean and quick-eyed, with wiry dark hair. He disappeared and came back with some sort of folding contraption as well as another bag. I guessed he'd got those out of the ambulance.

'You wait here,' the Scouser told me again. He and the younger paramedic headed up the lane.

I heard a shouted conversation somewhere at the front of the Landy, but I couldn't make any sense of the words. More firefighters were intent on doing things around their engine. They didn't need me getting in their way. I stayed where I was. To be honest, I wasn't sure that my legs would hold me if I tried to stand up.

The chemical smell of the foam rose over the stink of burning plastic and scorched metal. I looked up at the sky and wondered when the sun had risen. I hadn't noticed. I looked down at my phone. The battery was on its last legs. My first thought was relief. If I couldn't phone anyone, I wouldn't have to explain...

The guilt came surging back. I'd agreed to this plan, thinking I was running most of the risks. That was okay. That was my choice, and I can take care of myself. But Aled had been attacked. Not for what he had done but because he was working with me. He sure as shit didn't deserve any of this.

That wasn't even the end of it. The shapeshifting creature who had made him crash said this was a warning. It said I had to make amends. How the fuck was I supposed to do that, even if I wanted to, with the sodding harp on its way to Ireland? What more could the scary fairy do to hurt other people, thinking that would force my hand? Who the hell would be next?

The paramedics reappeared, carrying Aled on a sort of folding chair. The firefighters stood aside so they could get past the engine to the ambulance. I went after them. No one tried to stop me. I didn't get in the way as the paramedics lifted Aled into the back of their vehicle and got him onto a hospital trolley. I couldn't see his face. That was completely covered with a thick white mask now. I could see he was moving to help shift himself though. He was still conscious.

The paramedics had already sliced through the arms and legs of his overalls. I guessed that was to see how badly he had been burned elsewhere. They weren't slapping burn dressings on him, so there couldn't be anything too bad. Right?

Aled lay back on the trolley as the bald paramedic got a needle into his arm and started a drip. He was nearly as quick at doing that as Gillian's friend. I wondered if they knew each other.

'So how are you?' The younger paramedic was standing in front of me.

I blinked. I had no idea where the hell he had come from. 'I'm—' My mouth was so dry I could hardly speak.

The paramedic handed me a bottle of water. 'Let's get a better look at you.'

He was as Welsh as Aled, and he sounded as if he was smiling, though I couldn't see that through his mask. I drank the bottle of water as he checked me over. I lowered it when he reached for my chin and tilted my head back so he could look up my nose.

'You were lucky, mate. I've seen worse cases of sunburn on Harlech Beach. Get something to take the heat out of your face and arms at the chemist and you'll be fine.'

He sounded relieved. So was I. In the ambulance, the older paramedic stood up to adjust Aled's drip and looked at us. 'Time to be on our way.'

'Where are you taking him?' I asked quickly.

'Ysbyty Gwynedd, Bangor.' The younger paramedic hesitated. 'Are you, like, family?'

'No, a friend.' Thankfully, that bottle of water had really helped clear my head. 'I'll follow – when I can get my Land Rover out of here.'

'Are you sure you're okay to drive?' The paramedic looked for his older partner's opinion about that.

'I am,' I told them both firmly. 'I need to know how Aled is, once a doctor's seen him. There are people I'll have to call.' That was the truth, although I knew they would read a different meaning into what I was saying.

'As long as you're sure you're okay.' The older paramedic gave me a measuring look. 'You'll have a bit of a wait, mind, till they're finished up here.' He jerked his head at the fire engine.

His partner offered me a blue disposable mask. 'You'll need this to get into the hospital.'

I took it with a nod. 'Thanks.'

'Right then,' he said briskly. 'We'll be off.'

They closed up the back of the ambulance and drove away. I couldn't see Aled, but the paramedics didn't race off with sirens and blue lights. I really hoped that meant his burns weren't too bad. I had to wait before I could follow them though. I stood there and watched the sky brighten. Birds started to sing in the hedgerows on either side of the lane. I tried not to think how tired I was.

A bit later, a gloved hand tapped my shoulder. As I turned around, a firefighter took off her helmet. Her dark hair was sodden with sweat. I quickly put on the blue hospital mask I had in my hand. It seemed the polite thing to do.

'That's your Land Rover, right? If we back up to the last passing place, do you think you can turn around and get it out of here? Or one of us can turn it for you.'

'Yes, sure, I'll do it, thanks.' I rubbed my face and regretted it instantly, as the flash burns on my cheekbones stung.

The firefighter looked at me. 'That was your fire extinguisher, was it? And the bottle of water on the victim's burns? The first aid kit?'

'Yes.' I wondered why she was asking.

She pursed her lips. 'I should probably tell you not to put yourself at risk, but that was good work.' She put her helmet back on and walked away.

That was some consolation. Not much, but something. I made my way past the fire engine to the Landy and closed up the back. Another firefighter came over as I got into the driving seat. Something about his gear and his attitude made me think he was in charge.

'Do you have any idea what made your friend crash?'

'There was something in the road, a sheep maybe? I think he swerved to avoid it?' I managed a smile and quickly closed the door before he could ask me anything else.

Shit. Of course they would assume I was a witness to whatever had happened. There were going to be questions, and the firefighters or the paramedics would have made a note of the Landy's number plate. Aled and I needed to get our story straight before either of us talked to the cops, the fire brigade, his insurance company or anyone else. I had no idea how we were going to do that in a hospital. Even if I was allowed to see him, there would be nurses and doctors around.

First things first. I had to find out how he was. I'd left my keys in the ignition, so I started the engine. As the fire engine started reversing down the road, I hauled on the steering wheel. The lane was so narrow, I didn't manage a three-point turn, but I made it in about six or seven, which was good enough. Not that the firefighters were paying attention. They were still busy around the burned-out van. That gave me something else to feel guilty about. I'd been able to salvage my Landy, with Simon's help and my savings. Aled's van was a write-off. Even with good insurance, he wouldn't get paid what that had been worth to him.

Further down the lane, the fire engine had pulled into a farm entrance that I didn't even remember passing. I raised a hand to acknowledge the driver. He waved to me. As soon as I was past, I put my foot down. I wanted to be well out of sight before I pulled over to ask the satnav where the hell I should be going. Thankfully, when I did that, it found the hospital the paramedic had mentioned easily. I also remembered to put my phone on charge. I put it on silent too. I kept yawning, and honestly, I wasn't at all sure I should be driving. Since I didn't have a choice, I had better keep distractions to a minimum.

I opened my window as well. Away from the blaze and in this enclosed space, I realised my clothes were saturated with fumes. The harsh reek caught in the back of my throat. At least the mask helped filter it out and the cool wind in my face helped keep me awake.

Thankfully, it wasn't far to a decent-sized road, and there was sod all traffic about. Once I got close to Bangor, the road signs as well as the satnav directed me to the hospital. Miraculously, the parking was free, and this early in the day, there were plenty of spaces. I parked and wondered what to do next. I've never had anything to do with hospitals. I wasn't even born in one. Seeing signs to the main entrance, I followed those. I went through the double doors, but there was no one at the reception desk. I followed the signs to A&E.

A lot more people than I expected were sitting on hard plastic chairs looking miserable. Plenty were clearly in pain, though no one seemed to be bleeding. I went up to what I guessed was the main desk, where a young nurse was busy with a computer. She looked nearly as exhausted as the patients waiting to be seen. I waited for her to finish what she was doing.

She managed a tight smile as she assessed me with an expert eye. 'The current waiting time for non-urgent cases—'

I raised a hand. 'I'm fine. A friend of mine was brought here in an ambulance a while ago. Aled James. He was burned in a car fire.' Saying that sent a chill down my back. 'Can you tell me how he is? There are people I need to call.'

'Oh, right.' Now the nurse realised I hadn't come to A&E after a sleepless night with sunburn, her smile was more friendly. 'I'll see what I can find out.'

She headed off to an area with curtained-off beds and a whole load of busy people. I looked around for a coffee machine, but I couldn't see one. I didn't dare go anywhere, so I waited. Then I waited some more.

A different nurse appeared, looked around, and headed straight for me. She was older and her face was stern. 'You were asking about Aled James?'

'Yes. I know I'm not a relative, but I was with him at the accident. I need to let people know what's happened.' I wished I knew how to deliberately turn on some charm like Fin and her sisters. Though from the nurse's expression, I wasn't at all sure that would work. This was a woman not to be messed with, no matter who you thought you were.

'Do you have some ID?'

'Yes, sure.' I wasn't sure why she was asking, but I got out my wallet and showed her my driving licence.

'Thank you, Mr Mackmain.' She sniffed as she reached into a pocket. 'Mr James asked if I could give you his keys if you came here. He says, can you take them up to the centre first thing and give them to Daisy? He said you'd understand?'

If she didn't think so, I'd be in trouble. I nodded as I reached for the keys. 'Thank you very much. Yes, I understand. Please, tell him I'll do that. Tell him not to worry.'

If Aled was talking and able to think about his shop, that had to be good news. I was impressed he'd had the presence of mind to take his keys when he was fighting his way out of his burning van. Then I remembered his blistered face and felt sick with guilt again.

'Please, can you tell me how he is? Daisy will want to know.'

The nurse considered that for a long moment. 'He'll be transferred to a specialist burns unit as soon as we know where there's a bed. That'll be in the Morriston in Swansea or the Wythenshawe in Manchester.'

Shit. How bad did burns have to be to need a specialist? I had no clue. 'Oh,' I said. 'Right, thanks.'

I was ready to leave, but the way she was looking at me made me uneasy. 'Is there anything…?' I wasn't sure what I was asking.

'He told me what you were up to.'

'Sorry?' What had he told her? Could I possibly persuade her he was away with the fairies on painkillers? Which was a poor choice of words after last night.

'You think you're invincible, you young men.' The nurse was calm and polite, and she sounded more and more Welsh as she went on. 'What's so enthralling about a cave full of junk? And don't give me some old flannel about going there in the middle of the night so no one else could follow you. What would have happened if one of you'd had an accident? How many first responders would have had to risk themselves to save you from your own stupidity? What if you'd both got stuck? The pair of you could be dead in there and no one the wiser for days. Did you ever stop and think about that?'

She wasn't raising her voice. Regardless, everyone could see I was getting a well-deserved bollocking. The people waiting on the closest chairs were watching with interest, welcoming any distraction from whatever accident or emergency had brought them here.

I looked down at the keys in my hand, hiding my relief. If Aled had been able to remember the story we had come up with in case I needed an alibi for the police, he couldn't be doped up to the eyeballs. Now I knew what he'd said, we could give the same version of events, more or less. We were owed a bit of luck.

'I'm sorry,' I mumbled, still looking at the keys. I could see these were his house keys, as well as the ones for the workshop. The striking red leather fob with a silver dragon's head on it had to be his own work. 'You're right. We didn't think. We won't do anything like that again.'

'Your friend won't be doing much of anything for the rest of the summer,' she said crisply. 'Think about that.'

I looked up to promise I would, and I hoped she would see that I meant it, but she was already walking away. I gave the closest man smirking at me a hard stare instead. He immediately found something to look at on a nearby noticeboard.

I stuck Aled's keys in a pocket and headed out. I really was fit to drop. I definitely wasn't fit to drive. I went back to the Landy and set the alarm on my phone for 7 a.m. That wouldn't give me much sleep, but anything was better than nothing. I'd seen signs for a superstore on my way here, and a quick search online told me that's when it opened. The cafe didn't open for another hour after that, but I could get something to eat off the shelves, and with luck, some clean clothes. This trip was getting expensive, I thought as I closed my eyes.

Not as expensive as the night had been for Aled. How long was he going to be off work? That was going to cost him, even if he had self-employed income insurance. If he didn't, I guessed he could claim some sort of benefits, but that would be a nightmare of forms and systems designed to make people give up. I felt guilty all over again. Right now, Aled would be safely asleep in his own bed if he'd never met me. That's the last thing I remember thinking before I fell asleep.

Chapter Twenty-One

The phone alarm startled me awake. After a moment of utter confusion, I realised where I was. I felt like absolute crap, and I had a thumping headache. I wound down the Land Rover's window for some fresh air. The stink of the vehicle fire, of stale sweat and whatever I'd picked up on my trainers last night was enough to make me retch. I took a few deep breaths, and thankfully that urge receded. My mouth still tasted like something had crawled in there and died though.

I was still absolutely knackered, but I reckoned I could go a couple of hours without crashing completely, literally or metaphorically. I scrubbed my face with my hands and realised I had fallen asleep wearing that hospital mask. I felt the sting of those flash burns I'd forgotten about too. Maybe I wasn't as awake as I thought.

At least my face wasn't as sore as it had been. Dryad blood means I heal fast. I really, really hoped Aled had inherited something similar from his mysterious ancestor. I pulled off the mask and took a few more deep breaths. I started the engine and left the car park. The superstore was only on the other side of the hospital.

There weren't many people wandering the aisles this early, though I couldn't avoid them all. When I got too close, I saw from their expressions that I must absolutely reek. I could see one of the security guards was watching me too. I found what I needed as fast as I could and headed for the self-checkout. Hopefully, seeing I was able to pay would reassure the security guard a bit. Grabbing my two bags of shopping, I headed for the toilets.

Seeing myself in the mirror, I was surprised the bloke on the door had even let me in. My face and hair were filthy and so were my arms and hands. My eyes were bloodshot and shadowed, making me look like someone to cross the road to avoid. Maybe the security guard hadn't wanted to risk challenging me. Maybe he was ringing for back-up.

I swallowed a couple of paracetamol with a handful of tap water and stripped off my foul T-shirt. If anyone came in, they'd just have to deal with my bare chest. I ripped open a pack of wet wipes and scrubbed every bit of me that I could reach. After using them all up, I looked and felt a whole lot better. Cleaning my teeth with a new brush helped even more. Blowing my nose was a bit disconcerting, when I saw how black that made the tissue from one of the toilet stalls. How much crap had I breathed in from the fire last night?

I chucked the tissue in the bin. What was done was done. I was still breathing, wasn't I? I had more important things to do than worry about stuff I couldn't change. I collected up the grimy wipes and binned them as well. I chucked the filthy T-shirt in there too. That was a waste, but I had no idea how long it would be before I could do some laundry. I couldn't get rid of the fire stink entirely though. The store didn't have jeans or joggers that would fit. I didn't even bother looking for trainers in a size 14.

I rubbed after-sun lotion onto my face, hands and arms, and pulled on one of two new T-shirts. My reflection was much less scary now. The security guard looked very relieved when he saw me heading out of the store.

Out in the car park, I opened the Landy's front windows to let the breeze blow out any lingering stink while I leaned on the bonnet and ate a Cornish pasty and a whole bag of jam doughnuts. Once I started the pasty, I realised I was absolutely ravenous. The store sold iced coffee in tins, and I drank two of those as well. Right now, I needed the caffeine jolt.

I got behind the wheel and checked my phone. The battery was charged, and I had no new messages. There was no reason there should be any, I realised. Aled and I were the only people who knew we hadn't got home safe last night. Fin and everyone else was probably still asleep, thinking we'd outwitted the scary fairy. I put down the phone. Wrecking their day could wait until I'd passed on Aled's keys. You do the job that's in front of you.

I wondered how Aled was. Had he spent the night in too much pain to sleep or was he sedated? Would he wake up to find himself at the other end of Wales or a hundred miles away in Manchester? Did he even have his phone? If he did, was it still working? Just thinking about the aggravation ahead of him gave me a hollow feeling in my gut. Resolute, I shook it off. If Aled couldn't tell anyone where he was, it was up to me to tell Daisy. I guessed she was the Goth-looking girl I'd seen on the till on Saturday. I turned the key in the ignition.

The traffic was getting heavier as I left Bangor, but this was a weekday rush hour rather than the tourist gridlock of holiday cottage changeover and day-trippers at weekends. Once I was out of Bangor, I made decent time back to Caergynan. I stopped at Plas Brynwen, where there were enough people up and about for me to drive the Landy through the site to Eleanor's tent without drawing too much attention. The tent was just as I'd left it. I wondered if the rowan rings and the yew soil were keeping more than the Cŵn Annwn away.

Asking the wise women or the dryads about that could wait. I got my washkit and towel and went for a shower. I'd had enough of smelling like a baby's backside, even if that was better than the reek of the fire. Once I was finally, properly clean, I put on the second clean shirt I'd just bought, clean underpants and the combats I'd worn last night when I was crawling through the caves. I wiped as much of the dirt off as I could with Eleanor's damp tea towel. The end result wasn't great, but the alternative was the ones that stank of the fire, so I didn't have a choice.

More than anything else, I wanted to pack up the tent and leave. I wanted to drive until I found a travel inn and lock myself in a room where shapeshifters and fairies couldn't find me. I needed a decent night's – day's – sleep before I headed for Blithehurst. I was so tired I could barely think straight. Instead, I walked up the hill to the Meilyr Centre. I'd make some phone calls once I'd kept my promise to Aled and handed over his keys. Then I could leave.

The courtyard gates were already open. The caffi was doing good business selling the traders their first hot or cold drink of the day. The sky was clear and it was getting warm. The sign on Aled's door still said 'Closed', but I could see someone moving around inside. Of course Aled wouldn't have the only key to this place.

I knocked, and the purple-haired girl looked around from restocking the display. She had the same dramatic dark eye make-up but no lipstick, which looked a bit odd. Then I realised there was no point in lipstick if she was going to be wearing a mask. She saw I wasn't Aled, and her smile turned from a hello for a friend to customer service for a tourist. She came over to twist the latch and opened the door a crack, using a thick-soled buckled boot to stop me pushing it wider.

'We're not open just yet—'

'Are you Daisy?'

That surprised her. 'Yes?'

'Aled asked me to give you these.' I held up his keys.

She recognised the dragon's head key fob and reached through the gap to take them. Now she was concerned. 'Where is he?'

'He's been in an accident.'

Shocked, she pressed her hand to her mouth. 'What's happened?'

I glanced over my shoulder to see several other traders watching us. 'Can I come in?'

'What? Yes, of course.' She stepped back quickly.

I went inside but stayed by the door. I didn't want to crowd her. She was going to have enough to deal with. 'He crashed his car last night.'

'Where? When?' She stared at me, confused. 'Sorry, but who are you?'

'My name's Dan.' That was as much as I wanted to tell her. Aled clearly hadn't said a word about what we were up to. 'Listen, he's in hospital.'

Her dark eyes filled with tears. 'Which hospital? How bad is he hurt?'

Shit. Was she Aled's girlfriend? I should have thought of that earlier. Aled hadn't said, but he hadn't exactly had the chance. I should have rung Fin and asked her for advice on how to handle this.

'He's at the big hospital in Bangor. Well,' I said hastily, 'that's where he was last night. They were talking about transferring him to Swansea or Manchester.'

'Why?' She stared, horrified. 'What's happened?'

'The car caught fire. He got out, but he got burned. I was following right behind him, so I rang for an ambulance. When I got to the hospital, a nurse gave me his keys. She told me that he said I should give them to you. He can't be too bad if he could do that, don't you think?'

I stopped talking. She wasn't listening to me any more. She went around to the back of the counter and unlocked a drawer. She straightened up and threaded her arms through the straps of a small black leather backpack. She wasn't crying, not really, but tears running down her face were dark with mascara. 'I have to go. I need to lock up. You have to leave.'

'Right.' I retreated to the door. 'Is there anything I can do?'

'Has anyone fed Enfys?'

'Sorry? I don't know—'

'The cat.' She shook her head. 'Never mind.'

I couldn't tell if she was irritated with herself or with me, but I backed out of the shop regardless. Daisy followed so closely that I thought she was going to push straight past me. Instead, she locked the door and hurried away.

I let her go, feeling guilty about her as well now. Once she found out where Aled was and what the doctors were saying, she would have to tell a whole lot of people and deal with all sorts of of hassle. There wasn't anything I could do about that either.

Around the courtyard, concerned faces watched Daisy leave. They looked in my direction, openly curious. I decided against buying a coffee. That would come with questions I really didn't want to answer. Besides, I had to make some phone calls. I had no more excuses.

I walked towards the archway. The Cŵn Annwn appeared and blocked my path. Just my path. No one else could see them. A man carrying a cardboard box walked straight through the one on my left, like some movie special effect. The hounds were no illusion as far as I was concerned, though. They were watching me, and one had its red ears pricked. It was more than ready to chase me down if I tried to run. The other didn't look quite so alert, yawning to reveal ferocious teeth and a lolling scarlet tongue. I wondered how the hell I was going to get past them.

'You owe me a new lock on my front door, forest boy.'

A little old lady was sitting at one of the courtyard tables. Her fluffy white hair was so thin I could see her shiny pink scalp. Despite the warm day, she wore a cream cardigan over a green blouse and dark blue stretchy trousers. I recognised the walker by her chair before I put a name to her face. She'd been asleep without her teeth in when I'd seen her snoring in her bed. What the hell was Annis Wynne doing here?

'You and me, we need to talk.' She might be five feet tall and who knew how old, but that sounded like a threat I had better take seriously.

What was she, really? I looked closely at her, searching for some hint. She stared at me and blinked, slowly and deliberately. I didn't see the telltale flash of an uncanny gaze. Her eyes were so faded they were almost colourless, but nothing suggested she was anything but a very little, very old lady.

'Make yourself useful and fetch us a tray of tea,' she snapped.

Her voice got the Cŵn Annwn's attention. They looked at her, expectant. She gestured with a wrinkled hand, and they lay down to watch us with their heads resting on their front paws.

Seriously, who the hell was she? Since I wasn't going anywhere until she told her dogs to let me pass, I might as well find out. 'Okay.'

I went over to the caffi counter, where the bloke serving drinks was more interested in me than ever. 'Two pots of tea, please.'

'Right you are.' He put mugs and a miniature bottle of milk on a tray. 'It's been a while since we've seen old Mrs Wynne in here. She doesn't get out much these days. You know her, do you?'

'First time we've met. Friend of the family.' That might even be sort of true. She knew enough to call me 'forest boy'. I took out my wallet and pretended to check how much cash I had.

The caffi guy took the hint and filled two teapots with teabags and hot water from the spout on the espresso machine. 'Everything all right with Aled James, is it? Daisy left in a hurry.'

'He was in a car crash last night. He's in hospital in Bangor with some nasty burns.'

Caffi guy's eyes widened as he put down the second teapot. 'Well that's no good.'

'No,' I agreed. 'I'll pay by card, please.'

'Oh, right.' He tapped his screen to put the teas through his till.

I brushed my debit card across the terminal. It bleeped. 'I was just passing on the news. Thanks.'

I picked up the tray and walked off before he could ask me anything else. I felt a real shit, but I couldn't help hoping caffi guy and the other people here would be distracted by Aled's accident, instead of wondering what Annis

Wynne and I might have to talk about. I put the tray on the table. She slapped down a handful of coins.

'You'll take that for the tea.'

I saw she was paying me the exact price. She wasn't going to be in my debt.

'Thank you.' I gathered up the coins and slid them into my back pocket. A charity box could have them, the first chance I got. Just to be on the safe side. I filled my mug and waited to see if she would ask me to pour her tea. She didn't, even though she had to use both stiff and shaking hands to slowly lift and tilt the milk bottle and then do the same with the one-person pot. She wasn't going to owe me the slightest favour. Though she had said I owed her a door lock. I could hardly argue with that. I sipped my tea and waited.

She lifted her mug with both hands and drank before putting the drink carefully back down on the table. 'Where's the harp?'

So we weren't going to bother with small talk. 'Somewhere safe.' I really hoped that was true.

She looked at me, scathing. 'You'll tell me what you've done with it, or I ring the police later today. I'll tell them you forced your way into my house and stole a valuable antique. Enough people have seen that harp in my house.' She waved a claw-like hand at the caffi guy. 'Bedo Jones has seen us together, so you'll be a liar if you say you don't know me.'

The glint in her eye suggested she was well aware the cops would know I wasn't telling the truth, even if they had no idea why they were so certain. Since I really didn't need that aggravation, I told her the minimum I thought I could get away with.

'It's been taken to Ireland.'

'Ireland?' That surprised her.

I waited, hoping she might say something else. I was also trying to assess her accent. She sounded Welsh, but not like anyone I'd heard around here so far.

She shook her head. 'Ah, well. Perhaps that's for the best.'

She reached for her tea again and narrowed her eyes at me. She was waiting for me to ask why.

'How so?' I couldn't see I had anything to lose, and I might finally learn something about the bloody thing.

'How many years do you think I've got left? How many months? There's no knowing at my age.' She shook her head. 'I never wanted it to fall into the wrong hands, but I couldn't find the right ones. Let's hope you did right, forest boy, otherwise that'll be on your head. No, I don't want to know any more. Best I don't. What I don't know, I can't tell.' She leaned forward to study my face.

'Who taught you to use the gorse to ward my door after you broke the lock? A grandmother? Your mother? Someone close to you knows the old ways.'

I didn't understand. 'Sorry, what about the gorse?'

'You don't know?' She tilted her head, bird-like. 'No, you don't, do you?'

Her withered lips tightened, and I could see her deciding whether or not to explain.

'Gorse wards off the Tylwyth Teg,' she said curtly. 'They'll circle around it if they can, but they won't touch it or push through its prickles, no matter how much they want what's on the other side.'

So the shapeshifters weren't only deterred by the chicken wire. But what was Annis Wynne doing with the harp in the first place? I noticed that she didn't call it 'my harp'. The scary fairy hadn't claimed it was hers either.

'Did you find the boy?' she asked abruptly. 'The one she lured into her hill with her flower maiden? Is that what brought you here?'

'Which boy?' I asked cautiously.

We looked at each other for a long moment. Suddenly, the old woman laughed. More accurately, she cackled. The courtyard was getting busier, and several people broke off their own conversations to see what was so funny. The old lady leaned forward again and beckoned with a chalky-nailed forefinger. As I leaned forward, she lowered her voice.

'Answer a question with a question whenever you can, that's the safest way. Your grandmother taught you well, forest boy, unless that was your mother's doing. But we'll be here all day learning nothing if we do that. I'll make you a deal. Ask me no secrets and I'll tell you no lies.'

She sat back in her chair and looked weary. 'I need a new lock on my door before anyone comes calling to ask me questions I don't want to answer. I'm not the one trying to trap you. Why would I? I'm as mortal as you are.'

I could hear she was telling the truth. Just as obviously, she knew the scary fairy would snare me if she could. Whoever she was, Annis Wynne was no ordinary little old lady.

I offered her some honesty in return. 'My mother taught me to watch what I say.' I remembered what Aled had called dryads. 'She's one of the fair folk of the wood.'

For a moment, her gaze grew distant with memory. 'Few of those remain, and fewer still have dealings with mortals these days.' Then her eyes focused. 'You say you got more than one boy out from under the hill? Tell me.'

Since she was right about us getting nowhere if we didn't stop pissing about, I told her about Tom, and about rescuing Tyler. I kept my voice down, and the tourists wandering around the courtyard were far more interested in seeing what they might buy.

Obviously, I didn't tell her everything, not by a long way. I said I was working with friends, and I didn't tell her anyone's name. She might be mortal, but she could whistle up red-eared dogs from the underworld or wherever they lived. The Cŵn Annwn were still watching us intently. People walking straight through them didn't even make them twitch.

The old woman started to smile. By the time I told her about snatching back the harp, she was grinning from ear to ear. She nodded at Aled's workshop. 'So the coblyn boy helped you, did he?'

That was barely a question, so I settled on a shrug for an answer. Annis Wynne might be no friend to the scary fairy, but I wasn't convinced that made her my ally, not yet. And it was her turn to give me some answers.

'Why did she want the harp so badly?'

Annis drank some more tea, thinking over what she might say. She put her mug down and scowled.

'I took it from her a long time ago, but I promised not to use it against her as long as she left the mortals here alone. That was our agreement. Then I realised she had started luring youngsters to their doom from further afield, to scare mortal folk away from these hills. She broke her word first, so I was no longer bound by mine. She was always treacherous and sly.' She really, really didn't like the scary fairy.

'It's a spiteful instrument, if you know how to coax it to sing. You had better tell your friends in Ireland to take care. Those who hear that harp's voice are forced to dance. They can't stop until they're too exhausted to stand, and the harp will play on as long as the last one in any gathering can stay on their feet. So I played it, and that kept those who live under the hill busy while my friends chased the boy you call Tom out of the hill and beyond their reach.'

She gestured at the Cŵn Annwn. One stood up as if it expected a biscuit or maybe someone's soul. When it didn't get a treat, it lay down again.

I tried to picture Annis with the harp balanced on her walker, inching down the path to the quarry in those shapeless black zip-up boots she was wearing. She must have been really pissed off with the scary fairy. That didn't tell me how she had known what was going on though.

'She was content to leave me alone as long as I didn't interfere with her games. Once I spoiled her plans?' The old lady shook her head. 'I knew she'd try to take back the harp. I had no idea how.'

'Until I turned up.' I grimaced.

To my surprise, Annis didn't sound too bothered about that. 'If you hadn't strayed into her path, she'd have found some other way. But she won't let this rest, especially once she learns the harp is out of her reach, taken across the water. You know that, don't you? Has she killed the coblyn boy? Is that the news you had for young Daisy?' She sounded horribly matter of fact.

'No, but she's put him in hospital.' I explained what had happened. 'Assuming she sent the shapeshifter that made him crash, and the thing that burned the van.'

'She did.' Annis had no doubt about that.

Again, how did she know? I had so many questions.

'When did you make this agreement with her? Why?'

For a moment, I didn't think she was going to answer me. Then she shrugged.

'We fell out a long time ago. She always tried to fight against change. I said she might just as well try to stop the phases of the moon, or hold back the seasons. She said she would teach me what change really meant, and she kept her word. She always keeps her word. She thought she was rid of me, so she stole the harp and brought it here to torment the village folk and their visitors. She wanted them to leave. She thought the folk who knew us, who were content to live alongside us, that they would come back. I knew they were gone for good.'

She looked sad for a moment. Then her eyes brightened with malicious satisfaction. 'She didn't expect me to take the harp. I told her I would use it to make her sorry unless she left the local folk alone. In return, I promised her I would keep them away from her hill.'

I don't know what she saw in my face, but she cackled again. 'Don't ask me how I've been doing that, because I won't say. I may be mortal now, forest boy, but that doesn't make me human.'

That was unexpectedly terrifying. 'So you and her—?' I couldn't work out what I was really asking.

'My sister, you mean? At least she was, once upon a time.' Sorrow flickered across the old woman's face before she looked at me, implacable. 'I won't betray her, even though she stabbed me in the back. But you will have to put an end to this. You've crossed her, and she will take her revenge on these people and any others she can reach. She won't wait for me to die now this has happened.'

She seemed oddly satisfied at the thought of me doing her dirty work. But she was right, damn it. Somebody had to do something. The scary fairy was a bloody menace. I remembered that dream I'd had, when I'd seen the dead boy on a mountainside. The Green Man wanted me to put an end to this. I wondered when he had got wind of what was going on. When the hikers had found Tom, or when Tom had talked to me? There had been oak woods in my dream, and there were oak trees in the valleys between these mountains.

'What were you hoping for when you used the harp to get Tom out of her clutches?' I asked her. 'That someone like me would get suspicious when he told his story? That someone would come to see what was happening here?'

She didn't answer, reaching for her walker. 'Bedo Jones must want his table back. Now, are you going to mend my lock or not?'

I wasn't sure if she was still going to call the cops if I didn't, but I wasn't about to take that chance. Besides, as far as anyone else knew, she was still a little old lady. I couldn't leave her with a busted front door. That would get social services asking awkward questions, even if I reckoned those hounds would give any burglar the fright of his life. If he lived to tell the tale. I wondered how she controlled the Cŵn Annwn. I didn't bother asking. I might not like it, but Annis Wynne had the right to keep her secrets, like me and Fin and Hazel Spinner and everyone else who'd helped steal the harp.

I watched her unfold the walker and get it settled in front of her chair. She tried and failed to stand up.

'Can I help you?' I got to my feet and reached for her elbow.

'Leave me be,' she snapped. 'Grab hold of my arm and haul me up and you'll snap my bones like twigs. I just need to take my time.'

I raised both hands and backed off. 'Sorry.'

She stood up at her next attempt, though she was bent into a question mark with age. She had to twist her head sideways to look at up at me. 'Don't be long getting whatever you need. I need my door secure before twilight.'

Chapter Twenty-Two

Annis Wynne made her way slowly out of the courtyard. She looked steady enough on her feet. Besides, I was pretty sure she'd reject any offer from me to walk her home. The Cŵn Annwn stood up as she reached the archway. I guessed they kept her safe from the scary fairy or her shapeshifters when she left the safety of Cerrigwen. As Annis walked on, the hounds turned to follow, though one gave me a lingering last look. I wondered if that was the one I'd threatened to hit with the harp.

Bedo the caffi guy came to clear our table. 'Everything all right, is it?'

'Fine.' I left him holding the tray.

I was grateful the walk to the campsite was downhill. I took down Eleanor's tent and packed everything away. I stuck the rowan rings I had left in my pockets, just in case. I couldn't see any trace of the yew earth in the grass. Presumably the local earthworms were now safe from fairy malice. More importantly, there was nothing for Mr Williams to object to.

By the time I'd sorted out the back of the Land Rover, I had a bag of rubbish and wrecked clothes to chuck in a bin when I was well away from here. I had no idea if anyone or anything could use stuff I'd once owned against me, but I wasn't taking any chances. I decided paranoia was safest when you were dealing with fairies.

When I was done, I thought very seriously about just driving away. I had better check in with Mr Williams though, in case he thought I owed him for another day. He had my name and the Landy's number plate. I couldn't stop yawning as I walked round to the conservatory office. The surge of adrenaline that had kept me alert while I was talking to Annis Wynne was fading fast.

'Just letting you know I'm heading off. Are we all square, or...?'

'What's this I hear about Aled James?' Mr Williams looked up from his phone. 'He crashed his car last night and you found him?'

Word travelled fast around here. I nodded. 'He was taken to hospital in Bangor with nasty burns.'

I felt that hollow twist in my gut again. I desperately wanted to know how Aled was, and where he might have been taken, but ringing the hospital when I wasn't a relative or anyone his family would know would mean more explanations and, most likely, making the authorities suspicious. I desperately hoped Mr Williams wasn't going to start asking questions. I hadn't got a hope of coming up with a believable version of events when I was this tired.

'I'm sorry.' I genuinely meant that, though not in the way he would think. 'I really need to get on my way.'

'Right, right, yes.' Mr Williams stood up and offered me a handshake, concerned. 'You take care now. Have a safe journey.'

I shook his hand and wondered what he had seen in my face. 'Thanks.'

That's all I could say as my throat tightened. I nodded again and headed out to the Landy. Driving down into the valley, I found a space in the supermarket car park and sat there staring at nothing for a while. Then I called Fin.

'Hi there,' she said cheerfully. 'Where are you? Knutsford services or somewhere closer?'

'What? Sorry, no.' My thought processes stalled completely as I tried to decide where to start.

'Dan? Are you there? Can you hear me?'

'Yes.' I still couldn't think what to say.

'Is there some problem? With the Landy?' Fin asked, anxious.

'We have a whole load of new problems.' I took a deep breath. 'Nothing to do with the Landy.'

'Hang on.' She interrupted before I could try to explain. 'I'm up at the house. Let me find Eleanor and Blanche. Then I can put you on speaker and you won't need to go through everything twice.'

'Right.'

Fin put her phone down with a soft clunk. I guessed she was in Eleanor's sitting room, staying out of the way of tourists. It was Tuesday, so Blithehurst would be open. How the hell was it only Tuesday? Was it seriously only a week ago yesterday when I'd first spoken to Gillian? I tried not to yawn while I waited. Thankfully, it wasn't long before Fin came back. I could hear Blanche and Eleanor too, with that echoey quality that told me I was on speaker.

'Dan? Are you still there?' Fin asked.

'Yes. Okay, now listen.'

The wait had given me a chance to get my brain in gear. I explained what had happened last night and then this morning. When I finished, there was stunned silence from the phone.

Blanche was the first to speak. 'What are you going to do?'

'Mend her front door. See what else I can find out. I reckon she knows how to sort out this mess.'

'I'll call Iris.' Fin's voice was taut with concern. 'Make sure she warns her Irish friends about that bloody harp.'

'I'll see what the wise women have to say,' Eleanor chipped in.

'We need to find somewhere to stay over there. That's not going to be easy at this time of year.' Fin was exasperated now.

'I don't want anyone coming over,' I said sharply. 'I can look after myself, but we can't risk the scary fairy going after anyone else, not until we know what we're dealing with.'

As long as I had anything to say about it, no one would come anywhere near here again. I'd thought having people to call on would make dealing with these weird situations easier. After what had happened to Aled, I realised that cut both ways. Seeing people I cared about getting hurt wasn't a price I was willing to pay.

There was another silence. Again, Blanche spoke first.

'What do you think you're going to find out?'

That was a stupid question. How should I fucking know? I stared through the windscreen and counted to ten.

'What I mean is, we need a proper plan.' Blanche sounded defensive. 'What do we need to know if we're going to deal with this scary fairy? What does putting an end to her even mean?'

'He knows that.' Fin spoke up before I could answer. 'Dan, as soon as I've spoken to Iris, I'll see what I can find out online.'

'I'll look for anything useful in the library, as soon as we close for the day.' Eleanor was speaking over a hissed conversation between Fin and Blanche.

'Give it a rest,' Fin told her sister curtly. 'Dan, are you coming back to Blithehurst tonight?'

'That's the idea.' I felt really tired now. I didn't want Fin arguing with her sister. 'But Blanche is right. Getting this done right, once and for all, is more important than getting it done fast. I don't want to have to worry about anyone else getting hurt because we've rushed things.'

'I'm more worried that you're going to crash on the motorway because you've fallen asleep at the wheel,' Eleanor said bluntly. 'Why don't I come over with Fin? She can drive you and the Land Rover back. We can meet somewhere well away from Caergynan.'

How far away was far enough for the scary fairy not to notice us? Until I had some idea, I wasn't going to take any risks.

'I'll see how I feel when I've mended the old lady's door. If I need to, I'll give you a call.' That was as far as I was prepared to go. 'If there's nothing else we need to discuss, I want to get on. The sooner I've fixed that lock, the sooner I can be on my way back.'

'Okay.' Fin didn't sound happy. 'Keep your phone with you, in case we need to get in touch.'

'I'll see you soon.' I clenched my fist before I jabbed a forefinger at the screen to end the call. Hearing Fin's voice made me want to head back to Blithehurst more fiercely than ever. At the same time, it made me absolutely determined to keep her as far away from here as possible.

I could do both of those things if I found out what we needed to know as soon as possible. Ideally, I wanted to put an end to the scary fairy today, before I drove back to Blithehurst. What did putting an end to her mean? Who was I trying to kid? I was going to have to kill her. Was I going to be able to do that?

The other vicious things I've killed for the Green Man, like the nix in the lake that I'd told Tom about, they had looked like monsters. The scary fairy might not be human, but she could look like someone I might meet on any street. Even when she wasn't disguising herself, she looked like a person, not a monster. I've been in ordinary fights, even though someone else usually starts them, but I've never set out to attack a woman. I couldn't imagine a situation where I would. Would instinct make me hold back, even though I knew what the scary fairy really was? Would a split-second's hesitation get me killed?

Do the job that's in front of you. I went online to find the nearest big DIY store. I drove over and bought what I needed to mend Annis Wynne's door. I bought a new torch for the Landy, as well as a new fire extinguisher and another first aid kit. There was still just about everything left in the one I had, but I wanted more of those burn dressings in case that fiery fucker turned up again. I dropped the money Annis Wynne had given me to pay for her tea into a cancer research collection box at the checkout. I tried not to think about my bank balance as I paid for everything with my credit card. Somehow, I didn't think the old lady would be paying me for materials or labour. I hoped the gift shop at Blithehurst was selling lots of my woodwork.

Searching online, I found the nearest supermarket with a petrol station, and went and topped up with diesel. I didn't want to have to stop for anything once I was on my way away from here. I bought some food and a six-pack of litre-and-a-half bottles of still mineral water. Annis Wynne might be mortal, but she said she wasn't human and I believed her. I wasn't going to eat or drink anything I was offered in her house. I'd ordered and paid for the tea at the caffi, and we'd poured our own mugs from separate pots, so hopefully that was okay. I also wanted more than one bottle of water to hand in case that fiery fucker turned up again.

Since I was there, I bought some chicken salad sandwiches and a packet of crisps for lunch. I was getting tired of eating snacks. I hadn't had a proper hot meal since Sunday lunch with Aled. I wondered how he was. Had Daisy been able to find out what was going on? I should have asked for her number. Then I could have rung to ask her... what? I couldn't explain what had happened. I had no way to know what Aled had said. If we told different stories, she would get suspicious. If Aled had been able to say anything to her at all. The sandwiches I'd just eaten sat like a lump in my stomach.

I told myself to get a grip. One of the wise women who worked in the health service might be able to find out something. If so, there was a good chance Eleanor would have some news when I got back to Blithehurst. I turned the key and drove back to Caergynan. I kept my eyes open all the way for any sign of anything lurking to leap out of a hedge. Nothing did.

When I reached the village, I drove past Plas Brynwen and went up the hill to the end of the tarmac. I didn't turn into the Meilyr Centre car park but carried on down the track to the Cerrigwen farmhouse. That barely counted as going off-road for the Landy.

I pulled up outside the metal gate at the back of the house. It was still solidly padlocked. I walked back up the track and climbed over the fence with the chicken wire, intending to knock on one of the little porch windows. Before I reached the steps, one of the Cŵn Annwn came through the front door. I don't mean the door swung open. The hound walked straight through the solid wood. It stood in the porch and stared at me. It might have been my imagination, but I was starting to think I could tell them apart. Not from their appearance but from the way they behaved. This was the one that would attack me the moment it had any excuse – or was given the order.

I stared back. 'I need the back gate opened.'

I have no idea if it understood me, but I spoke loudly enough to be heard in the house since the front door wasn't properly shut. The hound turned around and went back inside. I waited, and a few minutes later I saw the door move. It didn't get far before it wedged itself on the clump of gorse.

'Make yourself useful,' Annis Wynne said irritably from behind it. 'Get this open.'

Since her hound hadn't reappeared to rip my throat out, I stepped up into the porch. 'Mind yourself.' I bent down to rip the twiggy stems out from under the door and pushed carefully. I didn't hit anything. The door swung wide, and I saw Annis standing in the hall, gripping her walker.

She didn't look particularly pleased to see me. 'You took your time.'

I wasn't going to tell her why. 'I'm parked outside the gate at the back. If you don't want people asking questions, let me have the key and I'll pull into your yard.'

'You couldn't walk here?' She glowered.

'Carrying a toolbox and a load of stuff from a DIY store? You don't think that'll make anyone who sees me curious?' I jerked my head back towards the Meilyr Centre.

'Still answering questions with questions.' She narrowed her eyes at me before slowly circling around in the hallway. 'Come in then, if you're coming.'

She didn't wait to see if I followed her, inching towards the back of the house. I walked up the steps and through the hall. There was no sign of the Cŵn Annwn. In the kitchen, Annis was searching through a drawer below one of the glass-fronted cupboards. I hadn't bothered to look in those since they were too small to hold a harp.

'So how did you come to live here?' If she and the scary fairy had been sisters, whatever that meant, I guessed she wasn't really the widow of the last owner's lost son.

'I protected the people here from those who live under the hill. When I needed shelter, they offered it.'

Annis tossed a bunch of keys at me surprisingly hard. I caught them by reflex.

'Lock the gate behind you. You can unlock it when you're ready to leave.' She started trundling her walker towards me.

I stepped aside and watched her make her way to the sitting room. A few moments later, I heard voices from the telly. I looked at the keys in my hand. It was easy to see which one opened the rim lock on the back door and which was the one for the padlocked gate. I went out into the yard and saw the Cŵn Annwn watching me from the shadows of the derelict outbuildings. I had to turn my back on them to unlock the gate. I tried not to feel too uneasy. They must know I had Annis's permission to be here.

I drove the Landy into the yard, shut the gate and clicked the padlock to secure it. I looked up and down the lane and across to the field beyond the stone wall. I couldn't see anything that might be a shapeshifter. When I turned around, I couldn't see the Cŵn Annwn either. I couldn't decide if that was good news or not.

There was no point in wasting time wondering. I got my toolbox out of the Landy along with the other stuff I'd bought at the DIY store. I carried everything through the house and considered the best way to tackle this job. In an ideal world, I'd take the door off its hinges, strip out the whole frame and replace it. Better yet, I'd set up some scaffolding because there was no way the porch roof was going to take my weight, and I'd see where the water was getting in. If I was going to do a decent job, that needed sorting out first.

I couldn't do any of that, which pissed me off even though I didn't have a choice. For a start, I've worked on enough old houses to know that stripping something back to do one job generally turns up three unexpected things. You'll need to tackle those before you can begin whatever you actually wanted to do. If you're lucky, it's only three new problems. Often it's five or six.

For another thing, Annis wanted her house protected by iron locks before twilight today, and I could hardly blame her for that. Doing the job properly wouldn't be quick enough, not if I was working on my own, and I wasn't going to risk getting anyone else involved.

Lastly and most obviously, there was no way that someone doing that amount of work wouldn't be noticed by anyone who could see the house. Given the way local news travelled here, Bedo the caffi guy or someone else was bound to turn up, asking questions that neither Annis nor I would want to answer. So I had better get on and do the best job I could.

I found the lock keeper on the floor where I'd put it out of the way. That was one less thing to worry about. When there was solid wood to screw the keeper onto again, the door would be secure enough. I looked at the mess I'd made of the door jamb and tried to ignore what sounded like a quiz show on the telly in the sitting room. I'd need to take out a sizeable length of wood and piece in a new length. At least there wasn't anything fancy like architrave to complicate my life.

I couldn't see how I could avoid cracking the old plaster on the wall. Then the new wood would need painting, and so would the new door stop I'd bought to replace the wooden strip on the outside. Hell, the whole door frame needed sugar-soaping and repainting. The fresh white gloss would stick out like a sore thumb against the grubby old paint everywhere else in the house.

Well, explaining that would be Annis Wynne's problem. I keep an old tarpaulin in the Landy because you never know when you might need something to kneel on. I spread that out to catch the worst of the mess and to give me something less prickly than the doormat. I got to work with a hammer and chisel. A good chisel that I'd just bought. You can never have too many chisels. That's what I was telling myself. I forced myself to go carefully, but the plaster still cracked, especially where the paint on the door frame met the wall. I had bought some filler, but that would be all I could do to make good there.

I did have some overdue luck. When I'm putting a new door frame into a brick-built house, I'll drill holes and use screws and wall plugs. Doing that's a piece of piss with power tools. This was a stone house, and the local stone was incredibly hard. Even these days, making holes in this wall would be a challenge as well as expensive in drill bits. Well, when this house was built, carpenters didn't have hammer drills, wall plugs or machine-made screws. They got the masons to put blocks of wood in between the stones around the openings where doors and windows would go. Then they could nail wooden frames to those.

I worked an old nail free from the scrap of wood in my hand. It was flat on all four sides where a blacksmith had hammered the thin iron rod on his anvil before heating it a second time. Snip off a length, and he would clamp that in a vice to flatten the top with another few strikes of his hammer. Nails took work in those days. They were valuable things, not sold in plastic packs for a tenner a kilo. Any blacksmith's nail that could be salvaged would be handed to some young lad whose only job was to hammer every single one straight.

I tossed it into my toolbox and examined the wood it had been hammered into. The dark block of oak in the wall was as immoveable as the stones above and below it. Better yet, it was where I needed to fix the new bit of wood to repair the door frame. I measured the gap and measured and marked up the wood I'd just bought. I measured the gap again, just to be sure, and sawed the wood to length. I didn't need a new saw, so I'd bought the cheapest one in the store.

Using a Stanley knife, I shaped the ends. I was very careful not to cut myself. Absolutely the last thing I needed was another trip to A&E. After I had carved a few more slivers out of the door frame, I reckoned I had the snuggest possible fit. I coated the edges of the new piece with wood glue. I don't care what adverts say; glue is no substitute for nails, but just at the moment, I'd take all the help I could get. I rammed the new wood home and hammered in a couple of nails, top and bottom. Getting them through the new wood was no more difficult than usual, but I felt a jar through the hammer as soon as the tip of the first nail hit old, solid oak.

'Oh, come on,' I muttered.

To my surprise, when I hit the nail again, it sank deep into the old wood. So did the next one, and the ones after that. Had I split the bloody thing? Was I going to have to start all over again? I could see the edge of the oak where the plaster had cracked away from the wall. I pushed it with my forefinger, to see if I could feel any movement. I didn't. The oak block was as solid as it had been since it was set into the wall. For an instant though, I could smell the wood where the tree had grown. I heard the rustle of a breeze in its branches.

That was unexpected. I stared at the wall for a few moments. Then, since I was far too tired for any more weird shit that wasn't telling me how to kill a scary fairy, I used a rag to wipe away the lines of glue squeezed out of the joints. Picking up the lock keeper, I found the front door key on the bunch Annis had tossed me. I worked out where the keeper needed to go. A bit of work with the good chisel and a couple of screws took care of that.

Once I was satisfied, I took the keeper off again, sanded the joins smooth and washed the whole door frame down with sugar soap and a scouring sponge. While that was drying off, I gave the length of doorstop that would go on the outside a quick coat of primer. Of course, if I'd been properly awake, I'd have done that first and the bloody thing would already be dry.

Once that was done, I went out into the porch and took off what was left of the rotten strip of doorstop. The frame itself was in a better state than I expected, now that I saw it in daylight. I had a go with some sandpaper where I could see dark stains. It didn't take a lot of work to get down to reasonably clean wood. I washed the outside down as well.

Since that needed to dry off, I went out to the Landy for a drink of water and a couple of biscuits. I fetched my new torch as well. I found a battered wooden chair in the dining room that should take my weight. Back in the porch, I stood on that and took a thorough look at the underside of the roof. It wasn't good, though I supposed things could have been worse. I couldn't see actual daylight. I resisted the temptation to test the strength of the wood with a screwdriver.

I got down from the chair and found the roll of flashing tape I'd bought. If I couldn't get onto the roof of the porch, I could do a temporary fix underneath while the weather was dry. Make sure surfaces are clean and dust free, the instructions on the tape said. Prime porous surfaces first. I wiped everything down with a damp rag and went to eat more biscuits. Chocolate bourbons.

When I came back, I stuck a length of the tape along the underside of the beam where the porch met the house. I positioned it so two thirds of the width was stuck to the house and one third was stuck to the wood. Then I stuck another strip over that so the beam got two thirds and the house got the rest. I had enough tape left for a third strip, so I used that to reinforce the first one. I had no idea how long that would keep the rain out, but it had to be better than nothing.

I gathered up strips of backing paper before they could blow away and put the old chair back in the dining room. Now the door frame was dry enough for me to give the new wood and the old bits that I had sanded a coat of primer.

I went into the living room to tell the old lady I wanted to wait as long as possible for that to dry before I gave the door frame a coat of gloss. She was asleep in her big armchair with the TV remote in her lap.

That was unexpected, but not unwelcome. Far from it. I took out my phone and started taking photos of the bookcases that lined the room. When I'd been in here last night – no, the night before – I'd noticed a lot of these books were about folklore. I even recognised a few of the titles, but there were a whole lot more that I'd never heard of, and that wasn't counting the ones in Welsh. Maybe one of these could tell us what we needed to know. *A Beginner's Guide to Monster Slaying*. We had to know how to kill the scary fairy before I needed to decide if I could do it.

I tried to send the photos to Eleanor, but my phone didn't have a signal. Sod it. I crossed the hall into the old woman's bedroom and checked those bookcases. They were crammed with what looked like historical romances. I nearly didn't bother taking any photos, until I remembered we'd found useful hints in old songs and stories before now. Similar truths might be hiding in more recent fiction.

I took another quick look in the dining room. There was no way I could search in there. I'd end up covered in dust for a start. I wasn't too bothered since I couldn't believe I'd find anything useful in that junk. Moving as quietly as I could on the creaky stairs, I headed for the back bedroom where I'd found the harp. I took a quick look through the window towards the quarry. No sign of movement.

I opened the dressing table drawers. They were full of jewellery and old gold coins. Shit. No wonder Annis wanted to be sure her front door would lock. I wondered where this haul had come from. I wondered how she turned it into cash to buy groceries. I'm sure Sainsbury's don't give change for sovereigns.

The middle mirror on the dressing table was fixed, and the ones on either side were adjustable so someone doing their hair or make-up could check how they looked from different angles. For an instant I saw the Green Man's face reflected in all three mirrors. Then he was gone, and I heard growling behind me.

I turned around slowly and saw one of the Cŵn Annwn in the doorway. The one that really didn't like me. I spread my hands slowly and decided saying 'good dog' was probably pointless.

'I haven't taken anything. See? I'm just looking.'

The hound padded silently into the room without taking its eyes off me. It walked through the bed to stand by the window. Now my way to the door was clear. I got the hint. I took a step. The hound moved forward, still looking at me.

I kept my hands raised. 'I get the message.'

I went down the stairs. The hound followed. When I reached the turn, Annis was standing in the hall with her walker. She glared up at me. I went down the creaking steps and I made damn sure I spoke first.

'I didn't take anything. Do you think I'm stupid? I was looking for something to help me put an end to all this. That's what you want, isn't it?'

I sounded more aggressive than I meant to. The hound behind me snarled. I raised my hands again and forced myself to speak quietly and calmly.

'I'm sorry. But I need to know what to do. You called her your sister. What does that mean? Isn't it in your own interests to tell me what you know? She must know I've been talking to you. I'm sure her creatures have seen my Land Rover in your yard today.'

That had occurred to me when I glanced out of the bedroom window. If the scary fairy thought we were allies, perhaps that would force Annis Wynne's hand.

'I've said all I'm going to. I won't betray her.' Annis had been defiant before. Now she just sounded sad.

I felt exhausted. 'Then I'll finish up and go.'

Giving the door frame a fresh coat of gloss paint didn't take long. I cleaned the brushes in the kitchen, wiped down the sink and put everything away in the Landy. The only thing I kept in my pocket was the screwdriver to fix the lock keeper back on. The paint was still tacky, but I was careful. Once I'd turned the key, that was everything done.

I was pleased with my work. If you didn't know what you were looking for, that new bit of wood in the door frame was invisible. The fresh paintwork wasn't though. I glanced at Annis Wynne. She had been standing in the sitting room doorway, watching my every move since I came downstairs.

'Does this work settle what I owe you? For breaking the lock.'

One of the Cŵn Annwn was sitting beside her walker. The other one was lying on the half-landing on the stairs. They both pricked their ears, which made me nervous. Annis took longer to answer than I would have liked, but finally she nodded. 'Yes. We're quits.'

That was good enough for me. There were still potential complications. 'How are you going to explain the fresh paint?'

She surprised me with a cackle. 'What's to explain?'

I glanced at the door. The white gloss looked as dingy as everything else in the run-down house.

'No reason you couldn't do that yourself,' Annis grumbled as she trundled slowly towards the kitchen. 'Save me the bother.'

'Sorry, what?' I went after her. The Cŵn Annwn growled a warning. I stopped beside the big hall stand.

Annis circled around in the kitchen doorway, hunched over her walker. 'You could do a lot more than you realise, forest boy, if you stirred yourself. You shouldn't need me to tell you that.' She crossed the kitchen to open the back door. 'You be on your way. Just don't forget you have a task to finish under the hill. The sooner that's done, the better for everyone, and for you most of all.'

'But you're still not going to tell me how?'

The old lady twisted her head to look up at me. Her face was as hard as a blacksmith's hand-forged nails. 'I've told you what you need to know. Work it out, forest boy.'

Chapter Twenty-Three

I was running on fumes. I only got back safely to Blithehurst because I pulled into a lay-by beside a lake and called Eleanor to take up her offer to drive over with Fin. It was my own fault. I'd stopped at a pub for a burger and chips. I wanted a sodding hot meal. Even though I'd drunk a pint of Coke with the burger and had a coffee, I'd barely gone a mile further on when I realised my eyelids were drooping.

I pulled over as soon as I found a safe place to park and got out my phone. Eleanor was brisk and businesslike. She didn't say 'I told you so', which I appreciated. I got into the passenger seat, made sure the Landy was locked and took a nap while I waited. When they arrived, Fin got in and started driving without saying a word.

By the time we got back to Blithehurst, I was so solidly asleep I didn't stir when she stopped and got out to open the back gate to the estate. I only jerked awake when the Landy pulled up outside my cottage in the woods. I barely opened my eyes as I stumbled inside, stripped off and fell into bed. I have no idea when Fin joined me.

I cannot begin to describe how good it felt to wake up in a proper bed the next morning. Camping might have its plus points, but I was in no hurry to do it again. I stretched out under the duvet and breathed in deep.

'You're awake then. I'll make some tea.' Fin swung her legs over the side of the bed and sat up.

'Can that wait?' I reached up to run my fingers down her back. She was as naked as I was, apart from the downy white swan feathers that clung to her skin.

She shifted around to face me. 'What did you have in mind?'

I stretched out my hand to cup her breast and brushed her nipple with my thumb. 'Whatever you like.'

Feathers drifted down my hand and forearm as she leaned forward to kiss me, long and slow. I threw back the duvet and she lay down beside me. We kissed some more, and our hands explored each other's bodies. I knew every inch of her by now, and every time I touched her was every bit as good as the first time had been. Her skin was silky, smooth, warm and welcoming. She opened her thighs and I slipped my fingers into her.

'I have missed you.' I kissed the hollow between her neck and her shoulder.

'I can tell.' Her hand tightened around my cock.

I brushed her soft feathers away and began kissing her gorgeous tits.

Fin's hands caressed my shoulders. 'Condoms?'

'In the top drawer.' I teased her nipple with my tongue. 'What's your hurry?'

'Do you think your phone will ring first—' she broke off and lifted my chin to kiss me hard as my finger found her most sensitive spot '—or mine?'

'Good point.' I sat up and found a condom.

'Lie back.' Fin straddled me and took my cock inside her. I fondled her tits as she rocked forward and back. As she rode me faster, I moved my hands to her hips, holding her tight as she reached her orgasm. Those sensations brought me closer and closer to coming myself.

'Mmmmm.' She arched her back. A few moments later, she relaxed to lie limp on my chest.

I gathered her in my arms and rolled us both over. There's plenty of room in my bed, and we've had plenty of practice by now. Fin stretched her arms over her head, keeping her eyes closed. Her smile was sensuous and satisfied as she drew up her feet. I knelt between her thighs and made sure the condom hadn't slipped. I started slow as I began moving inside her, determined to make this last as long as I could, for both our sakes. It wasn't long before all I could feel was the warmth of her around me. The rhythm of my hips matched my quickening pulse. All I could hear was Fin's breath, coming faster like my own. Now we were moving together. Then there was nothing but the ecstasy I've never felt with anyone else.

'Mmmmm.' When I could think straight again, I lay down and rested my head between her breasts. Sweat cooled on my back. I could hear birdsong in the trees outside the window as I wondered idly what the time was. I couldn't be arsed to move and find out.

I was just thinking I could do with a cup of tea when my ringtone cut through the peace and quiet. About thirty seconds later, someone called Fin's phone. *Sisters Are Doin' It For Themselves* told me that had to be Blanche or Iris. Fin doesn't have a different ringtone for everyone, but she does group people together with particular songs. I just use the bell sound. We both started laughing. I knelt back on my heels and lifted Fin's leg past me so she could sit up. I found a tissue and bundled up the condom.

'It's Blanche.' She pressed the screen to interrupt the song. 'Hi, yes, we're awake. Well, just about.'

Whoever was ringing me had stopped trying. I went into the bathroom, binned the tissue, had a pee, washed my hands and came back to pick up my phone. I headed for the kitchen, returning Eleanor's call as I went. 'Morning.'

'Are you up?'

I grinned to myself. 'Pretty much. I'm about to get in the shower and then we'll have some breakfast.' I lifted the kettle to see how much water was in it. Enough, from the weight. I put it back down and hit the switch.

'Come and have breakfast with us.' Eleanor's suggestion was closer to an order, really. 'You need to tell us what happened at the farmhouse before the staff start arriving.'

'Right.' I looked at the kitchen clock. It had only just gone seven. I wondered what time I'd crashed yesterday. Not that it mattered. Being able to sleep for as long as I wanted was a welcome change after the last couple of days.

Eleanor was still talking. 'Fin and Blanche can make some calls today while we're working, and hopefully set up some online meetings for after we close.'

'Right.' I found the teapot and dropped in a couple of teabags. 'We'll be there in a bit.'

'Okay. Thanks.' Eleanor ended the call.

I noticed my overnight bag and the camping gear were stacked by the back door. Sorting that out could wait. Hearing water running, I went into the bathroom. My latest project improving this old cottage has been putting in a walk-in shower. My priorities were a shower head that's high enough for me and fixing a screen that gave room for us both. Fin was already washing her hair. Her feathers clung to her in sodden white streaks. Incredibly sexy, if you ask me.

I joined her under the shower head. 'What did Blanche have to say?'

'We're invited to breakfast up at the manor.' Fin turned around, wiping foam away from her eyes. 'Who was—?'

'Eleanor.' I reached for the shower gel. 'Same invitation. There's tea in the pot.'

We showered quickly. Back in the bedroom, Fin smiled at me as she hung her towel on the hook on the back of the door. I could see what she was thinking and grinned. I didn't need any persuading to put off discussions about scary fairies for a little bit longer.

'We really shouldn't.' She didn't sound convinced though.

'I can be quick.' I chucked my towel away to show her. 'How about you?'

'Let's see.' She jumped onto the bed.

I grabbed a condom and joined her. If the way we'd started our day could be called making love, this was a swift, physical fuck. That's okay, because that's what we both wanted and we both enjoyed ourselves. Though I never did get that cup of tea as we quickly got dressed afterwards.

'Where are my clothes from yesterday?' I couldn't see the combats I'd been wearing as I found jeans and a Blithehurst staff shirt.

'In the wash, with the dirty stuff out of your bag. I couldn't stand the smell.' Fin buttoned her shorts. 'I got everything out of the Landy last night, apart from what looked like bags of rubbish.'

'Don't ever get caught in the smoke from a car fire.' I would get rid of that trash later. 'Thanks. You're a star.'

'All part of the service,' she said lightly. She pulled a loose sleeveless top over her head and checked to make sure her feathers were tucked out of sight.

Outside, her Toyota was parked beside the Land Rover. 'Are we walking or driving?' she asked as I locked up.

I'd got out of the habit of locking my door when I was the only one here apart from the dryads and the shuck. Not any more. The maps of the official paths around the estate didn't bring visitors down here, but there was nothing to actually stop them if they wandered this way. I turned the key in the mortice lock and wondered if anything had tried getting into Annis Wynne's house last night.

'Let's walk.'

It was so good to be back. This was where I belonged, not necessarily at Blithehurst but under the sunlit canopy of broad-leaved woodland. I could almost feel the sap rising through the trees as I heard the soft whispers of their branches. Mountainsides of barren rock and parched turf were no place for me.

I kept my eyes open for Asca and Frai as we walked to the manor house. Neither of them appeared. Typical. Now that I couldn't put off thinking about the unfinished business I had in North Wales, I remembered what Annis Wynne had said about me being able to do more than I realised. I wondered if the dryads here knew more about my greenwood blood than they had chosen to share. I wanted to talk to my mum as well. Would I be able to find some skill that I could use to keep other people safe? I wouldn't mind being able to whistle up a shuck. Annis Wynne was mortal, and she had those Cŵn Annwn at her heels.

If I found something out, I'd tell Fin. Then we could decide what we were going to tell Eleanor, as well as who we'd share the news with in her family. Then we'd decide what we were going to tell the wise women. If we were going to tell the wise women. That made me think of something else.

'Did you ever get an update yesterday about Aled James? Does anyone know how he is? Where he is?'

THE GREEN MAN'S GIFT

Fin had been walking beside me, as deep in her own thoughts as I was. 'Oh, yes, sorry. I should have said. He's been transferred to that hospital in Swansea, the Morriston. He's doing okay, apparently. His face took the worst of it, according to what Melangell could find out, but they're hopeful there'll be minimal scarring.'

I wondered what the hell that meant. 'When you say "they", do you mean the doctors or the wise women or both?'

Fin shrugged. 'Both, probably.'

'Any word on Tyler?'

She nodded. 'He's in nothing like such a bad way as Tom. For the moment, they're telling him he was roofied, but they're trying to keep that quiet. They don't want some bright copper reading two similar reports and alerting his bosses. The last thing we need is a police operation hunting down a sex and drugs ring operating out of Snowdonia.'

'Do you think that they'll manage that? Keeping it quiet, I mean?'

'They seem pretty confident they can.'

I wouldn't bet against the wise women. 'Did you manage to talk to Iris about the harp?'

She nodded. 'Conn says thanks for the heads up. He'll be in touch.'

The side door at Blithehurst was unlocked. I called out as I followed Fin inside. 'We're here!'

'In the kitchen,' Eleanor called back from what used to be the scullery.

As we came through the door, Blanche poured hot water into a big cafetière. She raised her eyebrows at Fin as she put the coffee on a tray next to milk, mugs and a teapot. Fin answered her with a blandly uninformative smile.

I grabbed an oven glove as Eleanor took a baking sheet out of the oven where it had been keeping warm. 'Can I help?'

'Thanks.' She handed me the croissants. 'Everything's over there.'

'Right.' I slid the pastries onto a big plate on the counter, beside another two-handled tray with butter, jam, cutlery and side plates. I added a roll of paper towels. If there's a way to eat croissants without getting yourself covered in jam, I don't know it.

'They're out of the freezer, but they're pretty good.' Eleanor added another half-dozen from another baking sheet. 'Unless you'd prefer a bacon sandwich.'

'This is fine.' I would much rather have had a bacon sandwich, but I owed Eleanor after our delay getting up here. 'I'll take the tray if you can get the doors.'

Blanche went ahead of Fin, who was carrying the drinks, and we followed them through to the great hall and on up the stairs. We had breakfast in Eleanor's sitting room. In between mouthfuls, I told them everything Annis Wynne had said to me while I was in her house.

'That doesn't give us much to go on.' Blanche was unimpressed.

I didn't tell her thanks, I already knew that.

Blanche moved on. 'Where do you suppose she got that jewellery and stuff? What'll happen to her little hoard when she dies?'

'Can you go over what she said to you in the cafe, please?' Eleanor had finished eating. She had an A4 pad ready and her fountain pen was poised. She wrote down everything I told her. When I finished, she sat looking at her notes, intent, as if this was some code she could crack if she just stared at the page long enough.

Fin stood up. 'You said you took some photos. Let me get the jam off my hands and I'll download them.'

She soon transferred the pictures of the old woman's bookcases onto her laptop. Eleanor and I left her zooming in and reading off the titles she could make out so Blanche could make a list.

'I couldn't put you on this week's rota since I wasn't sure when you would be back,' Eleanor said as we went down the main staircase together. 'You know where things get busy. Just make yourself useful today.'

'Fine with me.' I carried the breakfast tray into the little kitchen and loaded the dishwasher before heading out through the side door.

I walked up to the car park, where a couple of the staff asked how my few days away had gone. 'Okay,' I said with a shrug. They were just being polite, so I don't think they were really listening to my answer. That was fine with me.

Thankfully, an early surge of visitors meant we were too busy for small talk after that. I helped direct traffic in the car park, then I did a stint clearing tables in the restaurant. I checked in with the gift shop and the garden centre and fetched the stock they needed from my workshop in the old dairy yard. Having plenty to do was good for me. The only time I stopped to feel guilty about Aled was when I went back to the cottage in a mid-morning lull, to get the rubbish I'd brought back in the Landy. I reckoned it was safe enough to chuck it in the big commercial bins behind the restaurant. They would be emptied tomorrow.

Janice asked me to take some paper cups down to the cafe in the castle. When I got there, Sarah asked me to mop up an orange juice spill in the gatehouse, and then to go up to the ornamental temple so Mark could help out in the courtyard. I was more than happy to do that, though the dryads still didn't appear. I tried not to let that annoy me. In any case, there were too many people around to have a serious conversation with either of them.

No one texted me to suggest we meet up for lunch. I went down the hillside and over the river to get a tuna mayo baguette and a cold drink from the castle cafe. The walk was more tiring than I expected. Maybe I hadn't caught up on the sleep I had missed over this past week. I had just got back to the temple when my phone buzzed in my pocket. Fin wanted to know where I was. I let her know, and she texted to say she'd come and join me. I had just finished eating by the time she arrived.

The ornamental temple is a round plinth with pillars holding up a dome over the statue of Venus that was modelled on sketches of Asca. Semi-circular white marble benches flank it, so people can sit and admire her, or they can take in the view over the shallow valley with the ruins down by the river and the Tudor manor house on the slope opposite.

Fin dropped onto the bench beside me. The lunchtime lull meant no one else was around. She heaved a sigh, and not just because it's a longer, harder walk than most people realise, up the path through the wooded pasture.

'We were able to work out quite a few of those book titles, though we couldn't find out much about them online. Until we can get hold of the actual books, we can't tell if they'll be any use. If we can even get hold of them, ideally without spending a fortune. We've emailed the list to Hazel and Gillian to see if the wise women can help. We asked them to forward it to Melangell, to see what she can do with the Welsh ones.'

'Has anyone asked her what she knows about Annis Wynne? Melangell, I mean.' I was an idiot. I should have thought of that sooner.

'We asked Gillian to do that. I typed up Eleanor's notes about the cafe and added what she said to you while you were fixing her door.' Fin stared across the valley. 'Let's hope somebody sees something we've missed.'

'Is there any update on Aled?'

She shook her head. 'No one's been in touch yet. Well, apart from a Zoom meeting invite for this evening from Hazel. But no news is good news, isn't it?'

'I suppose so.' That didn't make me feel much better.

'There must be a way to do away with this fairy. When we know how—'

'No,' I interrupted Fin. 'There's no "we" here. You're not coming with me. I have to do this on my own.'

'You want to do this on your own, you mean,' she shot back.

'It's what the Green Man wants. I saw him in a dream.'

'Whatever you saw might be a message for you, but that's got bugger all to do with what I decide to do,' she retorted.

I realised she could tell I was trying to find excuses. Whatever I was saying wasn't ringing true, even if I wasn't telling actual lies. There was nothing for it but brutal honesty.

'I'm not risking you getting hurt. I'm not going to do that. Forget it.'

'I'll choose the risks I take, thank you very much.' Fin reddened, indignant. 'I've managed all right so far, haven't I? With the nix, and against the giant. You couldn't have dealt with them without me.'

'That was different,' I said stubbornly.

'How?' Fin demanded.

Because she had been able to fly away. Because now I loved her so deeply that the thought of her getting hurt was paralysing. I couldn't think straight with that fear in my head. I couldn't even put that feeling into words.

'You didn't see what happened to Aled.' The fastest swan couldn't outfly fire. I tried not to picture one of the great white birds falling out of the sky with its feathers going up in flames. 'I did, I saw him being attacked, and it was fucking horrible. I am not going through that again.'

'But you're fine with me waiting for a phone call to tell me you've been in a car crash or a fire or fallen off a sodding mountain to break your neck?' She glared at me. 'Or not getting any sort of phone call, just being left wondering what the hell's happened to you. Am I supposed to break that sort of news to your parents? Thanks for that. Actually, no. No thanks. You're not the boss of me. We can deal with this bloody fairy together.'

Deal with her. Put an end to her. Do away with her. Fuck that. We were talking about me committing what was essentially a murder. Murdering a woman a foot and a half shorter than me. I had just about convinced myself I would be able to do it, for Tom's sake, and Aled's and Tyler's. But there was no fucking way I could do that if Fin was watching me.

'No.' I shook my head again. 'If you won't promise to stay here, I won't go. Fuck it. The scary fairy can stay under her hill.'

'Are you serious?' Fin asked, incredulous. 'You'll let her carry on wrecking lives? When you've seen what she can do? I don't just mean those boys. What do you think she'll do to Aled, now she knows that he helped you out? What will she do to that old lady? What will she do to that village?'

All good points. I still wasn't going to back down. 'It's up to you then.'

'What the hell do you mean by that?'

I shrugged. 'You want this sorted out? You let me go on my own. When we know what I've got to do.'

Fin stared at me. I looked down the path to the valley.

'There are people coming.' I pointed at the handful of oblivious tourists toiling up the hillside.

Fin slowly shook her head. 'You bastard.'

She walked away. She didn't look back. I didn't go back to the manor until the last cars had left the car park and Mike had locked the gates. I went up to Eleanor's sitting room. She was there on her own, busy with her laptop.

I cleared my throat. 'Where are Fin and Blanche?'

'On their way back to Dorset.' Eleanor didn't look up from her screen. 'How are things with you?'

'Fine.'

'If you say so.' Her tone asked, who was I trying to kid? She closed her laptop. 'We had better sort out something for dinner. We're going to be spending most of this evening on Zoom.'

She wasn't kidding. Online conversations with Gillian and Hazel were just the start of it.

Chapter Twenty-Four

I arrived back in Caergynan two Mondays later, just after midday. I was on my own in the Land Rover. I had absolutely refused to give in, no matter who offered to come with me. I'd told Gillian the same as I'd told Fin. After what had happened to Aled, I wasn't going to see anyone else put themselves at risk. If the wise women wanted me to put an end to this scary fairy, that was my price. They didn't like that, but they had agreed.

I gripped the steering wheel hard enough to make my hands hurt as I turned into the Meilyr Centre car park. I didn't want to go in there. I wanted Aled kept right out of this. The poor bastard had already paid a hellish price for helping us. He'd done enough. More than enough.

I'd had to give in on this one. The wise women insisted. Aled was the man on the ground. He was the one with local knowledge. He might have heard or seen something I needed to know before I went down to the quarry. Annis Wynne knew he was working with me. She might have said something to him when he got out of hospital.

At least he was out of hospital. That had to be good, right? I was still wondering what 'minimal scarring' meant. I guessed I was going to find out. I looked around as I pressed the key fob to lock the Landy. There was no sign of the Cŵn Annwn.

I gritted my teeth as I walked through the archway. The craft centre was nicely busy without being packed, but Bedo the caffi guy saw me over everyone else's heads. He smiled and raised a beckoning hand. No chance. He was bound to ask about things I didn't want to discuss. I forced a brief smile to acknowledge him and headed for Aled's workshop. I was relieved to see the sign on the door said 'Open'.

There was no one else in the shop. Daisy with the purple hair was polishing the glass display counter. She looked up. 'Good morning.' Her eyes were wary.

'Hello.' I wondered what Aled had told her. I still didn't know if she was his girlfriend or a friend/employee.

He was at work at his bench, though he had his back to the shop. I could see his hair was clipper-cut as short as mine. I wondered if he'd had any choice about that.

He stood up and turned around. 'Dan! Great to see you, mate. Melangell said you'd be coming over, but she wasn't sure it would be today. How was your trip?'

I couldn't think what to say. Aled laughed.

'I'm all set for Halloween, don't you reckon?'

He was wearing a mask. Not a paper hospital one to ward off infection or a medical dressing like the one the paramedics had used. This was transparent plastic, covering everything except his eyes and mouth. Underneath it, his skin looked rough and painfully reddened, especially on his cheekbones. His eyes and mouth seemed okay though, and it even looked as if his eyebrows had grown back. I wondered about his beard. That was gone, but the thought of shaving... My toes clenched inside my boots.

I don't know what he saw in my face. His expression couldn't change, obviously, but his voice was concerned. 'It's just for six months, mate. Honestly, I'll be fine. Looking a bit weather-beaten after, maybe, but some girls, they like the rugged look.'

Daisy snorted. She wasn't his girlfriend, I decided. 'Right,' I said.

'Come on through.' Aled opened a hinged section of the partition wall where it met the counter in the middle of the shop. 'I'll put the kettle on.'

Hidden from customers, I saw a small drop-leaf table with two stools in front of a sink unit on the back wall. A kettle and a microwave stood on a fridge beside it. Aled switched the kettle on and reached up to a shelf for two mugs.

'I'm so sorry.' It was easier to talk when he had his back to me. 'For all—' No, I couldn't go on.

He turned around holding a tin of teabags from the shelf. 'Dan, mate, you've got nothing to be sorry about. Everyone in the hospital, they kept saying I was lucky you were there. Without that water, and those burn dressings for my eyes? I'd have been a whole lot worse off, trust me. And Melangell's been bringing me some burn cream that she says will work wonders.'

'You wouldn't have even been there if—' I stopped, partly because I didn't know if Daisy could hear us, and mostly because I didn't know what to say.

Aled put down the teabags. 'That was my call, going out that night. You didn't make me do anything. No offence, mate, but you couldn't if you wanted to.'

The bell over the shop door rang. Daisy greeted some customers. Aled stepped past the table and lowered his voice. He sounded indignant all the same. I was glad the kettle was boiling noisily.

'This is my place, my people. Something dangerous needs dealing with, I'm in, and that's all there is to it. Now.' Clearly, as far as he was concerned, that subject was closed. 'Melangell says you know what to do in the quarry. That's right, is it? You need anything from me?'

I cleared my throat. 'That's right, and no, this is a one-man job.' Thankfully, that was true. It didn't mean it wasn't going to be dangerous, but I could handle that, as long as I wasn't having to worry about anyone else. 'I'm just checking in with you, in case you've seen anything of Annis Wynne? In case she's said something I should know about?'

'No.' Aled went to drop teabags into the mugs. He poured hot water. 'She's keeping herself to herself. Melangell did call around to the farmhouse, to leave her phone number, see if she could have a chat, but the old girl told her to get lost.' He opened the fridge and reached down for the milk. 'Threatened to set the dogs on her.'

He gave me a meaningful look as he finished making the teas and handed me a mug.

'You haven't seen anyone else heading down that way.' I guessed not, if the Cŵn Annwn were still around, but I wanted to be sure.

'Not a one.' He drank his tea carefully because of his mask.

I drank mine. We heard a customer exclaiming over some necklace or other.

'How's trade then, over by your place?' Aled asked. 'I had a look at the website, Blithehurst. Looks nice.'

'It is, and yes, we're doing well for visitors, and for sales. How about here?'

'Very good sales this month, for me anyway. That's welcome with a new van to buy. Everyone I've spoken to says the same, more or less. Of course, we need it, after, you know, everything.'

'I do.' I put the mug on the table. 'Thanks for the tea.'

'Stop in for another before you head off.' Aled's gaze strayed in the direction of the quarry.

'Thanks.' Let's hope so, anyway. If I didn't come back, I hoped he'd have the sense to phone Melangell and not come looking for me himself. I didn't say that. Not after what he'd said earlier.

Aled opened up the door in the partition. That startled the customers in the shop. He didn't follow me out, and I couldn't blame him. I'd want to avoid strangers as much as I could if I was wearing that mask. Most people probably wouldn't ask questions, but I bet they stared.

I drove the Landy down the track to Cerrigwen and pulled up by the farmhouse's back gate. The padlock was secure. I looked at the house. The dining room curtains were still closed and there was no sign of movement in the kitchen. The Cŵn Annwn were nowhere to be seen.

I walked back up the track and climbed the fence to knock on the front door. No answer. The curtains were drawn at both front windows too. I knocked again as I tried not to imagine the old lady lying dead or helpless on the floor. Crouching down, I pushed open the letter box and peered inside.

If Annis had collapsed, she wasn't in the hall. I couldn't hear the television. I stood up and looked around. Surely the Cŵn Annwn would do something if the old woman needed help. They knew I was someone who could keep her secrets. I checked the time on my phone. Maybe she was having a snooze in her armchair after an early lunch. There was no reason to imagine the worst.

No, but that didn't mean I had to be happy about it. I wanted to talk to Annis Wynne about more than the plan we had finally come up with. I still wanted to know what she meant when she'd said I could do more things than I realised. I hadn't had a chance to talk to my mum yet.

Mum still wasn't talking to my dad. She hadn't joined in any of our recent calls. We were in the same boat then. Fin still wasn't talking to me. Not directly, not outside some conference call with the others or one of the meetings online. I hadn't mentioned that to Dad.

He hadn't been thrilled when I'd told him what had been going on. Obviously he was pleased that Tom and Tyler had been rescued, but he didn't like the sound of a creature that could send a car up in flames. I could hardly blame him. I was glad that I'd be able to tell him I had seen Aled and his burns weren't too bad the next time we talked. I would also try to find some way to say I had some idea how Dad felt now, when he knew I was going up against something dangerous and there was nothing he could do to stop me getting hurt. When this was all over.

So I needed to get it over with. I walked around the farmhouse and climbed over the metal gate. I drove on down the track. This definitely qualified as going off-road by the time I reached the quarry. I stopped close to the thicker grass marking the gully carved by that on-again off-again stream. I could probably drive across it, but there was always a chance of hitting a boggy patch or worse under one of those tussocks. Even a Land Rover has its limits, and I couldn't afford any more repair bills.

I'd come prepared. Asca had braided freshly cut rowan twigs around both my wrists first thing this morning. I was carrying everything else I needed in the pockets of one of those green outdoor sports waistcoats. Eleanor had suggested that, finding it in the back of some wardrobe. I felt a bit of a pillock, but I had to admit it was useful.

I headed for the scary fairy's cavern. This time I'd brought my own hard hat, and when I reached the entrance I put it on. I looked around the quarry again. The only movement was a few weeds swaying as they were brushed by the breeze. I rubbed the scars on my arm. Not so much as a twinge. After a lot of conversation, the wise women had agreed the marks the hamadryad had left on me seemed sensitive when something hostile to me was around. No, they couldn't explain it.

For now, I'd take the lack of itching as a good sign. I switched on my torch and headed into the darkness. When I reached the right-angled turn, something crunched under my boots. I was wearing boots today, not trainers. My building site work boots with steel toecaps. Like I said, I'd come prepared. I shone my torch downwards and saw the shattered remnants of the one I'd dropped when I was trying to escape with the harp. I scanned the rocky floor with the bright white beam. There was no sign that the bits of glass and plastic had been trodden on or swept aside. It didn't look as if anyone or anything had gone in or out of here since that night. Was that good news or bad?

Since I couldn't tell, I carried on walking. My steps echoed in the silence. I swung the torch beam from side to side to show the tunnel walls. I wanted to know exactly when I was about to reach the cavern. Every time the light crossed the ragged rectangle of darkness ahead, I searched it for any hint of glittering eyes betraying creatures in the shadows.

When I reached the cavern, it was empty, apart from the blanket I had left behind, which was lying in a heap. No scary fairy. No golden chair. No shape-shifters. Not even the shallow pool of water she had made glow for my benefit. No one would know this had ever been anything but an abandoned mine working. Bugger.

I walked over to the blanket and kicked it hard, just in case. Nothing was hiding underneath it. I walked around the cavern, looking for other tunnels leading somewhere else. I wasn't going to follow them on my own, but I was starting to think we needed another plan. If I brought back some new information, this wouldn't be a totally wasted trip.

There were no other tunnels. I shone the torch upwards to check if the ceiling was solid. It was. When I stood still and listened, the silence was absolute. I turned off my torch and total darkness surrounded me. It didn't feel ominous or threatening, just empty. The scary fairy and her creatures had gone. Had they gone for good? How the hell were we going to find out?

I picked up the blanket and left. The daylight outside was still bright enough to dazzle me. If anything was going to attack, this was its best chance. I rubbed my eyes and felt for the rowan twig I had sharpened yesterday. An offensive weapon, officer? Oh, I remember. I was whittling the last time I went camping. I hadn't even remembered I had this in my pocket.

Nothing attacked me. On balance, that was a good thing. I mean, I didn't want to have to fight for my life. Been there, done that, got the bruises and the scars. But we'd come up with a plan and I was here to see it through. How was I supposed to put an end to this if I couldn't find the scary fairy?

Who could I ask, apart from Annis Wynne? Folding the blanket as I went, I walked back to the Landy. I'd try knocking on her door again, and then I'd go and tell Aled. Then I'd head back to Blithehurst and back to square one. I hoped the wise women would have some bright ideas.

I was a few metres away from the Land Rover when mist surged out of the damp gully. The cloud solidified into an unfamiliar shape with familiar turquoise eyes. Kalei is a naiad, a river spirit. Water can take any form it likes, so she can look like any woman she wants to. This afternoon, she was masquerading as a woman about my own age in hi-tech hiking gear. Only her shimmering gaze stays the same, for people who can see her true nature.

The Blithehurst dryads had got word to her. I have no idea what they'd said, but she'd come to see what was going on. When I had explained I wasn't coming back here with anyone who could get hurt, Kalei had agreed that was wise. The fiery fucker didn't have to be a problem though, according to her. She was more than a match for some miserable creature who got thrills from causing explosions or burning up cars.

As soon as she said that, Eleanor insisted I wait until Kalei found a way to get here, so she could back me up. I hadn't argued. I'm not an idiot, and I've seen Kalei in action before. As it turned out, it took her more than a week to work out a route using rivers and streams, which wasn't ideal, but we had to put up with that.

'Well?' I asked.

'Nothing.' She shook her head. 'Not a trace under the ground, in the woods or in the shadows.'

She wasn't just here to play fire extinguisher. We'd discussed the many different ways a naiad could be useful.

'So what do we do now?'

Kalei hadn't finished. 'It's worse than that.'

Oh shit. 'What do you mean?'

'I talked to some of my own folk. That was interesting.' She looked at me with her opaque, impenetrable gaze. 'News like you gets around.'

'What does that mean?'

'They've gone. Left. Departed. Done a bunk. You're a celebrity, Dan.' Kalei can blend in with ordinary people so well, she spends a lot of time around them. She grinned, then she was deadly serious. 'This queen under the hill, her creatures, her allies who dwell deep in the darkness, they've abandoned this place. You've proved you're dangerous. They know you've got allies who are no friends of theirs, who are ready to share their secrets. Why would they stay where they know you can find them? They've gone and they're not coming back.'

'Fuck.'

We'd come up with a plan. I'd come here ready for a fight. What were we going to do now? How do you beat someone who doesn't turn up to be beaten?

'This doesn't mean you've won,' Kalei warned. 'The queen under the hill will never accept she's been defeated. If she does, no one will ever dance to her tune again, with or without a magic harp. Everyone knows that, especially her enemies.'

'So wherever she's gone, she'll be plotting some revenge.' That was hardly a surprise.

Kalei nodded. 'She really hates you, Dan. You had better watch your back.'

'Back to the drawing board then.' I reached for the Landy's door handle.

'I'll see you at Blithehurst.' Kalei turned into a cloud of mist and vanished.

Sod it. I tossed the blanket onto the passenger seat, turned the Landy around and drove up the track to the farmhouse. If Annis still wasn't in, I'd leave the blanket on her porch with a note of my phone number. If she didn't want to talk to Melangell, maybe she'd ring me just out of curiosity, or maybe to gloat. She had to know the scary fairy had gone. I was sure of that.

Before I reached the farmhouse, a taxi came down the track. I braked and waited. The Ford people carrier pulled up by the padlocked gate. The driver came around to help Annis Wynne and her folding walker out of the back seat. I saw him look at the Landy, dubious. Annis said something to him, gesturing sharply with one crooked finger. The taxi driver spread his hands and got back into the Ford. He reversed back up the track with a confidence that told me he'd done that before. As he drove away, Annis was still standing by the gate, hunched over her walker and looking at me. I drove up to the edge of the out-buildings, grabbed the blanket and got out.

'I borrowed this the other night. I thought you might want it back.'

'You think I should owe you that favour? Not hardly.' She held out her keys. 'Make yourself useful.'

'Okay.' I hung the blanket over the gate while I found the padlock key. 'Is everything okay? Where have you been?'

'Optician, not that it's any business of yours.' She cackled, startling me. 'Never known a woman my age with such healthy eyes, they say.'

'Congratulations.' I wondered how old their records said she was.

I opened the gate, leaving the padlock hooked on the hasp. Annis trundled slowly through. I followed and waited for her to tell me what to do next. She reached the back door and twisted around to look at me. 'You can unlock this. Help me up the step.'

'Glad to.' I did as she asked, supporting her with a hand under her elbow very carefully. I could have picked her up with one hand if I wasn't afraid of breaking her old, brittle bones. Once she was safely in the kitchen, I put her keys on the table then fetched the blanket. As I took it off the gate, I heard the Cŵn Annwn growl a warning. I saw them crouching in the tumbledown outbuilding again. I wondered how they came and went so freely, when the Tylwyth Teg were kept out. I rubbed my forearm, relieved to feel no warning from those scars.

I took the blanket back to the kitchen. 'Where shall I put this?'

'Needs a wash.' Annis sniffed. 'Leave it by the door. What do you really want?'

If she was going to be direct, I was happy to oblige.

'I came to put an end to her, but there's no one under the hill.' I jerked my head towards the quarry. 'Do you know where she's gone?'

'No.' She scowled. She wasn't happy about that.

I hoped that would do us some good. 'Do you know how we can find her? Will you tell us if you do?'

'We and us, is it now? Choose your friends carefully, forest boy.' She stood in the middle of the kitchen, silent and thoughtful.

I waited. I waited some more. I was starting to think she didn't actually know anything, but she didn't want to admit it.

'You'll have to lure her out,' she said suddenly. 'You need something she can't resist. Bait.'

'Like what?'

She shook her head, cross. 'That's for you to work out, since you're so clever, you and your new friends. You'll get nothing more from me.'

One minute, she seemed to want to see the scary fairy beaten. The next, she was acting as if I was the enemy.

'Go on with you.' She flicked a wrinkled hand at the door. 'I've nothing more to say.'

That clearly wasn't true, but I had no idea what I could do about it. The Cŵn Annwn appeared in the hallway. They both growled, unfriendly, even if that didn't make my arm itch.

'All right. I'm going.' I had something to tell the wise women, I supposed, though just the word 'bait' made my blood run cold.

As I reached for the back door, Annis spoke up. 'Wait.'

I turned to see her smiling unpleasantly.

'When you've done the needful, if you truly know what to do, you bring what you're left with back here. That'll be worth your while, forest boy.'

Her cackling laugh made my skin crawl. I didn't answer as I hurried out of the house. Securing the gate with the padlock felt more like doing something to keep me safe from her, not the other way around.

I got back into the Landy and wondered what Aled might have to say. He could pass the news on to Melangell. By the time I got back to Blithehurst, maybe the wise women would have come up with something.

Bait, though. Fuck. After what Kalei had said, the one person that couldn't be was me.

Chapter Twenty-Five

After a lot of discussion and arguments, we worked out what we needed to do. I really didn't like this second plan, but I couldn't come up with an alternative. It took another week and more to sort out the details. A couple of Saturdays later, I was sitting on the side of a Welsh mountain beside Fin's cousin Will. We'd been up here since sparrow fart.

It turned out that Aled knew the outsides of these mountains as well as he knew the insides. He said this was the ideal place. It was hard to tell through the mask, but I thought his face looked a little bit better. Even so, I was relieved when he left us to it. It was hard to ignore abrupt memories of that dreadful night when he was around. We'd ring him later. All being well.

I didn't like being up this high, and I didn't like having to sit still. If we were lower down, there would be more room. I could be pacing to and fro. Since I wasn't a mountain goat, that wasn't an option here. Why had I thought about goats? I rubbed my arm and looked around for any hint that a shapeshifter was watching us from some crevice.

'Relax.' Will was holding what looked like a computer tablet clamped to a game console controller. He was intent on the screen, completely unbothered by the narrowness of this ledge or the slick of scree beneath us. It was all right for him. He could turn into a swan if he fell off.

My phone buzzed in my pocket. I checked the message. 'He's on his way.'

'Let's see if we can find him.' Will's shoulders hunched as he concentrated.

I edged closer so I could see the screen. The shine on the glass was a pain. I tried to shade it with my hand, feeling queasy as the image swooped and swayed.

'Careful,' Will warned as I accidentally nudged his arm.

I moved away and looked across the valley instead, trying to see the drone in the air. It had seemed enormous when Will unpacked it. Now, as I tried to pick out his technological marvel against the dappled grey rocks and the varied swathes of green, I didn't have a chance. I did have binoculars, but I didn't have any better luck with those.

Will had told me everything anyone could ever want to know about his new toy on the drive over from Blithehurst. He'd been looking for a way to photograph things he saw from the air when he was being a swan for ages, apparently. Then there were the various government-mandated training courses he'd been on, to learn how to use it. It turned out he had a real aptitude, according to his instructors. That wasn't much of a surprise. I don't suppose these courses get many people who are already used to seeing the ground from low altitude, and to dealing with thermals and wind shear. I did tune out when he started talking about the rules and regulations around restricted airspace.

Will stiffened. 'There he is.'

I shifted so I could look over his shoulder. The screen showed us the drone's live feed. Will did something and the camera zoomed in. I saw Tom scrambling up the bare scrape of a sheep trail on the other side of the valley. He was wearing the torn black jeans and faded T-shirt he'd had on when I met him. I hoped he'd got some better trainers.

'Where exactly did the hikers find him?' murmured Will.

'On that path, though Aled couldn't say precisely where.' I swallowed. My mouth was dry. We had brought a couple of bottles of water in my cool bag, but I'd held off drinking anything to avoid having to go for a pee.

'Let's hope he's close enough.' Will adjusted the drone's controls to keep Tom in the centre of the frame. 'What do we do if she doesn't show up?'

'No clue,' I said curtly.

We had no Plan C. It had been hard enough to come up with this one. Then we'd had to convince Gillian, and that had been ten times harder. I still wasn't sure why she had finally agreed. I was just glad she had, and not only because I wanted to put an end to the threats from the scary fairy. Tom needed this. I wanted to see this plan work for his sake.

I realised I was rubbing my forearm and forced myself to stop. My scars weren't itching, and that was good news. If we were too far away for me to sense any threat from the shapeshifters, we were far enough away for the scary fairy not to sense me. Kalei had said that watching from the other side of this valley should be okay. We had to hope the naiad was right. We had to hope for a whole lot of things to go our way.

'There she is.' Will's voice tightened. His hands shook. 'That is her, isn't it?'

'Hold that thing still. Yes,' I said a moment later. 'That's her.'

Even the worst-prepared hikers don't climb mountains in evening dresses. Though bizarrely, the fairy queen didn't look remotely out of place as we watched her confront Tom. These were her hills. This had always been her domain, and as far as she was concerned, it always would be.

'Come on, Tom,' murmured Will. 'Keep it together.'

After a lot of discussion with the wise women, we had agreed the scary fairy must have been telling the truth when she'd told Tom she would always know where he was after he had been her prisoner. She had no reason to lie, even if she had been able to. So we had gambled on her curiosity when she realised he had come back to these mountains. Surely she would have to see what was going on? There was every chance she would want to snatch him back. That would be a victory after losing Tyler as well as the harp.

We were right. She had taken the bait. This was the first thing we needed to happen for this plan to have any chance of success. I stared at the screen, not daring to look away.

'No sign of creepy creatures,' Will remarked.

I wasn't sure why he felt the need to keep up a running commentary, but he was right about that. Or rather, Kalei had been right, and the Blithehurst druids had agreed with her. They said the fairy's shapeshifting followers were creatures of darkness and shadow. They wouldn't come out in broad daylight. They wouldn't have any substance. They wouldn't be able to touch or hold on to anything or anyone.

So far, so good. The third and final thing we needed for this plan to work was for Tom to keep his nerve. Gillian had argued that this was asking far too much of the boy. She said he was putting his life back together. She said any new trauma risked undoing the hard work he'd done so far with his counsellors and tutors. I said that was his decision to make. Surely he deserved to make his own choices?

Gillian had pointed out that I had changed my tune. I'd been perfectly happy making decisions for other people up to now. I said I'd been doing some thinking. In any case, did she have an alternative? I asked her to let me talk to Tom, to lay everything out. It wasn't as if I was going to lie to him. He would know I was telling the truth. I would give him the facts and he could make up his mind. She said she would think about it.

Eleanor had shut down her computer and asked me to warn her if I was going to do a U-turn like that again. She didn't want to be sitting quite so close if I was going to be struck by a thunderbolt. I wasn't quite sure what she meant by that, so I didn't ask.

The next day, Gillian rang to say she agreed to me talking to Tom. I headed up to Oldham. I've no idea what explanations Eleanor was offering the staff for my comings and goings now. I was pretty sure I'd be covering a lot of days off for the rest of the year.

We met in a nice park with kids playing games and people walking their dogs. Tom listened to me, pale and silent. I told him everything that had happened since we had last met. I explained what we were asking him to do. I made certain he knew the risks. The scary fairy would be as solidly real as he was, and most likely twice as strong. I explained how we would be watching, and everything we would do to keep him safe.

I said it was up to him. No one was going to force him to do anything. Nobody could. If he didn't want to do this, we'd find another way. His life would go on the same as it had for this past month. He'd have the same help and support, as well as the wise women keeping watch in case anything ever tried to find him again. We weren't looking to make a deal. He didn't need to pay us back.

The skinny kid sat still for so long that I thought he was going to say no. Then a wicked smile lit up his eyes. 'Fuck yes, I'm in.'

Now I was the one muttering as we watched the little screen. 'Come on, Tom. Remember what we told you.'

He stood on the path facing the scary fairy. His back was straight and he thrust his chin forward, defiant. We could see she was screaming at him, though Will and I could only hear the thin, mewing cries of red kites wheeling overhead. The scary fairy's face twisted with anger. I could see that livid scar on her cheek. She raised her arms with her hands crooked like claws. Tom didn't back down. He stuck his hands in his pockets and shrugged.

She made a grab for him. We couldn't see what Tom did next, but the scary fairy collapsed to her knees. She wrapped her arms around her head. The wind tugged at her long black hair and ruffled her flowing skirts. It hadn't done that before.

Tom stood over her, looking down. He lifted his hand. The sun struck a glint from the blade we knew he was holding. It was only a penknife. That was all he needed. I had given him the one I'd accidentally used to destroy the flower maiden. Gillian had told us he'd practised and practised, to make sure he could get it open in one quick move.

'Oh shit,' Will breathed.

'Wait.' I didn't dare even blink.

Tom lowered his hand and stepped away from the woman cowering on the sloping ground. He put his hands back in his pockets. He had put the penknife away.

'Yes!' I was so relieved I felt dizzy. I shook that off and reached for my phone. I hit the screen to call Aled 'He's done it.'

'Right you are.'

As soon as he ended the call, I rang Gillian.

'He's done it.'

'Excellent. See you there.'

My phone went dark, and I looked at Will. 'You're okay here?'

'Yes, fine.' He was gazing out across the valley, bringing his drone back to pack it away in the case we'd carried up here. 'You get going. I'll wait for Melangell, like we said.'

THE GREEN MAN'S GIFT

'Right.' I grabbed the cool bag and started down the path to the grassy lane where we'd left the Landy. I forced myself to go slowly and to watch where I was putting my feet. The last thing we needed was me falling down the mountainside. Besides, there was no need for me to hurry. Aled and Gillian were far closer to Tom, and they were already on their way.

I reached the Landy and took a few minutes to drink some water. I sent Eleanor a text to let her know Tom had done it. Then I followed the looping road that wound around the end of the valley and headed up the other side. I parked behind Gillian's grimy Peugeot and took the path leading up the hillside. She was already with Tom, her reassuring hand resting on his shoulder. I didn't think he needed that. For the first time since I'd met him, his eyes weren't hollow and haunted. He could look forward instead of back.

'Here you go.' He grinned as he offered me the closed penknife.

I held up an open palm. 'You keep it. You earned it.'

It wasn't as if the coppers could call it an offensive weapon, even if it had put an end to the scary fairy.

Aled had arrived before me as well. He was looking at the woman huddled in a heap on the path. Her high-pitched keening was barely louder than the red kites overhead.

'That's all it took,' he marvelled. 'One little cut.'

'Finding that out took a great deal of work,' Gillian pointed out.

'How—?' The woman choked as she looked up at us.

Her black hair reached down past her elbows, or at least it would if the breeze stopped blowing it into tangles. Her hands and her face were pale, marked by that old scar between her left thumb and forefinger and the newer gash on her cheek where I'd punched her with the rowan ring on my fist. Her eyes were chestnut brown with clear, unblemished whites. Human eyes. She was mortal now. As human as me, Aled, Gillian and Tom. As human as her sister, Annis.

We had finally put the few clues the old lady had given us together with everything Eleanor and the wise women had ferreted out. They had been reading every source they could possibly find that mentioned the Tylwyth Teg and their dealings with humans. One recurring theme had been the fair folk's fear of being struck, even accidentally.

Annis had said her sister stabbed her in the back. We realised she meant that literally. We realised the blow had come from a steel blade to leave that scar on the fairy's hand. When we found the story of a Tylwyth Teg wife who had become mortal after being cut with a knife, we understood what had happened. We also worked out it didn't simply take a single blow. There must only be a single blow. If Tom or anyone else stabbed a fairy in a frenzy, which would be understandable given what they put people through, a second cut would undo the work of the first and the knife would have no more effect.

At least, that was the theory. We had run it past Asca and Frai, as well as Kalei. The dryads and the naiad had never heard of such a thing, and they were quick to point out that this most certainly would not work on them. Will had asked his girlfriend over in Norfolk. She's a nereid, the daughter of a river spirit and a merman. This was news to her as well, and the sea folk were convinced we were wrong. Too many of them had had run-ins with boats and fishing gear for it to be true. But the wise women and Eleanor went over their research and their reasoning again and again. They were convinced they had found a secret to use against the Tylwyth Teg. Now we knew they were right.

Tom was still grinning at me. 'Told you I could do it.'

I had stressed how vital it was for him to keep his temper. He must not lose control, no matter how badly he wanted to cut her into ribbons. One cut was all it would take.

'You were right.' I grinned back.

We'd still taken precautions, in case he froze and the scary fairy thought she could drag him away to some new nightmare. Kalei was lurking close by, hidden in a waterfall even though that was only a faint trickle in the summer heat. She insisted the scary fairy would never know she was there. She swore there was nowhere the fairy could go in these mountains where a naiad couldn't follow. She promised she would get Tom out of her clutches before the scary fairy knew what was happening. We could all see she was telling the truth.

The woman kneeling on the ground wailed. She raised her left hand and her red sleeve fell back. A trickle of blood showed us where Tom had stuck the penknife in her. The cut was barely a couple of centimetres long on the inside of her forearm. She touched the scarlet thread with a shaking forefinger and screamed with shock, outrage and pain. She looked at each of us in turn, lost for words. She looked afraid.

I snapped my fingers to get her attention. 'Your sister said I could take you to her. Or I'll take you anywhere you want and you can fend for yourself.'

That was something we had discussed several times. We agreed we couldn't leave her out on the mountain to die from exposure – unless she absolutely refused to go with us. That was simple enough. If she wouldn't go to Cerrigwen though? We'd have to dump her somewhere else.

None of us particularly liked that idea, but what else could we do? Take her home to live with one of us? Try to explain that to friends and neighbours. Try to explain away whatever she told them, which might well arouse suspicions about our own secrets. Try to teach her to be a normal person, contributing to society? How many years would that take, even if it was possible? No chance. There could be no fairy tale happily-ever-after ending for her. She would end up on the streets, labelled homeless and deranged, but that was no threat to us. No one would believe her story.

She looked at me, so confused that I wasn't sure she understood. Then she blinked and her face hardened. 'My sister betrayed me? She will pay for her treachery.'

That threat was a pathetic whisper compared to the chilling wrath she had summoned as a fairy. When she blinked, her eyes stayed fearful and human.

'No, she didn't.' I shook my head. 'She refused to, more than once.'

She might be mortal now, but she could still hear I was telling the truth. She looked more baffled than ever.

'Right,' Gillian said briskly to Tom. 'Let's get you home.'

He looked reluctant for a moment, then he nodded. 'Okay.' He leaned down to smile at the woman still cowering on her knees. 'Suck it, bitch.'

She recoiled as if he had hit her. She might not understand the words, but Tom's meaning was crystal clear. He knew he had won, and he knew that so did she.

Gillian was having trouble keeping a straight face. 'Come on, you.'

She walked off and Tom went with her. I looked at Aled. He was amused, as far as it was possible to tell through his mask.

'Not exactly the words a bard would use to celebrate a famous victory.' He held up his phone. 'You'll be all right here, will you? Melangell's on her way.'

'I'll be fine. See you in the pub.'

'Right you are.' Aled started down the path to the road.

I glanced around, but there was no sign of Kalei. She was probably already on her way to The Black Bull now that the threat was gone.

I looked down at the woman. 'So, are you going to walk, or do I have to pick you up and carry you?'

I honestly didn't mean to threaten her, but she gaped at me, utterly terrified. For the first time ever, she was completely at the mercy of someone far bigger and stronger than she was. As soon as I realised that, I felt an utter prick. Then I remembered what she'd done to Tom and to the others. The feeling faded fast.

She was getting to her feet, which was a relief. I didn't particularly want someone driving by seeing me manhandling a kicking, screaming woman half my size and strapping her into the Land Rover. Kidnapping a woman with no

ID or anything else but the clothes she was wearing. Good afternoon, officer. My passenger's name? Ah...

I took my keys out of my pocket. 'What do you want me to call you?'

She shook her head, obstinate.

'Okay then.' I gestured at the path. 'After you.'

She stumbled down the slope ahead of me. I realised her feet were bare. She winced every time she stood on something sharp. By the time we reached the Landy, she was whimpering with tears running down her face. No ID and not even wearing shoes? I really did not want to get stopped by a copper before I got her to Cerrigwen.

I opened the passenger door. 'Get in.'

She looked at me, scared. I looked back, unrelenting. She reached for the door, snatching her hand back almost before she touched it. She expected the metal to burn her, I realised. When it didn't, I saw her face crumple. Her new reality was hitting home. She was mortal and everything had changed.

I went around to the driver's side and got in. 'Seatbelt.'

She hesitated, then she copied me as soon as she saw what I meant. As I started the engine, I reminded myself that she had been sharp-eyed and quick-witted when she was the scary fairy. She wouldn't be stupid as a mortal woman, if Annis Wynne was any guide. She might be knocked off balance at the moment, but I still needed to be careful.

I drove to Caergynan observing every speed limit, constantly checking my mirrors and signalling at every turn. When we got there, the village was busy with holidaymakers and hikers, but whatever Annis was doing to make sure no one was interested in her house was still working fine. No one gave the Landy a second glance as I pulled up outside the back gate.

The woman threw the passenger door open and sprang out of her seat. She'd even remembered to undo her seatbelt. She ran away down the track towards the quarry. I got out of the Land Rover, hoping to see the Cŵn Annwn go after her. No such luck. Where's a hound of the underworld when you need one?

I followed her, and with my much longer stride, I soon caught up. She was limping now, and crying out as the sharp-edged slate cut her feet. I caught glimpses of her bare, bloody soles and winced. She had hard lessons to learn about being human, and it looked like she was going to learn the hard way.

When we reached the quarry, I took a good look around even though my forearm felt fine. The dryads and Kalei had been confident that she would lose her hold on her shadowy shapeshifter creatures as soon as she turned mortal. I hoped they were right.

She headed straight for the entrance to her cavern. I remembered the broken glass and plastic on the tunnel floor. 'Wait!'

She didn't hear me. A crack like a gunshot echoed around the quarry. She stopped dead. So did I. Was someone out on these hills with a shotgun? I had absolutely no clue what to say if they wandered in here now.

Another ear-splitting crack made me wince. That wasn't from a shotgun. Movement had caught my eye. A jagged lump of stone had toppled from the top of the spoil pile. Another followed. It made the same noise as it hit the quarry floor. That was far more noise than a rock that size had any right to make. There was no reason for any of these stones to fall off a heap that hadn't been disturbed for decades.

She looked back at me, horrified. 'Coblynau?'

'I guess they're cross about what you did to Aled.' I really hoped they weren't cross with me.

She said something, but I didn't hear it. The whole spoil heap was on the move now. Stones flowed over each other, as swift and slick as water. Plants that had been growing in pockets of windblown dirt vanished, ground into mulch. Faster than I thought possible, the entrance to her cavern was blocked.

She screamed with wordless fury and frustration. A sharp crack answered her. That had come from the other spoil heap, away on my right-hand side. Two more dark stones fell from the top of it, both making that menacing sound.

I was already backing away. If the knockers wanted her, they could have her, because there sure as hell wasn't anything I could do to stop them. If her shapeshifters were lurking in the old mine workings, which I very much doubted, they were on their own.

Like I said, she wasn't stupid. She started back up the track, running straight past me, even though her feet must have been agony. The rocks stopped moving, apart from a faint patter of little stones down the spoil heap. That sounded like eerie, distant laughter.

I followed her, breaking into a jog. We couldn't have her running into the Meilyr Centre. I would have to grab her and drag her back to the farmhouse before she reached the junction with the footpath.

I didn't have to. She stopped by the Land Rover. The metal gate was open and so was the house's back door. Hunched over her walker, Annis Wynne stood in the entrance to the yard.

'You said I should bring her here,' I began as I reached them.

Neither of them was listening. They were staring at each other. I could see they could have been twins, they had once looked so alike. Now though, Annis could have been the woman in red's grandmother, or even her great-grandmother.

As she cackled, her faded eyes never left her sister's face. 'We were never able to foretell the future, were we? Well, my dearest, take a good look. This is the fate that awaits you.'

I don't know which made me shiver more. The look of utter horror on the woman in red's face or the vicious exultation ringing through Annis's words. That's why she had told me to bring her sister here. Not to offer her shelter now that she was mortal. She had wanted this revenge, and she had got it. She wanted me to know it too, otherwise she'd have been speaking Welsh.

Still looking at the woman in red, she jerked her head at the back door. 'Get in there.'

Completely cowed, she did as she was told, leaving bloody footprints on the step.

Annis looked at me, still savouring her triumph. 'You can go. This is between me and her now.'

I heard growling and saw the Cŵn Annwn in the shadows of the derelict outbuilding. The faintest warning prickled in my scars.

'Fine.' I got into the Landy and drove over to The Black Bull, the pub where Aled had taken me for Sunday lunch. The others were there, and my first pint was waiting.

What else was I supposed to do? Force my way into Annis's house and play referee? For how long, assuming the Cŵn Annwn even let me through the door? Yes, the woman in red was younger and stronger than Annis, but the old woman had her hounds to protect her, as well as whatever powers she could call on. She'd had decades to learn to live with her unwanted mortality. Decades to wait for this moment.

Chapter Twenty-Six

I saw Will again a few weeks later. He came over to Blithehurst to photograph the silver displayed on the altar in the hidden chapel.

'Have you had a look?' Sarah asked as she came down the secret stair and through the hidden doorway.

'I helped set everything up.' I was in the manor house dining room with a clipboard and pen. It was a Monday, so only the staff were about, but everyone seemed to want to see the treasure. They couldn't all go up at once, so I was in charge of the list.

'My turn.' Briony went up the narrow stair like a rat up a drainpipe.

'It is a shame we can't let people see it where it belongs.' Sarah waved that away. 'I know. We could never afford the insurance.'

'Did you hear what the conservator said?' Eleanor had asked an expert if he had any concerns about setting up photographic lights in the confined space. He had immediately assumed she was planning to let visitors into the chapel on a regular basis.

'No?' Sarah looked at me, expectant.

'Access would have to be strictly managed to avoid moisture from people's breath lingering and damaging the fragile paintings on the walls and ceilings.' That's why I had been taking staff names for these timed slots.

Sarah snorted, amused. 'He didn't think it might be difficult to manage the house tours with a great big queue cluttering up the place. Not to mention everyone breathing on each other while they waited.' She shook her head. 'No, it's all for the best. The exhibition in the morning room will be great.'

'And the one down in the castle,' I reminded her. 'With your video.'

Personally, I hadn't been thrilled when Eleanor had explained her plans for a second display showing how we'd found the treasure in the hidey-hole under the kennel. At least I wasn't in the video very much. Sarah had been far more interested in the mysterious box. Blithehurst was paying her for the rights to use the video in the display and on the website, so that was a nice little bonus.

Will and I had already been down to the ruins this morning. He'd taken a whole load of photos showing the plinth with the kennel, without the kennel, with the slab lifted up and with the box where it had been found. A new notice would tell visitors politely and firmly NOT to move the kennel themselves and to visit the exhibition in the gatehouse tower room. That would also have photos and reports from previous archaeological surveys around the buildings and the estate, to convince anyone who fancied sneaking in at night with a metal detector that there really was no more treasure to be found. As well as warning anyone who didn't believe it that they would be prosecuted to the fullest extent of the law.

Briony's eyes were bright when she came down the secret stair. 'That's amazing.'

'Isn't it?' Sarah agreed as they walked off together.

'Dan!' Will called down to me.

'Yes?' I went halfway up the steps until I could see into the chapel. That stair's a tight fit for someone my size, and the priest hole is even worse.

The altar treasure did look spectacular, standing on the blue velvet cloth. If you didn't know there were specialist lights and reflective surfaces set up, you would think the silver was softly gleaming in the golden light from the two candles that flanked the cross.

Will was adjusting something on his camera. 'She's the last one coming in until this afternoon?'

'That's right.'

He licked his thumb and forefinger and snuffed out the candles. 'Let's take a break and see what I've got so far.'

I went back down and hit the switch on the extension cord we'd had to run up the stair. Everything went dark as Will appeared. I closed the door hidden in the panelling by the fireplace and we went over to the trestle table set up by the window that looked out over the gardens.

'Mind the paintings,' I warned Will.

Five portraits rescued from the attic or borrowed from other family members were stacked against the wall. Handwritten letters with faded ink as well as crisp black print-outs were piled on the table in plastic folders.

'This is all going in the exhibition?' Will glanced over as he connected his camera to his laptop.

'That's right.'

He pulled up a folding chair and hit a few keys, intent on his screen. 'I think Eleanor will be pleased with these. If any London picture editor thinks their snapper can do better, they can kiss my lily-white arse. Any idea when she'll be back?'

'Not sure.'

Eleanor was out meeting a journalist from one of the Sunday papers, hoping to interest her in the exciting story of the Elizabethan Beauchenes who had used the silver in the Catholic services held in their secret chapel by fugitive priests. A century and a half later, a renegade Georgian Beauchene who had known about the hidey-hole had hidden the family treasure from his stubbornly Protestant eldest brother who was going to inherit the estate. John had gone off to fight for Bonnie Prince Charlie, and he was killed before he could come home and prove he hadn't stolen the treasure to help fund the Jacobite cause. The staff were talking about the possibility of a drama-documentary. Word had spread that Eleanor was meeting some television people later today as well. I wondered what Anthony Hackshott's ghost would make of that, if it ever happened.

Will looked up. 'When's the security firm due?'

'Five.'

We only had the silver back here for one day and everyone was sworn to secrecy. Every story that would go in the papers and on the local news, as well as the pages waiting to go live on Blithehurst's website, would make it very clear that the altar set was in the safekeeping of a firm of London auctioneers. They would be selling these rare and valuable antiques in a few months' time, ideally after this publicity had helped bump up the price as well as bringing the manor loads more visitors.

My phone buzzed in my pocket. Aled was calling me. 'Hello?'

'Hi, Dan. Well, there's news I thought you'd want to hear, and pass on. I found the last missing boy yesterday.'

'Dead?' I had to ask even though Aled's flat tone made the answer clear.

'Yes.' He sighed. 'Not exactly a surprise, but you couldn't help hoping, could you?'

'How did you find him?'

'I took yesterday afternoon off, borrowed Daisy's car. Went for a hike to clear my head, have some time on my own, off the beaten track.'

Somewhere people wouldn't be staring at him, I guessed.

'The Cŵn Annwn were waiting for me when I parked.' He sounded as if he still didn't quite believe it. 'They did the whole "What's that, Lassie? Little Timmy's fallen down the well?" routine. You know what I mean?'

'They showed you where he was?'

'Up in a dead-end valley where no one hardly ever goes. Of course, it's packed with people now. I rang the police and reported it. Whoever he was, somebody must be missing him.'

I thought about Tom. 'Let's hope so.'

Aled hadn't finished. 'That's not all, and there's no other way to put it. She's dead too.'

He didn't need to tell me who. 'How?'

'Took a header off the top of the quarry sometime last night, looks like.' He sounded shaken.

'Did you find her?' That must have been unpleasant.

'Thanks to the Cŵn Annwn turning up to pester me first thing this morning, as soon as I arrived at the centre.'

I wondered if the woman in red had known her last victim had been found. Had she confessed where he was to her sister? Had Annis sent the Cŵn Annwn to make sure that Aled found him? Had the woman in red jumped, or had she been chased off that precipice as some sort of retribution? It wasn't as if she could be charged with murder by the police. I didn't imagine we would ever know any of these answers. 'So...?'

'Melangell says they'll take care of her. Half a dozen of them have turned up.' Aled lowered his voice, though I couldn't hear any hint of another person near him. 'She says dead bodies are a lot easier to deal with than live ones.'

'Remind me never to get on their wrong side,' I said with feeling.

'I know, right?' He managed a short laugh.

'Has someone told Annis the news?'

'Melangell. She came over for a coffee. She says the old lady seems very frail, compared to a month ago.'

I wondered how much longer Annis would cling to life, now she'd had her revenge on her sister. I wondered what had gone on in that decaying house with the two of them shut up together. I wasn't sorry we would never know.

'Thanks for telling me. I appreciate it. I'll spread the word.'

'Cheers.' Aled sounded a lot less stressed now he had passed on that burden. 'I'll let you get on. Always plenty to do, isn't there?'

'There certainly is.'

'I'll let you know if there's anything else, after, well, you know.'

'Thanks. Bye.' I ended the call.

Will was wide-eyed with curiosity. 'What was that about?'

We were on our own in the dining room, but I wasn't about to repeat what Aled had told me when one of the staff might walk in at any moment. 'I'll email everyone later.'

'Oh, right.' He looked at me thoughtfully. 'I've been meaning to ask, about you and Fin—'

'Ask what?' I gave him a look that I really hoped would convince him to mind his own business.

It worked.

'Nothing.' Will stood up so fast he knocked his chair over. 'Why don't I go and get us some lunch from the restaurant? You've got to stay here on guard, haven't you?'

He hurried off before I could answer that, or even tell him what I wanted to eat.

I arranged to meet Fin a fortnight later. I texted Blanche to check for some dates when she would be free. Then I booked two nights in a double room at the most expensive hotel in Chester, really posh, right in the centre. I forwarded the confirmation email to Fin and waited.

I got a text later that day.

Book a table in the brasserie for dinner 7pm Friday.

I did that and texted back.

I'll meet you in the bar.

I got there early. I still had an hour to kill after checking in, having a shave and a shower and putting on a new shirt and trousers that made me feel as if I was going for a job interview. I didn't want to talk to anyone, but I didn't want to be on my own, so I went down to the bar. I stuck to Coke. This was no time to start drinking to get my courage up. Besides, I have a very hard head, so getting drunk would cost me a fortune as well as being stupid.

Fin arrived at exactly five minutes to the hour. She came into the bar and looked around. I raised my hand and got off the bar stool. She waited for me to join her. She was wearing a pale yellow blouse and loose cream trousers. She didn't look as if she'd just driven up from Bristol. She had a handbag with her, but that was all.

'You look nice.' I waited to see if she made any move to kiss me. She didn't.

'Shall we go through?' She turned to see where we had to go to find the restaurant.

In the brasserie, the waiter showed us to a table and handed us our menus. 'I'll give you a moment.'

I wondered what he thought was going on.

Fin studied her menu.

'I'm sorry,' I said.

Fin kept reading the menu. 'For what?'

'For all of it.' I tried to tell her I wouldn't do anything like that again, but the words stuck in my throat. 'I will try to do better. I promise.'

'Blanche says—' Fin bit her lower lip, still studying the starters.

I bit the inside of my cheek to stop myself saying anything, especially about Blanche.

Fin kept her voice down out of consideration for the other diners, but I could still hear an echo of her fury when she had left me at Asca's temple. 'Blanche says you probably wouldn't have been such a colossal arsehole if you didn't love me so much.'

That was a surprise. 'She's probably right about that,' I said cautiously.

'Iris says I probably wouldn't have been quite so pissed off if I didn't love you so much.'

I looked at the flower arrangement on the table. I guessed Fin had stayed over with Iris in Manchester or wherever it was she lived before coming to Chester today.

Fin cleared her throat. 'She's probably right about that. She says we need to talk. Not her and us,' she added quickly. 'You and me. Just you and me. On our own.'

That was a relief. I looked up. 'I really am sorry.'

'Let's eat before we get into that.' Fin looked around for the waiter. 'I'd like the grilled plaice to start, please,' she told him when he arrived, 'followed by the ricotta and spinach raviolo with a mixed salad.'

'Ham hock terrine, please, and the chicken breast, with chips.' I handed him my menu.

'And to drink?' the waiter asked.

Fin took a look at the wine list. 'The Soave.' She pointed to show him the one she meant. 'A bottle, please, and some water.'

I waited until the waiter walked away. 'So you won't be driving, later?'

'You booked a double room, didn't you?' For the first time since she had arrived, Fin smiled. 'I left my overnight bag with reception.'

I wondered if she would have picked her bag up and left if I had said the wrong thing. Probably.

A different waiter appeared with a jug of water. Fin filled our glasses. 'So how are things at Blithehurst? Trust me, you don't want to hear about sewage over dinner.'

I told her about Will and the photo shoots, and the new displays telling the story of the altar silver. Our food arrived, and it was really good. We talked about what there was to see in Chester and decided to do the city walls walk next morning. We wondered about the interest the Cŵn Annwn were apparently taking in Aled.

By the time we were waiting for our incredibly fancy desserts, things felt close enough to normal between us for me to reach into my shirt pocket. I took out a small plastic Ziplock bag. The silver feather earrings were inside.

'These are for you. Aled saw me looking at them in his shop. He sent them to me a few weeks ago, but I haven't got pierced ears.'

It wasn't much of a joke, but it was the best I could come up with. I had also decided against putting the earrings into a fancy box. I didn't want to even think about the ways offering her something like that in this restaurant could go wrong.

'They're lovely.' Fin took the earrings out for a closer look.

'I really am sorry,' I said again.

She looked at me and smiled. 'I believe you.'

For the first time since she'd walked away from me, I reckoned we would be able to put things right.

Acknowledgements

As ever, I am indebted to the valued friends and colleagues who contribute so much to the success of this series. As my publisher, Cheryl Morgan is taking Wizard's Tower Press from strength to strength. Toby Selwyn continues to excel as an editor, keeping me up to the mark as a writer. Once again Ben Baldwin shows his incredible talent for distilling the essence of a story in his artwork.

My sincere thanks to Kari Sperring for her perspectives on the Welsh landscape and language in the first instance. Once this story was written, Toby and Cheryl drew on their own heritage to offer further advice and amendments which were very much appreciated. Any errors or infelicities that remain are my responsibility alone.

For this book in particular, I am profoundly grateful to the Milford SF Writers group for organising their writers' retreat at Trigonos in Snowdonia in May 2022. This offered me the chance to see the places I was writing about and to pick up fascinating local history. This time away from home also came exactly when I needed peace and quiet without distractions or obligations in order to focus on this story. Thank you to the Trigonos staff for looking after us so well. I am also grateful to my fellow writers for their stimulating and inspiring company during our stay.

I can't recall when a week last passed without some hopeful query about the next book reaching me through social media. Knowing readers are eager for Dan's next adventure is wonderfully encouraging, and thank you to everyone who shares their enthusiasm for these books. Word of mouth buzz keeps small press projects going!

My thanks also to the SF convention committees and other fan event organisers for taking on the added work of blending in-person attendance with online access as we build on the experiences of the past few years. Our community of readers and writers continues to sustain me.

About the Author

Juliet E McKenna is a British fantasy author living in the Cotswolds, UK. Loving history, myth and other worlds since she first learned to read, she has written fifteen epic fantasy novels so far. Her debut, *The Thief's Gamble*, began The Tales of Einarinn in 1999, followed by The Aldabreshin Compass sequence, The Chronicles of the Lescari Revolution, and The Hadrumal Crisis trilogy. *The Green Man's Heir* was her first modern fantasy inspired by British folklore, followed by *The Green Man's Foe*, *The Green Man's Silence* and *The Green Man's Challenge*. Her shorter stories include forays into dark fantasy, steampunk and science fiction. She promotes SF&Fantasy by reviewing, by blogging on book trade issues, attending conventions and teaching creative writing. In 2021, Juliet was elected to the Management Committee of the Society of Authors. She has also written historical murder mysteries set in ancient Greece as J M Alvey.

www.julietemckenna.com

@JulietEMcKenna

The Tales of Einarinn

1. The Thief's Gamble (1999)
2. The Swordsman's Oath (1999)
3. The Gambler's Fortune (2000)
4. The Warrior's Bond (2001)
5. The Assassin's Edge (2002)

The Aldabreshin Compass

1. The Southern Fire (2003)
2. Northern Storm (2004)
3. Western Shore (2005)
4. Eastern Tide (2006)

Turns & Chances (2004)

The Chronicles of the Lescari Revolution

1. Irons in the Fire (2009)
2. Blood in the Water (2010)
3. Banners in The Wind (2010)

The Wizard's Coming (2011)

The Hadrumal Crisis

1. Dangerous Waters (2011)
2. Darkening Skies (2012)
3. Defiant Peaks (2012)

A Few Further Tales of Einarinn (2012) (ebook from Wizards Tower Press)

Challoner, Murray & Balfour: Monster Hunters at Law (2014) (ebook from Wizards Tower Press)

Shadow Histories of the River Kingdom (2016) (Wizards Tower Press)

The Green Man (Wizards Tower Press)

1. The Green Mans Heir (2018)
2. The Green Man's Foe (2019)
3. The Green Man's Silence (2020)
4. The Green Man's Challenge (2021)

THE GREEN MAN'S GIFT

The Philocles series (as J M Alvey)

    1. Shadows of Athens (2019)
    2. Scorpions in Corinth (2019)
    3. Justice for Athena (2020)
    4. Silver for Silence (a dyslexia-friendly quick read, 2022)

Lightning Source UK Ltd.
Milton Keynes UK
UKHW022056181022
410709UK00012B/169/J

9 781913 892418

Naked Project Management

Naked Project Management

The Bare Facts

DENNIS LOCK

GOWER

© Dennis Lock 2013

All rights reserved. No part of this publication may be reproduced, stored in a retrieval system or transmitted in any form or by any means, electronic, mechanical, photocopying, recording or otherwise without the prior permission of the publisher.

Dennis Lock has asserted his moral right under the Copyright, Designs and Patents Act, 1988, to be identified as the author of this work.

Published by
Gower Publishing Limited
Wey Court East
Union Road
Farnham
Surrey, GU9 7PT
England

Ashgate Publishing Company
110 Cherry Street
Suite 3-1
Burlington
VT 05401-3818
USA

www.gowerpublishing.com

British Library Cataloguing in Publication Data
Lock, Dennis.
  Naked project management : the bare facts.
  1. Project management.
  I. Title
  658.4'04-dc23

  ISBN: 978-1-4094-6105-0 (pbk)
       978-1-4094-6106-7 (ebk)
       978-1-4094-6107-4 (epub)

Library of Congress has catalogued the print edition as follows:
Lock, Dennis.
  Naked project management : the bare facts / by Dennis Lock.
    p. cm.
  Includes bibliographical references and index.
  ISBN 978-1-4094-6105-0 (pbk.) -- ISBN 978-1-4094-6106-7 (ebook)
  1. Project management. I. Title.
  HD69.P75L627 2013
  658.4'04--dc23

2012029750

WEST SUSSEX LIBRARY SERVICE	
201174247	
Askews & Holts	30-Apr-2013
658.404	

MIX
Paper from responsible sources
FSC® C018575

Contents

List of Figures   *vii*
Preface   *ix*

1   Projects   1
    Project Types   1
    Project Life Cycles   2
    Principal Project Players   6
    Project Outcomes   8
    The Swings and Roundabouts Project   9

2   Getting Ready for the Project   11
    Project Definition   11
    Work Breakdown Structure (WBS)   12
    Costs and Cost Estimating   15
    Introduction to Cost Estimating Methods   18
    Work Breakdown and Cost Estimate for the Swings and
        Roundabouts Project   19

3   Organization   25
    Organizations in General   25
    Introducing a Project into an Organization for the First Time   27
    Coordinated Project Matrix   28
    Project Teams and Task Forces   29
    Matrix Organizations for Multiple Projects   32
    Organization Theory from the Project Manager's Point of
        View   34
    Organization of the Swings and Roundabouts Project   35

4   Planning and Scheduling   39
    Essential Requirements for an Effective Plan   39
    Diary Planning   40
    Bar Charts   40
    Introduction to Critical Path Network Analysis   42
    Resource Scheduling   48
    Planning the Swings and Roundabouts Project   49

5	**Contracts and Commerce**	57
	About Contracts	57
	Purchasing	58
	Contracts for Services and Construction	64
	Contract Administration	67
	Contracts and Purchases for the Swings and Roundabouts Project	68
6	**Taking Control**	73
	Managing Project Risk	73
	Controlling Project Changes	75
	Some Principles of Progress Control	76
	Some Principles of Cost Control	79
	Methods for Measuring or Monitoring Costs	80
	Attempts to Analyse Trends and Make Predictions Using Earned Value Analysis	81
	Controlling the Swings and Roundabouts Project	84
7	**Task Forces for Special Projects**	89
	Our Project is Sick: Send for a Doctor!	89
	Task Forces for Business Change Projects	92
	Task Forces as a General Solution?	96
8	**Round Up**	99
	Meetings	99
	Actions Necessary When a Project Comes to an End	102
	Final Project Meeting of the Swings and Roundabouts Team	103
	Conclusion	105
	Further Reading	105
	Professional Associations	106
	Structured Project Management Methodologies	107

Index   *111*

List of Figures

Figure 1.1	Phases of a typical project life cycle	3
Figure 1.2	Project management cycle	8
Figure 1.3	The swings and roundabouts project: plan view of the site	10
Figure 2.1	Top three levels of charity project work breakdown structure	14
Figure 2.2	Work breakdown structure for swings and roundabouts project	20
Figure 2.3	Initial cost estimate for the swings and roundabouts project	22
Figure 3.1	Understanding an organization chart	26
Figure 3.2	Coordinated project matrix organization	29
Figure 3.3	Project team example	30
Figure 3.4	Principle of a matrix organization for multiple projects	33
Figure 3.5	Organization of the swings and roundabouts project	36
Figure 4.1	Bar chart for a garden pond project	42
Figure 4.2	Plans for a tree project	43
Figure 4.3	A task in a critical path network	44
Figure 4.4	Task list for the table project	47
Figure 4.5	Network diagram for the table project	47
Figure 4.6	Network diagram for the swings and roundabouts project	50
Figure 4.7	Swings and roundabouts project time analysis from Microsoft Project	53
Figure 4.8	Detail from the swings and roundabouts project network diagram as plotted by Microsoft Project	54
Figure 5.1	Possible sequence of events for a very high-value project purchase	61
Figure 5.2	A bid summary form	70
Figure 6.1	Top of a risk register page	74
Figure 6.2	Schematic diagram for a change control system	77
Figure 6.3	Cybernetic feedback loop to control the quality and progress of a project task	78
Figure 6.4	Earned value analysis for an engineering department	85
Figure 6.5	A tabulated project cost report that includes an earned value assessment	86
Figure 7.1	Task force organization to relocate a company's head office	95

Preface

Project management has been around for millennia, although only in fairly recent times has it become known by that name. Now project management is an internationally regarded profession, in which it can be enjoyable and rewarding to take part. Books about project management are plentiful and more are published every month. But the best of those books are too comprehensive for the person faced for the first time with managing a small and relatively straightforward project, or for the student studying for a degree or business qualification in which project management is not the main subject. At the other extreme, the worst books treat project management too lightly and gloss over or ignore some essential processes.

It was with beginners and students in mind that I wrote this little book. It is a short introduction to the subject, intended to whet appetites. My aim has been to strip project management down to its bare facts – to simplify everything but to trivialize nothing. So there is practical advice here on how to organize and manage a small- or medium-sized project.

Project management processes depend largely on common sense and a logical, systematic approach. But that is not quite enough. It is necessary also to acquire a few special skills if one is to plan, schedule and control a project so that it produces the result that everyone wants and expects. The best project managers are good leaders, and they know how to motivate people and get the best out of them.

In the following chapters I am going to give a general account of project management principles and practices. By means of a simple case example I shall demonstrate how a mix of common sense, logic and appropriate management tools can get a small project finished to everyone's satisfaction.

Dennis Lock
St Albans

1

Projects

A project is a human enterprise that sets out to achieve one or more set objectives. Unlike routine work, projects break new ground and require many decisions. They are usually associated with risk.

Project Types

Roughly speaking, most projects that we see in our everyday lives fall into one of four types:

1. Construction projects. These can be anything from putting up a garden shed to erecting a 300m skyscraper. Most involve work at a site that is remote from the headquarters of the company managing the project. They are usually visible to the public gaze. Tunnelling, mining, quarrying and civil engineering projects also belong to this group. In these projects people often have to work in unpleasant or even dangerous conditions.

2. Manufacturing projects. Whether you design and manufacture a hearing aid, develop a defence system or build an ocean liner you are undertaking a manufacturing project. These projects can be conducted within the company's own enclosed or fenced premises. They result in a tangible product, which can be anything from a new kind of safety pin to an aircraft.

3. Management change projects. When companies change their working procedures, install new IT, reorganize or relocate they have a management change project. Company mergers and acquisitions are also management projects.

4. Scientific research projects. A pure scientific research project is truly an act of faith for its investor. Often no one can tell if the

research will produce a useful result or be a complete waste of time. Projects for pharmaceuticals, medical research and the quest for new man-made materials are examples that come into this category.

So why have I taken the trouble to make these different classifications? Well, I want to identify some of their similarities and their differences when it comes to project management.

Broadly speaking, projects in the first, second and third categories listed above can all be managed using the same project management methods for planning and control. But management change projects usually mean that workpeople have to accept changes to their working lives. People generally prefer familiar surroundings and work processes and they dislike or fear change. For these reasons management change projects can be particularly difficult to implement, so I have devoted Chapter 7 to that subject.

So almost any kind of project will benefit from recognized project management methods (like those described in this book). The only exceptions are projects for pure scientific research because they are difficult to plan and have usually unpredictable outcomes. There are ways in which control over research expenditure can be exercised periodically, but those are outside the scope of this book.

Project Life Cycles

Two things that set projects apart from other commercial and industrial activities are:

1. a project is new, usually having no exact precedent, and carrying all the risks that stepping into the unknown can bring;

2. projects have finite life cycles. Every successful project progresses through several life cycle phases from birth to death.

Figure 1.1 shows the life cycle of a typical project. Although no two projects are ever exactly the same, their life cycles share common characteristics and they all progress through a series of phases. The boundaries between these phases are not always well defined and some phases can overlap each other considerably.

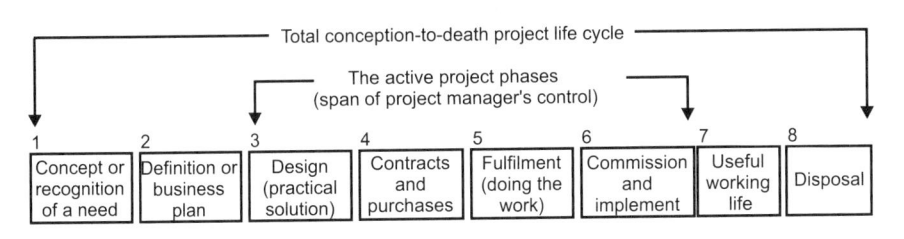

Figure 1.1   Phases of a typical project life cycle

LIFE CYCLE PHASES

Phase 1: concept or recognition of a need for a project

Now the project is merely a gleam in someone's eye. An idea has occurred for a venture that could bring benefit to an entrepreneur, an organization or a community. All that is known at this embryo stage is that something could and should be done to improve an existing situation, make a profit or produce some other kind of benefit. So far, no money has been spent on the project.

Phase 2: project definition or business plan

Now is the time for the initial project idea to be developed into a project definition or business plan. A person wanting a new home built can specify many things that an architect can later develop into a design scheme. A company wishing to expand its production facility can specify what new machinery it needs, so that a detailed order can be sent to a manufacturer. A person contemplating a business change must prepare a business plan that sets out what must be done, how long the project would take, how much it would cost and what the expected benefits should be.

Even at this early stage some money must be spent. How much money depends on the complexity of the proposed project. A straightforward machine replacement for a factory can be specified relatively easily. But developing a new oilfield or mining operation can require a feasibility study project costing millions of pounds.

Every business plan or study should look at how the main project activities will be funded. Possible sources of finance for a commercial project include:

- cash reserves (funds saved from previous company profits);

- revenue from current company operations;
- an issue of ordinary or preference shares;
- loans from banks or other financial institutions;
- an investment from a specialist investor company;
- a government grant or loan;
- a grant from the National Lottery.
- a public appeal campaign (particularly for a charitable project or a venture deemed to appeal to the general public for any reason).

The successful output of this project definition or business proposal stage is a management instruction for the project to go ahead. That will mean the issue of a contract or a purchase order when the project is to be purchased from a contractor or supplier of goods and services. If the project is an internal management change initiative, then senior management approval will be needed to launch the project.

Phase 3: design

Now the project has been approved it is time to establish the organization, appoint the project manager, carry out detailed planning, and produce drawings and specifications that will enable the project to be carried out. I'm sorry, but I did not have room in Figure 1.1 to list all these things, so I have lumped them all together as 'design', which is what many people do. Now the serious expenditure begins as people join the project organization to start work.

Phase 4: contracts and purchases

As design progresses, specifications can be drawn up for materials purchases and for contracted-out services. Now the bulk of the project expenditure must be committed when the purchase orders are released and contracts are signed. You will find some basic advice on contracts in Chapter 5.

Phase 5: fulfilment (which means doing the work)

This is the most active part of the project when the number of people engaged is at its peak. The project manager must exercise control over the progress and quality of the work.

Apart from possible technical difficulties and design errors, a well-known risk during this phase is that changes will be allowed which cause the project (and its costs) to expand beyond the original business plan. Project managers call this danger 'scope creep'.

Phase 6: commissioning and implementation

If the initial design was reasonably free from mistakes, and all the fulfilment work has been done successfully, the project should now be finished and fit for purpose. But, of course, there will often be some teething problems. So the active phases of most projects end with a period of trial, testing and adjustment to find and correct all the snags. Some project budgets become overspent and run late because this phase was not taken into account during cost estimating.

This phase is particularly important for management change projects, when all the people involved have to accept the change and learn to work with the new procedures and conditions.

Phase 7: useful working life

The project manager usually has no direct involvement in this phase, and should by now have moved on to another project or other things. However the project manager might be asked to sort out queries and snags during the first few months as defects and problems become apparent when the project is first put to use.

It is to be hoped that the project will have a long, profitable and trouble-free working life. But this lifespan might be brief for a project where the technology is moving fast (think of anything to do with computers). A new building might last for many hundreds of years.

Phase 8: disposal

For many projects this final phase lies well into the future, when the original project manager has long since lost interest. He or she might be retired or dead. However, project designers often have to take the environment into account when considering the original project design. Choices between recyclable materials or substances that could pose a threat to the environment upon disposal are considerations that have to be taken seriously. By far the most obvious example would be a project to build a nuclear-powered electricity generation plant. The time required for safe disposal can be very great, and the disposal costs might be greater even than those for the original project.

Principal Project Players

CUSTOMER AND CONTRACTOR

Every project is done because someone wants it. That 'someone' or customer might be an affluent individual, a commercial organization, a group of people, a government department – there are clearly many possibilities. The customer could be a group or person within the project company or other organization itself (for a management project). Now, this book could get incredibly complicated if in every instance I were to consider all these possibilities. So I am going to take the simple approach of calling any person or organization that wants a project *the customer*.

A similar argument applies to the organization that carries out a project for the customer. Depending on the type of project, this could a public company, a large joint venture company, a small contractor or a not-for-profit organization. For simplicity I shall refer to the organization with principal responsibility for doing the project as *the contractor*.

An internally conducted management change project is a special case, because the company is its own customer as well as being the project contractor.

SPONSORS AND STAKEHOLDERS

A stakeholder is any organization or person who can affect the outcome of a project or who could be affected by the project. Thus local residents, motorists and other road users would all be stakeholders in a project to drive a new road through green fields adjacent to existing housing. People and organizations who invest money in a project usually expect to see some return on their investment (in management projects this is often called benefits realization) and they are stakeholders. Some large projects, such as a new shopping mall, will have many stakeholders (including shopkeepers, shoppers and all those affected in any way by the new construction).

A project sponsor is a special kind of stakeholder who invests money in the project or otherwise helps to promote it. In a management change project, for instance, a senior manager within the company might have a particular role in championing the project and overseeing its progress – and so will be a sponsor for the project. Likewise a project investor (such as a bank) can have the dual role of stakeholder and sponsor.

It is generally accepted that a completely successful project is one that satisfies all its stakeholders. However stakeholders can have conflicting interests so it might not be possible to please everyone. For example, an expansion to London Heathrow Airport will benefit passengers and the airlines but not residents under the flight path. A project manager must learn who the stakeholders and sponsors are, decide whose interests are the most important, and then set out to finish the project so that as many stakeholders as possible are satisfied with the outcome.

PROJECT MANAGER

In manufacturing companies routine work flows continuously through the organization (raw materials in at one end and products out at the other). In service companies operations tend to be compartmented within functional departments (such as the claims department in an insurance company or the housekeeping department of a hotel).

Projects are different because they begin with the customer and end with the customer, and everything that happens in between has to be coordinated. Figure 1.2 shows phases 3 to 5 of a project life cycle in their true cyclical pattern. They are shown separately here for simplicity, but remember that in practice these phases can overlap. The active project cycle begins with the customer authorizing or placing an order for the project and ends when the project is handed back to the customer by the contractor, fully finished, tested and operational. The problem here is that companies are organized in departments (compartments is sometimes a more appropriate word), so that unless special steps are taken project work will not flow smoothly through the organization. Every project needs someone who can watch over it and guide it through all its stages. In other words a project needs its own manager.

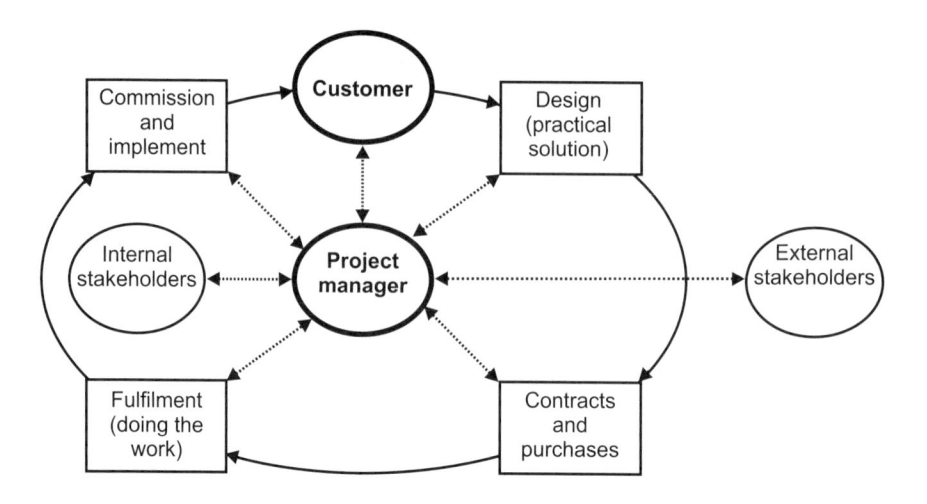

Figure 1.2 Project management cycle

Project Outcomes

Here's a popular buzzword – *deliverables*. These are the outcomes that a project is expected to deliver on completion, and for which the project manager can be held accountable. They can usually be grouped under three headings as follows:

1. Time – the date by which the project (and in some cases its intermediate events) have to be finished.

2. Cost – cost estimates lead to cost budgets, and the final project costs should not exceed those budgets. Note that profit is not always an objective because some projects are not conducted for profit. It is containment within cost budgets that is important.

3. Performance – the project should do what its investors expected it to do. For a management change project, performance is measured in terms of benefits realized by the company when the change has been fully implemented. For most projects performance can be defined by measurable quantities (for example the number of tonnes of cathode copper produced weekly from a new copper refinery). There is also an important quality element here. A new apartment block or office building should provide pleasant accommodation and trouble-free environmental services. A car should be designed primarily to be safe, whilst giving its owner

fuel economy coupled with suitable comfort, reliability and performance. I could give many more examples but all can be summed up by declaring that the project outcome must be fit for its intended purpose.

The Swings and Roundabouts Project

Now I am going to introduce a small project as a case example that we can follow through the following chapters.

A local authority has decided to set aside a plot of land in a public park for a new children's playground. The play area is to be rectangular, measuring 40 by 50 metres. The following facilities are to be provided:

- six tables and benches to form a small picnic area for parents and children;

- two identical sets of four swings for older children;

- one set of four small swings suitable for toddlers;

- one four-seat rocker;

- one turntable for small children (with its platform flush with ground level);

- a junior climbing feature with two small slides;

- one adventure slide and complex climbing feature for older children;

- six bench seats around the perimeter;

- six refuse bins.

The area is to be surrounded with square mesh steel fencing to keep children in and dogs out. Health and safety considerations mean that most of the apparatus will be built over 'falling surfaces'. Falling surfaces are areas of rubber, tan bark or other shock-absorbing material that will reduce the risk of serious injury should a child fall.

Figure 1.3 is a plan of the proposed playground, which I have based on a real playground in the beautiful Verulamium Park in St Albans. More details of this project and its management methods will be revealed in following chapters.

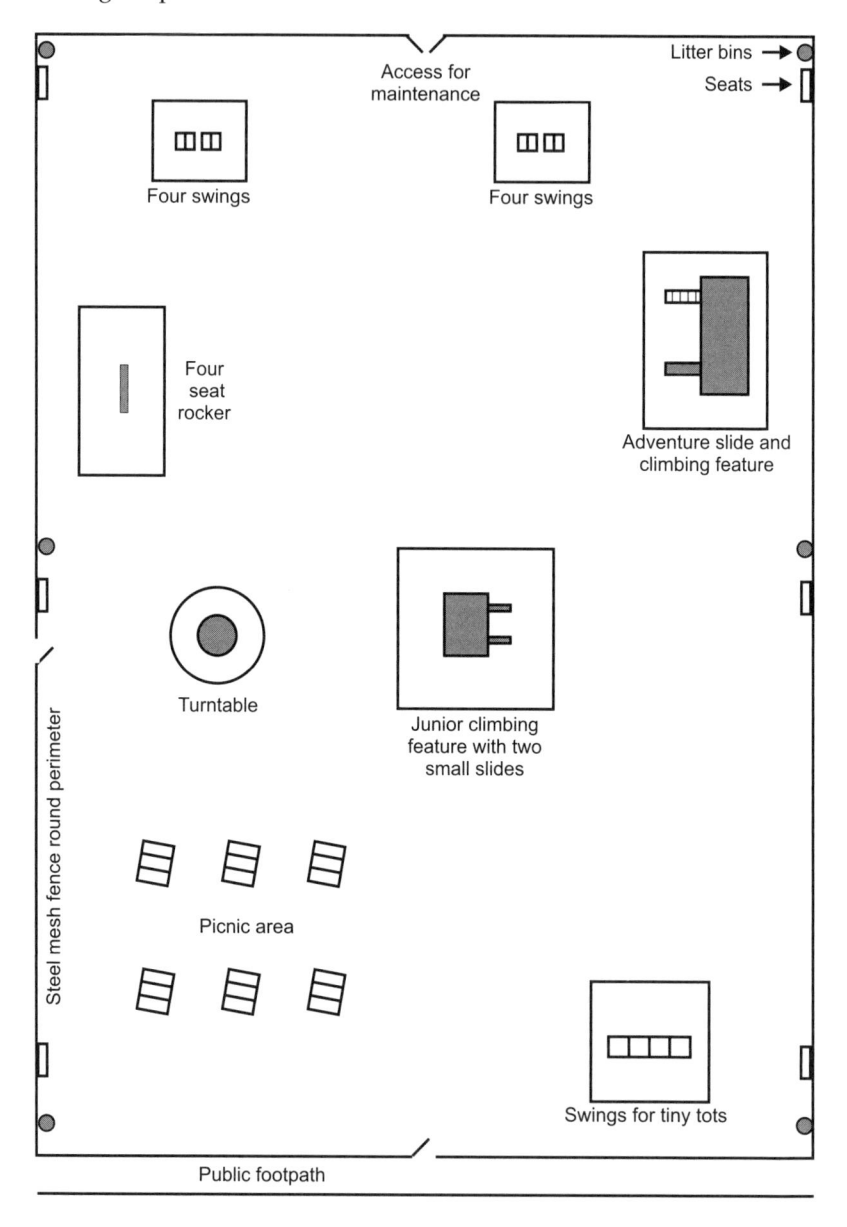

The scale is approximately 1/500.

Figure 1.3 The swings and roundabouts project: plan view of the site

2
Getting Ready for the Project

Every project should start from a project definition statement of some kind. For management change projects and all other projects funded entirely from within the project company that definition statement should come in the form of a business plan.

When a customer orders a project from a seller or contractor, then there needs to be a project specification that sets out everything that the customer expects from the project. Clearly project definition is important at the outset.

Project Definition

SPECIFICATIONS FOR COMMERCIAL PROJECTS

A customer that orders a project from a contractor usually has to specify requirements to support the purchase order or contract. In other words, the customer has to provide a technical and physical description of the finished project. That will form the basis of the contractor's own internal specification for the project.

Project definition can be made either by the customer or the seller. A customer might submit a technical specification to one or more potential sellers setting out what the project must do. Then each potential seller can make a proposal (including a project specification), telling the potential customer how that particular seller expects to meet the customer's requirements. Different sellers will propose different technical solutions and designs.

Customers having to choose between a number of different proposals should first eliminate those proposals that are technically inferior or which would not satisfy all the specified requirements. That should leave a shortlist of competent proposals, from which the customer can pick out the one that offers best value for money.

BUSINESS PLANS FOR MANAGEMENT CHANGE PROJECTS

Now consider how a business change project might be defined. There is no external customer, so there can be no purchase specification or sales proposal. Instead there has to be a business plan. That business plan should predict future benefits resulting from the project. These predictions have to be compared against the project investment costs and risks. So a business proposal or plan should result, and that will need to explain the following things:

- reasons leading to the need for this project;

- an outline description of the proposed project;

- a cost estimate (which can only be a rough guide at this stage);

- an estimate of how long the project will take to implement;

- some idea of the risks involved, if any;

- a quantified prediction of the benefits that will result. Techniques such as payback time, net present value and sensitivity analysis are often used, but these are outside the scope of this book.

Detailed procedures for preparing business plans and sales proposals need not be discussed here. However, whether a proposed project is very simple or a huge undertaking, it must be described as accurately as possible before work is authorized. If the project manager's job is to ensure that the project deliverables are actually delivered, how can he or she do that when those deliverables are not accurately stated at the outset?

Work Breakdown Structure (WBS)

Most projects have to be broken down into manageable parts before they can be planned and executed. For very tiny projects the work breakdown is little more than a 'shopping list' of jobs, but something more structured and detailed is needed for bigger projects. The work breakdown has to be as logical as possible. When you have done that it will be easier to plan and control all the project tasks and their costs.

Every project WBS is arranged in a pyramid or hierarchical structure. People who work in manufacturing design departments are very familiar with work breakdown charts, but they call them 'goes-into' charts. Those charts display the main product or assembly at the top, and then break that down layer-by-layer into sub-assemblies, sub-sub-assemblies and so on. If you want a spare part for your car, your service agent will have a parts breakdown for your particular model in their computer and that makes it possible to identify even the smallest part.

WORK BREAKDOWN STRUCTURE CASE EXAMPLE FOR A NATIONAL CHARITY PROJECT

Imagine that you run a national charity and need to raise funds for a special purpose. So you decide to plan and organize a project to conduct events in as many towns and villages as you can. You will encourage volunteers to have coffee mornings in their homes. Others can organize bring-and-buy sales. Flag days, with street collections, can take place in towns and cities throughout the land. You might be able to publicize your project in the media, so there will be a strong public relations aspect. Then you realize that as you will be dealing with money, you have to consider the security of all those who will be handling cash, so you have a banking and security dimension to your project.

Your charity project is not technically complicated and breaks no new ground. But it is big and dispersed over a wide area. It is complex enough for it to go seriously wrong. So you need a WBS. For this project there are several ways in which you might choose to break down the project. The WBS shown in Figure 2.1 is only one possibility. This shows the top three levels and you might need to go to at least one lower level. For example, you might want to split everything up into the different regions or towns and cities.

The WBS will help you to some extent in allocating responsibilities and you will be able to put someone in charge of each part (project managers call these parts 'work packages').

14   NAKED PROJECT MANAGEMENT

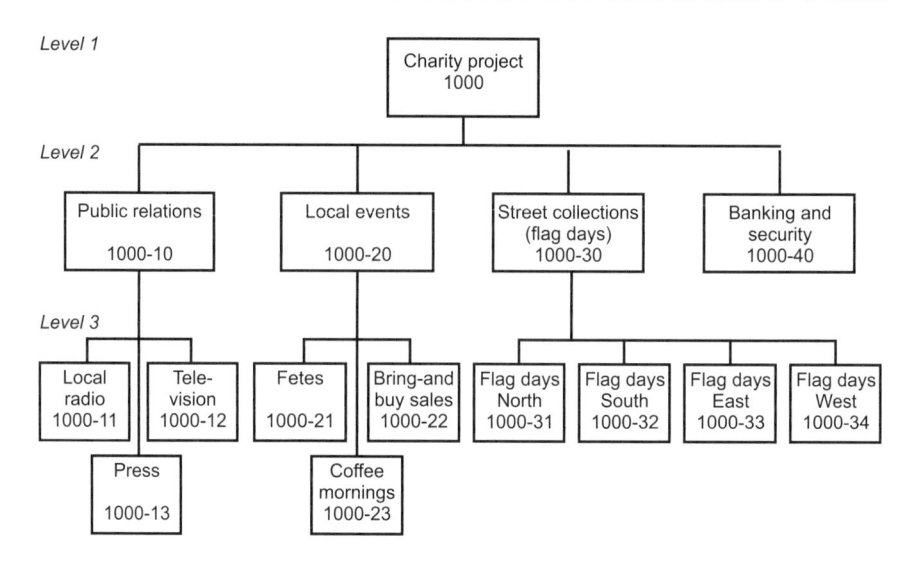

```
Level 1                    Charity project
                               1000

Level 2
         ┌──────────────┬──────────────┬──────────────┐
    Public relations  Local events  Street collections  Banking and
                                      (flag days)        security
        1000-10        1000-20         1000-30          1000-40

Level 3
    ┌─────┬─────┐   ┌─────┬──────────┐  ┌────────┬────────┬────────┬────────┐
   Local  Tele-    Fetes  Bring-and   Flag days Flag days Flag days Flag days
   radio  vision          buy sales    North     South     East      West
  1000-11 1000-12  1000-21  1000-22   1000-31   1000-32   1000-33   1000-34
    │                  │
   Press            Coffee
                   mornings
   1000-13          1000-23
```

Figure 2.1   Top three levels of charity project work breakdown structure

CODING A WORK BREAKDOWN STRUCTURE

You will notice that I have given every box in Figure 2.1 a number. These are code numbers that can be used particularly for collecting and analysing costs. The numbers are also useful for sorting and filtering jobs in the computer. Coding starts by giving the entire project its own code, which is 1000 in this charity project case.

Now look at the public relations box. This is coded 1000-10. The 1000 beginning of this code tells us that this relates to project number 1000.

Going down one further level, look at the box for 'Local radio'. This is coded 1000-11. The 1000 tells us that this is part of the charity fundraising project, the 1000-1 element identifies this as part of the public relations activities, and the 1 at the end is specific to local radio.

Codes in a project WBS can be extended to describe all kinds of things about each work package or task. For example, a company might decide to add a code denoting the department that would be most involved in performing the work. Such codes allow sorting and filtering by computer when project tasks are being scheduled, monitored and reported. But be warned. Always try to keep codes as simple as possible. People do not like working with long and complicated codes. If people have to write down or refer to complicated codes they will make mistakes (a problem that some organizations overcome by printing bar codes on documents and using automatic readers).

Organizations use coding systems in their accounts departments and for many other purposes (such as drawings and specifications). A sensible organization will attempt to make all its codes compatible, as far as possible using just one coding system. So in the WBS for this charity project, code 1000-12 could be used for collecting the costs of television publicity as well as for identifying all the associated tasks.

Costs and Cost Estimating

Every project proposal should have its cost estimate. So, a project manager has to understand something about how the costs of a typical project might be broken down into elements. The WBS is the most logical framework for project cost estimates and subsequent budgets. First it is necessary to understand a few fundamental things about costs and the way in which cost accountants treat them.

NATURE OF COSTS IN A DO-IT-YOURSELF PROJECT

If you are thinking about doing a project yourself, such as building some big garden feature or even your own house, all you need to know before you start estimating your project costs is that they will break down into the things you have to buy and the people you have to pay. So your private project expenses will break down as follows:

- materials – payments for materials you buy yourself;

- labour – payments you make to any individual people who help you;

- contracts – payments to companies that you engage for specialist work (such as roofing). These payments will cover both the people employed by the contractor and the materials they use.

- expenses – for example if you have to engage professional help from a solicitor or an architect.

You will need to start out with a budget to make sure you can afford your project, and for that you will need to make cost estimates. Then all you have to do is make sure that the money you spend on all the various items does not exceed your estimates.

That's all common sense, very straightforward, and you knew it already. But if you are employed by a company to manage a project for them, then costs have to be treated in a more formal way and you need to know a little about cost accounting.

NATURE OF COSTS IN A COMPANY OR OTHER ORGANIZATION

It costs money just to keep a company going. That can include things like:

- business rates;
- power consumption;
- maintenance of buildings and equipment;
- salaries and expenses of directors, managers and other administrative staff who do not themselves work on products, sold services or projects;
- cost of general stationery, IT equipment, communications and so on.

All those costs are classed as 'indirect costs', or 'overheads'. They are also mostly 'fixed' costs. They are 'indirect' because they cannot be charged specifically or directly to any product, project or sold service. They tend to be 'fixed' because they have to be incurred just to keep the organization in existence, so they do not vary much as the organization's workload fluctuates. In most cases the project manager has no control over any of these overhead costs. They will happen whether the project is busy or not.

'Direct costs' are those that can be identified and charged directly to a job or project. These split into:

- direct labour;
- direct materials;

- direct expenses.

'Direct labour costs' are usually expressed in terms of cost-per-hour-per person. Clearly not all people are paid the same amount of money, so direct labour costs are also split into different labour grades according to seniority. Within each grade, the accountants work out average costs of wages, employer's National Insurance payments and so on for each grade. Thus the cost estimator only needs to know the grade of person that will work on a job, not the name of each individual. A company should work with as few different grades as possible, so that (for example) clerks, typists, junior secretaries, are all bracketed in the same grade. Departmental managers, chief engineers and so on might also be grouped into one grade. I have known quite large companies that needed only six different grades, from directors down to manual workers.

'Direct materials costs' are the costs of all materials purchased or withdrawn from stored stocks for a project. Incidental costs of carriage and so on are often included.

'Direct expenses' are expenses incurred directly for the project, which can include travel, payments to specialists such as solicitors, charges made by materials testing laboratories and so on.

Other direct costs are those paid to contractors for services provided to the project.

Overhead recovery

I suppose some of you might be wondering how a company gets paid for its overhead (indirect) costs. After all, they are defined as costs that cannot be charged to a particular job or project. This is where the accountants apply a method known as absorption costing. All this means is that the accountants estimate how much will be paid out in direct labour costs in a year in total and compare that figure with the amount to be spent in overheads. It might be, for example, that the expected direct labour costs in the coming period will be £2,000,000. Now suppose that the total expected overhead costs for the same period will be £1,000,000. So the accountants will tell estimators to add 50 per cent to all estimated direct labour costs, and that should 'recover' the overheads. That 50 per cent is known as the overhead rate.

The accountants will do periodic checks to see if they have got their overhead rate right. If not, they can adjust it in future periods. Accountants call any differences between what they expect and what actually happens 'variances'.

Communication between the project manager and the accounts department

Project managers who began their working lives as IT specialists or design engineering might know little about commercial matters. This is often apparent when we read the books that they write. But if a project manager is to keep on top of expenditure and not let it get out of hand, he or she must have a close and friendly working relationship with the accountants. That might either be by direct communication, or through a project management office (a PMO, which will be described in the following chapter).

That's enough about cost accounting. When you have established your good communications with the accountants they can tell you more. Then you can learn about some complexities such as accruals, direct bookings by direct workers, indirect bookings by direct workers and so on.

Introduction to Cost Estimating Methods

Architects and others in the construction industry have access to published tables that can help them to estimate the costs of various operations, based on the quantities involved. But they are an exception, and I want to concentrate here on two different ways in which the direct costs of a project might be estimated by a project manager or cost estimator.

TOP-DOWN AND BOTTOM-UP COST ESTIMATING

In top-down estimating, the estimator considers the costs of the entire project, or at least large chunks of it, and simply estimates the project cost by making the best possible judgement. The estimator will usually be helped by the knowledge of what previous similar work cost. Estimates made in this way cannot of course be expected to be free from errors, and indeed might prove very inaccurate. But if little project design has been carried out this might be the only kind of estimating possible. The resulting estimates are sometimes called ballpark, and might be used in the early stages of compiling a business plan for a new project.

Bottom-up estimating is a far more detailed process and is often based on the elements in a WBS. If possible, quotations should be obtained from potential suppliers for the costs of bought services and highly priced materials. That leaves the direct labour costs to be assessed, and a common way of doing that is to obtain the estimates from all the supervisors who are going to be involved in the project.

Some people, understandably, find cost estimating difficult, but if they can be presented with records of similar jobs done in the past they should be able to make comparative estimates which, when adjusted for inflation, can hold good for the current project. That kind of estimating is quite common and is known as comparative estimating.

For any kind of estimate it is always best (but not always possible) to have the estimate made by the manager or supervisor who will later have responsibility for carrying out the work.

RECORDING COST ESTIMATES

Cost estimates should ideally be set out on some kind of standard forms, so that records can be kept for later budget setting and comparison of estimated costs with actual costs incurred. Figure 2.3 shows how this was done for the swings and roundabouts project.

Work Breakdown and Cost Estimate for the Swings and Roundabouts Project

This project to build a children's playground was introduced at the end of the previous chapter. This is an initiative by St Kevin Borough Council, and I shall have more to say about them and their organization in the following chapter.

Now it is time to get ready for the project. The first step I have taken is to draw the WBS and code each item. This is shown in Figure 2.2. You will see that the project breaks down into the following main areas or work packages:

- site preparation, which involves clearing the area of a few unwanted rocks, roots and so on, and then marking out the site;

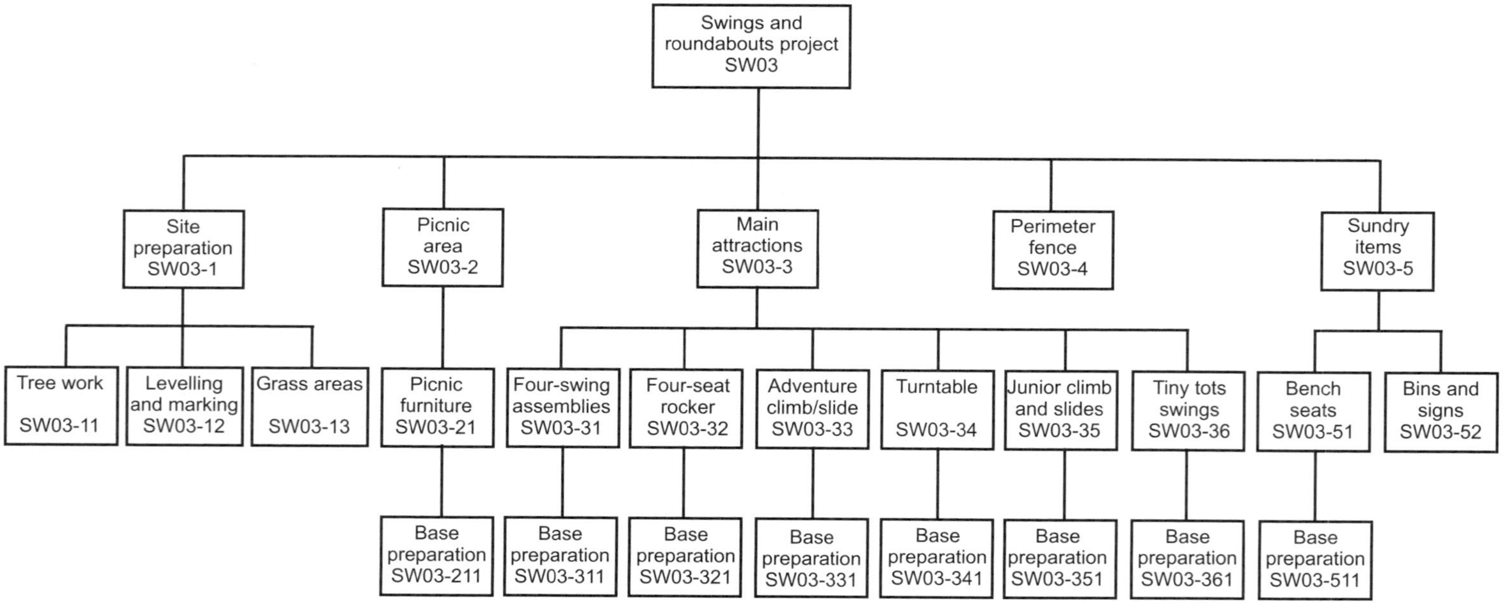

Figure 2.2 Work breakdown structure for swings and roundabouts project

- picnic area, in which six table-bench assemblies will be set out on paved bases;

- the main attractions, which were listed at the end of Chapter 1;

- perimeter fence and gates;

- sundry items, such as bench seats, rubbish bins and public notices.

This is a relatively easy project. Very little site preparation will be needed, because this is parkland that is already grassed and fairly level (just one big hump to be removed). There is a tree near the playground area, and it has been decided to cut one limb off this tree which would overhang the fence and could pose a threat if it broke and fell.

The various bases for the attractions have to be laid using shock absorbing materials (the so-called falling surfaces). Council staff will be able to do that with machinery that the council owns or can borrow from County Council. The council also owns lifting gear and raised platforms, so is adequately equipped for all the work. In fact, the council will be able to do most of the work, including assembling the rides, but some site work like levelling and turfing will be contracted out. The council have also decided to contract out the job of perimeter fencing.

Council employees on this project will include:

- one senior supervisor/engineer, grade 3, with a standard hourly cost of £20 excluding overhead;

- several skilled workmen, grade 5, with a standard hourly cost of £15 excluding overhead;

- several unskilled workmen (labourers), grade 6, with a standard hourly cost of £10 excluding overhead.

The overhead rate at the time of this project will be 50 per cent, relative to direct labour cost. Figure 2.3 shows the initial cost estimate for this swings and roundabouts project. This spreadsheet estimates that the project should cost a total of £91,393, which seems to be very reasonable for a project of this kind. Note that most of the cost is attributable to materials.

Cost estimate

St Kevin Borough Council

Date: Jan 2014
Estimated by: Ize Wong
Case number: One

Estimate for: Swings and roundabouts project, Project number SW03

Item code	Description	Grade 1 Hrs	Grade 1 £	Grade 2 Hrs	Grade 2 £	Grade 3 Hrs	Grade 3 £	Total (L) £	Materials £	Contracts £	Overhead 50% of L £	Total £
SW031	Site preparation											
SW0311	Tree work			2	30	1	10	40			20	60
SW0312	Levelling and marking out	3	60			3	30	90		1500	45	1635
SW0313	Grass areas (turfing)									2000		2000
SW0302	Picnic area	1	20					20			10	30
SW0321	Picnic furniture			2	30	2	20	50	4000		25	4075
SW03211	Base preparation			6	90	6	60	150	1000		75	1225
SW033	Main attractions	2	40					40			20	60
SW0331	Two four-swing assemblies			6	90	6	60	150	8000		75	8225
SW03311	Base preparation			2	30	12	120	150	2000		75	2225
SW0332	Four seat rocker			2	30	2	20	50	2200		25	2275
SW03321	Base preparation			2	30	6	60	90	500		45	635
SW0333	Adventure climb/slide	3	60	12	180	24	240	480	22000		240	22720
SW03331	Base preparation	2	40	6	90	12	120	250	2000		125	2375
SW0334	Turntable	1	20	6	90	6	60	170	6500		85	6755
SW03341	Base preparation			4	60	8	80	140	800		70	1010
SW0335	Junior climbs and slides	1	20	12	180	24	240	440	12000		220	12660
SW03351	Base preparation			6	90	20	200	290	1800		145	2235
SW0336	Tiny tots swings			6	90	6	60	150	4000		75	4225
SW03361	Base preparation			10	150	18	180	330	2000		165	2495
SW034	Perimeter fence and gates	2	40					40		10000	20	10060
SW035	Sundry items											
SW0351	Bench seats			6	90	6	60	150	3000		75	3225
SW03511	Base preparation			4	60	4	40	100	200		50	350
SW0352	Bins and signs			1	15	1	10	25	800		13	838
SW03	Project totals	15	300	95	1425	167	1670	3395	73800	12500	1698	91393

Figure 2.3 Initial cost estimate for the swings and roundabouts project

Most of those materials costs will be spent in buying the 'rides' from the manufacturers.

Although our cost estimate can tell us how many hours we expect to need in total for each labour grade, we do not yet know how many workmen will be needed on any given day. That requirement will only become apparent much later, when we carry out planning and resource scheduling. That subject is discussed briefly in Chapter 4.

Please note that all the estimates and methods described for this swings and roundabouts project are for the purposes of illustration only.

3

Organization

Once a project's description and cost estimates (or its business plan) have been accepted, the project can be authorized to start. So how will that project be organized? That's not always an easy question to answer, because different companies have their own ideas about what makes a good project organization. So this chapter will look at different ways of organizing projects. I shall also be introducing some of the key players, including of course the project manager.

Organizations in General

Before project organizations can be discussed and understood, it is necessary to have some grasp of how typical companies are organized. But there are almost as many organization patterns as there are companies, and these patterns become even more complicated when large multinational groups are considered. So here I shall confine my description to a fairly typical company organization pattern first, and then I can show different ways in which a company might accommodate one or more projects. We must not forget public sector organizations, so this chapter will end by looking at how the St Kevin Borough Council and its swings and roundabouts project could be organized.

ORGANIZATION CHARTS

All but the very tiniest organizations have to be depicted as charts if their structures are to be understood. So just in case any reader is not familiar with organization charts (which some people call organigrams), Figure 3.1 shows the essential elements. As yet, no project organization is shown on this example, which shows a company as it might exist when carrying out its routine, day-to-day, non-project operations.

```
                    ┌──────────┐
                    │ Managing │
                    │ director │
                    └────┬─────┘
                         ├──────────┬──────────┐
                         │          │ Secretary│
                         │          └──────────┘
    ┌──────────┬─────────┼─────────┬──────────┐
┌───┴────┐ ┌───┴────┐ ┌──┴───┐ ┌───┴──────┐ ┌─┴────────┐
│Marketing│ │Operations│ │Finance│ │Administration│ │IT and coms│
│director │ │director  │ │director│ │director     │ │director   │
└─────────┘ └──────────┘ └────────┘ └─────────────┘ └───────────┘
```

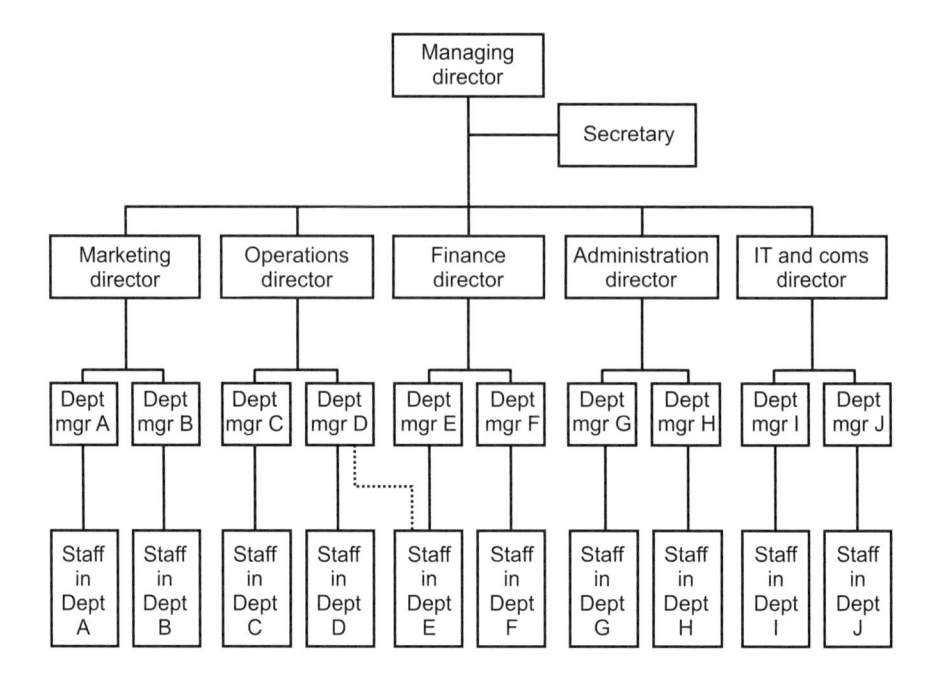

Figure 3.1 — organization chart with Dept mgr A–J and Staff in Dept A–J.

Figure 3.1   **Understanding an organization chart**

I have deliberately left all the job titles in Figure 3.1 vague. So this chart could represent the organization of any medium-sized company. It could be in the service industry (like an insurance company), it could be a manufacturing company or any other company that carries out routine work.

Charts usually place the most important people at the top level, and then put others in the organization at lower levels depending on their status. This often upsets people who believe that they have a higher status than their chart shows. Companies try to overcome that by putting a note on charts that reads 'Levels do not necessarily indicate status' (but no one ever believes that). Worst of all, some people get very upset when they are not shown on the chart at all.

Now I am going to describe everything that we can deduce from the chart in Figure 3.1. The most obvious thing is that a managing director heads the company's executive management, and several executive directors report directly to that managing director. I have not shown the chief executive or chairman here because I am concerned only with the executive operations.

Each executive director is responsible for one or more departments (or functions) and each of those departments is headed up by a departmental manager (they can also be called functional managers). Departmental managers are individually responsible for functions like sales, design, purchasing, customer services, human resource management (HRM), estates, maintenance, cost accounts and so on.

Solid lines on the chart represent lines of command when they are followed downwards. Following those same solid lines upwards shows that people are expected to report to their bosses. The dotted line joining department manager D to the staff in department E indicates that there is an especially important communication link here, so (for example) this might mean that a purchasing manager needs special and frequent access to staff working in the cost accounts department.

I need to say a little word about the managing director's secretary. She (please forgive me, but secretaries usually are women) reports to the managing director and has a high place on the chart. But she has no executive line authority herself. Instead she occupies what is known as a staff position. Although she has no organizational power, she does have status, because she reports directly to the managing director. Anyone who is disrespectful in any way to her is at risk of serious trouble from the managing director. Others who might occupy staff positions include a company's legal adviser, contract managers and internal consultants such as long-range business planning officers.

Introducing a Project into an Organization for the First Time

Now it's time to talk specifically about project organizations. The striking thing about the chart in Figure 3.1 is that it makes no provision for any project at all. So if this company finds itself having to conduct a project for the first time, there is no one in the organization who can logically manage that project and plan, guide and control it smoothly and successfully through the organization. One way of putting this is to say that a traditional organization has a hierarchical, *vertical* pyramid structure. But most projects have a strong *horizontal* dimension because they cross many departments. That horizontal dimension is missing here, and this organization at least needs a project coordinator.

You might argue at this stage that if the organization in Figure 3.1 is a service company (such as an insurance provider) why would it need to manage projects anyway? But every company has to manage a project at some time, whenever it wants to implement a significant change. That change could be anything from installing new IT to pulling up its roots and locating to a new town. So I can begin my explanation of project organization structures with the coordinated matrix. A coordinated matrix is not nearly as complicated as it sounds. It happens whenever a company like that in Figure 3.1 appoints a coordinator to plan a special one-off project and ensure that it progresses horizontally through all the company's departments.

Coordinated Project Matrix

Imagine that the company depicted in Figure 3.1 has been trading successfully from the same premises for many years. But now the company is about to undergo a complete reorganization of its procedures. The company's directors wisely recognize that this change has to be treated as a project. New IT will be involved, but the company will also have to redefine many jobs, so that this project cannot be managed by the IT department alone. Much coordination will be required across all departments, For example, some people will have to change where they sit, some will get new job titles, and others might have to take early retirement or be declared redundant. So HRM will certainly be involved. So will the facilities manager. In this case both the HRM manager and the facilities manager usually report to the administration director. But all company departments will eventually be involved in one way or another.

So this company has wisely decided to appoint a project coordinator. He/she will report to the administration director in this case, although it could have been to one of the other executive directors. A project coordinator is really another name for a project manager, but project coordinators rarely have any line authority. Instead they usually occupy a staff position, very much in the same way as the managing director's secretary. They have influence and status, but no line authority and thus no power. The coordinator can plan, advise, cajole, nudge, but has no executive authority. So he/she will carry out all the non-executive tasks of a project manager (like planning, control and reporting) but can only exert power by calling in the help of the boss.

Figure 3.2 shows the same company depicted in Figure 3.1, but now it has become a coordinated matrix for the life of this management change project. There are better ways of organizing a management change project, and one of these will be described later in Chapter 7. However a coordinated matrix is far, far better than no project organization at all.

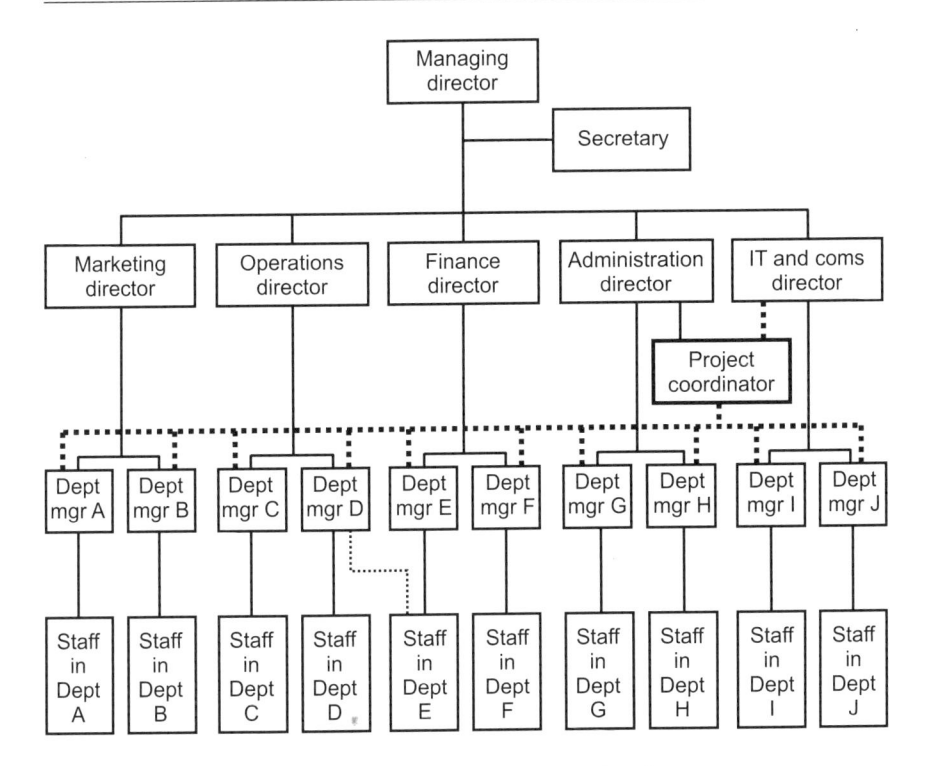

Figure 3.2   Coordinated project matrix organization

Every project coordinator and project manager has to be a good communicator, and I have deliberately emphasized those lines of communication in the chart of Figure 3.2.

A manufacturing company that produces routine batches of goods will find itself engaged in a project if it receives an order from a customer that departs widely from products in the company's catalogue range – in other words a special product that requires new design. A coordinated project matrix can solve that difficulty; with the company reverting to its normal routine operations organization after the project has been delivered. So the organization chart in Figure 3.2 covers that case.

Project Teams and Task Forces

A project team is the simplest kind of project organization to describe. A team is assembled to do all the project tasks, and when the project is finished the team is dissolved or, if it's lucky, moves on to another project. Projects in the construction industry, for example, are invariably organized as teams at their construction sites (even though their head office might have some other kind of organization). Figure 3.3 shows the elements of a project team. All members of this team report through a pyramid line structure to the project manager.

In most companies there will be departments outside the team, over which the project manager has no direct authority. Depending on the size of the project, those other departments outside the team will usually include functions such as finance, HRM, procurement, facilities management and general administration. However, I have to mention one exception to this rule. For a project involving huge capital investment, two or more companies might decide to share their technical expertise, resources (and project risk) to set up a separate joint venture company. A joint venture company usually exists for the life of the project. It is a supreme example of a project team, and the overall project manager might effectively also be the managing director of the joint venture company. Then all departments without exception will be in the project team. But joint venture projects are well outside the scope of this basic book.

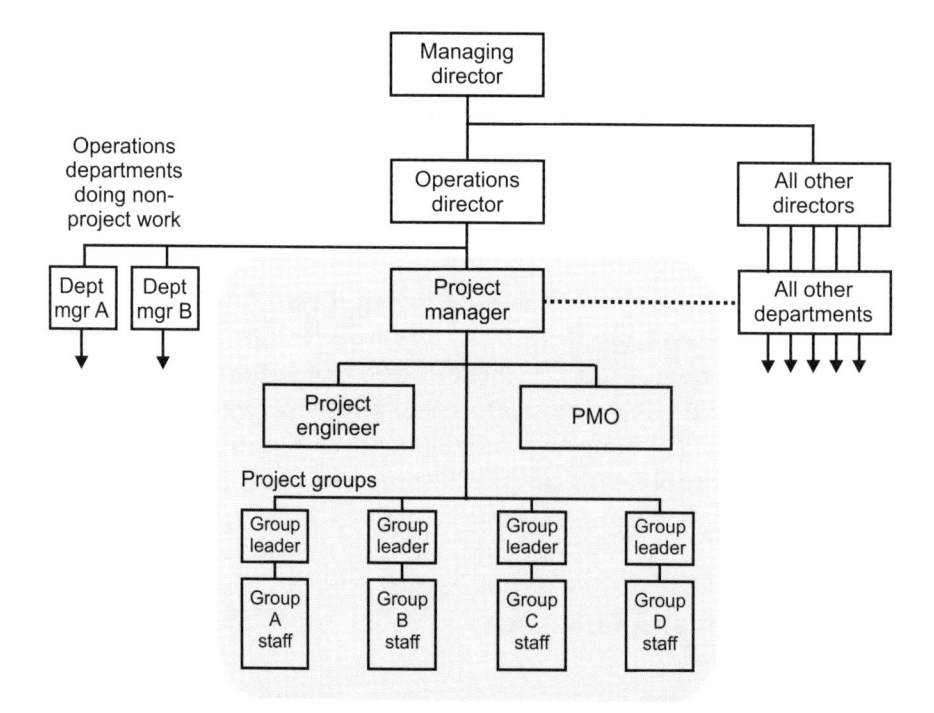

Figure 3.3   **Project team example**

Please have another look at Figure 3.3. You will notice that there are two boxes reporting to the project manager that need some explanation.

The project engineer in this example is typical of a large engineering project, and that engineer is there to support the project manager on technical issues. The project engineer might be responsible for approving drawings and specifications before they are released for production or construction and for maintaining overall technical excellence. A project engineer will usually occupy a staff position, but can deputize for the project manager. Many project teams will not include this role, which I have included here simply because I have at times worked with such organizations.

Of far more general importance is the box labelled PMO, which stands for project management office. On larger projects, the project manager will be far too occupied to deal personally with the preparation of plans, reports and so on and will need assistance from suitably qualified people. A PMO is the place for them. The PMO can include planners, cost and estimating engineers, progress chasers and clerical staff. Some projects require several registers to be kept of things like contract changes, design modifications, drawing numbers, purchase requisition and order numbers. Another function that the PMO can perform is the day-to-day follow up of work performed, task-by-task, against the project schedule. So it is clear that on a busy project, with a heavily occupied project manager, a PMO can be a vital asset.

MULTIPLE PROJECT TEAMS

Some companies spend all their time on projects and therefore can have several projects running at the same time. Each of those projects will probably have its own project manager, unless it is very tiny. When multiple projects are conducted simultaneously they are called a programme, and a programme manager or projects director might be appointed, to whom all the individual project managers report.

Often all projects in a programme (and all their project managers) will be served by a common PMO, in which case it will be called a programme management office.

ADVANTAGES AND DISADVANTAGES OF PROJECT TEAMS

The big advantage of a project team is that its organization is relatively uncomplicated. Everyone in the team reports to the project manager, and it is far easier to generate enthusiasm and a team spirit when a team actually exists. When a project is especially urgent, a team or task force can get the job done as quickly as possible. If a project is running late and becoming out of control, the best way to rescue it is usually to form a task force to do just that job,

Team organizations, because they can be self-contained and even located together, are the best option when project work is secret or confidential. Then all project information can be kept confined safely within the team. The obvious applications for this are for defence projects and also the development of new product ranges that the company wishes to keep under wraps and away from its competitors until a planned release date. However, a project task force can be useful also when a company is considering a big change that it wants to keep quiet to avoid the spread of rumours, and I shall deal with that aspect in Chapter 7.

So a project team has many advantages, but it also has some disadvantages. Problems with teams arise when the project ends, because what will happen to all the team members? That can be a demotivator when people in the shrinking and dying team worry about their futures.

Teams tend to use resources inefficiently, because specialists in a team will often find themselves unoccupied for part of their time, but if they were in a central functional department their time could be shared amongst all projects being handled by the company.

A technical person located in a functional department works among his/her peers, and can easily consult with them or the department manager for technical help. Also salary reviews are likely to be fairer when conducted by a departmental manager who understands the particular technical discipline. This aspect can be summed up by saying that a functional department concentrates expertise and enhances technical quality in a way that cannot be achieved by isolated technicians working in a team.

Matrix Organizations for Multiple Projects

Earlier in this chapter I described a coordinated matrix for a single project (Figure 3.2). That arrangement is fine for a company that handles a single small project on rare occasions. But the concept can be extended to suit a company that regularly handles several projects at the same time. Each project can have its own project manager, but the projects will be staffed from the functional departments. Figure 3.4 shows the idea.

A matrix organization such as this has several advantages, not least of which is that the company organization remains stable even though many projects might come and go. All members of functional departments work with their technical peers and so the company's technical strength is enhanced. For example, an engineer in the electrical engineering department might report to the chief electrical engineer. Regular performance and salary reviews will be conducted by someone who understands the engineer's profession. The individual engineer can even aspire to becoming the chief engineer in due time, and for the present is surrounded by colleagues to whom he/she can turn for technical advice. In this electrical department, the chief engineer is well placed to supervise all design work and ensure that it is of adequate quality.

A matrix is ideal for a company that regularly handles many small projects. But a matrix has problems of its own.

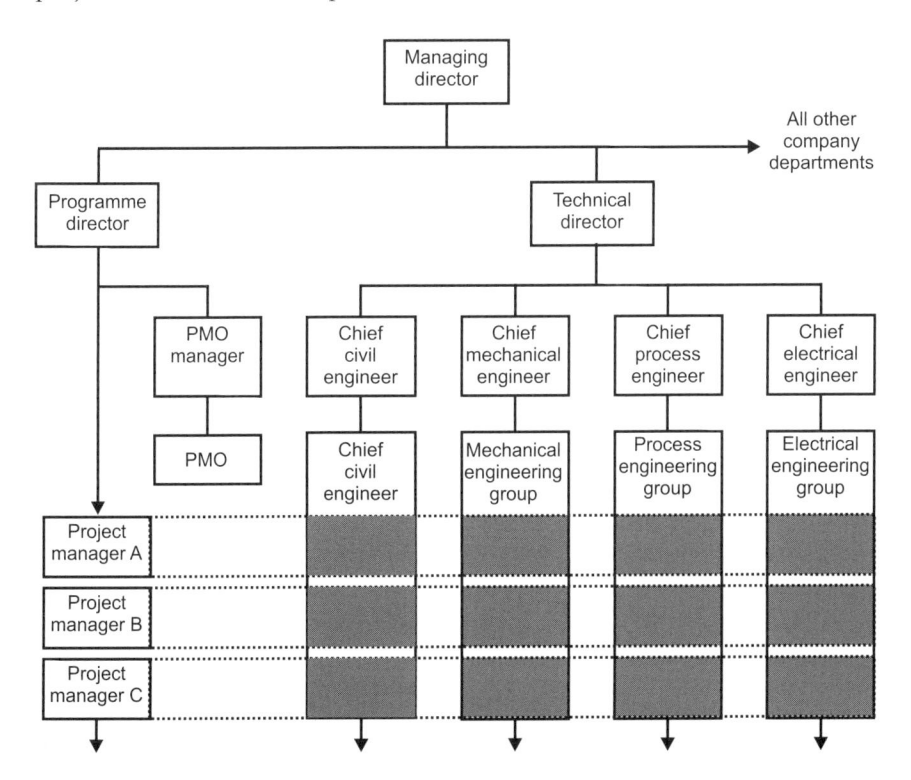

Figure 3.4   Principle of a matrix organization for multiple projects

One drawback of a matrix organization is that all the project workers are dispersed over their functional departments, so it is less easy to drum up a project team spirit. Each person's loyalty is divided between their functional department and the project, so motivation towards the project could be diluted.

A potentially more serious problem with matrix organizations is that they can engender conflict between project managers and departmental managers. Each project worker has two bosses, the project manager and his/her departmental manager (which management theorists recognize as violating the principle of unity of command). So problems can occur when the project manager wants one thing and a departmental manager wants another. Whose will should prevail? And what about the poor project worker in the middle of the dispute?

In a 'balanced matrix', the project managers and the departmental managers share power and are expected to cooperate for the best good of the company its projects. In a 'weak matrix', each project manager is little more than a project coordinator, and can only advise or request. At the other end of the power range, senior company management might decree that project managers have the highest authority, in which case the organization will be known as a 'strong matrix' and departmental managers must always try to bow to project managers' wishes.

Organization Theory from the Project Manager's Point of View

In most cases a project manager will be appointed to an existing organization and will have little or no say in whether that organization is to be run as a dedicated project team or as a project shared with others over a matrix. But although project managers might have no chance of choosing their organization structure, at least if they understand some of the theory outlined above they will be able to adapt their management style to get the best out of their people and work to overcome any organizational disadvantages.

One final word on organization design is a piece of advice that I often give. If you happen to be a senior manager given the job of designing your company's project organization structure, try putting yourself mentally in the place of people at various points in your proposed organization. Imagine how your attitude and work performance might be affected by the way in which the organization brings you into contact or conflict with others around you. That mental reflection could prevent a damaging and costly mistake, because projects stand a far greater chance of success when they are appropriately organized.

Organization of the Swings and Roundabouts Project

Now we are back with the St Kevin Borough Council, who have just given their swings and roundabouts project the green light to proceed. At the end of Chapter 2 we had a work breakdown structure (WBS) and outline cost estimate for this project. Now the project is being authorized to start we can think about its organization.

The St Kevin Borough Council actually comprises two organizations. One is the elected council members, who define council policy. But all the work of the council is performed under the direction of the permanent council body (the executive council): they are permanent staff not subject to the votes of electors. As our project will be built under the direction of the executive council, I need only describe that organization in any detail, and I can confine that description to those who will manage or work on our project. But the elected council (under the mayor) remains a key stakeholder. Figure 3.5 shows those elements of the executive council that will (in one way or another) be involved in the swings and roundabouts project.

At this juncture, please accept that the elected council body has approved the cost estimate and general plan for the swings and roundabouts project. So now the permanent council executive has appointed Theresa Green, the open spaces director, to manage this project. So she will have overall responsibility for planning and controlling this project and seeing it through to completion. She must fit this in with her other council duties, but she will have the full-time support of her site supervisor.

The shaded area in Figure 3.5 encloses the project team. But it is not strictly a team in the true sense. The road gang foreman Sally Forth has been seconded to Theresa for the duration of the project, to work when and as required, but Sally still reports also to her line manager Dusty Rhodes.

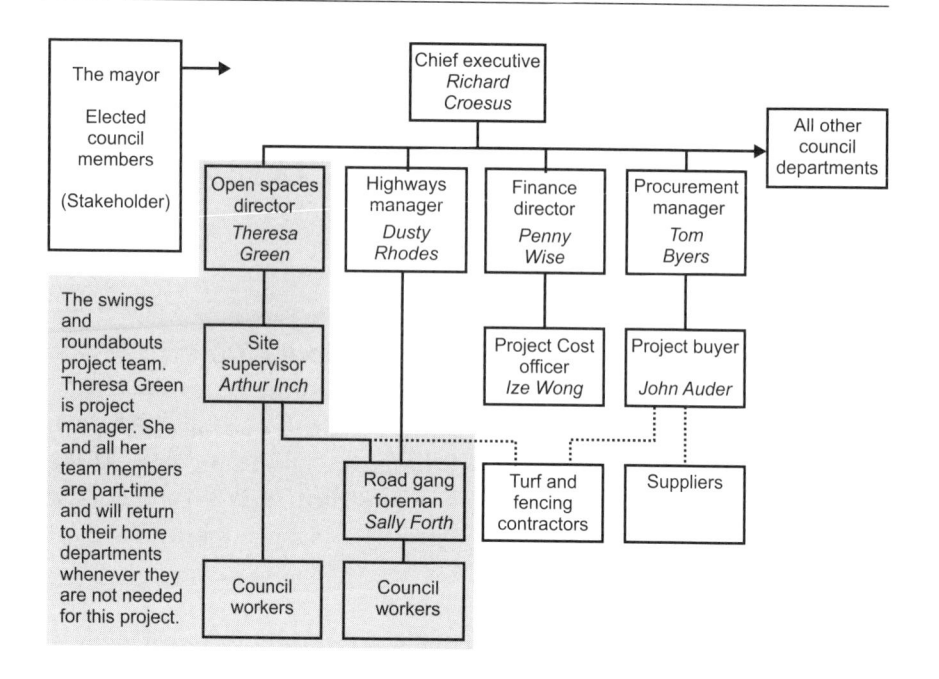

Figure 3.5 Organization of the swings and roundabouts project

[Organization chart showing:
- The mayor, Elected council members (Stakeholder)
- Chief executive Richard Croesus
- All other council departments
- Open spaces director: Theresa Green
- Highways manager: Dusty Rhodes
- Finance director: Penny Wise
- Procurement manager: Tom Byers
- Site supervisor: Arthur Inch
- Project Cost officer: Ize Wong
- Project buyer: John Auder
- Road gang foreman: Sally Forth
- Turf and fencing contractors
- Suppliers
- Council workers (under Arthur Inch and Sally Forth)

Note: The swings and roundabouts project team. Theresa Green is project manager. She and all her team members are part-time and will return to their home departments whenever they are not needed for this project.]

So this arrangement is really a very strong matrix (called strong because the project manager has overriding authority).

There is a further complication because the project will employ contractors, whose staff report back to their own companies as far as line management is concerned. When a project employs contractors to do much of the work, under the general supervision of a project manager or project management company, the arrangement is sometimes also known as a contract matrix.

So this organization, even though the project is very small, is somewhat complicated. But whenever was anything in local government easy to explain?

Other players in this simple project are the suppliers, and their progress will be monitored and expedited by the purchasing department under the direct supervision of John Auder, but he is not part of the project team and Theresa Green has no direct authority over him.

The project cost engineer, Ize Wong, made the original cost estimate for this project and, from his desk in the finance department, will monitor the costs and report them to Theresa. But once again Theresa has no direct authority over him. If this had been a large project it might have had its own PMO, with its own cost monitors directly responsible to the project manager.

So we have a workable project organization, but this example typifies the fact that many actual project organizations are complex and do not fit neatly into one of the categories described earlier in this chapter.

So now our project is ready to go – but first we need to schedule all the activities. That's Theresa Green's job in this case and fortunately she has had some project management training. The following chapter will outline commonly used planning and scheduling methods.

4

Planning and Scheduling

Planning can mean many things in projects, but here I am talking about setting out all the project tasks on their preferred calendar dates. Scheduling can mean the same thing, but it also has connotations in scheduling people so that they fit into the plan without being either too idle or overloaded.

Essential Requirements for an Effective Plan

An effective plan will be one that allows the project manager to set out the starts and finishes of all the project tasks at practicable times. Then the project manager can at least try to make sure that every task is started on time.

The plan must be set down in sufficient detail to allow monitoring and control. Suppose that the plan includes a task scheduled to last for 26 weeks. When that task has been in progress for ten weeks it can be very difficult to know whether or not it is on track to finish on time. But if that task were to be broken down into several tasks lasting (say) no more than two weeks each, that would give the project manager more reference points for progress checks. So a more detailed plan will provide more dates on which progress can be checked with some degree of accuracy.

When I am asked how much detail a plan should contain I always give the following answer. No task should be so long that it follows through more than one department under the control of more than one supervisor or manager. In other words, there should be a break in the plan every time responsibility for a task passes from one supervisor or manager to another.

Another essential requirement is that all the tasks are planned to follow each other in a logical sequence. For example, a plan should not show a roof being put on a building before the walls have been built.

The plan must communicate its message to all those who are going to work to it. If the plan contains hundreds or thousands of tasks, the project manager must ensure that people are not confused by large volumes of data. That problem can be solved using a suitable computer system, and by filtering and sorting all the task information so that each manager gets only information needed by his/her own department or group.

Diary Planning

The easiest form of planning occurs when a few project people get together, pull out their diaries (or the electronic equivalents of their diaries) and write down a few key dates that they hope to achieve for their project. Such plans are usually made on a wing and a prayer and fail because not enough attention has been paid to detail. They tend to allow long periods between events, so that it is difficult for everyone to assess progress. Late running will only be discovered when it is too late to correct. Also, diary entries can only cover a few tasks, so this method would be hopeless except for the tiniest of projects.

Bar Charts

Bar charts can offer planning success for very simple projects. They are sometimes called Gantt Charts, because an American industrial engineer called Henry Gantt, who lived from 1861 to 1919, was very fond of using charts to plan and progress work in factories where he was trying to improve productivity. For many years in the first half of the twentieth century all projects were planned using bar charts, which were often seen displayed on office walls.

Anyone who can understand an office holiday chart can understand a bar chart. For a project plan, jobs are listed in a column down the left-hand side, and their times are represented by horizontal bars placed out to the right. The farther to the right they are placed, the later they are planned to start and finish.

Some wall charts were sophisticated mechanical affairs, with strips for the bars that could be adjusted for time (which means sideways) by the planner because they were:

- magnetized strips stuck on a steel board or;

- job cards dropped into in long slots or;

- plastic strips (looking remarkably like Lego elements) which plugged into a board drilled with a grid pattern of many holes.

Many managers still like to see project schedules displayed as printed bar charts, which computers can produce even when the underlying planning methods are more sophisticated. Bar charts can display simple project plans very well (which is another way of saying that they can be visually effective and good communicating tools). Whilst the length of each bar is scaled according to the duration of the task, bars can be coloured or shaded to impart more information, such as indicating the main type of skill or resource needed for each task.

Now let's plan a big garden pond – it will be about five metres at its widest point and a metre deep in the middle. This is a very simple project, but it does have to be planned. It will require marking out a section of the garden and then a large hole has to be dug and lined with sand. I have built such a pond myself and I disposed of the earth by spreading it along a very wide border that was 20 metres long, so I needed no builder's skip.

A heavy butyl rubber liner will ensure that the pond will have a long life free of leaks, but that liner will be made to order and delivery will take a week. I need not describe all the individual tasks, because they are shown in Figure 4.1 overleaf. However, putting fish in the pond usually has to wait until the plants have been in for a week or two. The solid black bars on this chart indicate when the gardener is working and the grey bars generally show times when things have to wait, for example whilst paving slabs are delivered or the pond fills with water. I have not included the installation of anti-heron measures or pumps and fountains.

Now look at how the black bars fall below each other in the various day columns. On day 13 three bars appearing together in this column show that three tasks requiring the gardener's time occur on the same day. Actually for this project the gardener would indeed be able to choose the plants, go out and buy them and then plant them at the water's edge on the same day. But if these were all full-time tasks you would either need three gardeners on day 13, or the project must be extended by two days. Sorting problems like that out comes under the heading of resource scheduling, which we can look at later.

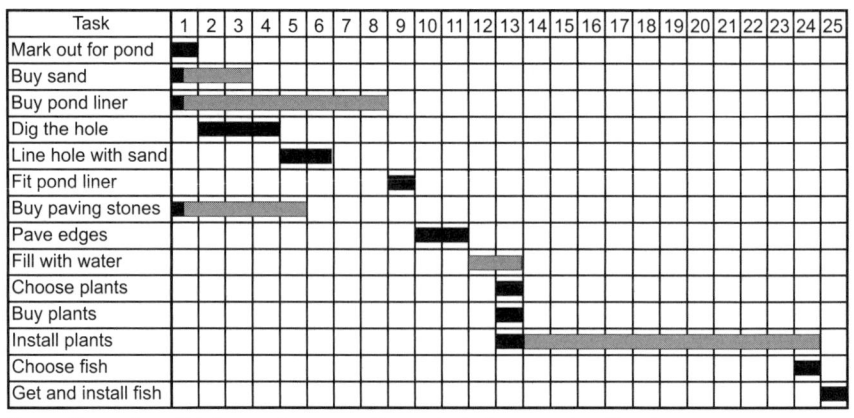

Task	1	2	3	4	5	6	7	8	9	10	11	12	13	14	15	16	17	18	19	20	21	22	23	24	25
Mark out for pond	■																								
Buy sand	■	▨	▨																						
Buy pond liner	■	▨	▨	▨	▨	▨	▨																		
Dig the hole				■	■																				
Line hole with sand						■	■																		
Fit pond liner								■																	
Buy paving stones	■	▨	▨	▨	▨																				
Pave edges									■	■															
Fill with water											▨	▨	■												
Choose plants													■												
Buy plants														■											
Install plants															▨	▨	▨	▨	▨	▨	▨	▨	▨	■	
Choose fish																								■	
Get and install fish																									■

Time units are days. This is a continuous working project with no weekend breaks.

Active tasks indicated thus: ■   Passive waiting time indicated thus: ▨

Figure 4.1   Bar chart for a garden pond project

This chart is fairly successful at displaying this project plan. But most of these tasks are linked and have to be performed in a set sequence. The chart implies this, but cannot show these dependencies clearly. Also, there are only a few tasks in this project, but most projects have hundreds or even thousands of tasks and cover a far longer time. Just imagine how confused a bar chart would become then. So whilst bar charts are fine for displaying and calculating plans for tiny projects, they are inadequate for larger projects. We need something better.

That 'something better' was developed in the middle of the last century. It is called critical path network analysis.

Introduction to Critical Path Network Analysis

Critical path network analysis emerged in different forms and from several sources in Europe and the US. This is not the time for a history lesson, so I shall describe the form of network analysis that is now in common use, and which is supported by all good (and some bad) project management computer systems.

TREE PROJECT

I have used this example countless times before to introduce critical path networks but it is a good way of explaining the symbols used. The 'project' is to plant a tree that someone has dumped on you as an unexpected

PLANNING AND SCHEDULING

Task	1	2	3	4	5	6	7	8	9	10	11	12	13	14	15	16	17	18	19	20	21	22	23	24	25	26	27	28	29	30
Dig the hole	■	■	■	■	■	■	■	■	■	■	■	■	■	■	■	■	■	■	■	■										
Put tree in hole																					■									
Fill in the hole																						■	■	■	■	■				

0	20	20
1 Dig the hole		
0	0	20

→

20	1	21
2 Put tree in hole		
20	0	21

→

21	5	26
3 Fill in the hole		
21	0	26

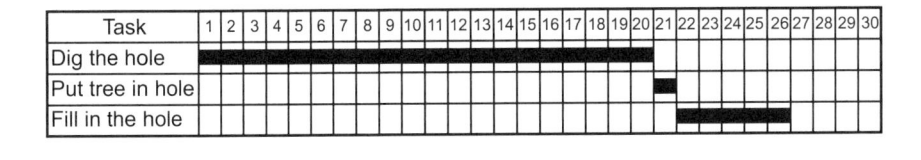

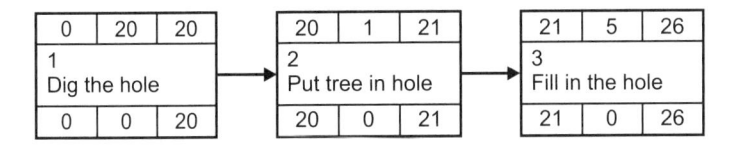

All times are estimated in minutes

This shows a bar chart and its equivalent network diagram. The network symbols and numbers are explained in Figure 4.3 and the text.

Figure 4.2   Plans for a tree project

present. So you don't have to choose the tree or go out and buy it, and there is only one place in your garden where you can plant it. All you have to do is dig a hole, put the tree in and then fill in the hole. Figure 4.2 shows how this plan would look as a bar chart and then gives its critical path equivalent. Each box in the network version represents one task.

A project network is drawn by placing all tasks in a pattern according to the sequence in which they should logically take place. There will be a start task at the extreme left-hand side and a finish task at the extreme right. We always like to start a project network with only one task, and run everything into just one task at the end. That will make subsequent calculations far easier. Nothing has to be drawn to any timescale.

No task can begin until all its predecessors have been finished. So in Figure 4.2, we cannot put the tree in the hole until the hole has been fully dug. That link is indicated by the arrow. You cannot fail to have noticed that there are some weird looking numbers in the little boxes in each task box, and now I have to explain those. For that, I must refer to Figure 4.3.

Figure 4.3 shows a common convention for depicting one task in a project network diagram. This is the way in which we sketch tasks when we draw networks by hand (for example during a project planning meeting). Sketching can be made far easier if we use Post-It Notes (one for each task) and I have known of at least one person who uses pads where each sticker has the task box and its lines pre-printed upon it.

Figure 4.3 A task in a critical path network

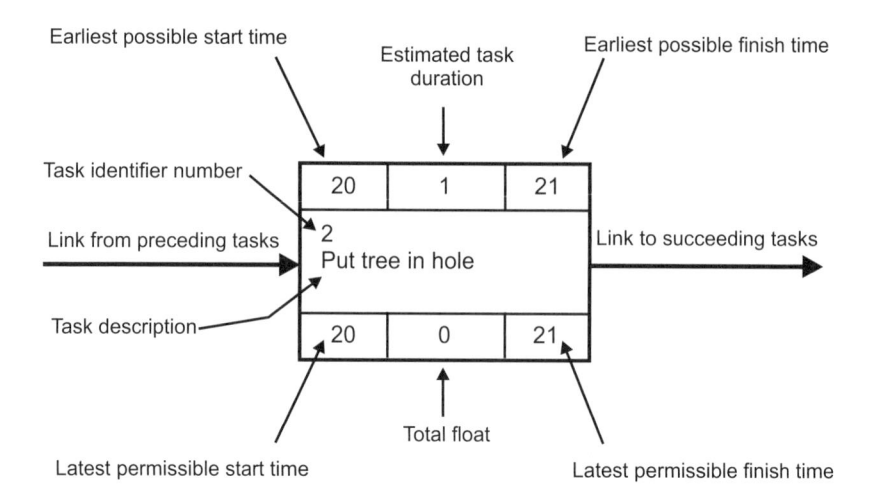

Diagram labels: Earliest possible start time (20), Estimated task duration (1), Earliest possible finish time (21), Task identifier number (2), Task description ("Put tree in hole"), Link from preceding tasks, Link to succeeding tasks, Latest permissible start time (20), Total float (0), Latest permissible finish time (21).

This is the convention for drawing a task on a network diagram. When networks are printed by a computer, space on the page will not usually allow for all this information to be included and one must rely instead for the associated tabular reports. All the terms are explained in the text.

Forward pass through the network diagram

Some things in Figure 4.3 are obvious, such as the task number, description and estimated duration. But now look at the numbers across the top of the box. At the left-hand side is the earliest possible start time for the task. This is determined by the earliest possible finish time of the preceding task. In the tree project we already know that we cannot begin to put the tree in the hole until the preceding task has been done.

Often in networks a task will have more than one predecessor, and then it is the latest of all their early finish times that will determine the earliest possible start time for the task being considered. In other words, the longest lead-in path will determine the earliest time when a task can start.

The earliest possible finish time for any task must, through simple logic, be its earliest start time plus the estimated duration.

So in a more substantial project than this tree planting job, the planner must work through the network, tracing through all its paths, to find the earliest start and finish times for all the tasks. This is known as the forward pass.

PLANNING AND SCHEDULING

At the end of the forward pass the planner will reach the end task, at the right-hand side of the network. That task depicts the end of the project, and its earliest possible finish date must be the earliest possible date at which the entire project can be finished.

That completes the forward pass. We now know the earliest possible time at which any task can be started and finished.

So far we are working in numbers and not calendar dates. So we have not yet concerned ourselves with complications such as weekends and bank holidays. Don't worry about that, because the computer can work all that out for us later. In fact it can also perform all the calculations described here, doing the forward and backward passes for us effortlessly. But we do need to understand the arithmetic and be aware of the process.

The backward pass

Please look again at the task depicted in Figure 4.3. The box in the bottom right-hand corner shows the latest permissible finish time for this task. If this happened to be the final task in the project network, then the earliest possible finish and latest permissible finish times will usually be the same because we normally like to finish our projects as soon as possible.

The latest permissible finish time for any task is found by looking at the following task, so the latest permissible finish time must be the same as the latest permissible start time for the following task (if the project is not to be delayed).

Often there will be more than one task immediately following the task being considered. Then one must trace back along the link arrows from all the immediately succeeding tasks. Each of those will have its latest permissible start time, and it is the earliest of those that must fix the latest permissible finish times for the task being considered.

Once we have found the latest permissible finish time for a task we have to determine its latest permissible start time, and that is easily done by subtracting the estimated duration from the latest finish time. That result is written in the bottom left-hand box.

Float and the critical path

Once the forward and backward passes have been made through a network there will always be a path where the earliest and latest times for each task in the path are the same. Those tasks must take place at their earliest possible times if the project is not to be delayed. Those tasks are thus critical and the path along which they lie is called the critical path.

Network branching can mean that there might be more than one possible path from start to finish that has the same duration, and then there will be more than one critical path.

Now consider a task which has an earliest possible finish date of (say) day 112 in a network, but that it has a latest permissible finish date of day 130. So that particular task could be delayed by 18 days without delaying the end of the project. We call those 18 days total float. Total float is found by subtracting the earliest possible finish time for a task from its latest permissible finish time.

There are other kinds of float, including free float and independent float but they need not concern us in this elementary book. However, if a task gets delayed for any reason, and uses up some of its float as a result, the float that is left is sometimes called remaining float.

TABLE PROJECT

Now I am going to describe a plan for making a table. This is going to be made by a carpenter, so the legs will be turned on a lathe and mortise and tenon joints will be used for the frame. Figure 4.4 lists the necessary tasks, with their estimated durations. All these estimated times are merely to illustrate the method, so there is some poetic licence here, and some of these tasks could no doubt be done more quickly in real life.

When planning, it is possible to use any time units from minutes to months. It is always best to use the same units of time for all tasks throughout a project plan and not mix different units. Days are very commonly used and are the default units in many computer programs. They are clearly the units of first choice. However, this table project is going to be very short, so I have chosen to use half-days. Half-days mean that you have ten units for a five-day week.

PLANNING AND SCHEDULING

Task number	Task description	Estimated duration	Predecessor tasks
1	Design the table	2	-
2	Buy the materials	2	1
3	Make the legs	4	2
4	Make the underframe	3	2
5	Make the table top	2	2
6	Assemble the table	2	3,4,5
7	Wait for glue to set	1	6
8	Sandpaper and varnish	2	7

All duration estimates are in half-day units (so that 2 = 1 day).

Figure 4.4   Task list for the table project

All the tasks are numbered, and those numbers are the task identifiers that could be used if we wished to process this plan in a computer. The end column in the task list (headed 'predecessor tasks') gives the identity numbers of all immediately preceding tasks. So, for example, task 6 (assembling the table) cannot happen before tasks 3, 4 and 5 have been done. Remember that project planning is all about logic.

The table in Figure 4.4 contains all the data we need to draw a network diagram for this simple project. That network is shown in Figure 4.5.

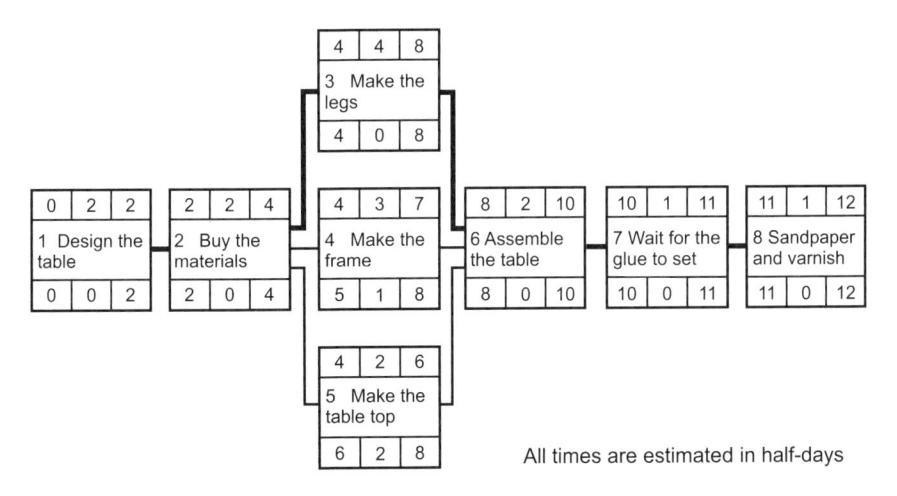

4	4	8
3 Make the legs		
4	0	8

0	2	2		2	2	4		4	3	7		8	2	10		10	1	11		11	1	12
1 Design the table				2 Buy the materials				4 Make the frame				6 Assemble the table				7 Wait for the glue to set				8 Sandpaper and varnish		
0	0	2		2	0	4		5	1	8		8	0	10		10	0	11		11	0	12

4	2	6
5 Make the table top		
6	2	8

All times are estimated in half-days

The critical path is highlighted by the heavy rule.

Figure 4.5   Network diagram for the table project

The forward pass through this network shows that this project could be finished, at the earliest, at the end of time period 12. Because I have used half-days as the time units, that actually means day 6.

The backward pass has revealed tasks 1, 2, 3, 6, 7 and 8 as having zero float, and thus being critical. The critical path has been drawn as a heavy line.

Now we have priorities for doing tasks 3, 4 and 5. Task 3 has to be done as early as possible, but task 4 could be delayed by one time unit (half a day in this case) and task 5 could be delayed by up to two units (which is a whole day).

So that demonstrates how the critical path can be calculated. Although this is an extremely simple example, it contains all the constituent elements for compiling even the largest project plan.

Resource Scheduling

Projects use resources of different kinds, such as materials, working space, money and so on. But the most important resource of all is usually people and, by a stroke of good fortune, their work is the easiest to schedule.

The plan for the table project assumes that all the tasks can be done at their earliest times, provided all the estimates were correct. But, of course, there is a snag. I have assumed that the carpenter can do two tasks at the same time. Clearly she cannot. If she did try she might have a very nasty accident with her machine tools. So either we need more carpenters for a limited time or the project must take a little longer. For the table project, of course, the resource restriction of having only one carpenter would add less than three days to the project time.

Many project managers ignore this aspect of planning and simply work to schedules that attempt to perform each task as early as possible. That often works, especially when the organization is large and has flexible resources. Indeed, many writers of project management books ignore the subject of resource scheduling.

There are two ways in which resources can be scheduled. For a very tiny project, if the project plan is drawn as a bar chart, and the bars are coded to represent the resource needed for each task, it can be possible to adjust the bars on the chart until no time column contains more than the number of each resource available.

Resource scheduling uses the results of critical path analysis and can give priority for the use of scarce resources to those tasks that are either critical or have least float.

The most practicable way to schedule resources is to use a computer program. Now we are beginning to step outside the 'bare facts' of project management upon which this book is based. So for detailed advice on resource scheduling, please refer to my larger book *Project Management* (which is also published by Gower). All the later editions of that book cover resource scheduling in some detail and also give advice on the choice of computer programs. A less comprehensive alternative is my smaller book *The Essentials of Project Management*, also published by Gower.

Planning the Swings and Roundabouts Project

The St Kevin Borough Council approved the cost estimate of £91,393 for the swings and roundabouts project in March 2014 and authorized it to go ahead. So project manager Theresa Green called a meeting of the key people to plan the project. The following people were invited to attend:

- Arthur Inch (site supervisor);
- Sally Forth (road gang foreman);
- John Auder (not a team member, but will be purchasing for the project).

More senior people from the executive council were not asked to attend, but Dusty Rhodes, Penny Wise and Ken Byers would be kept informed of the meeting's outcome (the council organization chart was given in Figure 3.5).

So four people met in a conference room and, using a large sheet of paper, sketched out the project network diagram. Only Theresa understood network analysis, but that did not matter, because she explained everything as the meeting proceeded. You will need to refer to Figure 4.6 overleaf to follow this discussion.

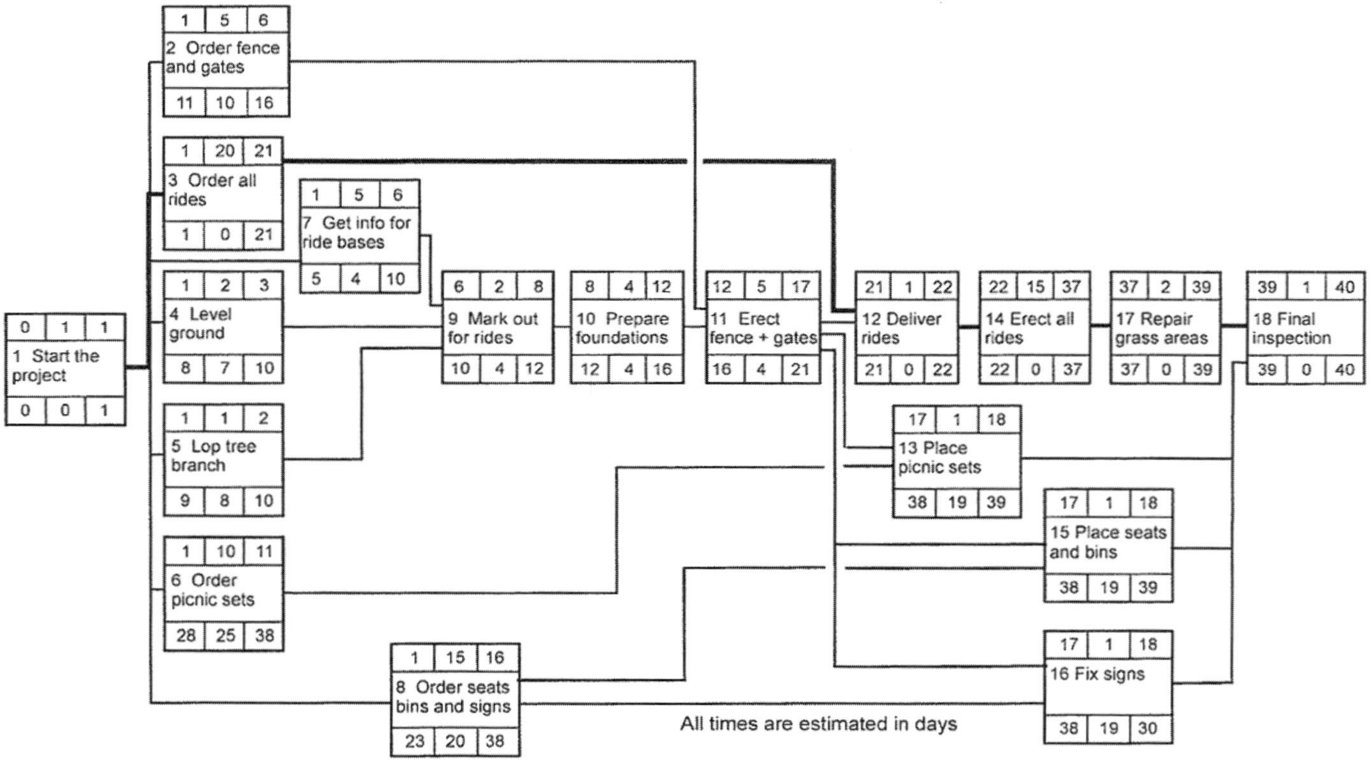

Figure 4.6 Network diagram for the swings and roundabouts project

DRAWING THE LOGIC DIAGRAM

Theresa placed the first Post-It Note at the extreme left hand edge of the paper. 'This,' she explained, 'is the start of our project. Now what must we do next?' So the people in the room and Theresa together decided what tasks needed to be done, and Theresa placed a Post-It Note for each task on the paper. Each sticker was put in its appropriate position in relation to the other tasks and Theresa pencilled in the linking arrows – although because everything always flows from left-to-right in a network, the arrow heads are usually not drawn.

One or two important decisions were made that affected the plan. Theresa pointed out that no expensive purchased goods could be delivered to the site until the fence and gates were in position, and Arthur Inch heartily agreed with that. But Sally Forth, who was going to have to use heavy machinery to put down all the foundations declared that the fence would be a hindrance and might even get damaged. So it was decided that the fencing contractors would not be allowed on site until all the heavy ground work had been done.

Arthur Inch wanted to mark out the site as soon as possible, and for that he said he would have to wait until the ground had been levelled (although the levelling would be easy because there was only one hump to level. He said he would need information from the supplier of the rides about fixings and foundations, long before the rides were actually delivered. Theresa said that this information could be obtained quickly over the Internet.

And so the meeting continued, with everyone being very cooperative, until Post-It Notes were in place that showed all the tasks in the agreed, logical work sequence.

ESTIMATING AND TIME ANALYSIS

Theresa's next step was to ask everyone to estimate how long each task would take. The units to be used were days, with no weekend working unless something ran late. So the project would be planned using five-day weeks. Every estimate was agreed by the person who would be responsible for the task, and so everyone accepted commitment to the agreed times. It is always important to get the commitment and agreement of people who are going to be held responsible for project tasks.

Note that the durations for all the purchasing tasks include delivery times, so (for example) task 6, for ordering the picnic sets, has been estimated at ten days duration. That means these sets could be on site if required ten days after placing the order. Arthur Inch reminded everyone that he wanted nothing delivered to site until the fencing was in place. This was proving a little difficult to show in the network logic diagram, so Theresa suggested to John Auder that he should advise all suppliers when it would be permissible for them to make their deliveries, and ask them to hold off until they got the green light. John readily agreed to that.

Theresa then carried out a time analysis and declared that the project should take 38 working days from start to finish if all went according to plan. So this project could be finished in just under eight calendar weeks.

Arthur Inch then expressed the concern felt by everyone else present that the plan only showed numbers, not calendar dates. Neither he nor his people could work to a timetable based on day numbers that he could not understand. Everyone agreed with that, but Theresa was quick to reassure everyone. 'Don't worry,' she said, 'we'll run it in the computer using Microsoft Project as soon as we decide our on-site start date. Then we shall have a schedule with calendar dates.'

So the next question was when could the project actually start? Everyone present said they would like a week in which to prepare themselves and clear up tasks upon which they were currently engaged. Sally Forth pointed out that she would have to get her boss, Dusty Rhodes, to arrange with the County Council for the loan of some heavy equipment.

So it was agreed by all that the project should start on Monday morning, 7 April 2014.

TIME ANALYSIS AND SCHEDULE USING MICROSOFT PROJECT

There is an abundance of software that can perform project scheduling. Microsoft Project, whilst not the best, is certainly by far the most popular. It is available, for example, to most university students. So Theresa used Microsoft Project. Her project schedule is shown in Figure 4.7. This should be the control document for this project, because all dates are set out clearly, whereas a bar chart would have to be interpreted from the scale. Notice that Microsoft Project uses the term 'Total Slack', which is an alternative name for 'Total Float'.

	Task Name	Duration	Early Start	Early Finish	Late Start	Late Finish	Total Slack
1	Project start	1 day	Mon 07/04/14	Mon 07/04/14	Mon 07/04/14	Mon 07/04/14	0 days
2	Order fence and gates	5 days	Tue 08/04/14	Mon 14/04/14	Tue 22/04/14	Mon 28/04/14	10 days
3	Order all rides	20 days	Tue 08/04/14	Mon 05/05/14	Tue 08/04/14	Mon 05/05/14	0 days
4	Level the ground	2 days	Tue 08/04/14	Wed 09/04/14	Thu 17/04/14	Fri 18/04/14	7 days
5	Lop tree branch	1 day	Tue 08/04/14	Tue 08/04/14	Fri 18/04/14	Fri 18/04/14	8 days
6	Order picnic sets	10 days	Tue 08/04/14	Mon 21/04/14	Thu 15/05/14	Wed 28/05/14	27 days
7	Get info for ride bases	5 days	Tue 08/04/14	Mon 14/04/14	Mon 14/04/14	Fri 18/04/14	4 days
8	Order seats, bins, signs	15 days	Tue 08/04/14	Mon 28/04/14	Thu 08/05/14	Wed 28/05/14	22 days
9	Mark out for rides	2 days	Tue 15/04/14	Wed 16/04/14	Mon 21/04/14	Tue 22/04/14	4 days
10	Prepare foundations	4 days?	Thu 17/04/14	Tue 22/04/14	Wed 23/04/14	Mon 28/04/14	4 days?
11	Erect fence and gates	5 days	Wed 23/04/14	Tue 29/04/14	Tue 29/04/14	Mon 05/05/14	4 days
12	Deliver rides to site	1 day	Tue 06/05/14	Tue 06/05/14	Tue 06/05/14	Tue 06/05/14	0 days
13	Place picnic sets	1 day	Wed 30/04/14	Wed 30/04/14	Thu 29/05/14	Thu 29/05/14	21 days
14	Erect all rides	15 days	Wed 07/05/14	Tue 27/05/14	Wed 07/05/14	Tue 27/05/14	0 days
15	Place bench seats and bins	1 day	Wed 30/04/14	Wed 30/04/14	Thu 29/05/14	Thu 29/05/14	21 days
16	Fix signs	1 day	Wed 30/04/14	Wed 30/04/14	Thu 29/05/14	Thu 29/05/14	21 days
17	Repair grass areas	2 days	Wed 28/05/14	Thu 29/05/14	Wed 28/05/14	Thu 29/05/14	0 days
18	Final inspection	1 day	Fri 30/05/14	Fri 30/05/14	Fri 30/05/14	Fri 30/05/14	0 days

Figure 4.7 Swings and roundabouts project time analysis from Microsoft Project

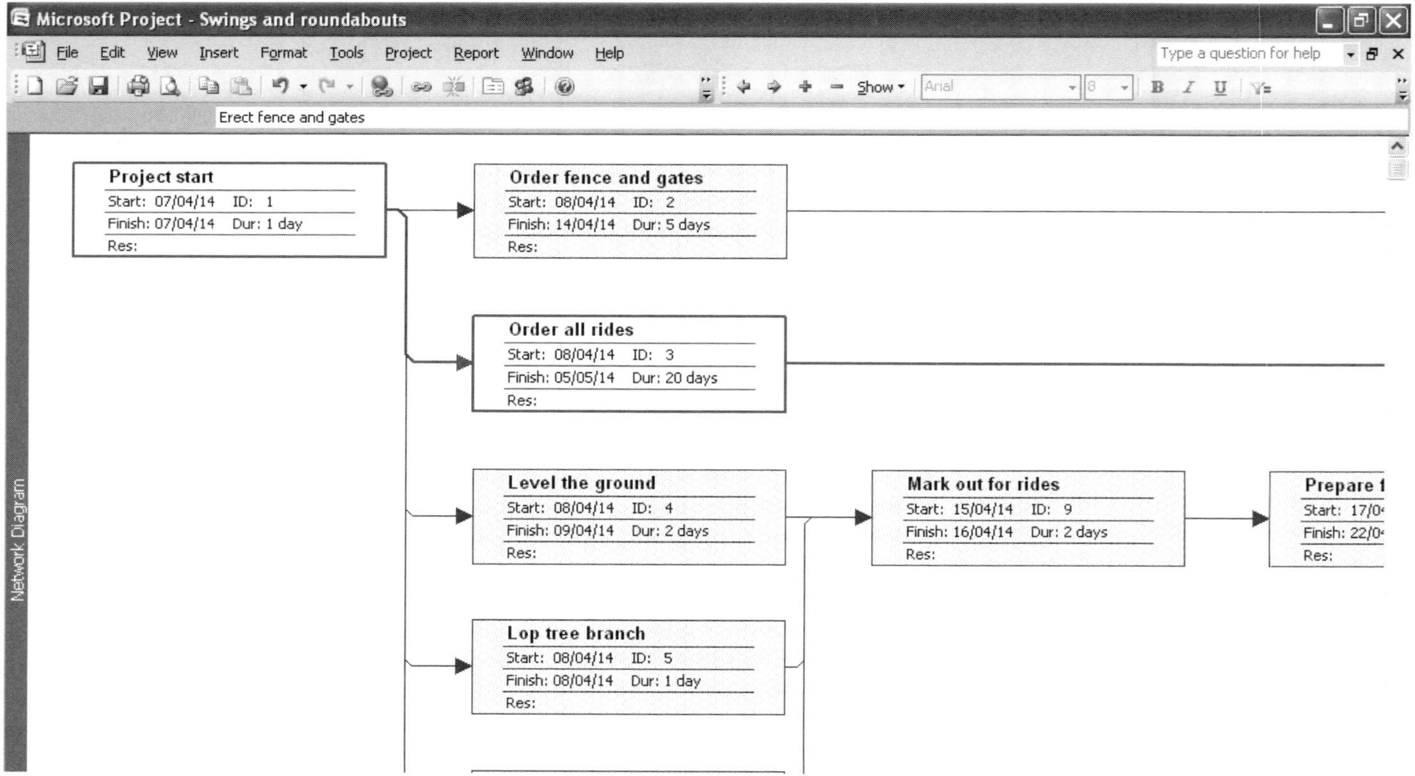

Figure 4.8   Detail from the swings and roundabouts project network diagram as plotted by Microsoft Project

PLANNING AND SCHEDULING

Figure 4.8 opposite shows a small fragment of the network diagram, but Microsoft Project needs large areas of paper to plot whole networks.

MISTAKES

It's very easy to make mistakes when using a computer to process a network diagram. The most common mistakes happen when people forget to enter something when they are typing data into the machine. To understand what I mean, turn back to Figure 4.6 and look at tasks numbers 9 and 10. Suppose I had forgotten to enter the link joining these two tasks. Then the computer, being an automaton, would regard task 9 as an end task and task 10 as a start task. This kind of mistake is very common, and it even has names associated with it. So task 9 would become an 'end dangle' and task 10 would be a 'start dangle'.

Clearly such mistakes would wreck the calculations and cause a bad schedule. The more advanced computer programs recognize that such mistakes can be common and so they will report all the start tasks and all the finish tasks for a project schedule. Now, if you have followed my earlier advice and drawn your network logic with just one start and one finish, you will know something is wrong if your computer tells you that you have more than one start and more than one finish task.

Other mistakes that used to be common are now prevented by the computer, which will recognize if you try to enter two tasks with the same ID, or if you attempt to specify a link that would create not a linear path but a continuous loop.

One mistake that the computer cannot recognize is when you enter the wrong duration. So it pays, provided the network is not too big, to run a mental calculation through just to find the critical path and get an idea of the estimated project duration. Then if the computer disagrees with you, you can start looking for the mistake.

On large networks, which might contain 1,000 or more tasks, mistakes are almost inevitable. In those cases it helps if one person keys the data into the computer whilst the other reads it off the network. With two people cross-checking each other, mistakes can be minimized or prevented. In my very long career in projects I have seen some terrible mistakes made that took days to sort out. So be careful and check your input data.

5

Contracts and Commerce

This chapter is about project purchasing and contracts – a subject that many writers tend to ignore. I have known brilliant engineers who have little interest in commercial matters, or even costs. Maybe they find these topics boring. They can be boring – until something goes wrong. Writers generally seem to share this disinterest. If you do not believe me, go to your library, pick up as many project management books as you can find, and look through their contents lists for any sign of purchasing or procurement. Too often you will search in vain.

In some companies the design departments and purchasing departments do not cooperate as they should. Technical people will happily pick up their telephones or go online with suppliers and contractors to commit their projects and their companies to contracts without first talking to the experts on these commercial matters.

When you consider that the costs of materials and bought-out services for a project can be as high as 80 per cent, all this neglect is astonishing. So in this brief chapter I must try to do something to capture your interest in this important subject

About Contracts

Our lives are surrounded and pervaded by contracts. Whenever we buy goods or services a contract is made between ourselves and the provider. However, in projects we are usually concerned with contracts between companies, so I must outline the essential ingredients that make a commercial contract.

When two companies agree to exchange money for goods or services the following four conditions are necessary for a legally binding contract to be made.

1. *Offer and acceptance.* One party has to make an offer to the other party to provide goods or services and the other party has to accept the offer.

2. *Intention to be legally bound.* There has to be evidence that the parties intended to make a legally binding contract.

3. *Capacity.* This condition applies particularly to contracts between companies. The company that makes an offer to contract has to have the capacity to make that offer. That capacity is determined by the objects clause in the company's memorandum of association. For example, a company that was set up in business to sell foodstuffs would be acting beyond its powers (the legal Latin term for that is *ultra vires*) if it offered to build a warehouse. The company can sell food to store in the warehouse, but it cannot legally contract to build the warehouse.

4. *Consideration.* This has nothing to do with politeness or concern for the other party's welfare. Consideration in this case means money or something else of value that is exchanged between the parties in return for the goods or services provided.

There are exceptions to all rules, but the above definitions generally apply.

Most contracts in projects will be contained in a written document, such as a specially prepared contract, a supplier's standard purchase order, or some model form of contract.

It is always best to make contracts in writing, with signatures on the documents. But contracts can be made verbally and do not have to be enshrined in written documents. Many service providers and other companies now routinely record telephone conversations 'for training purposes'. Discussions in meetings can result in verbal contracts that are made in front of witnesses who can later testify in court that there was intention to form a legally binding contract. I just mentioned the word 'court'. Let's try to conduct all our project business so that the courts never have to be involved.

Purchasing

I opened this chapter by mentioning the importance of purchasing with relevance to project costs. But purchasing is about far more than buying goods and services within budget. In fact, for many years manufacturing and project managers have chanted a mantra based on the word 'right'. It goes something like this. Materials have to be delivered:

- to the right quality;
- to the right specification;
- at the right place;
- at the right time;
- in the right amount;
- in the right condition;
- at the right price.

Sometimes there is tolerance on one or more of these issues, but if a road tanker full of ready-mixed and rapidly setting concrete arrives on a construction site where the formwork for the concrete has not been erected, someone has immediate problems. I know of several such instances from my own long career, sometimes happening in full view of the public gaze.

So, by now in this chapter, I think I have made the point that project purchasing is a process that has to be taken seriously.

INITIAL DISAGREEMENTS OVER CONDITIONS OF PURCHASE

Many purchasing contracts are made when the buyer issues a purchase order using a standard company form. Printed on the reverse side of most purchase orders are the standard conditions of purchase that the purchaser wishes to impose on the supplier.

These standard conditions can conflict with the terms that the supplier wants to impose on the purchaser. So the supplier's acceptance of the order might come with a different set of conditions attached. That difference of opinions can lead to correspondence between the two parties to decide which set of conditions shall apply. Such correspondence can go on for some time, until one party gets tired of the exercise and gives up. I have been told by legal experts that in such cases it is the last unanswered letter that will set the conditions because, by not answering it, the other party is deemed to have accepted the conditions by default.

For purchases made online this argument is usually cut short because the purchaser has to tick a little box accepting the supplier's conditions, and the screen will not move to the next page until that has been done.

I have to say that I have never personally had any trouble at all with conditions of purchase. Most honest companies are just too keen to do profitable business with each other.

PURCHASE ORDER PROCEDURE FOR SPECIAL OR EXPENSIVE ITEMS

Many purchases for projects are made by choosing items from suppliers' standard products as listed in their catalogues or web pages. But the following sequence of events will often take place for an order of very significant size, especially for non-catalogue goods or services and when the buyer wants to open the order to competitive bidding. The procedure is summarized as a flow chart in Figure 5.1 and is as follows.

1. The designer, engineer or other technical person who needs the goods or services for the project will write a detailed purchase specification of what is needed. Sometimes, for commonly used items, project companies will keep standard purchase specification forms that the technical person can use as a pattern.

2. When the specification is first sent to potential suppliers it is issued as an enquiry specification. The enquiry specification might also include special packaging and delivery requirements (sometimes goods have to be delivered to a site that is different from the purchaser's offices or packed to withstand export to some far-off land).

3. The purchasing department will send the enquiry specification to a number of possible suppliers, attaching its own standard enquiry form. That standard enquiry form will set out the

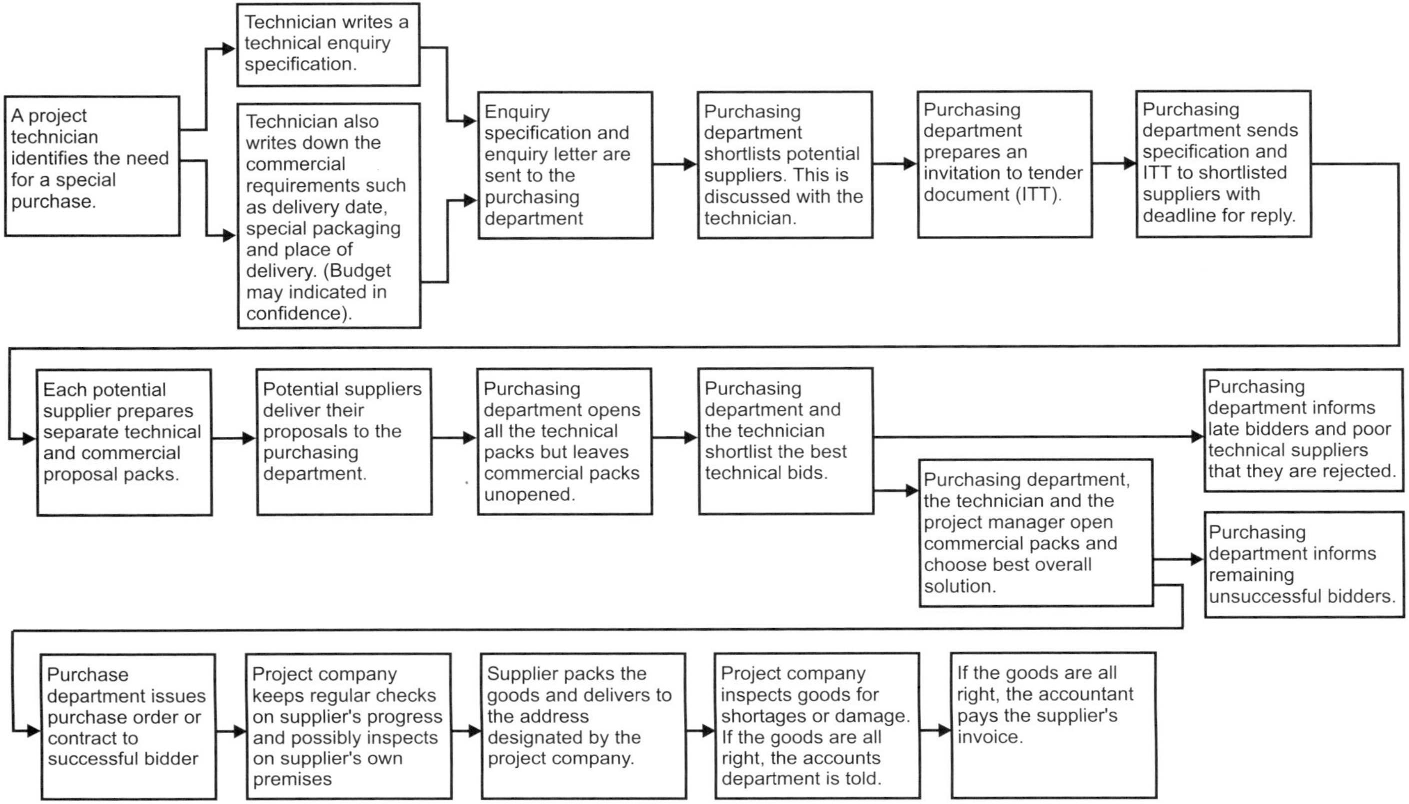

Figure 5.1 Possible sequence of events for a very high-value project purchase

commercial conditions expected, such as place of delivery, terms of payment, inspection arrangements and so on. Sets of documents like this sometimes constitute what is known as an invitation to tender (ITT).

4. All the potential suppliers who receive the enquiry will be asked to respond with their proposals by a certain date. They know that they will be disqualified if they miss the deadline date for any reason.

5. The project company receives, considers and compares all the proposals. Some companies use a standard summary form to make this easier for themselves. That summary form can list and compare salient facts from all the tenders received. For example, they might compare the expected delivery time, and the price to the purchaser (which means the total price including any essential items charged as optional extras and all handling, shipping and insurance costs). An example of a bid summary form is given later in this chapter (Figure 5.2).

6. The purchasing department and the technical person who originated the enquiry must now consult and decide together which proposal offers the best combination of technical performance and commercial terms. For very large contracts this is sometimes done in two stages, with the technical proposals being considered first. When the proposals that would fail on technical or quality grounds have been eliminated, the surviving proposals are compared for price, delivery and other commercial details.

7. Another stage can sometimes intervene here if the technical details have altered as a result of discussions between potential suppliers and the project company. Suppliers often make helpful suggestions and some of those suggestions can result in a change to the specification. In those cases the original enquiry specification will have to be amended before it can become the purchase specification.

8. Some project companies ask their technical people to reissue the purchase specification to the purchasing department with an accompanying purchase requisition. A purchase requisition in this case gives authorization from the technical people to the purchasing department to place the order and commit funds from the project budget.

9.   Finally the purchasing manager signs a purchase order and the contract is made with the supplier.

For public sector projects within the European Union (EU) further procedures apply when seeking tenders for goods and services valued above specified threshold values. These procurement directives are intended to promote fairness and open opportunities for suppliers and contractors throughout the EU. They can have the unfortunate consequence of delaying a project for many months. More on this can be found on the Internet. A very helpful site is at http://www.tameside.gov.uk/procurement/eudirectives.

EXPEDITING AND INSPECTION

Many weeks or months might elapse between the issue of a purchase order and the expected delivery date for the goods. During that time, a competent purchasing department will maintain regular contact with the supplier to check that everything is proceeding to plan. At all costs, one does not want the project to be held up because the goods do not arrive on the promised date. Surprises like that indicate poor management.

For very complex technical goods the purchaser might even wish to visit the supplier's premises to check that progress is indeed on track, and that the goods are being made to the required standard of quality. Of course such visits can only be made with the supplier's agreement but purchasers sometimes insist on the right to inspect in this way as a condition of purchase.

GOODS RECEIPT

When the goods are received they must be checked for possible damage or shortages. Of course they must also be checked to make sure that they are the goods which were actually ordered. Companies in the manufacturing and construction industries will have goods inwards inspection departments specially to make those checks.

If the goods are satisfactory, they are placed in store or at or near the point where they are to be used. The goods inwards department will send a note to the accounts department to release payment of the supplier's invoice. Clearly if the goods are received damaged or with shortages, the purchaser will be in urgent touch with the supplier and payment on the invoice will not be allowed.

PURCHASE ORDER AMENDMENTS

Sometimes it is necessary to change the requirements specified in a purchase order. The usual way for doing that is first to contact the supplier to ensure that the change can be made. If the change causes the supplier to scrap work already started there might be a justifiable amendment or cancellation charge.

Once the purchaser and the supplier have agreed that the change is possible, the purchaser will usually have to prepare and issue a purchase order amendment.

It is possible on large projects for an initial purchase order to be festooned with amendments, to the point that it is difficult to find out what exactly is on order. Sometimes the remedy for that is to talk to the supplier and agree that the initial order should be cancelled and replaced with a brand new order that incorporates all the amendments.

Contracts for Services and Construction

A contract might be agreed between two companies for the execution of an entire project. Many more contracts and subcontracts are usually made by project companies who need the services of specialist subcontractors. But because all contracts are governed by similar rules and practices, I need only set down some general information here.

Some industries are associated with professional organizations (the Institution of Civil Engineers, for example) and many of these have developed model forms of contract that companies within the particular profession are able to use. For example, I once had to place a contract for the installation of an elevator in the offices where I was employed as a manager, and my chosen contractor simply presented me with a proforma contract, complete with a standard set of conditions that applied throughout the elevator industry. The conditions were fair and reasonable, so I had no difficulty in accepting them.

Many companies prefer to draft their own contracts where special goods and services are concerned, and then it is always good practice for both parties to have their solicitors run through the document to ensure that it is fair and reasonable. That process is made more difficult when the contractor and the client or customer speak different languages.

TERMS OF PAYMENT

One of the most important sections of a contract will concern the agreed terms of payment. Very often the contract will give not only a total contract price, but will set out a series of stages when parts of the total contract price must be paid by the purchaser or client. This is usually done to ensure that the supplier has a steady income to support the purchase of materials and pay wages whilst the work is in progress. If that were not to be agreed, the supplier might be spending considerable sums with no counterbalancing revenues, and so could suffer cash flow difficulties.

A typical contract might provide for the customer or client to pay a cash deposit on signing the contract, with further payments according to progress measured as the project proceeds. That progress might be gauged by the achievement of particular tasks (often known as milestones), which could be for such identifiable events as the installation of a building's roof or (for a management change project) delivery to site of specified IT equipment.

Stage payments are typically made on the basis of a contractor's claims for the quantity of work done. Before clearing any invoice for payment, the client will need to be assured that the amount of work claimed on the invoice has actually been done. So each claim for a stage payment might have to be accompanied by a certificate signed by an independent expert who can verify that the amount of work claimed for has in fact been done.

On a construction project an independent assessor known as a quantity surveyor can certify that a claim is fair, in which case the invoice becomes known as a certified invoice. For soft tasks, such as engineering design, an independent technical expert such as an independent engineer will sometimes be engaged to assess the amount of work done.

In the case of the elevator installation project that I mentioned earlier, stage payment terms were agreed approximately along the following lines:

- due on contract signature: 10 per cent of total contract value.

- due on client approving the layout drawings: 10 per cent.

- due on delivery of main materials to site; 20 per cent

- due on start of commissioning: 20 per cent

- due on handover to client: 30 per cent

- Total paid up to handover: 90 per cent

- Retention, due three months after handover: 10 per cent.

A retention payment is to the purchaser's advantage. A small amount of the total contract payment is withheld until the customer or client is assured that all work has been carried out properly and no snags remain.

PRICING

There are several different ways in which a contract might be priced but I shall list the two most common here, which are fixed price or fixed rates.

Fixed price (lump sum)

Most purchasers prefer to be quoted a fixed price for the job. Then they know what their commitments are and should get no nasty surprises – unless they should be so silly as to change the scope of the contract. The contractor will use a formula to set the fixed price, and will bear the risk if the work costs more than estimates. A contractor might make a fixed-price quotation based on the following formula:

Estimated direct materials costs	£££
Estimated direct labour costs	£££
Overhead at x% of direct labour costs	£££
Below-the-line costs	£££
Mark-up for profit	£££
Quoted fixed price	£££
Provisional cost items	£££

Direct costs and overheads were described briefly in Chapter 2, but a couple of new terms in the above formula need a little explanation.

Below-the-line costs are added by the contractor's cost estimator to cover possible unforeseen additional costs. The most common two items in the below-the-line costs are as follows:

- *Escalation*, which is an allowance for cost inflation in labour and materials. This only applies for contracts that will run for a long time (like several years).

- *Contingency sums*, which contractors might add as a small percentage of the total above-the-line costs to cover themselves in case they find themselves having to do small amounts of extra work that they failed to include in the main estimate. Most cost estimates have small errors and it is reasonable to add a small amount to the initial estimates as a safeguard. Five per cent can be a reasonable amount.

Provisional cost items are sometimes advised to contract purchasers. The contractor has no initial intention of charging any amounts specified here. They are merely quoted to allow the project purchaser to budget in case these sums do have to be charged later. Here is an example. Suppose that a contractor has quoted a fixed price to refurbish a building, but can have no access to some hidden areas of the building, such as roof spaces, until the contract is made and work starts. No one knows if the roof is riddled with death watch beetle or some other infestation. Additional work will be needed if such problems are discovered when the hidden areas are eventually exposed as work proceeds. So the contractor might estimate the cost of such treatment and report it as a provisional sum. But if the roof structure proves to be sound, the client can breathe a sigh of relief and the provisional item will not happen.

Contract Administration

Most projects undergo changes as they proceed. The bigger the job, and the longer it lasts, the more changes can be expected. Changes can arise for many reasons and controlling them is important (something that will be discussed in the following chapter).

Changes to an original contract, when agreed between the two parties, are detailed in documents such as purchase order amendments, variation orders, or contract variations.

Very small changes to construction contracts can be taken care of locally, by agreement between the contract's site foreman or manager and the client. Suppose for example, the client knows that the contract covers repainting all the window frames in a wall. But there is one window frame in an opposite wall, outside the contract scope, that is going to look distinctly shabby by comparison with all the newly painted windows. Painting one extra window frame is hardly a subject for a contract variation. Far more likely, the client will say to the contractor, 'While your painters are working along that wall, do you think they might paint this window too?' So the two agree and the extra window gets painted. But the site foreman will record the additional time and material used on a document called a dayworks sheet, which the client will sign.

A big construction-type project, and other kinds of projects too, can attract many such small additional amounts of work on dayworks sheets. All of these must be accounted for at some time before or when the project ends.

So, whether from contract variations or dayworks sheets, a large project can finish up with many additional cost items that were not envisaged when the original contract was signed. Sorting all these variations and dayworks can be a nightmare at the end of a big project if both parties have not kept accurate records. Keeping such records is part of a process known as contract administration. A project management office (PMO) is usually the best place for a project manager to register and keep all those records.

Contracts and Purchases for the Swings and Roundabouts Project

On looking at the cost estimate for the swings and roundabouts project (shown in Figure 2.3), you will notice that the total project cost is estimated at £91,393, of which £73,800 was for purchased materials and a further £12,500 was for payments to contractors. So the total payments for goods and services on this project were estimated at £86,300. So goods and services were expected to amount to a massive 94 per cent of the total project cost.

That reinforces the arguments with which I opened this chapter about the importance of these commercial issues.

This project will involve three external contractors. One contractor will carry out a little ground levelling, which principally involves the removal of a hump. Using heavy machinery, the contractor can do this in just over one day. This was not an expensive contract and the council chose a firm that had served them well in the past.

Before the swings and roundabouts project can open to the public, areas of grass damaged during the various groundworks and foundation preparation will need to be repaired. Again, St Kevin Borough Council were able to choose a local turfing contractor that they had used successfully before.

The contract for erecting the fencing and gates gave the project buyer John Auder a little more to think about. He would liked to have appointed Auder Fencing Ltd., but that company was owned by his brother and there were some council rules which would have made that appointment difficult. In the end John Auder took advice from County Council colleagues and appointed Hemmitin Ltd, on the basis of their reputation for reliability and fair trading. This was a particularly important task because, with site security in mind, project manager Theresa Green wanted the fence in place after the heavy site work had been done, but before delivery of the expensive rides. So a penalty clause was inserted in the contract that would 'fine' Hemmitin Ltd £100 for every day by which the required fencing completion date of 5 May 2014 was exceeded.

Contracts do sometimes contain such penalty clauses, although their effectiveness is often questioned because contractors can look for extenuating circumstances that might let them off the hook. Also, penalty clauses can be difficult or impossible to invoke when the client has delayed the project, or has introduced changes.

PURCHASED MATERIALS FOR THE SWINGS AND ROUNDABOUTS PROJECT

By far the most significant purchase for the swings and roundabouts project was the rides. Because the total order value was expected to be well under 125,000 euros, this purchase would not be subject to the European Public Sector Procurement Directives.

St Kevin Borough Council			BID SUMMARY		
→	A	B	C	D	E
Country of origin					
Bid reference					
Bid date					
Period of validity (days)					
Bid currency					
Project exchange rate					
Item / Qty / Description	Price	Price	Price	Price	Price
Total quoted ex-works					
Discounts (if any)					
Packing and export prep cost					
Shipping cost					
Customs duty and tax					
Local transport cost					
Estimated total cost on site					
Delivery time ex-works					
Estimated total transport time					
Total delivery time to site					

RECOMMENDED BY THE BUYER:

For the purchasing department

RECOMMENDED BY THE ENGINEER:

Project/ senior engineer

RECOMMENDATION:

Project manager

Specification title:	Specification number:

Figure 5.2 A bid summary form

John Auder identified four companies that might each be able to supply all the rides in one lot. He prepared a simple ITT and sent that off to the four companies. He did this well in advance of the project start, so that all tenders would be received before the authorization date of 7 April 2014. In all cases suppliers were asked to quote on the basis of their standard catalogue items.

When the tenders were received, the results were set out on a bid summary form (see Figure 5.2). This allowed the information in the tenders to be set out and compared on the basis of total cost, delivered to site. It also compared the promised delivery times. A Chinese company sent in a very good tender, but with sea transportation of the goods they could not meet the onsite delivery date. In the end, a British company, Fragonard Swings and Things Ltd, was chosen and the purchase order was issued.

6

Taking Control

Controlling a project means trying to do everything according to the plans you have made and then measuring what is actually happening. Control happens when steps are taken to correct anything that shows any sign of deviating from what you want. But can you control everything? There will always be risks, and the prudent project manager will try to anticipate those. Risk management has come more into prominence as part of a project manager's skill in recent years. Project managers should think about the risks before the project starts and then review those risks at regular intervals.

Managing Project Risk

Control is perhaps the wrong word when talking about risk, because some risks cannot be controlled. But if a project fails because of an 'unforeseen risk', the project manager might be told that the risk should have been foreseen. So here, in a nutshell, is how risks can be approached by a project manager. Like all project management procedures, common sense and logical thought have to drive this process. Here are the necessary steps:

Step 1. Identify and list as many possible risks as you can. A brainstorming session with key people is recommended.

Step 2. Consider each risk and think about the probability of it occurring. Give your probability assessment a ranking number (from one to five). For example, an earthquake in Surrey would be unlikely, so you could rank that at the bottom end. But the risk of your project manager being struck by lightning if she happened to spend all her leisure time on the golf course might be ranked with a probability of three.

Step 3. Consider how serious it would be for the project if the particular risk actually materialized. Again rank that from one to five. For example, if your project customer were to fail and go bust, that would be so serious as to be ranked as five.

Step 4. Now think about how difficult it would be to detect the risk if it happened. Clearly if some scaffolding were to fall down, that would be detectable. On the other hand, a software glitch in a vital computer program might be very serious, but difficult to detect (so that would rank as five).

Step 5. The final step is to consider how you might take action to avoid a risk, or to mitigate its effects should it happen. You need also think about who would be put in charge of dealing with each risk (for prevention, cure or mitigation).

If you have a project management office (PMO), someone in there should be asked to compile a risk register (or risk log). Some projects are big enough to justify a full-time risk manager. Figure 6.1 shows what the top of a blank page in a risk register might look like. The method of use should be self-explanatory.

Risk ID No	Risk description and consequences	Probability P=1-5	Impact severity S=1-5	Detection difficulty D=1-5	Ranking P x S x D	Mitigating or avoiding action	Action by:

Figure 6.1   Top of a risk register page

Always remember that some risks can be insured against by paying a premium to an insurance company. Theft of tools or materials is one example. Most project management texts ignore the possibility of insuring against risk which, once again, shows how some project people seem to despise commercial issues (as I remarked at the beginning of Chapter 5). You, of course, would never make that mistake.

Controlling Project Changes

A project change is any change that would affect the scope or nature of a project, as defined in the original project definition (as contained in a business plan or a contract). Changes come in two main types, as follows:

1. Changes requested by a paying customer or client. Such changes usually have to be carried out, but the project manager or contractor should be able to negotiate additional revenue and, possibly, an extension to the project completion date. Of course a customer's change might request a reduction in project scope, in which case the contractor will be expected to make some price reduction. However, price reductions always have to be offset by the costs incurred for any work that has to be scrapped because of the change. The costs of work already performed are sometimes referred to as sunk costs.

2. Changes requested from within the project organization, for which clearly no outside customer or client could be held responsible. This could result from a design mistake. So the project organization itself would have to fund such a change and also explain to the customer or client why the project is going to take a little longer than at first thought. These changes are often called 'unfunded changes' (which means unfunded by the customer).

Changes in general are likely to cause more disruption and expense when they occur later in the project life cycle, when of course there is the probability that a greater amount of rework will be needed.

OUTLINE OF A CONVENTIONAL CHANGE CONTROL PROCEDURE

Every proposed change must undergo consideration by at least one responsible person in the project organization before it can be approved. Otherwise every Tom, Dick and Harriet might be changing things all the time. Companies that regularly conduct projects will have well-established procedures for handling changes, usually involving having a panel of experts called a 'change committee' or 'change board' to consider all the effects of any change before approving it. That 'panel of experts' should contain at least one senior representative from each project function.

The possible effects to be considered will include any effect on technical reliability, scrappage of work already done, implications for the project completion date and responsibility for paying for the change. In general, customer-requested changes will be approved unless technically very difficult or undesirable. Internal unfunded changes will be approved if they are essential for safety or reliability. If an unfunded change is considered to be only 'desirable' rather than 'essential' it should usually be rejected, because every change is disruptive and can generate hidden expenses in addition to the obvious costs.

Every request for a change should be logged into a change register and be summarized on some kind of standard form (a change request form) that sets out all the details and implications. Administration of this procedure is another job that can be placed logically in a PMO, where a change coordinating clerk might be given responsibility for registering and progressing each change request through all its stages to rejection or acceptance and action.

If a change is authorized, the change coordinator must follow it up to ensure that all drawings and other documents are revised accordingly – and, of course, to ensure that the change itself is actually implemented.

If a change is not authorized, the person who originally requested it must be told and informed of the reasons for rejection. A summary of a typical change control procedure is shown in Figure 6.2.

A significant number of customer-funded changes means that contract administration will have to be taken seriously, so that both contractor and client can agree at all times on the total current contract price and the project completion date. That's another job for the PMO.

Some Principles of Progress Control

All control depends on checking actual occurrences against plans or budgets. On a large project, that can involve many communication channels and all kinds of observations and reports. In other words, a large volume of data has to be digested.

However, for control purposes it is the things that go wrong which have to claim management attention. So in all progress reports and other communications intended to control progress and costs it is a mistake to include vast amounts of things that are going according to plan. Rather, the manager must concentrate on the variances or exceptions, because it is by putting those right that the project can be kept on track. This is known as the principle of management by exception.

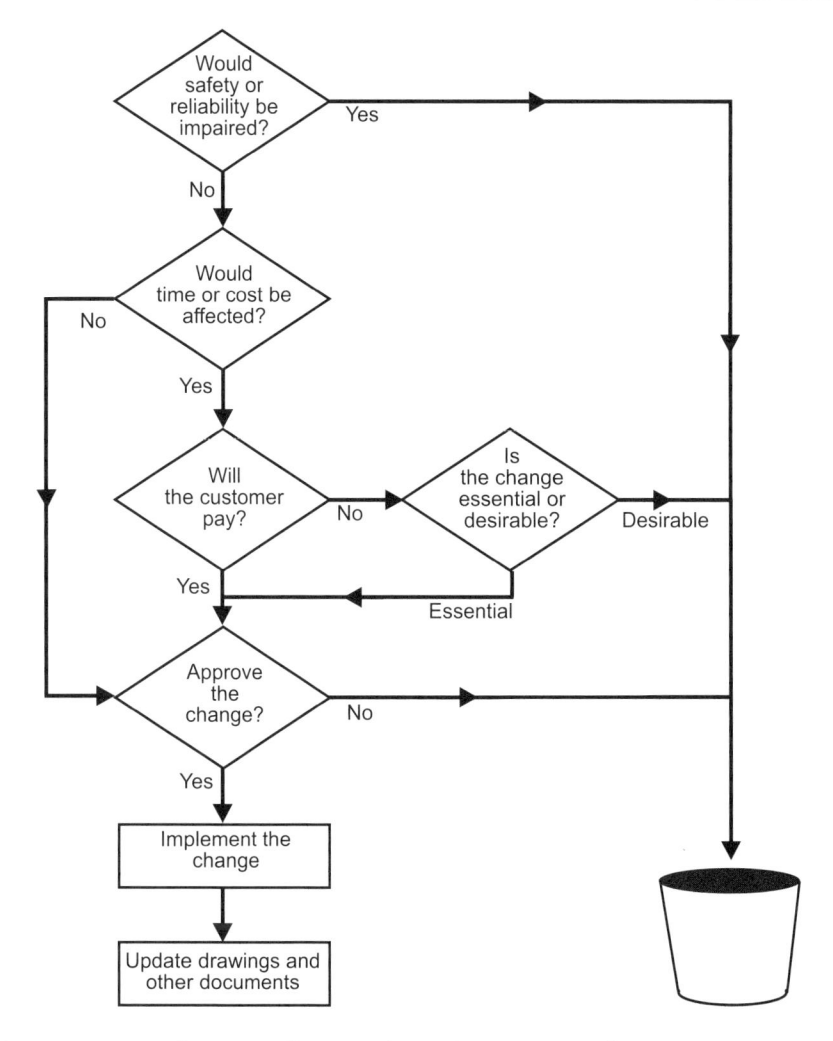

Figure 6.2   Schematic diagram for a change control system

A very good example of management by exception is seen in shortage lists for materials. These are documents compiled by supervisors to inform the purchasing department of materials that are not available at the workplace when they are needed, so that progress is delayed or stopped. Clearly the purchasing people will take these reports very seriously and put all reasonable measures in hand to obtain the materials so that work can resume.

PROGRESS CONTROL OF A SINGLE PROJECT TASK

Whether one is monitoring costs or progress, there is a recognized sequence for control. That sequence is as follows:

- measure;

- identify any difference between planned and actual quantities (which means an exception or a variance);

- take action and attempt to modify the work to correct the variance.

This is a cyclical process that is sometimes known as a cybernetic control loop, because it mimics a process familiar to electronic engineers where an error signal is fed back to the system input terminal of an amplifier to correct distortion. Figure 6.3 illustrates this process in relation to the progress of a project task. Of course this would not apply to a task of very short duration.

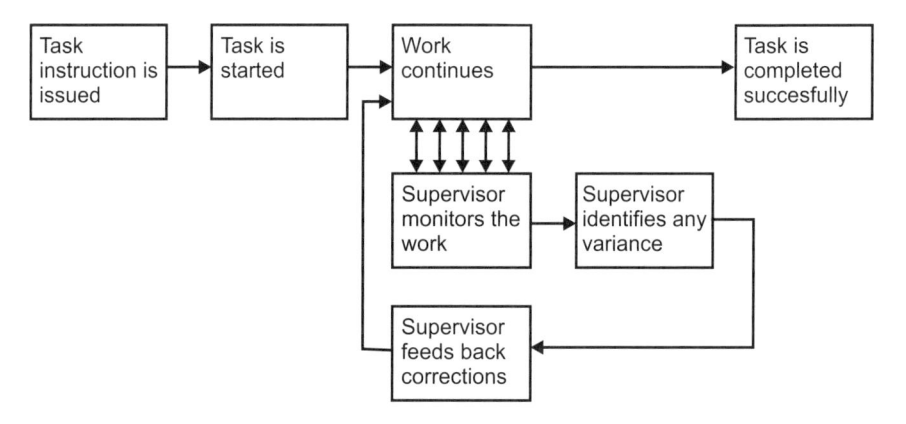

Figure 6.3 Cybernetic feedback loop to control the quality and progress of a project task

If a task is running late, then it must be checked against the project schedule. There, the project manager can discover whether the task has any float or is critical. If the task is critical (which means it has zero or even negative float) overtime or weekend working can be considered, or (where practicable) more people can be drafted in to work on the task.

A task that is running late but is not critical (which means it has some total float) should still be finished as soon as possible because every day that the task runs late will rob following tasks of their total float to the point where they might also become critical or even late.

PROGRESS CONTROL EXTENDED TO THE ENTIRE PROJECT

Just as it is necessary to monitor every single task for progress, so it is clearly necessary to measure all the tasks collectively against the project schedule. The principles are the same, but the scale is different.

Monitoring an individual task involves communication between a supervisor or manager and the person or group that performs the task. The project manager might not be involved directly in this process. But when progress measurement and control are scaled up to the entire project, although the principles of 'measure', 'identify exceptions' and 'take corrective action' still apply, many more people will be involved. External suppliers and contractors might also have to be brought into face-to-face discussions.

So a feature of any project lasting for more than a few weeks is that it will need fairly regular progress meetings throughout its life cycle. Meetings can be unpopular because of their time and costs, but they do have the advantage of allowing immediate face-to-face communication and the ability to get problems resolved on the spot, with collective agreement.

Progress meetings are by no means the only kinds of meetings needed for larger projects, so you will find a general section on project meetings in Chapter 8.

Some Principles of Cost Control

INDIRECT (OVERHEAD) COSTS

It is generally acknowledged that a project manager can only be held accountable for things over which he or she has the authority to control. Indirect costs are a function of the way in which a company is administered in terms of its general management structure, accommodation expenses and so on. So clearly these indirect costs cannot be the project manager's responsibility.

But, please stop and think about that. A project will attract overhead costs for as long as it is being conducted, because of the space needed for its people and equipment. Thus the longer a project takes, the more overhead costs it will attract. So, controlling progress will have an effect on the indirect costs associated with the project. Putting all this in a different way, a project that overruns its schedule will almost certainly increase its share of indirect costs. Always remember, as Benjamin Franklin put it a long time ago: 'Time is money.'

DIRECT LABOUR COSTS

Jobs that take longer than planned will almost always use up more direct labour costs, simply because people work on those tasks for longer than planned. So they will be paid more wages. Thus, if you can control the progress of all the tasks successfully, you will also be helping to keep labour costs down. Putting that in different words, the best way to control direct labour costs is to keep all tasks on schedule.

COST OF MATERIALS

The cost of any purchase is committed when the order is placed. Thus the way to control materials costs is to ensure that every item is purchased within budget. Thereafter, provided no changes are made, all the materials should come into the project within budget.

On many projects some large items can be estimated and budgeted by checking prices or getting quotations in advance from possible suppliers. That removes guesswork when making project cost estimates and helps purchasing within established budgets.

One risk occurs when a long time elapses between making the project estimates and authorizing the project to start. If this interval is more than one or two months, suppliers' quoted prices might have escalated. Suppliers generally will put a fairly short time limit on the validity of their quotations.

Methods for Measuring or Monitoring Costs

DIRECT LABOUR COSTS

In many project organizations, everyone from the lowest worker to the project manager will fill in weekly timesheets to record the hours worked on each task. This is where the work breakdown structure (WBS) and its cost codes come into force, because these are used to identify the tasks on which time is spent. The cost accountants will convert these times into costs using the standard cost rate for each labour grade.

Timesheet cost records are important for many administrative reasons. They will be of direct importance to a project that is being charged out to the customer on the basis of time and materials used.

MONITORING THE COSTS OF DIRECT MATERIALS

There are three different ways in which the costs of materials can be recorded. These methods are as follows:

1. The cost accountants tot up the costs of all goods issued from stores by valuing the relevant stores requisitions. This type of costing is particularly common in manufacturing. It has the disadvantage for the project manager that the information is gathered very late – far too late to correct any trend towards overspending.

2. The cost accountants tot up the cost of all suppliers' invoices relevant to the project. This again produces a lag between purchasing the materials and totting up their costs.

3. The method which I recommend and prefer is for the PMO and purchasing department to set up regular communications. The purchasing department can feed back the total cost of all orders placed for the project. Then the project manager gets a cost record that builds up as the materials costs are actually committed. That method can identify adverse trends as early as possible. Of course, if materials do have to be purchased at costs higher than the original budgets, there might be no corrective action possible.

Attempts to Analyse Trends and Make Predictions Using Earned Value Analysis

During the course of projects lasting more than a few months, project managers and their seniors are often consumed with curiosity about what their total project costs will be, using current performance as a guide. For example, if a job is halfway through but has already used up its entire budget, the implication is that the final job cost will be double its budget. That argument might be based on shaky foundations, but is the basis for a system in current vogue that is known as earned value management.

Before explaining this procedure, it is necessary to understand that this is a measurement and prediction process. It manages nothing. So it is not really a management process at all and earned value analysis is a better name. Also, the procedures can take considerable clerical effort, which adds cost to the project without adding any value. However, earned value analysis has its disciples and I have used the method myself in the distant past. It can be useful provided that it is conducted with common sense, and that everyone recognizes that the results may not be accurate.

So this is how it goes. Let's start by considering a single task of very long duration (let's say 16 weeks). Now suppose that the task has been going for eight weeks. So if one could quantify the amount of work done, that should amount to 50 per cent of the total, and it should also have cost 50 per cent of budget. But if the job has already cost 100 per cent of budget, then one could extrapolate that measurement and say that it would probably cost 200 per cent of budget on completion.

Earned value measurement uses the following expressions and formulae.

ACWP – the actual cost of work actually performed at the measurement date.

BCWP – budget cost of work performed, which is what the work actually done should have cost according to the original budget or estimate.

BCWS – the budget cost of the work scheduled at the measurement date. This is the budget cost or value of the work that should have been done on the measurement date.

CPI – this is a cost performance index, an index proportional to cost performance against budget.

SPI – this is a schedule performance index, proportional to measured progress made against scheduled progress.

The CPI and lesser used SPI are calculated using the following formulae:

CPI = BCWP/ACWP

SPI = BCWP/BCWS

A simple example will explain the process for one task. We have to build a brick wall 1,000m long, and the estimated total cost of this task is £40,000. We have been given ten weeks in which to build the wall. Some simple arithmetic tells us that, working a five-day week, we have 50 days allowed for the work at a budget cost of £800 per day. We have planned to build 20m of wall each day. The budget cost of each metre is £40.

So now consider day 20 of this project, when we should have built 400m of wall but have actually only built 360m. Further, that work has already cost £18,000.

Putting all of this into earned value expressions, we get the following result for day 20:

- ACWP = £18,000 (the actual costs recorded at the end of day 20).

- BCWP = £14,400 (360m of wall at the budget cost of £40 per metre).

- BCWS = £16,000 (20 days at £800 per day).

So, the CPI (BCWP/ACWP) for this wall project is 14,400/18,000, which is 0.8.

This means that the work has been done at only 80 per cent efficiency. By extrapolation, the total project cost is likely to be £(40,000/0.8), which is £50,000, an overspend of £10,000 on the original £40,000 budget.

Now if we needed to ask how long this project will actually take, we have to consider the SPI. Using the formula given above we get SPI (BCWP/BCWS) = 14,400/16,000 = 0.9. So progress is at 90 per cent efficiency and if the current work rate is continued the project will take not the originally planned 50 days, but 50/0.9 days, which is about 56 days.

Now, if you found that difficult to follow for just one task, imagine the amount of work involved in performing earned value analysis on a project with thousands of tasks. Of course computers can take the strain, but if no progress has been made on a job the computer finds itself having to divide by zero, which can cause all kinds of distress. I had some misgivings about including this process in a book that claims to confine itself to the bare facts. But some people love earned value analysis and have even written books about it. Also some senior managers like to see the resulting reports and predictions.

Figure 6.4 is very loosely based on a project that I managed many years ago, to show how earned value analysis can be made to work for a single department. Figure 6.5 is a total project report format that allows a form of earned value analysis which does not involve drilling down into every small task, and which takes into account the effects of project or contract changes.

Controlling the Swings and Roundabouts Project

The budget estimate for the swings and roundabouts project was shown in Figure 2.3, allowing for a total cost of £91,393. According to the schedule in Figure 4.7, work was due to begin on site on Monday, 7 April 2014. This project had the advantage of a good project manager in Theresa Green, and all her team members were dedicated to making the project a success. So clearly this project was well founded.

Most of the cost estimate was made up in the value of purchase orders for buying the rides, and since these were purchased at fixed price the project budget was fairly secure. Only bad progress could cause costs to overrun, but Theresa Green was determined that progress would be kept on plan. So all the early tasks took place as scheduled. There were, of course, a few difficulties. The contractor due to spend two days levelling the ground arrived on site late. Urgent telephone calls and emails established that this contractor was late finishing another job, so work on the playground site began one day late. It also finished one day late, on Thursday, 10 April instead of on Wednesday, 9 April. However, as this task had a total float of seven days this delay did not hold up the project.

Another difficulty facing Theresa was that it rained heavily for the two days Thursday, 22 May and Friday, 23 May 2014, preventing work on erecting the rides. Since this was a critical task, Theresa persuaded the gang to work over the weekend of 24 and 25 May to pull the task back on

Earned value analysis

Dept: Engineering
Project: Sensor and servo controller
Date: May 2014
Sheet 1 of 1

Task		Budget hours	Per cent achieved	Earned value BCWP	Actual hours ACWP
001	System design	350	100	350	255
002	Write system specification	35	100	35	35
003	Design +25v power supply	105	100	105	140
004	Breadboard stage	70	100	70	35
005	Package	70	100	70	40
006	Prototype	35			
007	Write test specification	35			
008	Design +10v power supply	105	100	105	65
009	Breadboard stage	70	100	70	50
010	Package	70	50	35	25
011	Prototype	35			
012	Write test specification	35			
013	Design -15v power supply	105			
014	Breadboard stage	70			
015	Package	70			
016	Prototype	35			
017	Write test specification	35			
018	Design sensor circuit	350	100	350	288
019	Breadboard stage	105	100	105	124
020	Package	105	40	42	50
021	Prototype	70			
022	Write test specification	35			
023	Design servo and controls	175	20	35	15
024	Breadboard stage	140			
025	Package	70			
026	Prototype	105			
027	Write test specification	35			
028	Design main frame	70	25	17	20
029	System test	70			
030	Environmental tests	70			
031	Write production specification	140			
032	Write operating manual	105			
	Department totals	2975	46.7	1389	1142

Figure 6.4 Earned value analysis for an engineering department

Project cost report summary

Project title:

Project number:

Page   of

Report date:

A Item	B Cost code	C Original budget	D Authorized budget changes	E Authorized current budget	F ACWP	G BCWP (assessed)	H CPI	J Forecast costs remaining (E-G)/H	K Forecast costs at completion F+J	L Forecast variance at completion E-K

Figure 6.5 A tabulated project cost report that includes an earned value assessment

schedule. For that, overtime premiums had to be paid, but that was a small portion of the overall project costs, and finance director Penny Wise had taken the prudent measure of adding a contingency allowance of £5,000 to the project estimates, most of which was not spent.

There were a few anxious moments for site supervisor Arthur Inch and the workers when attempting to assemble some of the more complex rides from the manufacturers' instructions. Modern communications came to the rescue here. A series of emails and telephone calls to Fragonard Swings for advice solved all the problems within a matter of hours. Modern communications have revolutionized much project work, especially when people are separated by very long distances.

It is worth noting here that weekend and overtime working should not be planned into normal schedules, but should ideally be held back as a reserve contingency. Theresa was very glad she had adhered to that rule in this case. Had any other delays occurred, she had other weekends available during which work could be conducted to bring any late tasks back on schedule.

And so the swings and roundabouts project progressed smoothly, with Theresa visiting the site at least once every two days to see progress for herself and give encouragement to all the workers. This was a well-planned, well-budgeted and well-estimated project. All credit for this was due to Theresa, who had followed all the rules (she had been well trained in project management methods). No surprise, then, that the swings and roundabouts project finished on time, within budget, to give delight to all the stakeholders.

Most noticeable among these stakeholders were the parents and children who enjoyed their new playground. Ratepayers in the Borough of St Kevin were quietly satisfied that at least this job had been finished within budget. Another stakeholder that took satisfaction for this project success was the proprietor of a refreshment café in the park, because their takings increased, as did those of an itinerant ice cream vendor.

7

Task Forces for Special Projects

Chapter 3 described some possible organization patterns for projects. Generally speaking, a project manager's authority and freedom to act decisively is likely to be highest in a team, rather than in a matrix organization. The strongest kind of team is a project task force, which is the organization indicated when it is necessary to drive a project to a successful finish in the face of difficulties. In this chapter two specific applications for a task force approach will be described. The first of these is for a project that is heading for disaster and needs a rescue effort to save it. This second case is a very disruptive management change project.

Our Project is Sick: Send for a Doctor!

There are occasions when a project gets out of control. Reasons for that usually include poor definition and bad planning, probably with no work breakdown structure (WBS) and no critical path analysis. Too many changes cannot help, either. An inappropriate organization structure can add to the havoc.

Provided it has not been left too late, there are some decisive actions that senior management can take to ensure that an ailing project is rescued. Of course, much depends on the importance of the project and whether or not it needs to be rescued – sometimes it might be more prudent to 'pull the plug' and put the project out of its misery. But in this book we do not want to contemplate failure, so what can we do?

PROJECT RESCUE STEP 1: FIND A HERO PROJECT MANAGER

There exist among us a few specially gifted project managers who have vast experience, impeccable decision-making skills and enough drive to power two ordinary mortals. These are the so-called 'hero project managers'. A company with a project in trouble could do far worse than hire one of these heroes on a short-term contract. One route to that solution is by approaching one of the specialist project management recruitment agencies.

PROJECT RESCUE STEP 2: SET UP A TASK FORCE

The organization chart for a project task force will look very much the same as a team organization. But a task force has one important difference. Not only does the project manager enjoy all the direct power and authority deriving from the team structure, but each member of the team also has considerable authority in his or her own right. So a project task force is a concentration of authority. It is a power house. Put a hero project manager in charge of such a task force, and you can almost guarantee to rescue an ailing project.

Consider, for example, a task force that has an electrical engineer as one of its members. Normally that engineer might report back to a chief engineer and be part of an electrical engineering department. But with the authority of the task force behind that engineer, he or she can even overrule the chief electrical engineer, especially when it comes to demanding priority to get design work through the electrical engineering department. And so it is for every other member of the task force. Backed by the authority of senior management and led by a hero project manager, everyone is unstoppable. How can the project fail now?

Well, of course the project can still fail. It depends just how bad the situation has been allowed to become.

PLANNING TO RECOVER A LOST PROJECT

So, we now have a determined task force led by an expert. But the original plan is now rubbish. Clearly we need a new plan. If time allows, the WBS also needs to be either established or put right, but that can be a procedural process needing time that the project simply does not have. So a new plan is the priority.

I am going to relate a case from my own experience when I was asked to rescue a project that had gone completely off track. It was so bad that no one even knew what the current state of progress was, or which jobs should be done next.

My project example concerned the design and manufacture of prototype products that had to be ready in time for display on an exhibition stand in central London. Just under three months remained to the exhibition date and the three product ranges concerned were:

- heart–lung machines and associated hospital operating theatre equipment;

- electronic patient monitoring devices;

- big autoclave sterilizers.

My first step was to call a meeting of the engineers and supervisors responsible for all this equipment. Fortunately everyone was keen to make the project a success and I also had full support and encouragement from the divisional manager. 'We need to make a new plan' was my first statement, but no one could tell me what they thought needed to be done next. So I had to do what everyone in such a difficult position must do, which was to give everyone present a vision of the future, with the project ending as a glorious success.

So I asked everyone to imagine the opening day of the exhibition, with all our products proudly on show as planned. I went to the whiteboard in the room, and at the right-hand side drew the last task in our network plan 'Exhibition opened'.

In only a couple of hours, working backwards and using their imaginations, all the people in the room were able to tell me everything I needed to draw a reliable network diagram. That ended at the left-hand side in a series of ragged start dangles (tasks with no predecessors). Now we had identified the current state of progress.

I returned to the whiteboard and joined all those start dangles up into a new project start task at the extreme left-hand edge. Effectively, we were indeed starting a new project.

The next step was to ask everyone how they proposed to perform each task and how long it would be expected to take. So I was able to add time estimates to the network diagram.

The network was not particularly big and I was able to carry out time analysis and have a project schedule with calendar dates issued by the following morning. Fortunately, time analysis proved that we would be able to meet the exhibition date. And of course, we did.

This project moved smoothly to a successful finish because now everyone had a new, practical and feasible plan. Equally as important, with the backing of the divisional manager, every task force member (which meant everyone who had attended the planning session) had power within his/her department to get the tasks done with high priority. All tasks to be done by outside departments were also given high priority, and that was helped by the support of the divisional manager.

SUMMARY OF ACTIONS THAT CAN RESCUE A PROJECT FROM DISASTER

Not every project can be rescued from failure, but the following steps will give you the best chance:

1. establish a task force;

2. give the task force an office that it can use as a 'war room' for the project duration;

3. put a hero project manager in charge of the task force;

4. give the task force teeth in the form of maximum possible authority;

5. make a rescue plan immediately (based on a critical path network);

6. motivate everyone on the task force by creating a vision of a successful future;

7. ensure that the task force gets enthusiastic senior management support.

Task Forces for Business Change Projects

Modern project management methods can be used for projects of all kinds but projects intended to change organizations, introduce new IT, or otherwise alter the way in which people work, have an important extra dimension. In other kinds of projects, the job is usually done when the project manager hands the project over to a client or customer. But in a business change project the IT and procedural design tasks are the relatively easy part. The real work comes when the project goes live and people in the organization are expected to accept the change, adapt and work with it. People are important in all projects, but in business change projects their acceptance of change is critical to successful implementation.

A management change might be something simple, such as a new invoicing procedure. On the other hand it could be a complete reorganization of the company, coupled with relocation to a different town. It is well known that people do not like change. Most of us prefer the familiar, steady life, with no unpleasant surprises.

When a change comes, people might have to learn new methods, Habits and beliefs of a working lifetime that have brought status, security and mental comfort could have to be discarded. Some people will be given promotion or the challenge of a new role in the organization. Others might have to leave, accepting redundancy, and that can seriously demotivate not only the leavers but also those who remain, because they lose friends and also realize that their own jobs might not be secure.

There is wide recognition that people in a changing organization can go through a series of emotions, ranging from shock and anger to despair. However, as time passes, if the change has been properly planned people can come to accept the change, possibly even seeing some benefits and gaining hope and optimism. The successful project manager will attempt to minimize the bad effects and emphasize the positive aspects. One way of giving people encouragement is to create a positive vision of the future, getting everyone to imagine in vivid detail how their jobs will be improved after the change.

HANDLING INFORMATION BEFORE A MANAGEMENT CHANGE

It is well known that one certain way to induce unrest in an organization is to allow two strangers in dark suits with clipboards to wander through all the offices taking measurements with tape measures. They might only be doing a survey for insurance purposes, but the alarmed staff will undoubtedly view them as a sign of approaching Armageddon.

So if you are planning to make a significant business change, it is best to keep everything confidential whilst various proposals are considered. I am certainly not advising deception – merely taking reasonable steps to keep all tentative proposals confined to the knowledge of those taking part in the studies until a business plan has been formulated and agreed. That kind of confidentiality can be very difficult to achieve and it is surprising how little snippets of information can get leaked to cause very big and disconcerting rumours.

Of course a time will come when change has to be announced, probably followed by consultation with staff members, giving counselling and practical help for those who must leave the organization. Those are areas outside my own expertise, and will involve senior management and HRM people, often with the help of specialist external consultants. Those issues go beyond the bare facts of project management and so need not be discussed further in this book.

CASE EXAMPLE

Here is a case example to illustrate in practical terms how a management change project might be conducted in its early stages. The company is fictional, but the case is based on fact. For the purposes of this example I am going to assume that this is the headquarters of an insurance company that is contemplating relocating its office from the City of London to a city or market town where operational costs will be far less. The organization of this company before this project was even considered is shown in the top section of Figure 7.1.

This company occupies rented offices and has just been subjected to a periodic rent review that saw its annual rent increase from £500,000 to £550,000 per year. Local business rates have also gone up, and another high cost factor is the London weighting applied to staff salaries. So the senior management have decided to investigate moving, but at present have no fixed idea of where to relocate.

The company's first step is to engage an advisory consultant from a company that specializes in company relocations. A steering committee

(a) Before the project

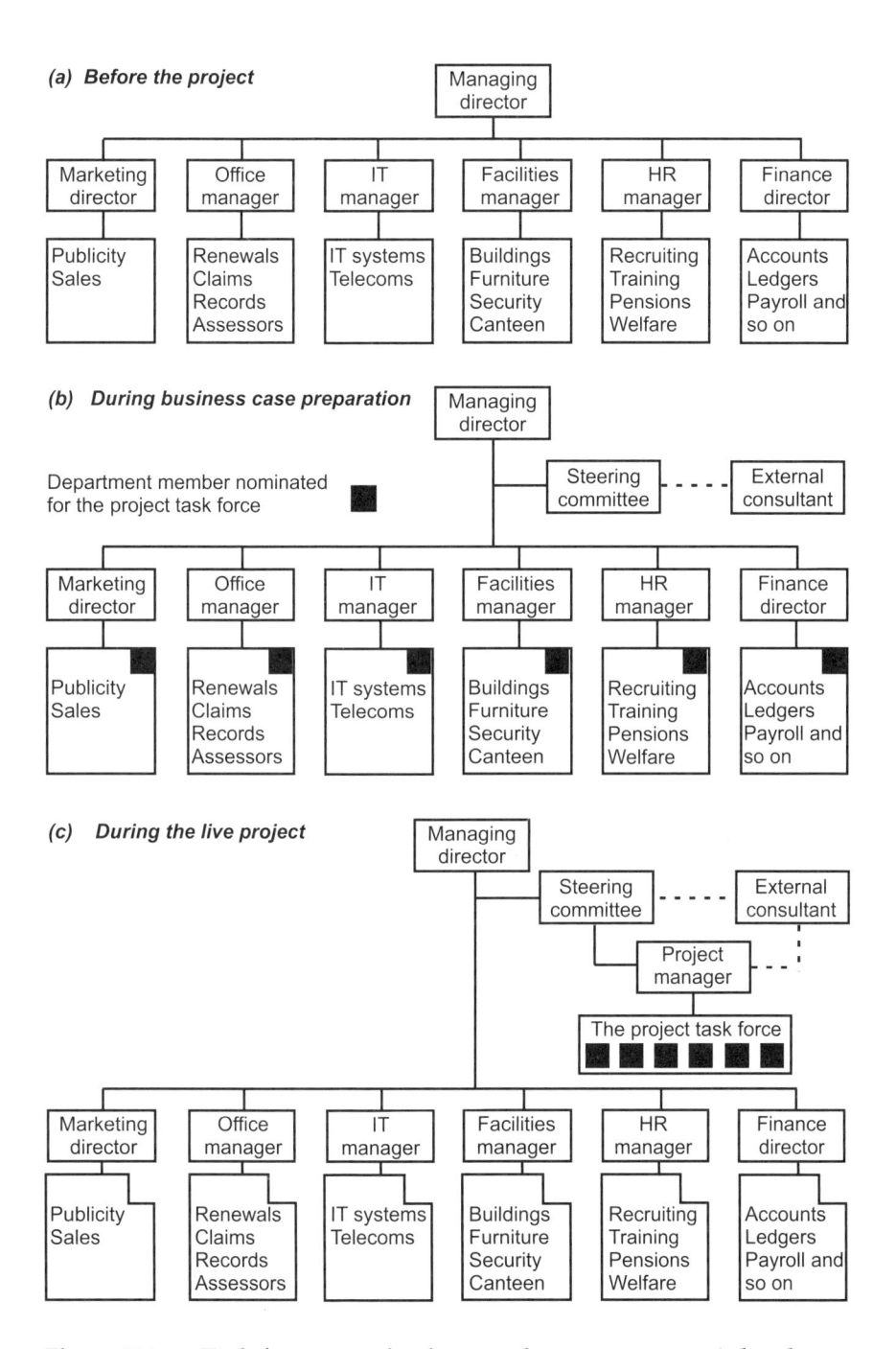

```
                          Managing
                          director
┌───────────┬───────────┬─────┴─────┬───────────┬───────────┐
Marketing   Office      IT          Facilities  HR          Finance
director    manager     manager     manager     manager     director
│           │           │           │           │           │
Publicity   Renewals    IT systems  Buildings   Recruiting  Accounts
Sales       Claims      Telecoms    Furniture   Training    Ledgers
            Records                 Security    Pensions    Payroll and
            Assessors               Canteen     Welfare     so on
```

(b) During business case preparation

```
                          Managing
                          director
                              │────────Steering──────External
                              │        committee      consultant
Department member nominated ■ │
for the project task force    │
┌───────────┬───────────┬─────┴─────┬───────────┬───────────┐
Marketing   Office      IT          Facilities  HR          Finance
director    manager     manager     manager     manager     director
│           │           │           │           │           │
Publicity ■ Renewals ■  IT systems■ Buildings ■ Recruiting■ Accounts ■
Sales       Claims      Telecoms    Furniture   Training    Ledgers
            Records                 Security    Pensions    Payroll and
            Assessors               Canteen     Welfare     so on
```

(c) During the live project

```
                          Managing
                          director
                              │────────Steering──────External
                              │        committee      consultant
                              │            │
                              │        Project
                              │        manager
                              │            │
                              │    The project task force
                              │    ■ ■ ■ ■ ■ ■
┌───────────┬───────────┬─────┴─────┬───────────┬───────────┐
Marketing   Office      IT          Facilities  HR          Finance
director    manager     manager     manager     manager     director
│           │           │           │           │           │
Publicity   Renewals    IT systems  Buildings   Recruiting  Accounts
Sales       Claims      Telecoms    Furniture   Training    Ledgers
            Records                 Security    Pensions    Payroll and
            Assessors               Canteen     Welfare     so on
```

Figure 7.1 Task force organization to relocate a company's head office

formed of the managing director, the HR manager and the finance director will spearhead the initial investigation, assisted where necessary by one senior staff member from each of the company's departments (depicted by the black squares in Figure 7.1(b). These senior staff have been picked because their discretion can be relied upon. They have all been asked not to discuss the proposed project with anyone. At this stage they form a consultation group. To preserve confidentiality, all initial project meetings are held away from the company's offices.

During this investigative period, various members of staff will visit suggested towns and cities that might be suitable for the new headquarters. They will collect information on local labour availability, standard of schools, quality of life, places of worship, prevailing business rents and rates, and so on.

Over the course of about two months a dossier will be assembled detailing the advantages and disadvantages of all the possible relocation centres until the steering committee and senior management can make a choice of the best place.

During this time it is almost certain that rumours will begin to circulate among the staff, but all steps must be taken to keep these to a minimum.

Eventually a business plan will emerge, detailing the preferred relocation site, proposed costs of the move, estimates of the staff who will be prepared to relocate and those who would prefer to remain in London and be compensated with a redundancy package. Also to be considered would be counselling and possible assistance for redundant staff. Another important consideration would be the relocation expenses package to be offered to those prepared to move. Keeping all that confidential is a tall order, but it can be done.

If the business plan is approved by the board of directors, the plan must be announced and staff must be reassured that their interests will be considered. A consultation period should follow.

At the same time as the project is approved, the original members of the consultation group move full time into a project task force to carry out all the executive tasks needed for the move. That development is shown in Figure 7.1(c). Now the project has a dedicated task force, whose members are closely familiar with the aims of the project and also with the detailed operations of all departments. Together this task force can plan and execute the move with least possible risk of any material factor being overlooked.

When the relocation has been completed successfully, the project organization can be disbanded and the task force members will return to their home departments.

Task Forces as a General Solution?

'Now,' I imagine you thinking, 'if a task force organization is so wonderful and can achieve magic results, why not organize every project as a task force?' Well, that might work just fine provided no two projects happened to be running at the same time in the same company. But two or more task forces in the same company fighting over common resources would be a recipe for conflict. Just imagine if several all-powerful managers were in competition for common, scarce resources. Blood would flow. So in general, a task force project should be a special case. Otherwise cooperative teams or a matrix organization should be chosen.

What about the swings and roundabouts project though? That was a single project. Why might that not have been organized as a task force? Well, if you look back over the case and regard its organization chart in Figure 3.5 you might consider that it was indeed a task force. Any team operating alone in an organization can take on the strength and characteristics of a task force if all its members are sufficiently motivated, as they clearly were for the children's new playground. One of the essential skills of a project manager is to develop that strong team spirit across the project, even when the organization might be dispersed over several departments and no organization team has been defined.

8

Round Up

Meetings and projects seem to go hand in hand, so I want to begin this final chapter with a few tips about project meetings. Then I shall add some notes on what should be done when a project comes to an end, so that it is closed down without leaving too many loose ends.

Meetings

Communications between people are all-important in projects and thus most projects abound with meetings. Increasingly, these days, virtual meetings can save people time and travel, especially on international projects. However, in this book I have been discussing relatively simple projects so I shall confine this section to face-to-face meetings where all or most of the people can be physically present.

Among other things, project meetings can be used to:

- inform;
- gather ideas through brainstorming;
- consider proposed changes;
- review progress and decide actions;
- celebrate successful project completion (by which, I mean, having a party).

Three kinds of project meetings are of particular importance. These are:

1. the initial kick-off meeting when a project is launched;

2. brainstorming sessions;

3. periodical progress meetings called to review problems and progress.

Of course there will also be technical meetings, but strictly they lie outside the scope of project management.

PROJECT KICK-OFF MEETING

When a new project has been authorized and its project manager has been appointed, good practice is for senior management to display their support for the project and its manager by inviting all key people in the project organization to a 'kick-off' meeting. This gives everyone an opportunity to meet and greet the project manager, and for the project to be described in outline terms.

After introducing the project manager, senior management might wish to stress the importance of the project and ask everyone to give the project manager their full and willing support. If the project is for an external customer, the value of gaining that customer's business might also be stressed.

The project manager can then outline the project, giving a summary of its expected duration and cost, and describing the outcomes expected.

A project kick-off meeting will have served its purpose if everyone leaves the room fired with enthusiasm and keen to start work on the project.

BRAINSTORMING MEETINGS

Brainstorming sessions demand active participation from all those present. In projects they can be held to identify possible risks as part of the risk management process, and also to seek solutions for difficult problems.

In a brainstorming meeting the chairman or 'facilitator' asks everyone to come up freely with ideas relevant to the subject being discussed. All those ideas, no matter how relevant or sensible, are written on whiteboards or flip charts. No one should be discouraged from making suggestions, and no one should be criticized for making what might seem to be a silly suggestion.

The idea is to get as much collective brainpower focused on the matter in hand. Then, when the meeting has dispersed, the chairman or facilitator has plenty of thoughts and ideas to choose from in obtaining guidance towards the required solution.

PROGRESS MEETINGS

It could be said that the initial meeting called to plan a project schedule is the project's first progress meeting. But that first planning meeting needs plenty of imagination, and it also needs a skilful facilitator who is capable of sketching the plan in the form of a critical path network in full view of all those present.

One important feature of such a planning meeting is that those who will eventually supervise the various tasks should take part if possible in estimating the durations and costs of those tasks. Cost estimating is often done at an earlier date, but when the durations of tasks are estimated by those who will eventually supervise those tasks, the supervisors will have accepted commitment and should be more motivated towards achieving their tasks on time.

Subsequent progress meetings might be held monthly or more frequently, depending on the duration of the project, its complexity, and the number of problems being encountered. All managers with significant responsibility for project tasks should attend, and sometimes outside suppliers and contractors will also be needed.

Customary protocols for meetings mean that everyone invited should be given an agenda in advance, with sufficient time allowed before the meeting for people to gather facts and have their answers ready or otherwise be prepared for the meeting.

As each item is discussed, fresh action might be agreed and entered in the minutes, which become a kind of action plan. Ideally, the minutes should be written as the meeting proceeds and then everyone can be given a copy as they leave. Otherwise, the minutes should be distributed as soon as possible. If anyone who was not at the meeting is listed in the minutes for taking action, clearly they, too, should be given a copy of the minutes.

Every action required should be explained succinctly and precisely, with calendar dates and without ambiguous phrases such as 'as soon as possible'.

When a meeting breaks up, it will have been successful only if all the members feel that they have achieved some real purpose and that actions have been agreed which will benefit the project. Demands made of members during the meeting must be achievable, so that promises extracted can be honoured.

Time and money spent on progress meetings will be wasted if the actions agreed collectively are not followed up by the project manager or some other responsible person.

CELEBRATION

In some industries it is customary to have some kind of celebration or party when the project ends, which gives some of those who have worked hard an opportunity to relax and reflect on their success. Sometimes clients will be invited to such gatherings. So, now we are contemplating the end of a project it is time to end this book with some thoughts about the closing down activities.

Actions Necessary When a Project Comes to an End

Projects can be closed for a variety of reasons, not all of which are connected with success. However, here we cannot contemplate failure and must assume that our project has satisfied all its stakeholders.

The project contractor has to undertake a few administrative actions so that the project is closed down in a methodical and efficient way. So the work of the project manager can extend for a week or two after all the project outcomes have been delivered successfully. Here are the more important closing down steps that need to be taken.

1. Make a staff announcement to the effect that the project has been closed and that no more time may be booked to it on timesheets. Junior staff sometimes find themselves waiting between jobs, and they seek imaginative ways of describing that time on their timesheets. They have a tendency to book their time to familiar cost codes. If the computer has been programmed to reject those bookings, they will have to book their time to the appropriate code for waiting time.

2. Manage the files and archives. Much of the information collected during one project might be of use in later projects

(especially some designs). Also some records must be kept for at least six years in case of subsequent investigations from tax authorities, or should a post-project dispute develop with a client or some other stakeholder.

3. A project contractor has some duty of care to a client in providing post-project services or advice, and will need to retain records of the project (drawings and specifications) to help in that task. Even such things as instruction manuals from the vendors of equipment built into the project might have to be retained.

4. Another reason for keeping project documents is that the contractor will need them if the original client comes back wanting an extension to the original project. That can apply particularly in projects such as construction and mining.

5. Above all, every project adds to the fund of experience that a company builds. So the company must retain all significant documents in which that experience is documented.

Some project managers are encouraged to keep a project diary, in which significant events and decisions are recorded. This need not be an elaborate document, but it can prove invaluable should a post-project legal squabble break out between the project company and its client or one of its suppliers or subcontractors.

One final thing that is commonly recommended is that the project manager organizes a get-together with key project staff to write down any lessons they have learned during the project, either from mistakes or from particularly good performance.

Final Project Meeting of the Swings and Roundabouts Team

After the final inspection day and opening of the swings and roundabouts project, project manager Theresa Green decided to invite the following people to a final project review meeting:

- Site supervisor, Arthur Inch;

- Highways manager, Dusty Rhodes;

- Road gang foreman, Sally Forth;

- Finance director, Penny Wise;

- Project cost director, Ize Wong;

- Procurement manager, Tom Byers;

- Project buyer, John Auder.

Dusty Rhodes and Tom Byers did not attend the meeting, but Theresa was delighted when chief executive Richard Croesus dropped in on the proceedings.

Theresa began by thanking everyone who had helped to make the project a success. She then asked some of the people, in turn, about their personal experience of the project and the way in which it had been managed. One universal answer that emerged was that everyone involved at the site in the park had been impressed at the regularity with which everything seemed to happen. Unlike previous ventures, there were no panic days and all the materials and services appeared at the right time. Theresa explained that the critical path network had much to do with that.

Penny Wise remarked that it was good to see a project that had finished almost exactly on budget. That was far better than St Kevin Borough Council's experience with projects in other departments. Theresa explained that working to a sensible schedule, with everyone clear about what they had to do, coupled with controlled purchasing, was the reason for that success. Ize Wong commented that having such a detailed work breakdown structure (WBS) had helped him to make the original cost estimates, and had also enabled him to record the actual costs as they arose and compare them with the estimates.

Chief executive Richard Croesus now spoke up. He congratulated the team and said that their project success would create a good impression with the public, and with users of the new playground. He said that other council departments should take note of this success and consider whether they should adopt similar project management methods. Richard made it clear that he would encourage that.

As everyone was dispersing, Richard took Theresa on one side and said he would like her to train people from other council departments and show them how they might improve the management of their projects. He asked the beaming Theresa if there was anything she needed to help in future projects. 'Well,' she replied, 'we would need some more advanced software. Microsoft Project is fine for small projects, but I would like to do things like incorporating the work breakdown codes in all project task identifiers, and have a timesheet facility for recording costs. Also, this was a small project and we managed without resource scheduling, but we really need software that can do all that well, and also produce well-designed but compact reports.' Richard was somewhat taken aback, but asked Theresa to submit a proposal and cost estimate to him. Theresa suggested Primavera or Deltek's Open Plan, as two of the many competent software packages that might be considered (you can use Google to find their contact details), She thought the initial cost would be in the region of £5,000 to £10,000. They would run on the council's existing computers. So Theresa left the room with her head buzzing with pleasure, thoughts for the future, and what she might write in her software proposal.

Conclusion

Project management can be a very rewarding and satisfying career. So, if you have read this little book and would like to know more, I have provided a short further reading list and the names of the two principal professional organizations that might help you to get started.

Further Reading

There is a bewildering amount of literature available on project management and related topics. So I shall just list a few recommended titles here. Many other books not listed here are also excellent.

Devaux, S.A. (1999), *Total Project Control: A Manager's Guide to Integrated Planning, Measuring and Tracking*, New York, Wiley. Stephen Devaux is a personal friend. He writes particularly clearly on the logical construction and use of network diagrams.

Hartman, F.T. (2000), *Don't Park Your Brain Outside*, Newtown Square, PA, Project Management Institute. I once had the pleasure of writing a review for this book which is packed with common sense and advice. However it does assume some prior knowledge and is not for the beginner.

Kerzner, H. (2009), *Project Management: A Systems Approach to Planning, Scheduling and Controlling*, 10th ed., Hoboken, NJ, Wiley. Professor

Kerzner is a dedicated scholar who writes with great authority. He is highly respected.

Lock, D. (2009), *Project Management*, 9th ed., Aldershot, Gower. This book is revised from time to time and a tenth edition had gone to press as I write this. However, the ninth edition remains adequate and gives good coverage of its subject. Both editions come as a paperback and as an alternative hardback tutor's version.

Meredith, J.R., and Mantel, S.J. Jnr., (2008), *Project Management: a Managerial Approach*, 7th ed., New York, Wiley. This book is also updated from time to time. It contains many detailed case examples from real life, which give useful insight. The index is not of the best, which makes navigating for subjects a little difficult. However, the book is authoritative and very good value.

Gower Publishing, which is an imprint of Ashgate Publishing, has specialized in project management for many years and publishes highly regarded titles covering every conceivable aspect of project and programme management.

Professional Associations

INTERNATIONAL PROJECT MANAGEMENT ASSOCIATION (IPMA)

The International Project Management Association was founded in 1965 and is the world's oldest project management association. It was originally known by the initials INTERNET but, 20 years later, the Association switched to the initials IPMA for obvious reasons. 26 IPMA International Congress events have been held in several cities held since the IPMA was formed, with each attracting many speakers and delegates. The IPMA is a not-for-profit federation of over 50 national project management associations. Individual membership is made by joining the relevant affiliated national project management association. People living in countries with no national association should contact the IPMA direct for advice. Contact details are as follows:

IPMA,
PO Box 1167,
3860 BD,
Nijkerk,
Netherlands.
Telephone: +31 33 247 3430

For email enquiries go to the website and then click the email button on the relevant page. The website is http://ipma/ch.

THE ASSOCIATION FOR PROJECT MANAGEMENT

The IPMA-affiliated association for UK readers is the Association for Project Management. The APM offers many professional services, publications, and support for project managers and students as well as administering professional qualifications. For details of corporate or individual membership, their address is:

The Association for Project Management
Ibis House,
Regent Park,
Summerleys Road,
Princess Risborough,
Buckinghamshire, HP27 9LE.
Telephone: 0845 458 1944
Email: info@apm.org.uk
Website: www.apm.org.uk

PROJECT MANAGEMENT INSTITUTE

The American-based Project Management Institute (PMI) has a large individual membership worldwide, with active chapters in many countries. It administers project management qualifications and publishes associated books and journals. Their contact details are as follows:

PMI Headquarters
Four Campus Boulevard,
Newtown Square,
PA 19073-3299,
USA.
Telephone: +610-356-4600
Email: pmihq@pmi.org
Website: www.pmi.org

Structured Project Management Methodologies

To end, I have to mention some project management methodologies, each of which embodies the combined expertise of many experts. These go well beyond the bare facts outlined throughout this book, and will enable readers to enrich their understanding of our profession. Each of these standards of methodologies was born (and has since evolved) from the work of various committees. It has been said that a camel is a horse designed by a committee, and that is intended to be a derogatory statement – but if you found yourself stuck alone in the middle of a sandy desert which would you rather have as your means of escape – a horse or a camel. So committees can produce good results. It all depends how well they are controlled.

BODY OF KNOWLEDGE FROM THE PMI

The best way to learn about this methodology is to buy a copy of PMI's *Guide to the Body of Knowledge*, which at the time of writing was in its fourth edition. The title is always abbreviated to *PMBoK Guide* (PMBoK is a registered trademark of the PMI). The body of knowledge is not a teaching textbook, but instead defines the principles that govern best practice in project and programme management. This has evolved over many years to take account of developments in project management and it encompasses the combined wisdom of many contributors. A feature of this publication that I always find particularly useful is the glossary of project management terms, but now PMI publish a *Lexicon of Project Management Terms*. Go to the PMI website at www.pmi.org to learn more about these publications.

BODY OF KNOWLEDGE FROM THE ASSOCIATION FOR PROJECT MANAGEMENT

Again this is a statement of project management best practice, rather than a textbook. The APM actively encourages its members to suggest improvements, so effectively the design committee is as big as the membership. I contributed in a very modest way to the current sixth edition. The coverage is authoritative and comprehensive. For more details, or to buy a copy go to www.APM.org.uk.

INTERNATIONAL STANDARDS ORGANISATION (ISO)

The International Standards Organisation is chiefly known for its ISO9000 series of quality standards, However ISO also applies itself to best practice in project management and publishes several project management standards. Also relevant to some project managers are standards dealing with subjects such as environmental best practice. For more details about ISO and its publications go to their website at www.iso.org.

PRINCE AND PRINCE2

PRINCE is an acronym for **pr**ojects **in c**ontrolled **e**nvironments. Unlike the bodies of knowledge listed above, PRINCE gives direct advice on how to organize and control projects. The system was originated by a UK Government-sponsored committee of experts and was originally slanted towards IT projects. At one time any company wishing to obtain a UK government contract might have been encouraged to follow PRINCE recommendations.

PRINCE2 came about because of criticism that PRINCE was too prescriptive (especially regarding project organization) and PRINCE2 is now more widely accepted.

Although I do not personally advocate all aspects of PRINCE2, it has some valuable features, and in the past I have been impressed by some of its standard documentation templates.

Many training establishments run courses on PRINCE2, and it carries its own widely recognized qualifications. It does not enjoy universal support among all experts, but its popularity continues to grow. PRINCE2 qualified candidates can be at an advantage when applying for certain vacancies.

Because PRINCE and PRINCE2 have been sponsored by UK Government departments, there have been several changes over the years in its ownership as different elected governments have abolished various departments. PRINCE2 now has its own website at http://www.prince-officialsite.com.

Index

Actions when a project comes to an end 102–3
Association for Project Management (APM) 107

Bar charts 40–43, 48, 52
Below-the-line costs 67
Benefits realization 7
Bid summary 62, 70–71
Body of Knowledge
   APM 108
   PMI 108
Brainstorming 73, 99–101
Business plan 3–5, 11–12, 18, 74, 94, 96

Contract administration 67–8, 76
Contractor 6, 11, 17, 36, 63, 65–9, 75–6
Contracts 4, 57–8, 64–5
   see also Purchasing
   changes and variations 68
   penalty clause 69
   pricing 66–7
   swings and roundabouts project 68–9
   terms of payment 65–6
Cost estimating 18–19
Cost control
   principles 78–9
Cost measurement and monitoring 80–81
Costs (nature of) 15–18
Critical path network analysis 42–55, 89

Cybernetic control loop 78

Deliverables *see* Project outcomes

Earned value analysis 81–86
European Public Sector Procurement Directives 63, 69

International Project Management Association (IPMA) 106–7
Meetings 99–102
   brainstorming 73, 99–101
   celebration party 102
   planning 43
   progress meetings 101–102
   project kick-off meeting 100
Microsoft Project 52–5

Organization
   charts 25–27
   coordinated project matrix 28–29
   matrix organization for multiple projects 32
   swings and roundabouts project 35–7
   teams and task forces 29–32, 89–97
Organization theory from the project manager's point of view 34–35
Overhead recovery 17–18

Planning *see also* Bar charts *and* Critical path network analysis

diary planning 40
essential requirements 39–40
swings and roundabouts project 49–55
PRINCE and PRINCE2 109
Professional associations 106–7
Progress control 76–9
Progress meetings 101–102
Project changes 75–7
Project definition 3, 11–12, 74
Project kick-off meeting 100
Project life cycles 2–6
Project Management Institute (PMI) 107–8
Project management office (PMO) 18, 37, 68
Project manager 7, 76, 79, 81, 84, 89–90, 92–3, 97, 100, 102–3
Project risk 73–4
Project teams and task forces 29–32, 89–97
Project types 1–2

Purchasing 27, 36, 51, 57, 59–64, 77, 80–81, 104

Resource scheduling 41, 48–9, 105
Sponsors 6
Stakeholders 6–8, 35–6, 87, 102–3,
Structured project management methodologies 108–9
Swings and roundabouts project 9–10
  contracts and purchases 68–71
  control 84–7
  final project meeting 103–5
  organization 35–7
  planning 49–55
  work breakdown and cost estimate 19–23
Table project 46–8
Tree project 42–4
Work breakdown structure (WBS) 12–15, 19, 35, 81, 89–90, 104
  case example 13–14
  coding 14–15

Other Titles from Gower and Dennis Lock

Accelerating Business and IT Change: Transforming Project Delivery
Alan Fowler and Dennis Lock
978-0-566-08809-4

Advanced Project Management
Frederick Harrison and Dennis Lock
978-0-566-07822-4

Aviation Project Management
Triant G. Flouris and Dennis Lock
978-0-7546-7395-8

Managing Aviation Projects from Concept to Completion
Triant G. Flouris and Dennis Lock
978-0-7546-7615-7

Project Management
Dennis Lock
978-0-566-08772-1

Project Management in Construction
Dennis Lock
978-0-566-08612-0

The Essentials of Project Management
Dennis Lock
978-0-566-08805-6

The Gower Handbook of Management
Dennis Lock
978-0-566-07938-2

GOWER